# SKIN AND BONES

A PATRICK FLINT NOVEL

PATRICK FLINT
BOOK 8

PAMELA FAGAN HUTCHINS

SKIPJACK PUBLISHING

# FREE PFH EBOOKS

BEFORE YOU BEGIN READING, you can snag a free Pamela Fagan Hutchins ebook starter library by joining her mailing list at https://pamela-fagan-hutchins.myshopify.com/pages/the-next-chapter-with-pamela-fagan-hutchins.

# PROLOGUE: DESCEND

Cloud Peak Wilderness, Bighorn Mountains, Wyoming
*Then*: Sunday, September 18, 1977

*Patrick*

Patrick Flint stood atop Cloud Peak, fists on hips, and took in the view from the highest point in Wyoming's Bighorn Mountains. The world looked at once vast and incredibly small, and a lot lower than his perch. *This is how a bird of prey views the world.* Snow. Rocks. Treetops. Valleys. High plains. Even the interstate and distant pinpricks of buildings. Everything bathed in sunlight softer and more diffuse than just a few weeks before, as the earth's tilt caused the rays to hit it at a lower angle and September marched toward autumn.

"You're like an old mountain goat, Dr. Flint." Loren Freemason held up his hand for a high five. The climber—one of the two other people in their small group—wasn't many years past twenty. He had a lean, hungry look accentuated by loose-fitting clothes and unkempt hair. "Far out."

"Call me Patrick. Please." He smacked Loren's palm. He would have preferred to be compared to a bighorn sheep instead of a goat and without tacking on *old*. But he knew what made him adept at climbing. "Slow twitch muscles," he said. Slow-twitch muscle fibers are fatigue resistant and focus on sustained, smaller movements and control of posture, because they contain more mitochondria and myoglobin. Because of an abundance of good slow-twitch fibers, Patrick had always done well in endurance sports, like mountaineering, which they were perfect for.

Loren gave him a blank, confused look.

Whitney Saylor retied a red bandana around her forehead and curly brown hair. "Kathy was right about you, Dr. Flint." Nurse Kathy Bergman had connected Patrick with the younger climbers. Kathy had introduced Whitney to him as her best friend since nursing school, although Whitney had taken a job in Sheridan and Kathy one in Buffalo. "Why don't you climb Mount Rainier with us next August? It's gonna be a-mazing."

A frown creased Loren's forehead for a brief second, then cleared. He nodded. "Yeah, sure. Come, why don't you?"

Patrick took the invite seriously. He did need a new goal. He'd completed a few half marathons and studied up on mountain climbing in the last year. While Mount Rainier wasn't the tallest peak in North America or even in the lower forty-eight states, it was considered the premier warm-up climb for McKinley in Alaska—the tallest peak in North America—and a launching point for the tallest peaks on each of the other six continents, collectively known as the Seven Summits. Rainier boasted accessibility from Seattle, yet had altitude, technical elements, and conditions that mimicked the taller peaks.

Would his wife mind, though? Susanne had just begun her first semester at Sheridan College. She planned to increase her hours to full time in the spring. Years ago, she'd quit college when they'd started a family. As far as he was concerned, that had been the best move she could have made for their kids and for him. And for her—to spend that time with their children was irreplaceable.

This new direction for her didn't seem sustainable. Not right now with the kids still at home. He'd carried that kind of load before when he was in medical school, and he secretly believed she'd sideline it until the kids graduated from high school, after she got a taste of how hard her fall would be. *As she committed to me seventeen years ago.* Before she'd changed her mind and decided she couldn't wait any longer to become a teacher.

Based on his analysis, climbing Rainier next summer wasn't going to be a problem. He nodded. "Sounds good."

"It's settled. Time to chow down, then," Loren said.

Patrick unbuckled his backpack and let it slide to the ground. Loren and Whitney had claimed two flat rocks as seats, but Patrick didn't want his muscles to tighten up. He would stand. He'd left the house at three that morning so that he, Whitney, and Loren could begin their climb at five a.m. at the West Tensleep trailhead. It was twelve thirty now. They were on schedule for a one o'clock turn-around, to avoid the usual afternoon thunderstorms. He'd consumed a series of snacks to keep himself fueled. Food wasn't his problem. Water was.

Patrick had forgotten one of his canteens at home. The other had spilled out on the trail because Patrick hadn't tightened the cap appropriately and then carried it upside down. There were plenty of stream crossings, but, after catching giardia from mountain water two years ago, he hadn't dared risk it again. Nor was he going to rob the other two of any of their water unless it became an emergency. They needed it as much as he did.

And he sure wasn't going to mention his mistake. He didn't want to seem like a novice. Or a bonehead. To that end, he took out his canteen and pretended to sip from the empty container. Then he dug into his pack for his peanut butter and jelly sandwich, swallowing down nothing but cotton mouth. He was feeling the early signs of dehydration. Dry mouth, lips, and tongue. Thirst. Lightheadedness.

And in the last two hours, he hadn't needed to visit the bushes. *Great. Just great.*

A sudden gust of wind ripped through the climbers. It was strong and shockingly cold.

"Whoa," Loren said with his mouth full. "Where did that come from?"

Wind buffeted them again. Then a third time. By the fourth blast, the temperature had dropped twenty degrees from what had been a balmy sixty. Whitney rose to her knees and braced against it. She pulled a sweater out of her backpack and slid it on.

Patrick squinted upward. The wind had pushed in clouds. Around them, the world darkened at a speed he wouldn't have believed possible if he wasn't witnessing it with his own eyes. No precipitation or lightning, but that could change fast, too. "This feels like more than an afternoon squall. We need to get down."

"Almost done." Loren brandished half a sandwich. A slice of bologna fell onto the ground, and a marmot wobbled over and snatched it. "Hey, dude, quit stealing my chow."

"I think we should leave *now*." Patrick stuffed his sandwich wrapper into his pack and yanked out a weatherproof jacket and a wool cap. After he had them on, he zipped up his gear.

"I'm with Dr. Flint." Whitney was buckling her backpack into place around her chest and waist. "This weather is freaking me out."

"Hold your horses." Loren raised his arms overhead and arched his back. "Hydrate or die." He opened his canteen and tipped it up. Water dripped down the sides of his mouth.

Patrick gritted his teeth, partly at Loren's ridiculous nonchalance, and partly at the waste of water. He hefted his backpack up and slid his arms through the straps then began buckling up.

Whitney's voice was strained. "Hurry up, Loren. It's snowing." White flakes dotted her sleeves and hair.

Loren rolled his eyes. "Snow isn't the end of the world. It's September in the high country, Whitney. Look around."

Small patches of snow remained on the ground from a storm two weeks before. It was normal for snow to fall here this time of year. But the forecast today had predicted warm, dry weather. The trio wouldn't have made the ascent if they'd expected a winter storm. At least, Patrick wouldn't have.

He'd had it with Loren's attitude. "I'm leaving. Whitney?"

"Me, too," she said.

Patrick nodded at her and strode out in the direction of the trail they'd taken up.

"Jeez Louise, wait up, you guys," Loren said.

But by then, his voice was a faint irritant in the distance behind Patrick.

# CHAPTER ONE: CHASE

Buffalo, Wyoming
*Now* (nine months later): Saturday, June 17, 1978

*Patrick*

Patrick Flint stood at the edge of their pasture. Sunlight dappled the waving purple, blue, yellow, and green blanket of spring flowers in the foreground of the snow-capped Bighorn Mountains. Three horses grazed on new grass amongst the flowers. A red barn stood off to one side, doors thrown open to air out winter's stuffiness. The rushing water of Clear Creek provided thrilling background music. Was there any more glorious month of the year in Wyoming than June?

He raised his arms over his head and leaned first left, then right, stretching for the effort ahead of him. The horses ignored him, tails swishing. "My dad used to give me a quarter for every armadillo I'd catch back in College Station."

His willowy daughter Trish frowned. "Grandpa Joe's too cheap to do anything like that." At seventeen and going into her senior year of high school, she argued with almost everything her parents said. Patrick still remembered the days when he'd been her idol.

He lowered himself into a runner's lunge. He'd been training for high altitude climbing all winter, and he still stretched and warmed up before any physical exertion. *Especially* after all his training. He couldn't let an injury derail his plans to climb Mount Rainer in August. Or doubts about the wisdom of doing it. Whether it was safe. Whether he was ready. Doubts were more crippling than an injury, and they were absolutely forbidden.

He pulled his mind back to the present, his kids, and the task at hand. "Have you ever seen what an armadillo can do to a yard when it digs for grubs? Your grandfather did the math. Paying me was a lot cheaper than buying sod." He smiled. "Because Gramma Lana didn't ask for much, but she did enjoy a well-kept lawn."

"Tell me you didn't kill the armadillos," Trish said.

"I can't speak for your grandfather, but I did not."

"You won't kill a marmot either, right?"

Patrick considered the perfection of a yellow-bellied marmot. They were adorably destructive little creatures. *No, I'd never kill one.* "Repatriation only."

"What does that mean?" Perry asked.

"Study some vocabulary, Perry. It means he'd move it somewhere else," Trish said.

Perry mimicked her behind her back.

"Why not just trap them?" Trish pointed to the cage Patrick had placed by the pasture gate.

Patrick winked at his daughter. "Where's the fun in that?"

"Do you think a marmot is going to be easier to catch than an armadillo?" Perry's fourteen-year-old voice broke on the last word. If it bothered him, his shining blue eyes didn't show it.

"Son, an armadillo can run up to thirty miles per hour. A marmot waddles along at about three." Patrick made a muscle and grinned. "No problem."

Trish rolled her eyes. "But marmots are rock chucks. With big teeth."

Perry sang out, "How many rocks would a rock chuck chuck if a rock chuck could chuck rocks?"

*Chip off the old block.* Patrick tried to ruffle his son's hair. Perry ducked. "Those teeth are nothing compared to the digging claws on an armadillo. But I'm going to grab the marmots at the base of their tails." He exhaled forcefully a few times, making room for the oxygen required for sprinting at the mile-high altitude of their Buffalo, Wyoming home. He did respect the teeth on the little suckers. They'd done serious damage chewing through the electrical wires under the deck. Their electrician, George Nichols, didn't seem to mind the extra work, though. "Your mom is spitting mad at the little boogers."

As if on cue, Susanne stuck her head out the front door of their home, her voice raised to cover the distance across the wide driveway and parking area between house, barn, and pasture gate. "Can I let Ferdie out?" The enormous wiry-haired dog strained against his collar beside her. Music blared out the door as well. The Jackson 5. "I Want You Back." The kids must have left the stereo on because Susanne was stuck in the late fifties with the Everly Brothers.

"No," Patrick shouted. The dog wouldn't make marmot catching an easier sport.

Susanne waved, and she and Ferdinand disappeared behind a closed door.

"How are you going to get the marmots out of their dens?" Perry asked.

Patrick felt a thrill as he considered his strategy. This was going to be fun. "I'm not. I'm going to wait until they're sunning and intercept them before they go underground."

Trish folded her arms across her chest. She sounded like she'd rather be watching paint dry on a rainy day. "I don't think this is a good idea."

"There's one!" Perry's whisper exuded excitement that matched Patrick's.

A marmot had wandered away from the cluster of rocks nearest Patrick and the kids—where Patrick assumed its den was located—and was settling itself in a patch of sun near the deck and the scene of the electrical wire crime.

*Perfect positioning*, Patrick congratulated himself.

With one last deep exhale, he shook his hands, rocked onto his back heel, and started running, attempting a faster version of the American Indian fox-walking technique he used for stealth. He had to get between the marmot and the sanctuary of the deck before the animal noticed him, or it would disappear under it. He focused on staying low with his hands near his knees, raising one foot high, setting the outside of the foot down, rolling to the inside, and putting the heel down, toe down, and weight down. Repeating it. It became harder as he gathered speed. He slowed down and angled harder toward the house.

The marmot woke with a jerk of its head, emitted a shrill squeak, and burst back towards its den.

Perry screamed, "Go, Dad, go!"

Patrick abandoned all semblance of fox running. He cut sharply and sprinted after the rock chuck. He liked his chances of catching the animal. The fastest man in the world can run twenty-five miles per hour at top speed. The average man running for his life, twelve. Patrick figured at his age and fitness level he could do ten. That far outpaced the little animal only fifteen feet ahead of him, with fifty to go.

Patrick had scoped the entrance to the burrow and had good trajectory. He closed the gap quickly. Trish's voice joined Perry's in cries of encouragement.

Their cheers spurred him on, but his breathing grew labored, heart slamming against his ribcage. Training for climbing versus sprinting worked to different ends, it seemed. Ten feet from the marmot's burrow, Patrick knew it was now or never. He dove, arms outstretched, hand reaching for the base of the animal's tail. His fingers made contact with fur—soft golden fur, so silky—and grasped. Victory is mine! A victory for thirty-something, not-so-young-anymore men everywhere!

For a split second, his mind flashed on the book he'd been reading. *Zen and the Art of Motorcycle Maintenance.* To him, it seemed to explore the concept of quality. A man knows it when he sees it. And he knows it when he achieves it. This was a quality catch.

Until it wasn't.

The heel of his palm bore the brunt of his landing on the ground too hard to be dirt. Rock. *Nooooo.* As the marmot shrieked its shock and displeasure, Patrick heard the crunch of bones breaking. Or maybe he just imagined the sound. But he didn't imagine the feeling. Pain. Sudden. Sharp. His fingers released the marmot tail of their own volition even before his body made full contact with the earth. His teeth ground together. Air whooshed out of his lungs. An OOMPH burst from between his lips. He held back inappropriate words and a guttural scream. They resounded in his brain anyway, as clearly as if he'd released them.

"Dad, he's getting away!" Perry yelled, his voice hot with the thrill of the chase. Then, "Hurry, Dad! Get up!"

Trish sang out, "Too late. Marmot down the hatch." Did she sound pleased?

Patrick rolled to his back, cradling his right hand. The grade of the slope surprised him, and his roll extended to two, then three rotations. At that point, unfortunately, the ground dropped away to the creek, and his roll turned into a free fall. The sensation of air and gravity ended with a thump on the back of his head. The ringing of bells. Splashing. Wetness. Cold, all over his body. On his face.

He was in Clear Creek.

Patrick spewed water from his mouth and sat up. He wasn't sure what hurt worst. Hand. Head. His skin everywhere. He was aware of sounds like voices shouting as if they were outside a glass dome, with him on the inside. He'd figure them out in a second. But before he could do anything to remedy his current situation, something bumped into his leg.

It bumped him again.

And then a third time.

Moving slowly, he used his uninjured hand to hold his ringing head and looked down to see what was thumping him. Nothing that he could see. Not above the water anyway, which was less than a foot deep. He strained, lifting further, and then he saw it. It was a log, or something like a log, floating but not floating. Half in, half out of the water. Long and narrow. With moss billowing around one end. Stubby branches halfway down its length.

*No.*

*That's not moss, and that's not a log.*

Crunched hand bones forgotten, Patrick scrambled to his knees for a closer look at the body of a lifeless young woman.

"Oh, no. Oh, no, no, no." The words escaped his lips on a moan. Because he knew her. He knew her very well. He'd trained with her. He'd planned to climb Mt. Rainier with her.

It was Whitney Saylor, apparently dead in their backyard creek.

# CHAPTER TWO: PROTEST

Buffalo, Wyoming
*Now*: Saturday, June 17, 1978

*Ronnie*

Johnson County Deputy Veronica Harcourt tapped a pencil against her lips. "Run that by me again, Patrick." She'd responded to the Flint home as soon as she heard about the situation on her radio. The city police had jurisdiction, but a suspicious death in the county drew out all the area law enforcement, especially if the law enforcement officer in question happened to be one of the best friends of the man who found the body.

Patrick was sitting on the steps to his backyard deck, head lowered, one hand cradling the other, while cops and EMTs milled around on the bank of the creek, gathering evidence, taking photographs, talking, and preparing to transport Whitney Saylor to the morgue. She'd be bypassing the county coroner, Hal Greybull, and going straight to forensic pathologist Dr. Coop Evans in Sheridan. Dr. Evans was technically assigned to Sheridan County, but he assisted the small neighboring counties as well.

Patrick looked up with red-rimmed eyes. "Whitney is my mountain climbing partner. We were planning on making the Rainier ascent together in August."

"How'd that come about? She seems... "

"Young. Yes. Kathy Bergman—she's a Buffalo nurse—"

"I know Kathy." In fact, Patrick had introduced them, but Ronnie understood the impact of stress on a brain.

"Sorry. Yes. Well, Whitney and Kathy are—were—best friends. Kathy introduced us because we're both into climbing. I went up Cloud Peak with her and Loren Freemason, last September. You remember that incident?"

Ronnie nodded. "You nearly didn't make it down."

"That was our first climb together. It was near winter, so we couldn't climb after that, but we've met up for some training sessions. Running bleachers in weight packs, things like that."

"Okay."

"We're scheduled for some fourteeners in Colorado this summer." He shook his head. "Or we were."

Ronnie knew Patrick was referring to fourteen-thousand-feet and higher peaks. Wyoming had none. Colorado had more than fifty. Susanne Flint had bemoaned the number over coffee just last week when she'd told Ronnie about Patrick's summer training plans. "We'll barely see him all summer," Susanne had said. "Not that the kids seem to notice whether either of us is around. But I don't understand why he's so obsessed with activities that don't involve us. Or at least me. And I could use his help with the kids now that I'm working in Sheridan. I'm praying he'll purge the mountain climbing bug from his system with Rainier."

Down at the creek's edge, Ronnie heard someone count down from three. A few seconds later, she saw the EMTs carrying Whitney up the creekbank on a stretcher. "So, you and Whitney were friends?"

Patrick caught sight of the stretcher. Ronnie heard his shaky exhale. "Sure. Not close friends, but friendly enough."

"Was she friends with Susanne?"

"Susanne isn't a fan of my climbing, or anyone associated with it."

"I'll take that as a no."

Patrick sighed. "It's not that Susanne is a jealous wife. This is about the demand on my time, not Whitney herself."

Two city officers had walked up. They stood to the side, watching and listening to her conversation with Patrick, heads together, whispering.

Ronnie held up her hand. "I get it. But you know it looks very strange that she died here?"

"If she died here. She could have floated downstream."

"You know what I mean." The body of an attractive woman a decade younger than the prominent and married doctor friend at whose house she turns up dead? It was more than strange.

Patrick rubbed his forehead, leaving red marks. "Yes. Yes, I do."

"You're going to get questions."

"But I don't know anything, Ronnie."

She doubted that would matter.

The cops stepped forward. Ronnie had been leaning against the deck railing. She straightened. "Eli. Cliff."

Eli Welch spoke first. She'd gone to high school with him. He still had the same baby face and peach fuzz he'd had then, making him possibly the only male over the age of twenty in Johnson County who didn't wear a winter beard. In his case, couldn't. "What brings you out to our scene, Ronnie?"

"Death. I thought maybe I could lend a hand."

Cliff Appelt sneered down at her from his impressive height—Ronnie guessed six foot five. "Maybe you can help your buddy here figure out why Ms. Saylor had his business card in her wallet."

Patrick stood. He stuck out his uninjured hand to Cliff. "Patrick Flint. I don't believe we've met."

Cliff didn't take Patrick's hand. "I know who you are. I may be the only person in this town who doesn't think your shit don't stink just because you're a doctor. And I asked Ronnie a question."

Ronnie's eyebrows stretched her forehead. "It wasn't really a question for me." Or a question at all. Cliff wasn't the kind of cop that made people think officers were there to help their communities. *He makes it harder for the rest of us.*

Patrick said, "I gave her my card."

"How'd you come to do that? Seeing as she don't live in Buffalo and is closer to the age of that pretty daughter of yours I see peeking out the window than she is to yours."

Patrick's head whipped around. Ronnie saw Trish watching them through the glass by the dining table. The back door opened, and Susanne emerged. Curvy and petite with long, wavy brown hair and an outgoing, magnetic personality, Susanne drew the eyes of the two cops.

"Patrick, what's going on?" Her face was drawn. Her lipstick chewed off.

"Your husband was just about to tell me how Ms. Saylor came to die with his business card in her wallet." Cliff watched Susanne, not Patrick, as he waited in the pause after his words.

Ronnie winced.

Patrick said, "We were trying to hire her."

"At the hospital? Or at your house? Because your home phone number is written on it." He turned a plastic baggie toward Patrick. "That is your home number, isn't it?"

Patrick frowned. "Yes, but—"

"Do you give all prospective employees your home number?"

"Not usually. But we were sort of mountain climbing partners. . ."

Cliff's eyebrows shot up. "Partners?"

"Whitney—"

"Is your girlfriend? Or should I say was?"

Susanne gasped.

Patrick frowned. "What? No! She organizes training sessions and climbs."

"For the two of you?"

"We had a third to our group, but—"

"How'd you hurt that hand you're babying?"

Patrick looked confused and embarrassed. "Trying to catch a marmot."

"Are you sure it didn't happen when you killed your girlfriend?"

Susanne had moved closer. Her face was red and splotchy. "She wasn't my husband's girlfriend, and he didn't kill her."

Cliff turned to her. "You think not? I was wondering who else might want her dead? Like a jealous wife, maybe?"

"She's not the first woman to admire my husband."

"Just the first one who ended up dead at your house." He held up the baggie with the card. "And the first one to write 'his wife knows—she threatened me' on the back of your husband's card, I'd guess?"

Both Flints gasped, but Susanne lunged forward with her hand out, reaching for the baggie.

Ronnie threw up an arm between Susanne and Cliff. "Let's take a breath. Cliff, the Flints have had a terrible shock, as have their kids. I think Patrick needs medical attention for his hand. Maybe if you'd like to talk to Patrick and Susanne, we can come into the station later?"

Cliff's voice was malevolent. "There is no 'we' here, deputy. This is our case. Eli, could you escort Ronnie to her vehicle? Mrs. Flint and I were just about to have a chat."

# CHAPTER THREE: FEAR

Buffalo, Wyoming
*Now*: Saturday, June 17, 1978

*Trish*

Trish shuddered as she watched her parents and the cops. Her mom and dad seemed upset, and the Buffalo cops looked aggressive. The tall one was waving things in their faces and hovering over her mom in a threatening manner. What the heck was going on? She knew the woman who her dad had found in the creek—Whitney—was someone he'd climbed with before. But she didn't understand why the police would be giving her parents a hard time. She was glad Ronnie was with them, at least.

The phone rang. Not tearing her eyes away from the scene outside, she picked up the receiver. "Flint residence. Trish speaking."

The girl's voice on the other end was snotty. It wasn't a nice word, but that was the only one for it. "You'd better have a darn good excuse for missing practice this morning."

Jillian. The captain of the cheerleading squad and the bane of Trish's existence lately. "Uh, yeah, as a matter of fact, I do. We found a dead woman in the creek behind our house. There are cops everywhere."

"Unless that dead woman was you then—wait, what? A dead woman? Who is it?"

"A nurse from Sheridan. Her name is Whitney something."

"Is she pretty?"

"She's dead, Jillian."

"I'm just trying to picture it. It's, you know—so tragic and everything."

Trish shook her head and didn't respond. One of the cops was walking away from the deck with Ronnie. She followed with her eyes until they were out of her sight.

"Anyway, we're working on a new dance routine for the first pep rally. You'll have to learn it from one of the other girls."

"Shouldn't be a problem. That's not until August."

"I choreographed it myself. It's to that really cool Steve Martin song. 'King Tut.'"

"Great."

"We even practiced our makeup and talked about costumes for it after practice. And Bella Crooke was there. Our new sponsor. She's buying us new uniforms for this year. And you missed it all."

"Sorry."

"Well, don't let it happen again."

"What, women dying in our backyard?"

Perry walked in. "I need the phone, Trish. Off."

Jillian said, "Is that your little brother?"

Normally, Trish wouldn't do anything Perry told her to do, but he'd given her a convenient excuse. "Sorry, Jillian. Gotta go. See you at Monday practice."

Just before Trish hung up, Jillian shouted, "Wait!"

Trish closed her eyes in frustration. "What?"

"Tonight. Dabbo is taking me to the movies. His friend needs a date. I told him about you."

Her stomach clenched. "No."

"What? I haven't even asked you anything. Yet."

"No. Way."

"Please? My parents won't let me go out with Dabbo unless you go, too. They think you're like a good influence or something."

"Dabbo and his friends are too old."

"He's only twenty. And his friend is younger. Like maybe eighteen or nineteen, I think."

"I'm supposed to hang out with Marcy."

Jillian's laugh was cutting. "Marcy will be fine with rescheduling. Or whatever crumbs you throw her now that you're one of us."

Trish frowned. Marcy wasn't a cheerleader, although her desire to be one was the whole reason Trish had even tried out. It had been hard on Marcy when Trish made the squad and Marcy didn't. But despite making it, Trish wasn't one of the popular girls—she was a bookworm. A nerd. Encyclopedia Flint. Or was she popular now? She didn't want to be. She wanted to be friends with Marcy like always. Or at least like always before Trish spent so much time with Ben that Marcy had felt abandoned. Well, that was over, and Trish wouldn't let a boy come between them again.

"I won't mark this missed practice against you if you'll just come tonight. Just think of it as a free movie and popcorn. You can go home as soon as the movie is over."

"You promise?"

"Thanks! You're a doll!"

There was a click as Jillian hung up. Trish growled. She'd never actually said yes.

Perry grabbed the phone. "Are you ditching Marcy?"

Trish turned toward him. "No. I have to reschedule her."

Perry began dialing. "You've really changed since you made cheerleader."

"I have not! What about you? You've been acting like a big shot since you got picked to practice with the varsity football team."

Perry grinned and put the phone to his ear. "That's because I *am* a big shot."

"Big head more like it. But still in a shrimp's body."

Perry peeled back his fingers and held all but the middle one down with his thumb.

Trish tossed her hair. "Good luck finding anyone who wants to go out with you tonight, dork."

She returned to the window. Her parents were gone. Frowning, she walked to the front door, opened it, and stood in the doorway. The cops were putting her mom into the back seat of one of their trucks. The tall one had his hand on her head like she was some criminal.

"Dad," Trish screamed. "What's going on?"

Her father didn't answer. He was arguing with the tall cop. She ran toward them, straining to hear.

"Back off, Mr. Flint, or you're going with her," the cop said.

"This is ridiculous. She hasn't done anything wrong."

"Unless you have something to confess, you need to step away from our car, right now."

Her dad took one step back. The cop slammed the door as he got in the driver's side.

"Dad?" Trish said. Her voice was wobbly with tears. Her throat was tight.

He acted like he didn't hear her. The police car drove away with Trish's mom in it.

"Dad!"

Finally, he turned to her, his face pale. "I have to go to the police station."

"I don't understand. Why did they take Mom?"

"Because of the woman who died. Whitney."

"Is Mom under arrest?"

"I don't know."

"That makes no sense."

"Exactly." He stormed toward the house, holding his right arm and hand to his midsection. "I have to make a call before I leave."

Trish ran after him. "What about your hand?" The marmot chasing and his fall seemed days ago, not hours.

"I'll worry about it later." Susanne came first, even though breaking his dominant hand was a big deal. As a doctor, it was a very big deal.

She opened the door for him, and he barreled through it. He rushed toward the kitchen, tripping over the phone cord stretched into the downstairs half bathroom. Luckily, he didn't fall.

He pushed down the plungers in the phone cradle. "Perry!"

From the bathroom, Trish heard Perry saying, "Hello? Hello?" The door swung open. He saw his father and sister. "Did one of you hang up the phone?"

Their dad held out his good hand. "It's an emergency. Give it to me."

"Geez, Dad. You could have just said something."

Trish shook her head and made a slashing motion across her throat.

Patrick snatched the receiver from Perry and stalked back to the phone book, hand still pressed against his stomach. He stuck the receiver between his ear and neck, flipping through the pages, lips moving. Then he dialed his call. He seemed to have forgotten Trish and Perry were even there.

Perry whispered, "What's going on?"

Trish shushed him with a hand outstretched.

Her dad said, "May I speak to the county attorney please? Tell him it's Patrick Flint. Patricia's brother."

Perry whispered, "He's calling Aunt Patricia's boyfriend?"

Trish put a finger to her lips, then pointed at her ear to tell Perry to listen to their dad.

"Max, this is Patrick. The police took Susanne. It's all a big mistake. What do I do?" Their dad's voice didn't sound like the man

Trish was used to. This man sounded scared and uncertain. Her pulse sped up until it was thundering in her chest. He paced, listening. Then his words came out in a rush. "A woman died. Someone I climb with. I found her behind our house in the creek. The police tried to insinuate I was involved with her and that Susanne had been threatening her and killed her." Again, he was silent. Then he wrote something in the margin of the phone book page. "Stu Ryan." He repeated a phone number. "Okay. Thank you."

He hung up the phone.

"What did Max say?" Trish asked.

Her dad was already dialing again. "He gave me the number of a defense attorney."

"But what is he going to do for Mom?"

Her father looked her dead in the eye. "There's nothing he can do, Trish. He's the county attorney. He's not on our side of this."

# CHAPTER FOUR: DODGE

BUFFALO, WYOMING
*NOW*: SATURDAY, JUNE 17, 1978

*Susanne*

SUSANNE STARED AT THE GRAY, windowless door to the interview room. *Any minute now, someone will come through that door and tell me this was all a big mix-up.* Patrick would be there, and he would be mad enough to spit. The police would apologize. Ronnie would come over later and explain what had happened. They'd all laugh about the confusion. Susanne would forgive and forget. Mistakes happened, right?

But the door stayed stubbornly closed. The room was cramped, humid. The walls seemed to close in on her more with each passing minute. And the smell—like sweat and body odor. She sniffed her armpits. It was her. She was the smell. Warmth creeped up her chest to her neck and face. She felt like a caged animal.

She stood. She wasn't handcuffed. No one had told her she was under arrest, although they'd made her feel like she had no choice except to come with them. All of this over something Whitney had written on Patrick's business card that Susanne knew nothing about? She'd thought she could clear everything up quickly. Cooperation and openness would work in her favor.

Instead, there had been no talking. They'd dumped her in here half an hour ago without offering her an explanation, the bathroom, a drink, or a phone call. It was ridiculous. She was free to go, wasn't she? She wished she'd taken criminal procedure as an elective last spring. It had been that or geopolitics. All she'd gotten out of geopolitics was a professor who hit on her and every other female student in his classes. But that wasn't the whole truth. She'd also gotten a job as a research assistant—with course credit—that had been honored even after she lodged a complaint against her professor, and he had been fired.

A job she was supposed to be at today. She hadn't even had a chance to call her boss to let him know she'd be late. Or possibly not coming in at all.

Taking a deep breath, she walked to the door. *Just open it and leave.*

She reached for the handle, but the door moved away from her. She gasped and jumped back, hand to her chest.

The two officers—she remembered their names, Welch and Appelt—blocked her path. Appelt was the tall one who wasn't nice. Welch was quiet. She didn't have a read on him yet.

Appelt narrowed his eyes. "Where do you think you're going?"

Susanne's mouth went dry. "I was going to get a drink, use the lady's room, and call my husband."

Appelt pointed at the chair she'd just vacated. "Take your seat. We'll talk first."

Welch's face turned pink, and his lips pursed, but he didn't say anything. He leaned against the wall.

She tried to catch his eye, but he was looking at his feet. She addressed them both. "May I have some coffee, please?"

Appelt laughed. "This isn't the Busy Bee Cafe."

Susanne backed up, not sitting. "I want to talk to my husband."

"And I want a Corvette, lady. Sit down."

Susanne tried to remember her rights. As a lifelong good girl, she'd never thought they'd be at issue. Thus, she'd never paid much attention to what they were. Didn't even watch *Perry Mason* on TV. Something about remaining silent and legal counsel? "I'd like a lawyer, please."

Appelt pointed at the chair.

She sat and tried to hide her trembling hands by clenching them in her lap.

Welch took a chair catty-corner from her.

Appelt remained on his feet, hands on his hips. "Susie, you can call a lawyer when we're done. You can get coffee with your girl friends when we're done. You can get your hair styled and nails manicured for all I care, but it will be when we're done."

"I thought I had a right to a lawyer?"

"Not unless you're under arrest. Eli, did you tell her she was under arrest?"

"No, sir." Eli found something on the table more interesting than her or Appelt.

Appelt smirked. "Yeah. So, no. You don't have a right to anything."

Appelt was a bully. It helped her find her courage. "Since I'm not under arrest, I can leave when I want to."

"Now, why would you want to leave? It's almost like you don't want to help us figure out who killed your husband's girlfriend."

Anger flared inside her. "She's not his girlfriend."

Appelt snickered. "You know what we've been doing while you've been in here? We've been investigating. Talking to people who told us a completely different story than we heard from you and the 'good' doctor." He used his hands to pantomime quotation marks.

"Now, why don't you cut the crap since we already know about it, and tell us when you found out about their affair?"

Susanne was about to defend herself—where was he coming up with this nonsense?—but she was interrupted by a commotion outside the door.

A woman's voice squeaked, "Sir, you can't go in there."

The door swung open into the wall with a loud crash. Patrick barged in. He seemed high on adrenaline, but he was still holding his hand to his midsection. "This interview is over."

Appelt stuck a finger at Patrick's face. "You. Out."

Patrick advanced on the finger. "If my wife is not under arrest, then this interview is over."

"I'm not." Susanne jumped to her feet. "He said I'm not."

Patrick had eyes only for Appelt. "You're not going to get away with treating my wife this way."

"Are you making a threat against an officer of the law, Flint?" Appelt said. He looked amused. Happy.

Susanne put her hand on her husband's elbow. He was vibrating with anger. "I'm okay, Patrick. Let's just leave." He resisted. She applied pressure. "Come on, Patrick, or you're the one they're going to arrest."

Finally, he reached for her hand. The two of them walked out. Susanne held her breath, expecting Appelt to arrest her at any moment.

Behind her, the cop laughed. It wasn't a nice sound. "Take a little time to get your stories straight. But this isn't over, and both of you know it."

Susanne picked up her pace to keep up with her husband. Patrick's grip was grinding the bones in her hand. But she didn't care about the pain. She cared about only one thing. Answers. And as soon as they were in the car, Patrick would be the one answering questions.

Hers.

# CHAPTER FIVE: DRINK

Buffalo, Wyoming
*Now*: Saturday, June 17, 1978

*Perry*

Perry ran for the front door the second he heard the horn beeping outside.

"Where are you going?" Trish shouted.

"You're not the boss of me," he shouted back, slamming the door.

It opened behind him as he reached the old Chevy truck idling in the driveway.

Trish put her hands on her hips. "Mom and Dad will want to know. Will you be home for dinner?"

Perry made a face at her and opened the passenger door. Music blasted out like a sound bomb. "Boogie Oogie Oogie." The song hadn't grown on him yet, but it was all over the radio.

Chuck Peters got out. Chuck was an offensive lineman, a junior, and he equaled two or three of Perry. "You're in the middle, frosh."

Perry expected the middle, but he hated it. He was usually the smallest. Plus, upperclassmen hazed the new lowerclassmen on the team. As the only freshman on varsity, Perry was catching more hazing than anyone else. Noogies to the head. Tripping. Even being chased around the locker room and whipped with clothes hangers. Perry really hated that one. But he liked being part of the team. And he was tough. He would take whatever they dished out. He was just glad senior and team captain Wyatt Evans wasn't with them. Wyatt had stolen Perry's girlfriend Kelsey. His first girlfriend. Sometimes it was hard to pretend that didn't sting, and yet he had to.

Chuck slammed the door. "Your sister is hot."

"Great legs," Billy agreed. He barely ever talked, so the fact that when he did speak it was about Trish in that way made Perry uncomfortable.

The mail carrier pulled to a stop at their mailbox near the end of the driveway. Billy whipped the truck around, driving wild and fast. Two empty beer cans rattled around on the floorboard. The carrier honked and backed up to avoid being hit. Billy didn't seem to notice. Perry kept his face down. His parents were going to hear about that.

Perry changed the subject. "Where are we headed?" He honestly didn't know, which is why he hadn't answered Trish. He didn't care either. Today had left him a little bit out of sorts if he was being honest. He just wanted to get away from that feeling.

"An old cabin out at the Nelsons' ranch. They've got a keg." *People were drinking this early? It was barely the afternoon.* Chuck leaned down and pulled a beer out of a partial six-pack. He popped the top and chugged.

"Hand me one," Billy said.

Chuck freed two beers. Only one was left in the webbing. Chuck opened a can and passed it to Billy. Billy drove with one hand and chugged from the can with the other. Chuck put the other beer in Perry's hand.

Perry had never drunk a whole beer. He'd had sips of his dad's beer at his house before. His dad liked the taste. Perry would rather have a Coca-Cola, but he wasn't about to say that to Chuck and Billy. He pulled off the pop top and piled it in the ashtray with the others. Foam spilled out the mouth.

"People are saying a woman got murdered in your backyard and that the police took your mom to jail today," Chuck said. "What's up, man?"

Had they taken his mom to jail? Perry wanted to forget about the dead woman. Whitney. A friend of his dad's. He didn't want to think about his mom at the police station. He gulped beer to keep from answering. The taste was bitter. Something felt wrong in his throat, and he had trouble swallowing. A cough formed. He tried to resist, but it exploded out of him. Beer spewed onto the inside of the windshield.

"Dude, why'd you do that?" Billy yelled. "I can't see."

Chuck busted out laughing. "Are you a beer virgin, Flint?"

Beer ran down Perry's chin. His shirt and jeans were soaked. It was all over the dashboard. It was kind of hard to even see the road ahead. There was no point in answering Chuck. He was close enough to being a beer virgin, and everyone in the truck knew it.

"You're gonna clean that up, frosh," Billy said.

"Yeah. I'm sorry."

Chuck said, "You're trippin'. Finish the rest of your beer without wasting it, and then your punishment is that you have to shotgun the next one."

"Shotgun? What's that mean?"

The older boys snickered.

Chuck's smile was a little scary. "Don't worry, beer virgin. I'll show you how. You're going to love it."

# CHAPTER SIX: LOSE

Cloud Peak Wilderness, Bighorn Mountains, Wyoming
*Then (nine months earlier)*: Sunday, September 18, 1977

*Patrick*

Patrick was shivering violently. Sweat from exertion plus freezing temperatures and wind was a bad combination. He was exhausted—even sleepy—and his brain felt sluggish. A little confused. His movements were lethargic and clumsy. Add to all of that the blinding snowfall and storm-induced darkness around him, and he was in trouble. All three of them were.

"I knew we took a wrong turn at the top," Loren said. He'd stopped and was gesturing around him. "Dead end."

Rock walls. A narrow ledge. A sheer cliff edge. Everything about this route was wrong. Dangerous. Cloud Peak was not a technical climb. Sure, there was bouldering, but it was in essence a twenty-three-mile, 5300-foot elevation gain roundtrip endurance climb.

They didn't have the right gear for a descent down rock cliffs. Or icy cliffs. Or both.

"Should we turn around?" Whitney asked.

Loren sighed. "Probably. Although finding our way back isn't going to be a cakewalk."

Patrick cleared his dry throat. His voice came out as a croak. "I need water."

"Hey, man, drink your own. I don't carry extra."

Patrick shook his head. A mistake—it made him dizzier. "I didn't have any. Long story." He leaned back against the rock wall. His eyes fluttered closed.

Whitney's voice was inches away. "You haven't had fluids all day?"

He opened his eyes. "No. Would have been okay except for this storm. Getting lost." He lifted a hand. It dropped to his side.

"How are you feeling?"

"Dizzy. Dehydrated. And I've got a headache."

She reached for his wrist and pressed two fingers against it. She shook her head. "Your pulse is high."

Loren threw his hands in the air. "Great. Just great."

"Hush, Loren." Whitney handed Patrick her canteen. "You take it, Dr. Flint. I've already had all I need."

Patrick knew he had to accept it. He was a liability to the group in his condition. Would be more of one if he didn't address the problem now. Still, he felt guilty taking it from her. He swigged a few sips and tried to hand it back.

She pushed it away. "Uh-uh. You may be the doctor, but right now, you're my patient." She turned to Loren. "We need to find shelter."

"Are you crazy? We could be snowed in for the season in a few hours. We need to find a way down." Loren's face was an ugly scowl.

"Just for half an hour. Dr. Flint is going to fall off this mountain if we don't give him time to recover."

Loren threw his hands up. "Fine. I think I saw a cave or a crevice not too far back."

"We'll follow you then."

Loren took off without a second's hesitation.

"Just a minute, Loren. Wait for us. We can't get separated."

He huffed and stopped.

Patrick drained the water and handed the empty canteen back to Whitney.

She took his elbow. "Are you okay to walk?"

Patrick was seeing spots at the edges of his vision. Something big swooped across the sky, close to his face. He felt the flutter of a wing. A rush of air against his cheek. He squinted at the object as it moved away. An enormous wingspan. White with brown feathers interspersed. Ear tufts in the shape of horns. An owl? But what would an owl be doing at this elevation, out in this weather? And a snowy owl if his eyes didn't deceive him. They were rare outside the arctic tundra, but he'd heard tell of sightings of them all along the Rocky Mountains and into Mexico. Still, he had to be imagining things. If he was, he sure didn't want it to be an owl. They were harbingers of death in some cultures. But something niggled at his brain. There were other interpretations for owl sightings. Wisdom. Patience. He needed those now.

"I'll take it slow. That water will do its work on me fast."

"Good. You go in front of me, then." She released his elbow and called out, "Okay, we're ready, Loren."

Loren didn't acknowledge her, but he took off again.

Patrick shuffled along the narrow path, careful not to look down to his right. In the state he was in, the body followed the eyes. His would concentrate on the slippery rocks under his feet, the ones he wanted to stay on. There was no way he was going to die in a climbing accident. Susanne would never forgive him. Fourteen-year-old Perry would have no male role model. Trish, his seventeen-year-old and the human most like him, would test her mother past her limits without him there to referee. And who would take their Irish wolfhound Ferdinand on the long mountain hikes he so dearly loved?

Suddenly, the world seemed to tilt. He listed to the right, overcorrected, and slammed into the rock wall on his left.

Whitney screamed. "Dr. Flint!" She slammed him against the rocks with her own body.

# CHAPTER SEVEN: RECEIVE

BUFFALO, WYOMING
*NOW*: SATURDAY, JUNE 17, 1978

*Trish*

TRISH DANGLED her legs over the arm of the living room chair and flipped forward a page in *The Diary of a Young Girl*. She loved this book. Anne Frank had lived through the worst horrors imaginable and yet felt many of the same feelings and worried about a lot of the same things Trish did. But it was hard to concentrate on Anne right now. Her mind kept wandering to her parents. They'd been gone a long time.

Ferdinand barked, deep and loud, and ran to the door. He sniffed and snuffled. It had to be the mail delivery. The dog loved mail delivery. It was always at the same time. Three thirty every day except Sundays. Sometimes one of her grandparents posted her a letter, but not often. She used to love to race out to the mailbox when she was little, but not anymore. She almost didn't go outside for it, but then she thought about how stressed her parents were. She should do what she could to make things easier for them. She could make dinner for them, too. Maybe fry some hamburgers and bake some potatoes?

She tucked a bookmark—Josie and the Pussycats, a gift from Marcy when Trish made cheerleader—in her book, then shut it and set it on the coffee table.

She walked to the door. "Back, Ferdie." She used her hip to keep the tall, wiry dog at bay and slipped outside. The driveway and house felt so empty. She shivered. She wished one of her parents would call home with an update. Or that they'd come home.

Behind the door, Ferdinand whined. She almost let him out—sometimes she did—but he'd been really keyed up ever since the cops had been there. She was afraid he'd run off. So, she walked alone to the mailbox. It was all the way out at the corner where their driveway met the road. She pulled its little door open and retrieved a passel of mail. A Good Housekeeping magazine for her mom, which made Trish happy. She liked to read the short stories each month. A big manilla envelope to her dad. Some bills.

And a letter addressed to Trish. Her heart lodged in her throat. She recognized the handwriting on the envelope.

It was from Ben.

A sound escaped her lips. Not a moan, not a cry, not a scream, but a weird combination of all three. Ben, the boy whose promise ring she'd worn on a chain around her neck for four months after he ran away, claiming he would never be good enough for her. Then, in April, she and her family had driven all the way to Ketchikan, Alaska, when they'd heard from the Sibleys that he was there. But when the Flints had arrived, Ben was gone. He'd quit his job on a fishing boat and moved out of his lodging house. During the long drive back to Wyoming, Trish had decided she had to try to start living again. She had taken off the promise ring and put it in her jewelry box. It had been time to let him go.

And now she had a letter from him.

She ripped it open, dropping the rest of the mail. She tried to read it, but the sun was too bright in her eyes. She scooped up the mail that had fallen to the ground and ran back to the house as fast as she could go, her heart pounding out of her chest.

# CHAPTER EIGHT: CONSULT

Buffalo, Wyoming
*Now*: Saturday, June 17, 1978

*Patrick*

"Thanks for seeing us over the weekend, Mr. Ryan." Patrick took in the one-room office. There'd been no receptionist. Ryan's walls were lined with gilt-stamped law books on listing shelves. Diplomas—but nothing else—hung on the one shelf-free wall. University of Wyoming for a political science undergrad and a law degree. Double U-W. They were the right credentials for these parts.

"My pleasure." Ryan put out his hand. He was young. Fresh-faced. Bright-eyed. Patrick felt like Methuselah next to him, knowing the last few years had seen crow's feet and laugh lines etch into his face and gray encroach into his dark brown hair. The younger man also smelled like drugstore cologne. A lot of it.

"Sorry." Patrick held his injured right hand against his chest, slightly elevated. Every movement was painful. He needed an anti-inflammatory. Probably a splint. Maybe a cast.

"Our next stop is the ER," Susanne said. "Doctors make the worst patients. But I can shake." She offered the attorney her hand and glanced at her husband. Her expression wasn't warm.

Ryan smiled. "Call me Stu. And it's no problem. You delivered my sister's third baby last year, Dr. Flint. It was a breech birth in the middle of the night. My whole family owes you one."

"You already paid that back by explaining that if Susanne wasn't under arrest, I could simply go pick her up. The police were none too happy about it."

"Appelt is a bully. I'm not surprised he tried to pressure you, Mrs. Flint. Please, both of you, have a seat."

Susanne sank into the chair, and her shoulders drooped. "I don't know what he thinks he could have learned from me. I have no clue about what happened to Whitney."

It broke Patrick's heart for her to face suspicion over this, his—in her words—"hobby." Mountain climbing. As he sat—careful not to jostle his hand—his mind returned to the drive from the police station to the attorney's office. Susanne had been emotional, and she had questions. A lot of them. The police had gotten under her skin and into her head, which he was certain was what Appelt had intended.

Patrick had tried to convince her that he'd never had any feelings for Whitney. That their relationship was about rocks. Mountains. Endurance. Still, harsh words had been exchanged.

"You brought this on yourself. You shouldn't be hanging out with a young woman instead of your wife and kids," she'd said, her eyes flashing.

"What about all the people you've met and spent time with at the college? This could just as easily have been one of them," he'd shot back at her. "And are you forgetting the impact your former professor had on our family?" Her words stung. She was usually his biggest champion. Whitney dying in the creek behind their house was not his fault.

"My education so that I can pursue a career is not the same thing as you working out with a young woman in pursuit of a hobby."

He'd parked the car and slammed the door, as angry as she was.

But in the aftermath, he was reeling. He did feel responsible. It was his fault she was in this position. His climbing. His friend. It was the guilt that had made him a defensive porcupine, and he regretted comparing the situation to her college classes and job. And deep inside, he hurt, too. For himself, for his wife. For the tragic death of Whitney, a young person with a promising future ahead of her.

He wished he'd found the right words to say to her in the car. Now here they were, with a gulf the size of Crazy Woman Canyon between them forming a barrier as hard as its pink granite walls.

Stu said, "Why don't the two of you give me the facts as you know them, from the beginning."

"It's really not my story," Susanne said.

*She's right.* Patrick told Stu about finding Whitney in the creek, his association with her, and the police zeroing in on Susanne. "To my knowledge, they don't even know how or when she died yet. They based all this on my business card and home phone number being in her wallet. And something Whitney wrote on it, that neither of us understand."

"Which was?"

"His wife knows—she threatened me."

Stu's mouth tightened and his eyebrows rose. "What does that mean?"

"I have no idea."

"Nor do I," Susanne said. "All I knew was that Patrick and Whitney climbed together."

"What did you tell the police?" Stu asked.

Patrick said, "I told them I gave her the card when she interviewed at the Buffalo hospital, and that she had my home phone number to contact me for training and climbs."

"They have nothing, then." Stu wove his pen through his fingers.

"They're fishing. Susanne, what was your relationship to Ms. Saylor?"

Susanne's lips tightened. "I didn't even know her. I'd never met her. I was jealous of the time Patrick spent away from his family on things like mountain climbing, but that was how I felt about *Patrick.* It had nothing to do with her. She can make any choices she wants on how to spend her free time."

"Did you ever have harsh words or a disagreement or altercation with her?"

"No."

"Did you tell other people you disliked her or wished her harm?"

"I've told my friends Ronnie Harcourt and Vangie Sibley how I feel about the time Patrick spends climbing."

"Did you ever threaten her?"

"Never. I would never. Even if I hated someone, I wouldn't do that. It's not who I am."

Stu nodded and made some notes.

Patrick leaned forward. He hated hearing the pain and fear in Susanne's face. "What do we do now?"

Stu set his pen down. "Nothing, unless they arrest one of you. Do you have reason to think they will? And remember that anything you tell me is protected by attorney-client privilege."

Susanne said, "I didn't kill her, if that's what you're asking."

"Good to know. But you don't have to confess anything to me."

Patrick broke in. "Neither of us has anything to confess."

"Can you find out what evidence they have?" Susanne asked.

Stu smiled. "None, or you wouldn't be sitting here now. And if I ask them what they have, it makes them think there's something to find."

"There isn't," Patrick said, his voice firm.

"All right. I'll give them a call. Let them know I represent Susanne—"

"Represent both of us," Patrick corrected.

Stu's brow knit. "I can do that, for now. But how would you like to handle it if a legal conflict arises between you?"

"What do you mean?" Susanne asked.

"Well, let's say that one of you has information that could exonerate the other but would get you in trouble. In that case, you'd either have to waive the legal conflict, or one of you would need to get another attorney."

Her response was quick. "There won't be any conflicts."

"Patrick?"

"There won't be any."

Stu nodded slowly. "Good to know. And it's always something we can address later if a situation arises. So, as I was saying, I can call them and let them know I represent the two of you and that you're willing to cooperate, within reason, but that you have no more information than what you've already provided them. It won't stop them from showing up to arrest you if they find evidence, though."

"They won't find any because it doesn't exist," Patrick said.

Susanne put her hands in front of her, palms out. "The police led me to believe someone is saying Whitney and Patrick had... had... were... in a romantic relationship."

"Were you?" Stu asked Patrick.

Patrick shook his head vehemently. "Absolutely not."

"Any idea who would have that impression?"

"None." Stu kept looking at him. Patrick added, "Honestly, none."

"I think this is the moment I should let you know that I can only help you if you tell me the whole truth. Everything. Openness and honesty. No surprises. No lies. Can you both agree to that?"

Patrick couldn't recall the last time his truthfulness had been challenged. His left fist balled. His right one tried and got nowhere except into a state of instant regret.

"I can," Susanne said.

Patrick tried to relax. Stu wasn't the enemy. He was trying to help them. "Yes. Me, too."

"Good. Anything else then?"

Susanne finally looked at Patrick, her gaze wary, as if she was afraid of what he'd say next. It cut him to the quick.

"Nothing."

"Go home then. Try to forget about this. And let's hope this is the end of the police's interest in you. With any luck, they'll determine there was no murder, and you'll never hear from them again."

Patrick put his good hand under his wife's elbow and guided her toward the door. Her arm was stiff, but she didn't pull away. He pondered Stu's last words. No murder would be the best resolution. But there was a second best one as well. He muttered, "Or that the police believe someone else besides us did it."

# CHAPTER NINE: READ

Buffalo, Wyoming
*Now*: Saturday, June 17, 1978

*Trish*

Back in the house, Trish took the mail up to her room. She flopped onto her unmade bed and read Ben's letter once, then a second time with tear-filled eyes.

Dear Trish:

My boss Cap and my landlord said you and your dad came to see me. When I'd left, I wasn't sure whether I'd ever be coming back.

I'd gone home to Buffalo. I was there to apologize for running off and ask you to forgive me. I have not had a single date with another girl. I was promised to you. Even though I had to leave, I still felt the same way about you the whole time.

But when I went to your house, I saw you with your new boyfriend Wyatt. I watched you through the window. You were wearing his jacket and playing board games with Perry and Kelsey. You broke my heart.

I am confused why you came to Alaska if you are seeing someone else?

Henry and Vangie told me that the charges against me in Laramie were dropped. That is good. But I have decided that college is not for me, and I am not going back to UW. I like Alaska. I make good money fishing.

If there is a future for us, you can write to me. If you're still seeing Wyatt, don't bother. I'm in Ketchikan. I got back not long after you were here.

I really am sorry about running off without talking to you. And I really have loved you with everything I am.

Ben

WATER MARKS MARRED THE PAPER. Hers, wet. Others, dry. Ben's?

A strangled sound erupted from deep inside her, and Ferdinand shoved his cold, wet nose under her arm. How had Ben managed to arrive at her house at the exact moment Wyatt and Kelsey had been stranded there during a freak spring snowstorm? Wyatt had never been anything to Trish. He'd just given her a ride home from one of Jillian's awful parties, then gotten stuck at her house. There had been no one but Ben for her, ever since she met him.

Trish gently set his letter aside. She went to her desk and pulled a box of pink monogrammed stationery from the bottom of a drawer. It had been a birthday present from her mother when she was sixteen, and she rarely used it. She lifted off the lid. A scent wafted out. The Blue Jeans perfume that had come in a separate box. She remembered spraying it in a mist over the sheets.

She put a page on her desktop, then smoothed her hand over the loops of her raised initials. She fished out a pen and wrote, "Dear Ben."

Before she got any further, the doorbell rang. Ferdinand dutifully bounded away to investigate. He sounded the intruder alarm as he flew down the stairs.

"Hush, Ferdie." She looked at the clock on her bedside table. How had time flown by so fast? It was already five o'clock. Jillian, Dabbo, and his friend were due to pick her up any minute. Their double date to an early movie had been pushed forward to include grabbing a quick dinner.

Double date? It wasn't a date. Not even a blind date. It was just her giving in to pressure from Jillian because the girl was the squad captain.

But now, after the letter from Ben, Trish couldn't go. Besides, she wasn't ready. She hadn't showered all day. Not that it mattered what the guy thought. But her mom had raised her to care about how she presented herself in public. Trish didn't always like it, yet still she found herself unable to completely ignore the lesson.

She had to answer the door, though. She ran down the stairs to where Ferdinand was barking his fool head off. "Calm down, dog." She put a hand on his head. Peeking out the sidelight window, she groaned.

There were three people standing there. Jillian, dark-haired Dabbo, and a blond guy she didn't recognize. He looked older than Jillian had promised. He had a mustache, for Pete's sake! Thank goodness her parents weren't here. Or maybe it would have been better if they were. They would never let her out the door with this group. She would have had a built-in excuse for canceling: the parental no.

She opened the door, holding onto her dog's collar. Ferdinand still lunged toward the newcomers, dragging her with him. His barks turned to snarls.

"Whoa! Get that dog off of me." Dabbo raised a knee, without much success. The dog was as tall as a Shetland pony.

"Sorry." Trish didn't know Dabbo very well. He was constantly with Jillian, but he didn't interact with the other cheerleaders. She yanked Ferdinand back. "Jillian, could you come in alone? He knows you."

"Hi, Ferdie," Jillian crooned as she slipped in the door. "You're like a big wrecking ball, aren't you?"

Just before the door clicked shut, she heard Dabbo say, "I told you she's good-looking. And fresh as the driven snow, too."

*Whatever that means.*

"Is that what you're wearing?" Jillian said.

Trish barely glanced down at her cut off jean shorts and old Buffalo Bison t-shirt. "Jillian, I can't go."

Jillian crossed her arms over her chest. "Uh-uh. No way you're backing out."

"Please, Jillian. It's just a bad time for me."

Jillian's pixie face turned to stone. "You promised. You will not do this to me, Trish Flint."

Trish closed her eyes. She had promised. *Sorry, Ben.* "Just dinner and a movie, right? Then straight home?"

"If that's what you want, yes."

"It's what I want."

"We'll see." Jillian nudged Trish in the side with her elbow. "Jimmy is pretty foxy. You might change your mind."

"I won't."

The girl shrugged. "Whatever. Just be ready in five, okay?"

Against her better judgment, Trish nodded. This wasn't a date. It was a favor to stay in Jillian's good grace.

And, most importantly, Ben would never know.

# CHAPTER TEN: CONFRONT

Buffalo, Wyoming
*Now*: Saturday, June 17, 1978

*Susanne*

Back at home, Susanne walked in to find an agitated dog and a note on the dining table.

I'm going to a movie with Jillian. Perry out with guys on the team. I'm sorry you had such a hard day. Hope everything is all right. Be in by 10:30. XOXO Trish

The door closed. Patrick's footsteps approached. They'd stopped at the emergency room after they met with Stu Ryan. Patrick had cracked a bone in his hand, which he'd told her was as minor an injury as he could have hoped for. He'd splinted and wrapped it, refusing a cast because it would interfere with his training. He had left with a good supply of anti-inflammatories, though. Now, he put his good hand on her waist and read the note over her shoulder.

"The dog needs to be fed," she said, moving away.

In response, Ferdinand picked up his metal bowl and began circling them with it in his mouth, his big tail whacking her legs each time he passed.

"Susanne..." Patrick's voice was soft. The defensive edge from earlier was gone.

She wasn't ready to forgive him. "Can you take care of Ferdie? I have to make dinner." She searched inside the refrigerator for something fast and easy. Hamburger meat. She'd make a beef succotash. She ran tap water into a pan and added rice and salt, then put it on the stove to bring it to a boil.

"Stop for just a moment." Patrick walked into the kitchen.

She felt him stop directly behind her, and she froze. He guided her gently to turn and face him. When she didn't meet his eyes, he tilted her chin with a finger.

"I'm sorry this is happening. I know you don't love the mountain climbing or that I've been doing it with Whitney—"

She spoke through teeth gritted to hold back sudden tears. "She's too young."

He sighed. "It's a sport best not done alone, and there's no one else to climb with around here."

"You haven't looked hard enough."

"Maybe so. I'll try again now. But I promise that—"

The doorbell rang. Ferdinand abandoned his metal bowl and skidded to a noisy stop at the front door.

She frowned. "Are you expecting someone?"

"No. I'll be right back." He walked to the door.

*Please God, not the police.* She put on a pot of water to boil then positioned a cutting board where she could see out of the kitchen into the great room and dining room.

"Who is it?" Patrick said.

Patrick held on to the dog and opened the door, letting the soft night sounds in. The rustling of leaves from wind in the treetops. Birdsong. Crickets. "Hey, Ronnie."

Relief flooded Susanne. It was an officer, but not the bad one.

Her face was grave but friendly. "I just came to check on you guys."

Patrick waved her in. "We've had a bad day."

"I heard." Ronnie walked to the kitchen and leaned a hip against the L of the breakfast bar. "I'm sorry, Susanne."

"I survived," Susanne said. She didn't want to rehash her feelings. She was still raw from fighting with Patrick.

"Did you get any information on cause of death during your visit?"

"Nothing. All they did was badger me."

"Did you form any impressions when you were with the body, Patrick?"

He shook his head. "I couldn't tell. She could have fallen or had a medical event. Aneurysm. Stroke. Heart attack. Rare in someone her age but not impossible. She might have drowned. Or someone could have killed her. Drowned her or hit her, although it would have been a closed wound. I didn't see any blood. Someone could have poisoned her. The possibilities are endless at this point. The forensic pathologist will figure it out."

"I heard they have a witness." Susanne felt Ronnie's eyes on her. "Susanne, I'm sorry to bring it up, but we need to talk about it."

She nodded, lips pressed together, and added rice to her pot and hamburger meat to a skillet turned to medium high. She broke it apart with a wooden spoon more forcefully than necessary.

"That's what they told Susanne. Do you know who it is?" Patrick's voice was preternaturally calm.

"Her old boyfriend, I'm told."

"I didn't even know she had one. What is he saying?"

"That you and Whitney were close. That Whitney would have liked it to be more. That she had a thing for older guys."

"That's not true. About us being close. I—I don't know about the rest."

Susanne slammed the wooden spoon on the counter. "Why would he say that, Patrick?"

"I don't know! Whitney never gave me any indication of... inappropriate feelings. In fact, when I met her, I thought she was dating Loren. You know, the other climber. From last fall."

Susanne paused stirring to watch Patrick's face. She didn't like thinking about that time. About Patrick not coming home by the end of the day as he'd promised. About her frantic calls to Ronnie and Wes. The sleepless night wondering how she could go on without him if the worst had happened on the mountain. Search and rescue deployed at first light. That call. That wonderful call when word came back that he'd made it off the mountain safely. Meeting him at the ER. His windburned face and exhausted eyes. And their hug. Their wonderful hug and the kiss from his chapped lips. The other climber who hadn't been as lucky. She'd held her husband's hand while he was rehydrated with IV fluids, then they'd gone home, and, despite how tired he was, they'd come together in the sanctuary of their room in the way they always did. With so much love. She had to believe that he hadn't betrayed that love with Whitney.

But she wasn't stupid. "What aren't you telling me?"

Patrick's lips were moving, like he was talking to someone, but no sound came out.

"What?" she said.

"Nothing. This is just news to me. And not good news. I never led her on. I am married." He smiled at her. She didn't return it. "Happily married."

Susanne wanted to throw the wooden spoon at him. She turned the rice down to simmer and stirred it instead to make sure it wasn't sticking to the bottom of the pan.

Ronnie cleared her throat. "The opinion of a jealous ex-boyfriend isn't fact. If that's all they've got, it's nothing. He also said she was working on something new."

"You mean her application to work at Buffalo?"

"He told the Buffalo police it was a project outside of work. A thing she'd been working on since last fall. I thought maybe she talked to you about it?"

Susanne thought Patrick looked relieved. "We were nothing but climbing partners. I knew nothing about her personal life."

She had let a long moment pass. The silence became awkward. Manners forced her to speak, with Ronnie in their home. She reached into her cabinet and took out cans of green beans, corn, and crushed tomatoes. Luckily Ronnie spoke first so she didn't have to.

"Patrick, are you still on for Rainier now that Whitney is gone?"

"Our first climb of the season was supposed to be a return to Cloud Peak."

Susanne's fists balled and her lips pressed together. Patrick looked at her. She turned her attention to opening the cans.

"It's too early for it yet, right?"

"A bit. But soon. As for Rainier, I'll have to talk to Susanne."

"Okay. Well, I need to get home before Will goes to bed. And Jeff said he made dinner for us. That's a rare event, so I'm supposed to make a big deal about it." She rolled her eyes, but she laughed. "You guys call me, though, if you need anything."

"Thanks. We will." Patrick walked Ronnie to the door.

She waved and disappeared into the night.

"Smells good." Patrick returned to the kitchen and leaned against the counter. "I know that was hard, but I think it was a necessary conversation."

All of the emotion that had been rattling inside her, good and bad, blew like the top off a pressure cooker. She whirled to face him. "Stand in front of me."

He frowned but stood and moved to do as she asked. "What's up?"

"Raise your right hand and repeat after me."

"Susanne..." He shook his head. "What is this about? This is silly."

She drilled him with her eyes. "I mean it."

His hand went up.

"I, Patrick Flint, do solemnly swear..."

He repeated, "I, Patrick Flint, do solemnly swear..."

"That I was never given any reason to think..."

"That I was never given any reason to think..."

"That Whitney had anything other than platonic feelings for me."

"That, uh... "

Her heart sank. "That's what I thought." She turned back to the stove and stirred blindly, deaf to the flood of words now pouring from her husband.

# CHAPTER ELEVEN: DISGUST

Buffalo, Wyoming

*Now*: Saturday, June 17, 1978

*Trish*

Trish walked out of the theater, keeping Dabbo and Jillian between her and Jimmy. That was the blond guy's name. Jimmy. Jimmy Gross. And it fit. During the movie, he'd spent the first hour trying to kiss her—he'd even tried to touch her!—and the second hour muttering to himself about wasting his money. Meanwhile, Jillian and Dabbo had their tongues in each other's mouths the entire time. It had been the most awkward night of Trish's life. She'd really wanted to see *Grease*, too, but they'd ruined it for her. All three of them, but mostly Jimmy. Even dinner had been awful. Fast food burgers with limp lettuce and cold French fries. Flat Pepsi. The guys talking to each other like the girls weren't even there, and Jillian hanging on Dabbo's arm and simpering up at him.

Trish just wanted to go home. She was worried about her parents. Her mom especially. And she wanted to write back to Ben.

Jillian was singing the words to "Sandra Dee" as she and Dabbo climbed into the back of Jimmy's Cutlass, where they started sucking face again. Trish huddled in as close to the door as she could get in the front passenger seat.

"Sandra Dee. It's a song about you, Trish," Jimmy pulled forward out of their parking place.

Jillian laughed and leaned across the seat. "Oh, my gosh, that's so true. Think about it Trish. You're blonde. You're smart. You're—"

Jimmy cut in. "She's a prude."

Trish took a deep breath. She was halfway between mad and embarrassed. "I'll take that as a compliment."

Everyone laughed. Then the sucking and rustling noises resumed in the back seat.

"Stop, Dabbo. Not in here," Jillian said, in a mock whisper.

"Then where?" Dabbo drawled. "Because wherever that is, I'd like to get there fast."

"Somewhere private. Sometime later."

JIMMY SNORTED. "At least someone is having fun tonight." Then he said, "Windows down. It's hot, and I'm not wasting my gas money on air conditioner."

Everyone cranked down their windows. Jimmy hung his left arm out the side and leaned his seat back a little. Moments later, they were cruising past the Occidental Hotel where Trish and her family had stayed a few months before when their heating system was broken. The June air felt great on her skin and downtown looked pretty, but Trish just wished Jimmy would drive faster.

She wanted—no, she *needed* to get home. She thought about the letter she was going to write to Ben. They'd wasted so much time over misunderstandings. Him not knowing the charges against him had been dropped. Her not realizing Ben had the wrong impression about

Wyatt. She wished she knew his phone number. She could just call him and explain. Of course, her parents would probably never let her spend all that money on a long distance call. But waiting for a letter to get to him and then a response to come back from him—if he sent one, he might not—would take *so* long.

She realized she'd been daydreaming and that Jimmy hadn't slowed down at Fort, the street out to her house. He'd blown right past it.

"You missed my turn," she said.

"You missed my turn," he repeated in a high-pitched voice.

"Ha ha." She crossed her arms over her chest. "I'm serious."

"Me, too, and I don't really care." He turned to the back seat with his hand up for Dabbo to slap a high five, but Dabbo didn't come up for air. Jimmy dropped his hand.

Trish shifted from irritated to nervous at his words. His tone. "Where are you going?"

He tapped a gauge on his dash. "First, to get gas. After that, I dunno—where do you wanna go, Dab?"

But the only sounds coming from the back seat were the disgusting smacking noises.

Trish tried to keep her voice firm. Was it shaking? "I need to get home. I have a curfew."

"You're nearly a grown woman. Too old for curfews, aren't you?"

She turned to face him. His yucky mustache. His floppy blond hair. The glint in his eye that spoke of trouble she didn't want any part of. "A woman died in our yard today. The police made my mom go in for questioning. I can't give my parents any trouble. They have enough already. Please take me home."

He winked at her. "I heard your dad was getting a little on the side and your mom took out the competition."

Her brow furrowed. Had he said what she thought he said? Yes, he had, and it was awful. Unforgiveable. "Stop this car right now."

Jimmy laughed, then reached over and chucked her face with his knuckles. It wasn't like he punched her, but it still felt menacing. "Come on, Sandra Dee. I'm just joshing you."

"It wasn't funny. Let me out. I'll walk home."

He turned into a gas station and pulled up to a pump. "We're already here, and I need fuel. After this, I'll take you home." He slapped the top of the front seat between them. "Dabbo, quit making out with your jailbait. Let's go, uh, take care of the bill inside."

"Hold that thought, Hot Lips," Dabbo said.

Out of her side vision, Trish saw Jillian blow her boyfriend a kiss. Dabbo wasn't as disgusting as Jimmy, but she still didn't understand what Jillian saw in him. She could date nearly any boy at school if she wanted. What was she doing with a guy so much older than her? One who didn't go to college but barely even worked? Trish stuck her face out the window. Strong gasoline odors made her nose wrinkle. Could she trust Jimmy to take her home after this? It was a very long walk. It would take her an hour or more. She'd for sure be home after she'd told her parents in her note.

She decided to give him one more chance to do the right thing.

The car doors slammed, and the guys walked to the station. Jimmy punched Dabbo in the arm. The two of them scuffled for a moment, laughing. Trish saw something in Dabbo's hand. It was long and wooden. A baseball bat. That was odd. She didn't know he played baseball. Or that it had been in the car this whole time. There were some summer leagues, though. Perry was on a team. She used to play, too. Maybe there was one for old guys who couldn't keep jobs.

"So, what do you think of Jimmy? He looks like Sam Elliott, doesn't he?" Jillian said.

"Who's Sam Elliott?"

Jillian laughed. "You're kidding, right?"

Trish shook her head.

"That actor from *The Lifeguard*? The one with the great mustache?"

"Didn't see it." Trish held her eyes closed for a moment. How could Jillian think there was any planet on which Trish would dig

Jimmy? This is why she and Jillian weren't friends. The girl was completely oblivious to anything outside of the center of the universe —herself. "I'm not in the market to date anyone."

"Why not? Come on—you have to have a boyfriend for the summer. We could have so much fun hanging out if you dated Jimmy."

*Because I already have a boyfriend.* Just because she and Ben had been having trouble didn't mean she didn't love him. Her heart belonged to him. When she'd gotten ready that night—quickly, with Jillian, Jimmy, and Dabbo waiting outside—she'd put the chain with the promise ring back around her neck. Now, she pulled it out from under her shirt. She unhooked the chain, slid the ring off it, and slipped it on her finger. She wasn't taking it off again unless he asked for it back.

There was a loud crash and the sound of shattering glass.

"What was that?" Jillian said.

Trish turned toward the station. The front window was broken out. Someone was shouting. Screaming, really. Suddenly, Jimmy and Dabbo were sprinting to the car, laughing like maniacs. Just as they reached it and jumped inside, a man ran out after them, shaking his fist. Trish couldn't understand what he was saying, but she got the gist of it. Jimmy and Dabbo had made him really, really mad. She assumed they were the ones who broke the window.

"Go, go, go," Dabbo yelled.

The engine roared to life. Jimmy shifted and accelerated at the same time. The tires squealed. The car jolted off the curb as Jimmy turned and headed back toward town. The bounce shot Trish in the air. She hit her head on the ceiling.

"Dabbo Kern, what in the world is going on?" Jillian demanded.

He ignored her. "Drive faster, Jimmy."

And then Trish heard the wail of police sirens.

# CHAPTER TWELVE: REFUGE

Cloud Peak Wilderness, Bighorn Mountains, Wyoming
*Then (nine months earlier)*: Sunday, September 18, 1977

*Patrick*

"Are you okay?" Whitney grasped Patrick's shoulders as they huddled against the rock wall beside them, away from the yawning emptiness on the other side of the narrow trail.

"Sorry." Patrick grimaced. He hated being a burden. He hated it with every fiber of his being. "Better now. Thank you." He wasn't. Not much, anyway.

She forced air out of her mouth, expressing excess adrenaline. "You scared the pee waddling squat out of me."

That made Patrick smile. An old timey expression from such a young person.

Then there was a shout ahead. Through the falling snow, Patrick could just see Loren waving and pointing. Had he found the cave?

Patrick pulled himself up straight and took a few deep breaths. "I'm ready."

"I'll be right behind you."

With renewed purpose and focus, he forged ahead. The snowfall was heavier now. The ground starting to cover. He cursed the weatherman for a bad forecast. Himself for bad preparation. He shuffled to a stop when he reached where Loren was waiting for them by a low, narrow opening.

"I don't know how big, but it's a cave." Loren waved Patrick ahead. "I haven't gone in yet. Watch out for grizzly bears."

Patrick didn't have the energy to tell him that the last grizzlies had been hunted out of the Bighorns half a century ago. Or that no bear of any type would be hibernating in September when there were still berries and nuts to forage on at lower elevations.

Using one hand to brace himself, he leaned over. The opening was still too low for him. He sunk to his hands and knees and crawled forward, blinking his eyes at the immediate, complete darkness. His backpack scraped the rock above and threatened to wedge him in place. He backed out, removed it, and dug out his flashlight. He turned it on and shone it inside. The light bounced back at him.

"What do you see?" Loren said.

"Not a thing yet. I'll have to get inside to see."

"If it looks like there's room, I'll push your pack in after you."

"Okay. Thanks." Patrick tucked the flashlight in his jacket pocket and started crawling again. The walls and ceiling were tight. They should have sent Whitney in. She was the smallest, and she wasn't mentally compromised by dehydration. At least he wasn't claustrophobic. As he moved forward, the space began to open up. He sniffed. The odor was quintessential mountain cave, without a subterranean musk. Clean, clear, dry. And cold.

He stopped, grabbing the flash light and shining it in. The beam illuminated a spacious, high-ceilinged interior ahead, plenty big enough for the three of them. A narrow shaft of light was making its way in from somewhere above and to the right. The floor was rock, but pebbly, dusty, and littered with small animal scat. A dark area in the back appeared to be an opening. Maybe an anteroom? But he was too tired to check it out.

Over his shoulder, he shouted, "Looks fine. Plenty of room." Just the effort of raising his voice made him lightheaded. *Dammit.* He'd let the dehydration go on far too long.

"Roger that," Loren said.

Patrick heard scraping, grunting, and heavy breathing noises behind him. He moved out of the way as his backpack appeared, then his climbing partners. He pulled the pack over to him and positioned it as a pillow. Solid as a rock, it felt like goose down at that moment. He sighed and put the flashlight on his lap, switching it off.

He closed his eyes. "Wake me in fifteen."

"Hey, can I borrow your flashlight, man?" Loren asked.

Patrick grunted and held it up. After a moment, he felt it removed from his hand. Then it switched on. He shielded his eyes from the light.

Whitney handed him her canteen. "There's still a few sips."

"Thanks." Patrick drank slowly and carefully, then handed the canteen back to her.

"This cave goes on a way. Let's see what's back there," Loren said.

"Shouldn't we rest?" Whitney sounded nervous. "We don't know what we have ahead of us."

"Well, I know I'll never be back to this cave again and I want to explore a little. You don't have to come if you don't want to."

"Five minutes," she said.

Patrick just wished they'd keep it down. The "old mountain goat" would do better on the climb down with a little shut-eye.

Just as he was drifting off, Whitney screamed. The sound reverberated off the rock walls of the cave.

Patrick sat up. "You okay in there?"

There was a pause. He was about to jump to his feet when Loren said, "Yeah, man, we're cool. Just, uh, ran across something... unexpected."

Whatever it was, it would have to wait. Patrick was melting with exhaustion. He let himself drift off toward slumber again. Just before it overtook him, voices beside him jerked him back from the brink.

Whitney was whispering. "Do you think we should tell him?"

Loren's voice was louder, although he was whispering, too. "Hell, no. This is ours."

*Are they talking about me?* But if they said anything else that would have answered his question, Patrick didn't hear it as he fell into a deep sleep.

# CHAPTER THIRTEEN: SPEW

BUFFALO, WYOMING
*NOW:* SATURDAY, JUNE 17, 1978

*Perry*

PERRY'S FOREHEAD whacked on something hard. He groaned. Or he thought he did. But his thinking wasn't working very well, so he couldn't be sure. He'd been with Chuck and Billy. They'd gone to a party. After that, things got fuzzy. He was pretty sure they'd left and that he'd fallen asleep in the truck. But what had he hit his head on? Where was he now? And why was everything spinning?

"Flint, wake up. We're at your house," Billy said from right beside him.

"Okay," Perry mumbled. He felt sick to his stomach. Really, really sick.

"Get him out of here before he pukes in my dad's truck."

He heard a door open. Something moved away from his head.

Then rough hands pulled Perry up and out of the truck by his armpits. He landed in grass. Hitting the ground hurt his head a little, but the grass was cool and soft on his face. It felt so good. So, so good. Maybe he could sleep here. But, no—his parents would find him, and he'd be in big trouble. He had to go inside. Sleep in his own bed.

The thought of standing up reminded him how sick he felt, though. The long walk inside and up the stairs seemed impossible.

"What do you think of shotgunning beers, frosh?" Chuck's mouth was close to Perry's ear.

"Ugh." Perry tried to crawl to his feet. He made it to his elbows and knees with his cheek on the ground. *Have to get inside.* He balanced there for a second then collapsed back onto his stomach.

"Later, Flint."

Footsteps crunched gravel. The truck door slammed. The engine revved. Little rocks spit out from under the truck wheels and pelted him in the back. Then the truck was gone.

He sighed. Just a short nap. Then he'd go inside.

The outdoor lights came on.

"Who's there?" Perry's dad said in his tough guy voice.

Perry pushed up. *Have to stand up. Have to show Dad I'm okay.* He moaned as he lifted his head. *Not good.*

"Perry, is that you?"

"Yeah."

"Are you all right?"

A weird sensation in his head made it seem like the ground was moving. Like he was spinning. He rested his forehead on the ground. "Naht rilly."

He felt his dad's presence looming over him. "You smell like a brewery."

"Wuzzen my idea."

"Someone *made* you drink beer?"

"Upper... upper..."

"Upper classmen made you drink?"

"Sorda. Kinna."

Another set of hands under his armpits. These less rough than those in the truck but equally firm and one felt funny. Hard. His body rose. His dad muttered something about his hand. Perry scrambled to get his feet under him. His head lolled. He tried to hold it up straight and failed. Gave up.

"Can you stand?"

"Tryin' to."

Then, with no warning, Perry felt an explosion of beer make its way up and out of his mouth and nose. The hands under his arms didn't let go of him when his knees buckled. He reached down and propped his hands on his knees. One slid off, then the other and he hung from his dad's hands, fertilizing the lawn again and again until his body racked with dry heaves.

"Patrick?" His mom's voice.

"Hey, Susanne. I'm out here," his dad said.

"What's going on?"

"Just talking to Perry about his night. Go back to bed. We'll be inside in a minute."

"Okay." She sounded uncertain, but the door clicked shut.

"Better now?" his dad said.

Perry groaned. "A liddle."

"Good enough. I'm going to hose you off, then I'm taking you in the kitchen and get you something to eat and drink. You need to keep sipping water, no matter how sick you feel, all night. Got it?"

"Goddit."

"Now, take off your clothes. I'll hose you off."

This didn't sound like fun. Perry grabbed the bottom him of his shirt. The ground tilted and he took a few steps sideways until his dad pulled him back to center. He pulled the shirt up. It smelled awful. Gushy stuff was stuck to it. He gagged.

"Keep going," his dad said.

Perry pried the shirt over his head. His shorts were even harder, and he landed on one hand dangling from his father's grasp when he tried to step out of them. Finally, he was down to his birthday suit.

"Here it comes." His dad turned the hose on him.

The water was icy cold. Perry gasped and turned away, covering himself with his hands. *This hurts.* The water kept coming. But he felt better. Maybe it was helping. He shivered and his teeth chattered.

His dad turned the water off. "Okay, let's get you inside."

"I'm neck-ed."

"Nothing I haven't seen before. Move it."

Perry lurched up the steps. He braced himself on the doorframe, then the wall, then the furniture, and finally the kitchen table. His dad detoured to the laundry room with Perry's dripping wet clothes and came back with a towel, underwear, and a t-shirt.

Perry sat and dried off. He put on the t-shirt then held still until a wave of nausea passed before he stepped into the underpants.

His dad brought him a large water in one hand and a bowl of rice balanced on his other arm. He had something on his hand. A splint. *Oh yeah. The marmot.* "Thank goodness for leftovers tonight. Put salt on that rice. You need it. You eat while I add Alka-Seltzer to the water."

"Okay." Perry grabbed the saltshaker from the table, knocking it over and spilling it. Wasn't that supposed to be bad luck? He couldn't think well enough to remember. He picked up the salt and shook it over the rice. He could barely see if it was coming out, so he did it some more. Finally satisfied, he set the shaker down, leaned over the bowl, and propped himself up on his elbows. He spooned rice in his mouth then chewed very, very slowly, stopping altogether every few seconds as he fought down nausea.

His dad returned and dropped two pills in the water. It bubbled and fizzed. "Drink it all, one sip at a time, before you even think about going to bed."

"Okay." Perry took a sip. It tasted weird. It felt weird in his mouth. In his stomach. He set it down and put his forehead in his hands. "Thanks, Dad."

His dad snorted. "Don't thank me yet. I'm going to get you through tonight, but you've got a date with destiny in the morning."

Perry didn't have any idea what he meant. The way he felt, he probably wouldn't survive the night anyway, so it probably didn't matter.

# CHAPTER FOURTEEN: GETAWAY

BUFFALO, WYOMING
*NOW*: SATURDAY, JUNE 17, 1978

*Trish*

TRISH HADN'T UTTERED a peep since Jimmy's Cutlass had rocketed away from the gas station. She was too scared to talk. What had happened back there? Why were cops coming for a broken window? It must have been an accident. She wished Jimmy and Dabbo had stayed to deal with it. She didn't respect people who refused to take responsibility for their actions. But what she wished even more was that Jimmy had taken her home before this happened, or that she'd made good on her threat to walk.

Jimmy turned off Main Street into a residential neighborhood, tires squealing. "I know a guy who lives near here. We can park and hide behind his house."

"Whatever you're going to do, do it fast," Dabbo said. "Or the cops will be on us."

Jimmy switched off his headlights. He barely slowed as he whipped the car left into a dirt driveway. Trish gasped and held on. At the end of the driveway, he jammed on the brakes then pulled into an unfenced, grassy backyard, where he cut the engine. It was so quiet that all Trish could hear was her own panting breaths.

Seconds later, the scream of a siren split the silence, growing nearer and nearer. Blue and white lights strobed over the house behind the back fence. It was on Main Street. She held her breath, praying it didn't turn down the street they'd taken. That it would keep going.

The sound receded. Then it was gone altogether. But Trish couldn't make herself exhale.

"Are we okay?" Jillian said, her voice squeaking.

Dabbo howled like a dog at the moon. Then he let out a cackling laugh. "Never better as long as my man Jimmy outruns the law."

Trish's breath finally came rushing out. She hugged herself. She'd been scared before. Now she was terrified. Jimmy and Dabbo were afraid of the cops catching them. That meant they'd done something wrong. Broken the law. And she was caught up in it. She didn't like how Jimmy had lost his temper earlier. Or picturing Dabbo hitting that window with a bat. It was already past the time she'd told her parents she'd be home, but she didn't breathe a word.

"At least tell me it was worth it." Jimmy turned to face Dabbo, his eyes sharp.

Dabbo held up a stack of bills then started counting money under his breath. "Four-hundred and eighty-five dollars."

"Oh my gosh," Jillian said. "That's a lot of money."

*That's all she has to say?!* Trish shrunk into the seat. She wished she could imagine herself into invisibility. She had only thought breaking a window was bad. Jimmy and Dabbo had stolen money and run from the cops. How much trouble was she in if they got caught? Would she be considered an accomplice? *I could go to juvie. Like*

*Ben*. If that happened, could it keep her from getting a scholarship—from becoming a wildlife biologist?

"I wonder if that guy got your license plate number," Dabbo said.

"Not when the plates are in the trunk." Jimmy grinned. "I took them off this afternoon."

Trish gripped the hand rest so hard her nails dug into it. Jimmy had been planning this. It was a premeditated crime! Things just kept getting worse. She closed her eyes. She didn't want to get caught with these guys. She didn't want to pay for their mistakes. Then she had an idea. Her eyes popped open. "What if the guy at the gas station saw that you didn't have a plate and told the cops? That would be, like, the description of the vehicle. But if you put it back on now, you won't match his description."

Jimmy was nodding, grinning under his stupid droopy mustache. "That's not a half bad idea, Sandra Dee."

"Encyclopedia Flint strikes again," Jillian said. Her voice was excited. Not scared. Not disappointed. *She thinks this is fun*.

"I'll help you get the plates on," Dabbo said.

The two guys went outside. Trish heard the trunk pop open, then the sound of Jimmy shoving things around in it. She shivered. Was she guilty of aiding and abetting now? But she felt like she had to help them or risk getting caught with them. She just had to make it home. She never had to see Jimmy again. Never, ever. No matter what. And she wasn't going to do Jillian any more favors.

"So." Jillian reached over the seat and pushed Trish's shoulder. "Are you having a good time?"

Trish turned and gave her an incredulous look. "What do you think?"

"Jimmy really could be the Danny to your Sandy."

Trish shook her head. "I don't think so."

"Oh, come on. Loosen up. Live a little." Jillian laughed.

"Stealing is not 'living a little.' It's committing a crime." Trish turned back around. There was nothing more she could say to Jillian. The only thing they had in common was cheerleading. She wished she'd done something with Marcy instead. Or stayed home. She could have written back to Ben.

Ben! If the police caught them, Ben would find out she'd been out with Jimmy. Even though it had meant nothing, it would send the wrong message to him. About the two of them. Ben and her.

They just couldn't get caught. No matter what.

The Cutlass sunk as the two guys settled into their seats.

"I have another idea," Trish said.

Jimmy whistled. "Turning into a regular Bonnie Parker. What is it?"

Trish hated that she didn't have to ask what he meant. Bonnie to his Clyde? No way. Besides, Bonnie and Clyde had made mistakes. They'd been caught. "The store owner would have reported two guys in a Cutlass with no plates. Maybe a brown Cutlass, although it was a little dark and might have been hard for him to see the color. Maybe, if he saw Jillian and me, he would have said two guys with two girls. But what he wouldn't have reported at all was two girls alone in a Cutlass with plates."

Jimmy frowned. "Ri-ight..."

"So, you guys get in the trunk, and I'll drive."

Jillian whooped. Jimmy grinned. Dabbo mussed the back of Trish's hair, laughing.

Trish felt like she'd just sold her soul to the devil.

# CHAPTER FIFTEEN: WORK

BUFFALO, WYOMING
*NOW:* SUNDAY, JUNE 18, 1978

*Susanne*

EARLY ON SUNDAY, Susanne headed to Sheridan College to make up the work she'd missed on Saturday, leaving the wayward Flint teens in the hands of their father. She couldn't believe how the two of them had behaved the previous night. Trish had come home later than she'd promised. And Perry. Oh, Perry. Patrick had been cagey about their son at first but confessed all to her when they woke up.

Well—for once she would just let Patrick handle it. He was in for a fun morning.

But she couldn't help feeling responsible for it, though. The kids had never caused much trouble. Certainly not drinking and staying out past curfew. She shuddered. She'd been hauled into jail, and they'd immediately both fallen apart. She squeezed the steering wheel. But that would make it more Patrick's fault than hers. It was his pastime, his little friendship that precipitated this mess. *Stop being petty*, she chided herself. It *was* sad the girl died.

But Susanne had done nothing wrong, and she and the kids were paying a heavy price.

She glanced at the speedometer and slowed. She was in a hurry, but not enough of one to risk a traffic ticket. Susanne's professor didn't care *when* she worked, luckily. His only request had been that she make progress on her research before he arrived on Monday morning.

That would be no problem.

As she pulled off the interstate and drove cross streets to the college parking lot, Susanne felt free. She rolled the window down and let the breeze blow her hair. She'd never appreciated her ability to come and go as she pleased. Today she did. Being detained had been life changing. Something she never could have imagined would happen to her. At least their attorney, Stu, was optimistic that the police interest in her would wane. She prayed he was right.

She found a good parking place—ah, Sunday morning!—and shut off the car. She hated missing church, especially on a week where she would have wanted people to see her hold her head high. A shallow reason, but rumors spread like wildfire. She slammed the car door and tilted her face up to the sun as she walked in the building.

Five minutes later, she unlocked her professor's office with the key he'd given her. She propped the door open with the stack of books kept on the floor for that purpose. Susanne still had flashbacks to the previous occupant of this office, former Professor Renwick, and how uncomfortable his advances had made her. And it hadn't just been her. She'd led a charge to bring his atrocious behavior to light. Other women had come forward. There had been flak—students who claimed they were trying to get Renwick fired to avoid bad grades. Professors who whispered about the "cabal" that could cost them their careers. Some who suggested they would continue targeting professors the administration didn't like.

*Such rubbish.* This had been her year to be a gossip magnet, it seemed.

But Renwick's replacement, Professor Seth, had been great about everything. A grandfatherly man, he had emigrated from Egypt. He smelled like pipe tobacco and wore linen suits and a white mustache that wiggled like a caterpillar when he talked. And the projects he had her working on were fun. Researching current events didn't feel like a job. Or *recent* events, anyway. Seth was writing a paper on Egyptian President Anwar El-Sadat's relationship with the United States, which had been resurrected from the depths of severed diplomatic ties by a visit from President Nixon, the first US president to travel to Egypt since Franklin D. Roosevelt thirty years before. Two months after their meeting, Nixon had resigned over the Watergate scandal. But inroads had been made and were sustained. Seth planned to cover the historic thawing between the countries in his geopolitics course for the fall semester.

A stack of mail towered on the corner of the professor's desk. A note was taped to the pile. FOR SUSANNE. *My research is here!* The library at Sheridan College was light on current events and geopolitics. The librarian was helpful, though, and she obtained documents Susanne needed through mailed interlibrary loans and Xeroxed copies, although the wait time for them was lengthy. *Like waiting for Santa Claus.*

Susanne picked up the top envelope and shivered with a delicious sense of anticipation. It was addressed to her, care of the librarian. The return address was Library of Congress. Receiving these in northern Wyoming was the next best thing to reviewing them in D.C. She retrieved an ornate silver letter opener from a pencil cup. *Perfect for the occasion.* She slit the envelope and extracted the contents. Three paperclipped documents. She set them in a row, ran her hand over them. Picked up the next package. Repeated the process.

This was going to be the perfect distraction.

# CHAPTER SIXTEEN: MAIL

BUFFALO, WYOMING
*NOW*: SUNDAY, JUNE 18, 1978

*Patrick*

PATRICK PACED the bottom story of the Flint home. He'd run out of honey-do projects from Susanne's list an hour ago. He couldn't abide sloth and idleness. It was bad for his body and worse for his mind, which kept returning to the police rousting Susanne for questioning in Whitney's death. Yesterday had been his scheduled rest day from training, the day he'd take care of the home front while Susanne worked at the college. Those plans had gone awry, but he had another day away from work—a rare full weekend off for him. He'd planned to fill it hiking. Take two cars and the whole family so the others could stop when it wasn't fun for them anymore, and he and Ferdinand could continue onward. Check the snowmelt conditions and see how much elevation they could achieve. How soon summiting Cloud Peak was feasible.

Instead, Susanne was in Sheridan. Perry was sleeping off his hangover. Trish hadn't emerged from her room, although he could hear her piddling around up there. Ferdinand had galloped up the stairs and been granted admittance into the emotion cave. Trish had arrived home upset the night before, but that was normal in the last few months. Since Ben had run off. When Patrick had come out to check on her, she'd burst into tears and ran for her room.

He hadn't had the heart to scold her for being late. It had been a hard day for all of them.

He chewed the inside of his cheek. It was after seven a.m. He couldn't let Perry laze around any longer. The wages of sin are hard work early in the morning under the watchful eye of a parent, after all.

He stomped up the stairs, singing the Eagles' "Life in the Fast Lane," which turned out to be harder than when he was following their lead on the radio. He hmm-hmmed his way through the first verse and chorus, then rapped his knuckles on Perry's door. Left hand. Because pride goeth before a broken right one. "Up, Perry. Now."

The only response was a long, loud moan.

Patrick threw the door open. Perry was face down on top of the covers, one arm and one leg hanging off the bed. His head was balanced on the edge of the mattress, mouth aimed at a trash can. Based on the reek, it had been utilized. Patrick was used to worse at the hospital, but not at home.

He kept his voice cheerful. "I let you sleep in."

Perry squinted his blood-shot eyes. "What time is it?"

"Time to pay the piper."

"I can't."

"Factually inaccurate. You just think you can't."

"Dad, please." Perry's whine sounded nine years old instead of fourteen.

"I have fried eggs, toast, and sausage on the table. You're going to need your strength. And a gallon of water." He crossed his arms, raising his voice to a boom. "Get. Up. Right. Now."

Perry swung his feet to the floor without lifting his upper body. He slithered down to his knees and leaned against the bed.

Patrick slapped his hip as he burst into a new song. "Put one foot in front of the other, and soon you'll be walking cross the floor..."

Perry climbed to his feet and pushed off the bed. His face paled to gray. "I'm going to be sick."

"I doubt there's anything left in your tank. But you can bring the trashcan. You need to clean it out anyway."

"Where are we going?"

"After breakfast?"

"I can't eat."

"Then we're headed straight outside. I have a list of jobs for you." Patrick did a crisp about-face and nearly ran into his daughter. "Good morning, Sleeping Beauty."

"Hey, Dad." Her eyes were cast down, her voice listless. But at least she didn't appear hungover like her brother. He hadn't detected any alcohol on her last night either.

"What's the matter?"

"Nothing." She held out a stack of envelopes and magazines. "Yesterday's mail."

"Anything interesting?"

She shrugged.

"Want to tell me why you were late last night?" He didn't dare ask what was wrong. That was better left to Susanne.

"Jillian." Trish headed downstairs. She was holding two envelopes in her hand. He guessed she had gotten mail, too.

"Doesn't sound like she's someone you want to be hanging out with." He moved to the top of the stairs. Patrick's impression of her had started poorly because of the older guy she was dating. He'd met the two of them the previous winter. His opinion of her hadn't improved since.

"Tell me about it." She stopped at the front door.

"Where are you going?"

"To ride my horse."

"You may have to remind Goldie who you are as little attention as she's gotten lately."

"Very funny."

The front door opened and shut, and his daughter was gone.

He turned his attention back to his boy child. Perry was in the bathroom. The tap was running. Patrick grinned. He remembered being Perry's age. He remembered waking up in his condition. And he remembered how his own father had handled it. *This is going to be fun.*

Patrick glanced at the stack of mail in his hand. A magazine for Susanne. Some bills. And then he noticed the name and return address on a large manilla envelope. The blood drained from his face.

The envelope was from Whitney Gaylor.

It was addressed to him and postmarked two days ago. Before she'd washed up dead in the creek behind his house.

# CHAPTER SEVENTEEN: RIDE

Buffalo, Wyoming
*Now:* Sunday, June 18, 1978

*Trish*

Trish rocked in the saddle to the rhythm of Goldie's lope. Hooves drummed the grassy edge of the ditch that ran along the dirt road. The pen and the envelope holding Ben's letter and her reply rubbed against her chest. She'd shoved them in her shirt on her way out of the house. Because this ride wasn't about time with her horse, although that was a bonus. It was about finding a quiet place to finish writing the letter, uninterrupted.

She'd also wanted to escape her guilt about the night before. In the house, it had felt heavy enough to crush her. She hadn't robbed the gas station, but she had helped Jimmy and Dabbo get away, for her own selfish reasons. And even if her dad couldn't read it on her, her mom would when she got home from Sheridan, if Trish didn't manage to shake it off before then. Was she doing the wrong thing, not turning them in? Part of her wanted to make an anonymous call. But a larger part didn't want that call to result in the police charging her with something, too.

*Or Ben finding out.*

When she reached the last house before the creek crossing, she saw a "For Sale" sign in front. It had been empty for a month. Her mom said the family moved to Denver for a new job. But the kids had gone to her high school, and Trish had heard that it was more like when their dad got fired after he drank himself blind the entire winter. As she got older, she was realizing that wasn't an unusual problem in Wyoming.

"Walk, Goldie," she slowed her hips and eased back in the saddle while gently lifting the reins.

The palomino mare slowed, trotting a few steps, then matching Trish's body motion down to a walk. Goldie blew a few heavy breaths. The horse was out of shape. It had been a long winter with nothing much to do except munch grass. Then cheerleading had distracted Trish when the weather favored riding. Last summer, Trish had barrel raced Goldie at the Johnson County Fair & Rodeo, with Ben cheering her on. There was only two months left to prepare if the duo would repeat this year. Without Ben. She knew they could do better this year if they practiced, but they'd have to start immediately.

"I'm sorry, girl. I'll do better." She guided the horse with her legs, and they moved past the side of the house and into the unfenced backyard facing the creek. The yard was a lot like her house, except here the tall grass hadn't been mowed in weeks.

At the creek, she sat back. "Whoa." She swung off Goldie as the horse stopped, then walked her over to the water.

Goldie sucked noisy mouthfuls. She raised her head, water dripping out of both sides of her muzzle.

"Goofball." Trish hadn't brought hobbles, but she had left Goldie's halter on under her headstall. She slipped the bridle off and dropped the lead rope that she'd looped around the saddle horn. "Don't run off."

The mare was already munching greedily. Sprint grazing. With the grass as good as it was, Trish figured she had ten minutes or so before the horse would start to wander. It would give her time to finish the letter. She'd written most of it the night before. She just wanted to take another look at it before she signed it and sealed the envelope.

She re-read her own words.

Dear Ben:

First, I am so glad you are all right! And that you wrote to me! I have missed you more than anything, and I love you so much. You completely got the wrong idea about Wyatt. He is not my boyfriend. I never went out with him. He is dating Perry's old girlfriend Kelsey, and they were stuck at our house because of a blizzard. There is no one for me but you, Benjamin Jones. Please call me. Please give me a phone number to call you. Please come see me. Please write to me. Please just, well, please just don't forget about me. I don't care if you go to college. I don't care if you live in Alaska. I just want it to be you and me again, forever.

THAT WAS AS FAR as she had gotten. Even that much was covered with water marks from her tears. There was so much more to say, but also there was nothing else to say. Ben should never have run off without giving her a way to stay in touch with him, but he'd been desperate after his arrest, given the history of his time in juvie and the criminals in his family. He should have given her a chance to explain about Wyatt, but that was then, and he was asking for that explanation now.

The one thing—the only thing—she was uncertain about was whether to be open that she had been on one date. Last night. The disastrous evening with Jimmy. Not that it was really a date. She'd just been along so that Dabbo and Jillian could be together.

If Ben was in her shoes, would she want him to tell her?

She put her head in her hands for a moment. *Ugh. I don't know.* On the one hand it would crush her that he'd been out with someone else at all, and on the other if he swore it meant nothing, she'd believe him. It would still sting.

If it truly meant nothing, would the pain of him telling her be worth it?

*No. I am tired of hurting.* I wouldn't want to hurt anymore. I would just want him back. She traced the promise ring with the index finger on her other hand, eyes closed.

She stacked the page on the two envelopes and Ben's letter for padding. Then she pulled the cap off her pen and started writing, pressing lightly.

I AM WEARING YOUR RING. You are my one. The only one for me. I can't wait to hear from you and to see you again.

All my love,

Trish

SHE FOLDED the letter and put it in the envelope. She stuck the pen inside with it, then heard a crunching noise. At first, she thought it was Goldie, but when she glanced up, she saw the horse chomping grass and swishing her tail only twenty feet away, between her and the house. Between her and the *horse* was a steaming pile of horse nuggets. Uh oh. She hadn't thought about that. She'd have to kick it to spread it around as fertilizer.

But what had made the crunching sound? She looked in the other direction and saw that a car had pulled up in front of the house. Not just any car. A police car.

Had someone called to complain about her and Goldie? Or was this about last night? She stuffed the envelopes down her shirt, jumped to her feet with the bridle in her hand, and clucked to her horse. Goldie ignored her. Trish knew better than to charge at the mare—who would lead her on a game of high-speed chase if she did—but she walked briskly, trying to downplay the panic she knew Goldie would react to. Horses coming off winter rest were used to freedom and often didn't relinquish it easily.

Goldie jerked her head up and she snorted.

"It's okay, girl." Was her voice quivering? "Time to go." She held her free hand out, palm down, smiling, even if it was fake.

Goldie's tail went up.

"No, girl. It's okay."

But the game was on. The horse trotted around the back yard, her hooves digging into the freshly shorn ground, carving out chunks of sod. Chasing her in circles wasn't going to do any good. Trish would have to soften her approach. She hadn't brought any horse treats, unfortunately, which would have made this easier. She slowed down and plotted an intercept course, trying to make her voice soothing.

"Easy, girl. Easy now. Time to go home."

A man's voice said, "Did you lose your ride?" He sounded friendly.

Trish jumped and looked over her shoulder. It was a cop. No, it was two cops. Men. The same ones who'd hassled her parents and taken her mother yesterday. She recognized them even though she hadn't met them—had only watched them through the kitchen window.

His question had a literal answer, and she gave it. "Yes, sir."

"Did she take her own bridle off?" the other officer said. His tone was sarcastic. Cutting. Mean.

Heat rushed to her face. "I have to catch my horse." She kept moving toward Goldie, arm out. With the arrival of the two men and the tense change in the atmosphere, Goldie was having none of it. She wheeled and galloped away at full speed, disappearing around the house. *Great.* Trish sped up to go after her.

"Hold up a second, young lady. We're talking to you." It was the mean cop again.

Trish turned to face him.

The first cop said, "Cliff, her horse just vamoosed."

"I'm not blind," the officer said through gritted teeth.

"Could cause more damage. Or even a wreck."

The one named Cliff held up a hand. The first cop fell silent. "Are you vandalizing this vacant home?"

Trish wanted to run after Goldie. The horse was by then probably halfway to the interstate. She could get hit by a car or be gone for days. Or forever. She was a beautiful mare. Anyone who found her would want to keep her. "No, sir. I was just sitting by the creek."

"This is private property. An empty house that is on the market. Look what you've done. Do you think the owners will appreciate that?" Cliff waved his arm to indicate the uneven grass, torn up sod, and pile of manure.

"No, sir."

"Maybe we should haul you in for destruction of property."

"I didn't..."

"Didn't what?"

"I'm sorry. I didn't think that would happen. I'll fix it."

"We'll wait here while you take care of it then."

Trish froze in place, waiting for the worst. She opened and closed her mouth a few times. But then she realized that the cops hadn't mentioned the night before. The gas station. Jillian, Dabbo, and Jimmy. This might really just be about messing up this backyard. And she could fix it. "I'll need to go get a shovel and some other tools. At my house."

"Where do you live?" Cliff stared at her, hands on hips.

"Just down the road."

"What's your name?"

"Trish."

"Trish what?"

"Trish Flint."

Cliff's eyes glittered. "Flint. Are you the doctor's kid?"

"Um, yes, sir."

"We'll give you a ride home then."

"What about my horse?"

He shrugged. "You should have thought about that before trespassing and defacing property."

The other cop shook his head and mouthed, "I'm sorry," at Trish.

Cliff pointed vaguely in the direction of their car. "Well, let's go!"

Trish startled and trotted a few steps before slowing and walking to the front of the house. She hoped to find Goldie grazing in the front yard, but the horse was long gone. A truck was racing down the road at them, though. So fast that it was kicking up a tall dust trail behind it.

It drew closer and she saw it was her dad's truck.

"Get in the car," Cliff said. "Back seat."

She pointed. "That's my dad."

"Speeding."

The other cop said, "I expect her horse galloped into the barn without a rider. If my kid's horse did that, I'd be speeding, too."

Officer Cliff gave him a withering look.

Trish took a step toward the road and waved her arms over her head. Just as her dad was about to fly past them, he saw her. The truck skidded to a stop, then he turned in the parking area and rolled toward them.

Her dad turned off the engine and jumped out. "Trish! Are you okay? Goldie came running in all lathered up, without you."

"I'm fine, Daddy."

"Scared me to death. I'm glad someone was already helping you out."

Cliff said, "Oh, we aren't helping her, Dr. Flint."

Her dad squinted. Recognition crossed his face. A frown followed it.

Officer Cliff continued. "We were bringing her home to get some tools. We caught her in the middle of causing destruction to property. A lack of respect for the law seems to run in the family."

Her dad's voice was like ice. He put a hand on Trish's shoulder. "I'll take it from here, Appelt."

Cliff smirked. "We'll be by later to ensure she did the repairs. If not, we know where you live. We can come by with a ticket for her. Maybe talk some more with your wife while we're there."

Her dad squeezed her shoulder. "Let's go, Trish."

She hurried away with him. She couldn't be the reason the cops returned and hassled her mother again. "I'm sorry, Daddy," she whispered.

Through gritted teeth he said, "No, honey, I'm the one who's sorry."

# CHAPTER EIGHTEEN: HAZE

Cloud Peak Wilderness, Bighorn Mountains, Wyoming
*Then (nine months earlier)*: Sunday, September 18, 1977

*Patrick*

Patrick became aware of the cold. First in his feet. Then his nose. His ears. His hands. He wriggled his fingers inside his gloves and opened his eyes. It was pitch dark. Where was he? For a moment, he couldn't figure it out. Where he was now. Where he had been. What he'd been doing. Who he was with.

Then a woman's voice said, "I think he's awake. Patrick—" a warm hand touched his shoulder, "—how are you feeling?"

He paused, searching for a name to match the somewhat familiar voice. Climbing. He'd been climbing. Gotten dehydrated. And he was with someone. Two people. Whitney and Loren. Then a storm had come up. They'd taken a wrong turn. Sheltered in a cave. *Yes.* He sat up. He'd been lying down with his head on his backpack. A searing pain shot through his neck. He ignored it as he evaluated himself. No more dizziness. He was becoming more alert by the second. The danger of the dehydration had passed. "Better, I think."

She said, "I've been melting snow in my hands and putting it in the canteen when it's almost thawed. I think I've gotten it half full for you." There was a clank, and something hit him in the hand. "Drink up."

Patrick grasped the canteen with his gloved hands. He wasn't giving her any argument. He took slow sips, careful not to spill a precious drop, as he evaluated his stomach for signs of rebellion. If he developed a stomach issue, he could lose all the precious fluids he'd consumed. It growled in hunger, but not in protest. "Thanks." His eyes were adjusting to the dark. He capped the canteen and handed it back to the blob taking shape a few feet from him.

A second blob further back in the cave shifted and sighed. "The storm is howling." Loren. "I went out and checked on it about half an hour ago."

"Still snowing?"

"Ya know, I can't tell. The wind is so fierce it could just be redistributing it. But it's dark outside now. No visibility at all."

"Any idea what time it is?"

"Last time it was light enough to see my watch, it was about six. And that was hours ago."

Their short break in the cave hadn't ended up very short after all. They were spending the night on the mountain. Susanne would be frantic with worry. She'd report them missing. A search and rescue operation would have to wait for first light. Which, this time of year, would be before seven in the morning, at least.

He rubbed his face. "Man, I really passed out."

Whitney's voice held a smile. "That's a good thing. We need your brain and body strong in the morning."

"Besides making water, what have you guys been doing?"

Neither climber answered, and Patrick sensed a strange electricity in the air.

Finally, Whitney said, "Oh, nothing really. Napped a little. Checked outside occasionally. Explored some. Chatted a bit."

"Yeah, nothing, really," Loren said.

"Did you find anything interesting?"

"What do you mean?"

"Like a secret elevator shaft down to West Tensleep?"

Whitney's laugh sounded brittle. "I wish."

"I guess we'll have to climb down the hard way, then." Patrick shivered. He was warmer now that he was awake. Unfortunately, here above the tree line, there was no wood for a fire. The cave was as warm as it was going to get. "At the risk of sounding like a dad or the doctor of the group, we need to conserve our body heat."

"How?" Loren asked. "I have on all my clothes."

"Close contact. And as far as possible from that wind that's still working its way in here."

"I'm sorry, but I'm not snuggling with you, Dr. Flint."

"You could only dream of being so lucky. Chivalry, my dear Loren. You and I will get on either side of Whitney and keep her warm. We'll just have to hope we don't get frostbite on our exposed sides."

"I like the plan," Whitney said.

"You would," Loren grumbled.

She ignored his comment and said, "I think this side of the cave is out of the wind."

Patrick scooted his behind toward her, dragging his backpack with him. He sat close enough that his arm and leg was pressed against hers. "Is this good?"

"Toasty."

He positioned the backpack against his other side for a little more warmth. He'd already put on all his layers earlier.

"Me, too," Loren said, his voice now close on the other side of Whitney.

"Dr. Flint..." Whitney said.

"Patrick," he replied.

"Patrick. There's something we should tell you. Loren and me."

Loren's voice was hard. "No, there isn't."

Patrick frowned. "What is it?"

"Whitney," Loren said, his voice a warning.

Whitney sighed. "You're being rude."

"And you are being shortsighted."

Whitney cleared her throat. "Sorry for the weirdness, Dr., er, I mean Patrick. Loren and I have a ... relationship. He's very private about it. But I thought you should know."

The silence grew even more awkward.

Patrick couldn't think of an appropriate response. "That's nice." Their status was none of his business. Or even his interest. "We should start as soon as there's light. Good night to both of you." And he closed his eyes, hoping he wouldn't have trouble falling back asleep, but losing himself to the night before he finished the thought.

# CHAPTER NINETEEN: RECEIVE

Buffalo, Wyoming
*Now:* Sunday, June 18, 1978

*Patrick*

After helping Trish with the cleanup of the neighbor's yard and supervising Perry's mostly-not-working work, Patrick returned to the package he'd received from Whitney, which he hadn't opened yet. He took it into his bedroom and shut the door.

From the weight and size of the envelope, he knew there wasn't much inside. He worked his right index finger under the flap—hand protesting—and pulled out the contents. Only two pieces of paper. One was a map, hand drawn. The other was a typewritten letter on a plain white sheet of paper with Whitney's signature at the bottom.

Patrick,

I'm writing to ask a favor. Can you hold on to this map for me? It details an important memory. Of all the people in my life, you are the one I trust the most. I'll explain soon. Thank you and see you on the mountain!

Sincerely,

Whitney

Patrick stared at the note, gobsmacked. He flipped it over to see if she'd written anything else on the back. Nothing. It made no sense to him, but the fact that she'd sent it to him was troubling. According to her ex-boyfriend, Whitney had feelings for Patrick. The police seemed to believe it, or at least Appelt did. This package would make it seem like there was more of a relationship between Patrick and Whitney than existed. It would add credibility to Appelt's insinuation that Patrick had given Susanne a reason to be insanely jealous.

A reason to protect her relationship from another woman.

He set the letter aside and shifted his attention to the map, which appeared to be drawn in colored pencil. It was labeled "Cloud Peak" across the top. A tiny red flag marked the high point of the mountain, but instead of the usual route down, the drawing showed the trail away from the summit where their group had gotten lost. His memories of that ordeal, now nine months in the past, were hazy. They hadn't been all that clear even shortly after, given the condition he'd been in on the mountain—dehydrated, exhausted, and worried about the storm that had overtaken them. He'd been lucky to escape with his life from the tragic ordeal. *If I'd been alone, I wouldn't have.*

Whitney's drawing exhibited her better recall. She'd circled an area of the trail and marked it as "impassable." She showed the dead end at a wall of rock that had blocked their path and sent them back to the cave where they spent the night. She'd noted distance, landmarks, and altitude drop. From the entrance to the cave, arrows pointed straight down. She had written "dangerous." Patrick couldn't disagree with that.

The back of the map was a close-up of the inside of the cave. Whitney had included what looked like a person—maybe him?—sitting against a rock wall and holding a backpack or something in their lap, maybe even hugging it to their chest. It was hard to tell for sure. She wouldn't win any awards for artistic ability.

He rubbed his forehead, grazing it with the splint. Why had this been such an important memory to her? And why did she send it to him?

The phone rang, and he startled. He turned to the bedside table and answered it on the first ring, hoping it was Susanne. But it was the next best thing—Henry Sibley. Patrick had called his friend earlier when he'd reached his wit's end with Perry. The boy needed stern course correction after his wild night of drinking. In Patrick's mind, labor was the best possible means. But with Patrick's job, he wouldn't be around to supervise. The Flints' small property didn't afford enough physical tasks to suit Patrick's purposes anyway. But Henry's ranch would if Henry was in the market for free teenage help.

He explained the situation to Henry. "I can't promise his attitude will be great, but he's strong, and I'd give you complete authority to deal with him anyway you see fit." Patrick shoved Whitney's papers back in the envelope. He opened his top drawer and slid it underneath his underwear. Guilt immediately gnawed at him. He needed to tell Susanne about it. Of course he did, and soon. But he didn't want to leave it laying around where the kids might find it or Susanne run across it before he had time to think it through and come up with a logical, palatable explanation.

Henry's jovial voice tugged him back from the problem of Whitney to the problem with Perry. "You know I believe in labor therapy. When we first fostered Ben, hard work was our main strategy to keep that boy on the straight and narrow. Worked like a charm, too."

"That's why I thought of you. You did wonders with that young man."

"I can keep Perry busy until he's carting great-grandchildren around on his hip. Can you get him here by six in the morning?

That's when ranch work starts. Actually, that's letting him off easy. Blister starts at four thirty." Henry sounded amused.

"Blister?"

"We've got a new summer hand. That's not his real name, but it's what I call him on account of the fact that he has a way of showing up after the hardest work is done. He'll never have a real blister at the rate he's going."

"Sounds like he and Perry will get along real well."

"We've got an extra bunk with Blister if you'd like him to get the full experience. Save you driving him out in the pitch dark every morning, too."

Patrick heard the front door open, then Susanne calling a greeting. "That sounds perfect. We'll have him out there tonight. Thanks, Henry."

"Don't thank me yet. I've never failed before, but then I've never tried to get water out of a Flint."

# CHAPTER TWENTY: SHIFT

SHERIDAN COLLEGE, SHERIDAN, WYOMING

*NOW*: SUNDAY, JUNE 18, 1978

*Susanne*

THE DAY HAD FLOWN by so quickly that Susanne felt like she'd barely started reading the materials on Egypt and US relations before it was time to drive back to Buffalo. It was so engrossing that she hadn't thought about Whitney or the rude Buffalo cop or even kept track of time. Now, she needed to hurry home.

She filled her tote bag with research materials and lugged it out to her car. The days were getting longer, so at six it was still bright outside but would be falling dusk soon. She'd need to keep a watchful eye for deer in the highway.

Once in the car, she pulled her cassette player from the tote and put it on the seat beside her. She pressed play, then exited her parking space, and drove toward the interstate. A voice filled the interior, and she exhaled, willing herself to focus. She'd started tape recording her classes and re-listening to them on her drives to and from Sheridan during her first semester back in college. The repetition of the lectures was critical to her academic success. With the demands of the kids' schedules and running their household, she wasn't able to study much. Her job had only made things worse.

This cassette wasn't a lecture, though, and it wasn't a professor's voice. It was her own. *I'm Minnie Mouse! Tell me I don't really sound like that!!* She shuddered.

But as the miles of ranchland rolled by, it grated on her less. By the time she passed stark Lake Desmet, she was completely engaged in the running summary, thoughts, and questions she'd recorded during her research. Chief among her favorite discoveries? That Presidents Nixon and Sadat had reached an agreement for the King Tutankhamun exhibit to tour the United States in exchange for the U.S. funding improvements to the Royal Opera in Cairo. That tour was now ongoing and breaking museum attendance records nationwide. She couldn't believe she was being paid—not much, mind you, but some—to learn about topics like this.

To think Nixon left office only two months after he and President Sadat had met. It was the deal that almost hadn't happened. Without it, Steve Martin wouldn't be singing "King Tut" every time she turned on the radio. People wouldn't be standing in line to see treasures from the boy prince's tomb and learning more about Egypt than they had in their entire lives.

The tape ended as she hit the Buffalo city limits, and soon she was parking at home and let herself in the house, her mind still on mummies and jewels and priceless antiquities. Ferdinand was the only family member happy to see her. He snuffled her feet, wagged his tail, and twirled. Patrick was sitting at the kitchen table, talking to himself silently. Trish took one look at her and dashed up the stairs where she slammed her door. Perry was vacuuming the living room rug, his face in a deep scowl.

She went to Patrick and yelled over the vacuum. "What's going on?"

He motioned her out onto the deck. "It was a hard day with the kids."

She struggled to hold back a smile, amused and a little pleased the kids had made him work. "That's not surprising."

He recounted Trish's brush with the law and Perry's reluctant labor. "I called Henry. Perry is going to stay with the Sibleys for a few days and work at their place."

"What about football practice?"

"Trish will taxi him."

She raised her eyebrows. "Out of the goodness of her heart?"

"I'm paying her."

Susanne nodded. It was a lot of driving, and she didn't want to do it herself. She could support incentivizing Trish.

Patrick held up the Sunday paper. "And I just had time to sit down with this morning's paper. Brace yourself."

She read the headline aloud. "*Local physician's wife Susanne Flint a 'person of interest' to police in death of Sheridan nurse.* Oh, my goodness. This is bad."

"Yes. I'm so sorry. But I'm sure it will blow over."

"You can't be sure of that. And my reputation will be tarnished forever." She squeezed her eyes shut. Work had been blissful. Coming back to this was jarring. *Is this how Patrick feels about his job and hobbies?* She didn't love that bit of insight. "Is that all, or is there more bad news?"

A funny look crossed his face. "Um, well, something came in the mail Saturday. I just opened it today."

"And?"

"It's from Whitney. To me. Something she asked me to keep for her."

"You. Whitney."

"Yes. It's very strange. And I can't decide whether to call the police about it or not."

Anger was building inside her, the flames leaping. "What is it?"

"A hand drawn map of our misadventure on Cloud Peak."

She frowned. "What, was it some kind of precious memory for Whitney? She needed to remind you of your time together?"

"I don't think so. But I'm afraid that is exactly what the police will think if I share it with them."

The vacuum cleaner switched off midway through Patrick's last words, making it seem as if he was shouting.

Susanne tried to fight the fire inside her. She was no idiot. Her reaction was exactly why the police were suspicious of her. She dropped her voice. "Withholding it makes us seem unhelpful."

"If they ever find out."

For a moment she was tempted to suggest he burn it. Then the doorbell rang, followed immediately by sharp knocking—almost banging—so loud they could hear it outside through their open kitchen windows. Ferdinand rushed the door in a frenzy.

"Are you expecting anyone?" she said.

"No."

"Me either." And no one they knew would attack their door like that.

They walked back inside together, Susanne with a sense of dread.

"I've got it," Patrick said.

The knocking intensified. Someone rang the doorbell over and over, like a child being silly. Or a bratty teenager. But when Patrick opened the door, it was neither.

Appelt showed his teeth in a mockery of a smile then stuck a toothpick in his mouth. "Took you so long, I was beginning to think you were avoiding us. Mr. Flint. Mrs. Flint."

From behind him, Welch said, "Dr. and Mrs. Flint."

Susanne's stomach plummeted like she'd jumped off a cliff into a lake, something she'd done once to prove to her kids she wasn't the chicken they accused her of being. *They're here for me.*

Patrick and Ferdinand blocked the door. "What is this visit about?"

"We'd like to come in, if you don't mind," Appelt said, the toothpick bobbing with his words.

Patrick held his ground. "We're in the middle of something. State your business, please."

Appelt guffawed and shouldered his way past Patrick. "For starters, we're following up about your daughter as we said we would."

Welch's Adam's apple bobbed as he mouthed, "Sorry," but he followed Appelt in.

"I supervised her cleanup. She did a first-rate job." He moved quickly, putting himself between Susanne and the two cops.

On the landing to the stairs, Perry and Trish peered over the banister. Trish shrunk back at mention of her name.

"There's still the matter of her trespassing."

Susanne had had enough. Anger radiated through her and out of her. "I'd be happy to call our former neighbors. I'm certain they won't want to press charges."

Appelt turned all his attention on her, eyes gleaming. He put the toothpick in his breast pocket and licked his lips. "The ever-feisty Mrs. Flint."

"A mother protects her children."

"And her marriage."

"I would if I needed to. But Patrick hasn't given me any reason."

"You said earlier you'd never met Whitney Saylor."

Susanne felt better now that she'd drawn the attention from Trish to herself. And this was safe ground. She held the factual high ground. She drew herself up to her full five feet four inches. "Because I haven't."

Welch's face betrayed a trap. He flinched and looked away.

Appelt said. "Never been to her home?"

"No."

"Never fought with her?"

"Of course not."

"Never had a public argument?"

Doubt flickered inside her. Where was Appelt going with this? He seemed to be honing in on something specific. But all she could do was tell the truth. "I have not."

"I don't suppose your answer would change if you were under oath?"

She frowned. "It would not. What is this about?"

Appelt's smile was broad now. He strutted to the door, shooing Welch ahead of him. Just as he was about to exit, he threw one last comment over his shoulder. "You'll find out soon enough. Good day." He put two fingers to his forehead in a soft-wristed salute.

The door clicked shut. Before Susanne and Patrick could exchange a word, their phone rang.

Susanne picked it up. "Susanne Flint speaking." Her voice sounded shell shocked even to her own ears.

"Mrs. Flint, this is Stu Ryan." Was she being paranoid, or was there an edge to the attorney's voice? He'd been so warm and friendly during their visit with him yesterday.

"Hello, Mr. Ryan. A Sunday phone call. I'm impressed. And your timing is impeccable. We just had a very disturbing visit from the police."

"I'm calling to inform you that I will be unable to represent you or your husband."

Susanne sank heavily into a chair at the kitchen table, waving Patrick over. "I don't understand. Everything was fine yesterday. Why won't you help us?"

Patrick sat beside her and leaned in. She made room for both their heads at the receiver, so he could hear as well.

"It's come to my attention that you lied to me in our meeting. I told you I could only help you if you were open and honest with me."

Patrick gave an angry snort, but Susanne shushed him with her hand. "I told you everything I know. And I most certainly didn't lie."

"Mrs. Flint, there are multiple eyewitnesses to you publicly fighting with Ms. Saylor in the grocery store parking lot, not two weeks ago."

"What? I—" And then she stopped speaking. Two weeks ago, at the grocery store in Sheridan, a very hostile young woman had accused Susanne of scratching the side of her car with a shopping cart. Susanne had protested. Her cart hadn't touched the car. The young woman had pointed at a scratch and screamed at her until Susanne had backed away with her hands up. But the girl had followed Susanne to her own car. She demanded Susanne pay for the damage. At that point, Susanne smelled a shakedown. Hands on her hips, she'd flat out refused and told the younger woman to back off. Then she'd gotten in her car. The woman had hit her window with the side of her fist and yelled something that, at the time had made no sense. But now it did.

It had been Whitney Saylor, and she'd said, "This is about your husband and we both know it."

# CHAPTER TWENTY-ONE: AWAKEN

SIBLEY RANCH, STORY, WYOMING
*NOW*: MONDAY, JUNE 19, 1978

*Perry*

ACROSS THE ROOM, a loud ringing noise jerked Perry out of slumber. There was a THWAP sound. The ringing stopped. Perry wiped the sleep out of his eyes and blinked. It was pitch black inside the bunk house.

From a few feet away, the Sibleys' ranch hand groaned. Blister. That was his name. Perry had arrived at bedtime, so he'd barely met the guy before lights out, other than to notice he was scarecrow thin with wild, straw-like hair to match.

Blister said, "It feels like that damn alarm clock goes off earlier every day." Two feet hit the floor. "Better get your butt up and moving if you want to eat breakfast, Perry."

Perry wanted to sleep. He knew he deserved punishment for

getting drunk, but his dad was overdoing it, in his opinion. Giving him to Henry Sibley as free labor? And free labor that started before sunrise at that? Too much. Too, too much. What would be next, military school? He rose, reluctantly, stretching his arms over his head and twisting his neck to one side and then the other. Working on an empty stomach wasn't going to cut it.

Five minutes later, Blister knocked on the front door to the Sibleys' house.

The door opened. Vangie Sibley stood in front of them, one hand holding tight to the wrist of a struggling little boy. Her toddler, Hank. Vangie was pretty, although Perry felt weird for noticing. She was his mom's best friend. "Good morning, Blister. Hi, Perry. Henry's already out at the barn. Would you like breakfast?"

"Bekfust!" Hank shouted.

Perry smiled at the little boy. He almost said no. If Henry was already at work, that meant they were late. And that Perry would never want to be a rancher if this was the type of hours they kept.

But Blister wiped his feet on the mat. "We'll make it a quick one, Mrs. Sibley. Sorry we missed him."

"Oh, you know Henry. He woke up with a bee in his bonnet about something. I have to get Hank dressed. Help yourselves." She towed Hank behind her by the hand. The little boy was pulling back hard, trying to join the hands.

Perry knew the way from many dinners with the Sibleys in the past, but he let Blister lead.

"Mrs. Sibley makes good grub."

It was no lie. Perry loaded a plate with two giant cinnamon rolls piled high with bacon. When Blister poured himself a coffee, Perry decided to give it a try. He filled the cup halfway with cream first and added two heaping teaspoons of sugar.

At the table, he tasted his coffee first. A little bitter, but it wasn't bad. His mom drank hers black all day every day. He'd tried it once, and it was awful. The cream and sugar made a big difference.

"Okay, squirt. We need to set some ground rules for today."

Blister talked through a mouthful of cinnamon roll. "Number one, when I say I need my break, you take a break, too. And stay on break. Don't go back early. This includes lunchtime. Number two, you don't work harder or faster than me. For you, this is just a few days. For me, it's a long, hard summer, and I have to pace myself. And number three, when it's quitting time, we stop. No matter what. If you can follow the rules, we're going to get along. And I promise, you want to get along with me."

Perry washed down his cinnamon roll with more of the sweet coffee. It tasted even better that way. "Got it."

"How long you here for?"

"A few days. Maybe Friday. Maybe less."

Blister rolled his eyes. "It's not even worth the time to train you."

Perry nodded. "I'm sorry."

"Whose bright idea was this anyway?"

"My dad's."

"It's barely a summer job."

"Oh, it's not a job. I'm here as a punishment."

Blister paused with his roll in midair. "For what?"

"Drinking."

"What, are you like in middle school? That's way too young."

Perry stiffened and lifted his shoulders. "High school."

"Huh." Blister's raised eyebrows gave away his surprise.

"Anyway, my dad's a doctor and he's always at the hospital and my mom's in college in Sheridan, so neither of them had time to do the parenting themselves this week. They dumped me off on the Sibleys to make me suffer."

"Your pop's a doctor? I guess rich kids can afford to work for free."

"We're not rich."

Blister snorted. "Richer than me or my family. Wait, what's your last name?"

"Flint."

Blister's eyes widened. "Oh. I, uh, read something in the paper..."

Perry had seen the newspaper article about his mother the day before. He felt terrible for his mom. And defensive of her. He changed the subject. "Um, what time does Henry normally start?"

"Sunrise."

The sun hadn't been up when they got to breakfast, but he was sure it was now. "I'm ready whenever you are." He couldn't believe the hours Henry worked. He'd known the man was a hard worker, but this was insane. And now Perry would be living here round the clock until he'd earned his way back into the good graces of his parents. With football practice every evening, too, he was going to be exhausted.

"Let's go." Blister stuffed a few pieces of bacon into his mouth.

The door shut behind them, and they walked across the ranch yard toward the barn. The sun was easing over the eastern horizon, so it was bright enough for Perry to dodge cow and horse manure. The barn was in the center of the outbuildings, big and red, matching the feed storage silo, a few loafing sheds, and a big, metal building that he knew from past visits held the vehicles and mechanical equipment.

Henry came out of the barn carrying a square bale of hay dangling from hay hooks in each hand. He grunted. "I need two more. Perry, grab 'em and follow me out to my east paddock. Blister, you know what you need to be working on."

Blister said, "Yes, sir." He wheeled and walked toward a different outbuilding without another word.

Perry was used to a different sort of relationship with Henry. One with "Hey, kid, how are you, how's school, how's football." There was none of that this morning. Perry hurried into the barn, found more hay hooks and wrestled two bales of hay down from the loft. The bales were sparse after a hard winter. First cutting would be coming soon, Perry knew. Half the guys on his team would be working for their family ranches between practices, and they were already complaining about it. Most of the livestock was on straight grass by now. Perry wondered why Henry still had them hefting bales, but he hustled after his new boss. Or whatever you called someone you worked for when you weren't getting paid.

Henry was spreading hay into pens with individual animals in them. He handed Perry wire cutters then chinned at the line of metal fencing and gates. "Put three flakes in each."

Perry cut the baling wire then did as he was told. "What's going on with these animals?"

"These are the ones that are sick, hurt, or need dry lot."

"Okay."

Henry stopped and stared at the sunrise for a moment. "I'll have you done in time for football. Trish is coming to get you and drop you back off?"

"Yes, sir." And she wasn't going to be happy about it. It was not a short drive to make roundtrip twice a day.

"Your dad wants me to be tough on you." Henry's attention seemed to be captured by something in the grass outside one of the pens. He frowned.

"I understand."

Henry pulled something from his back pocket. Two things. A slingshot and a round metal ball. He loaded the ball in the sling, then pulled it back and let the shot fly. It hit something that flew into the air. Something long that whipped around, then fell to the ground.

"Rattlesnake. Been having some trouble with 'em." Henry cocked his head, watching to see if the snake moved. It did not. "I think I got it."

"Why didn't you just shoot it?" Perry saw the gun at Henry's hip.

"And startle all the animals that we have penned because they need peace and calm for birthing, healing, or doctoring? I've always liked a slingshot. And sometimes it's the least troublesome tool to get a job done."

Perry nodded. He hadn't thought of that.

Henry held it out.

"You want me to try it?" Perry took it from him. Henry added a handful of shot. Perry dropped them in his front pocket and stuck the slingshot in a back one.

"No. I want you to take it. Practice with it. It'll give you something to do in your down time. Plus, you can think about how to cause the least trouble possible every time you do. Because that's what your parents need right now. No trouble. Your dad lost a friend. Your mom is fending off some ugly allegations."

Perry looked at his boots. He'd stepped in manure after all. "Yes, sir."

"You going to give 'em any more of it?"

"No, sir."

"You going to give me any of it?"

"No, sir."

"Good. Then I expect we'll do just fine."

"I wish my parents felt like you."

Henry spat something in the grass. Chewing tobacco. Perry was dying to try it himself. "You do a good job for me and keep your nose clean. It'll work out."

"They treat me like I'm a baby. I'm not anymore. I'm practically a man."

Henry cocked his head. "Well, I suppose that's true. But they'll know you're a man when your actions show it."

Perry chewed the inside of his lip. He knew grown men that drank beer. But he suspected Henry was talking about more than not getting drunk. "What do I have to do to prove myself?"

Henry clapped him on the shoulder and propelled him toward the barn. "It's different for everyone. It's not something you do by pushing. Or that you'll learn from Blister—don't be using him as your example, although he's nice enough. But there'll be no doubt when it happens."

It didn't make any sense to Perry, and it sure didn't satisfy his sense of justice. There was nothing he could do about it this week while he was stranded halfway to Montana on this ranch anyway. He'd just have to work on it when he got back home.

# CHAPTER TWENTY-TWO: POST

Buffalo, Wyoming
*Now*: Monday, June 19, 1978

*Trish*

Trish pushed the speed limit driving to the post office first thing Monday morning. She waited in the short line to talk to a postal employee, not trusting her precious cargo to the uncertainty of the impersonal mail slot.

"Do I have the right postage to get this letter to Ketchikan, Alaska, the fastest way possible?" Trish asked the gray-haired man behind the counter.

He smiled at her, revealing brown teeth, probably from years of chewing tobacco. "Yes, young lady, you do. First class mail will get it there via air, or close to it. I don't imagine we have any postal services planes flying all the way into Ketchikan, now do we?" He winked. "I'll make sure it goes out with this morning's pickup."

"How long do you think it will take it to get there?"

"Shouldn't be more than a few days, end of the week at the latest. We don't have to worry about the weather this time of year."

Trish nodded. It was better than the Pony Express that had raced through this area a hundred years ago, but it still sounded like forever. How she wished she had Ben's phone number. "Thank you."

In her truck leaving the post office, Trish made a split-second decision. Instead of home, she decided to drop by Marcy's house. She had backed out of their plans Saturday night. Marcy hadn't been happy. She might slam the door in Trish's face. But Trish had to try.

As she navigated the whimsical steppingstones from the curb to Marcy's front door, she started having second thoughts. She almost turned back. Then the front door opened before she even reached it.

Marcy stood in the doorway, hair in messy pigtails, wearing a long night shirt. "What are you doing here?"

"I thought maybe we could do something today."

Marcy frowned. "What—is Jillian already booked?"

Trish winced. She deserved that. She hadn't wanted to ditch Marcy. And lately she'd been so busy with all the practices. But she'd also spent time outside practice with the others on the squad, and there was no denying that had impacted Marcy. Trish should have insisted on including her old friend with her new ones. "You are my best friend. I didn't ask her."

"Maybe I already have plans today."

*Wow, that stung.* "Okay. I can come back another time."

Marcy laughed. She kicked the door further open. "No, dummy. I was just messing with you. Want some cereal?"

Trish sighed with relief. She traipsed inside after Marcy. "Sure."

The two girls poured From Loops and milk into bowls. If sugar had a smell, it was Fruit Loops. *The best.* Out of years of habit, they sat at the same seats at the table that they always picked when they were together. It was comfortable. The whole house was like putting on your favorite sweater on a cold day. The dark wood paneling, the shag carpeting, the goofy family photos. Years of friendship, acceptance, and love here in this house.

"How is lifeguarding?" Marcy was lifeguarding at the creek-fed city pool that summer. "I've seen you in the chair when I've driven by."

"It's great, if you like screaming kids, cleaning up vomit, and seeing Mr. Hatchett in his Speedo."

Trish giggled. "Oh, my gosh, Mr. Hatchett still wears that tiny thing?"

"He must be like forty years old. So gross. But there's a new lifeguard. Marcus. He's going to be a senior with us. We've, uh, sort of been talking."

"Talking, like at work, or on the phone, or over burgers before a movie?"

"All of the above." Marcy smirked and tilted her head.

"That is so cool!"

Her friend exhaled a shaky breath. "I really like him."

"When do I get to meet him?"

"Soon, I hope."

Trish finished her cereal and put the bowl in the sink. "Do you mind if I call my mom and tell her where I am? I don't want her to freak out. I was supposed to go straight home from the post office."

Marcy flapped her hand in permission and poured more cereal into her bowl. "What were you doing at the post office?"

Trish hadn't told anyone else about the letter from Ben. It felt right to tell Marcy, though. "Answering a letter from Ben."

Marcy grinned and talked with her mouthful. "I *so* knew that the two of you would get back together. Now we both have boyfriends."

Trish dialed her home number. It hadn't just been cheerleading that had gotten in the way of her friendship with Marcy. Trish had spent a lot of time with Ben when they were together. Marcy had been dying to have a boyfriend and fought against her jealousy of Trish's relationship with Ben, sometimes unsuccessfully.

"Susanne Flint speaking."

Trish almost rolled her eyes at her mother's formal greeting. She'd even used it yesterday after the awful visit from the police. Nothing seemed to rattle her. Although that call had, and she hadn't been herself that morning. "Hey, Mom. I'm at Marcy's house."

"That's nice to hear. I like her better than your new friends."

"Me, too. I'm going to hang out here for a little while if that's okay."

"Fine by me. I'm about to leave for Sheridan. Oh, and Ronnie called. She wants you to babysit Will Friday night. She said you're welcome to keep him at our house since she's taking me out to dinner."

"Like a ladies' night? Or a girls' night out?" Trish giggled.

"It's belated congratulations for my new job."

Trish hadn't realized her mom's job was a big deal. Had she even said anything to her about it? "That's cool, Mom. I'd be happy to babysit for her."

"Thanks. I'll call her and tell her. Love you."

"Love you, too."

She hung up the phone. "I don't even know who that woman I just talked to is, because she can't be my mother."

"Did you say she's going on a ladies' night?" Marcy put her own bowl in the sink.

"Yes! It's crazy!"

"She's probably glad she's not in jail for murdering that woman who had a crush on your dad."

Trish opened her mouth to speak. It froze in place so long that she had to remind herself to shut it. When she did, it was with a clack.

Marcy clapped her hand over her own mouth. "People are —I mean, that's what I've heard but, oh my gosh. I'm sorry!"

"It's not true. Mom didn't hurt anybody. Dad didn't have a girlfriend. But that's not why she's going out. They're celebrating my mom's job. She just never does stuff like that. I don't get it. She would celebrate with my dad. Or he would go with them. Ronnie's husband Jeff would go, too."

Marcy's lips puckered and twisted in a funny face. "Maybe your mother is more upset about that Whitney girl than she's let you know."

Butterflies flapped their wings in Trish's stomach. She hoped Marcy wasn't right.

## CHAPTER TWENTY-THREE: QUESTION

BUFFALO, WYOMING
*NOW:* MONDAY, JUNE 19, 1978

*Patrick*

PATRICK HAD BEEN SEARCHING for Kathy Bergman since arriving at the hospital Monday morning. It wasn't until he sat down for an early lunch in the break room that she found him. He was opening his sack lunch. He couldn't believe after the awful police visit and attorney call of the evening before that Susanne had still packed it for him. Her sack lunches were a tradition dating back to his medical school days. Unfortunately, they were fewer and farther between since she had started at Sheridan College. The lunches he made for himself invariably consisted of a box of vanilla wafers, a jar of peanut butter, a squeeze bottle of honey, and a spoon. At first, he'd been delighted to eat his favorite snacks for lunch every day. It got old quickly, though.

He opened the bag and pulled out a Tupperware container.

Meatloaf, carrots, and mashed potatoes from the night before. A warmth suffused his chest. The thought of her long-fingered hands packing this for him felt like love. A sharp pain shot through his middle. The woman he loved had been gutted the night before, sobbing in his arms as she went over the meaningless interaction with the girl she hadn't known was Whitney. Meaningless then, not even worth remarking on over dinner that night she'd said, but now it meant so much. He hated this. Hated it, hated it, hated it. Had to make it right.

The young, pretty brunette nurse poured herself a cup of coffee. "I heard you've been looking for me." Kathy had started at the hospital in Buffalo a few months before. It had been a trial by fire, including a long and terrifying spring night snowed in at the hospital with a murderer. Sparks between Kathy and lab tech Wes Braten had ignited over the course of the ordeal, and the two had been dating ever since. Patrick and Susanne had enjoyed getting to know Wes as the other half of a couple, instead of the confirmed bachelor he'd been for years.

"Do you have a minute to talk?" he asked.

Kathy sat down across from him. "Sure. Is it about Whitney?"

Patrick nodded somberly. "I'm very sorry. I know the two of you were close."

"Yes." Tears welled in her eyes. She put her coffee mug to her lips, and Patrick thought it was more to regain her composure than to take a sip. "I'm going to miss her so much."

"I know you will. I'll miss her too. She was a good training and climbing colleague. And finding her like that in the creek behind our house... The only word for it is surreal."

"I've heard some things. About Susanne. About you and Whitney." Kathy looked him straight in the eye. She wasn't the kind to tread lightly.

"It's all ridiculous hogwash. Susanne didn't know her." He tried not to let his face betray him. Susanne and Whitney. The argument. Susanne swore she hadn't known it was Whitney, and he believed her. “And there was nothing going on between Whitney and me, even though the cops are claiming some guy she dated said she had a crush on me.”

Kathy took a deep breath. "She never said anything about romantic feelings to me. Did she ever... I don’t know—come on to you?"

"Never." He thought about the envelope in his top drawer. There was nothing romantic about that package, but it was perplexing. So were the words she’d written on the back of his card. *His wife knows —she threatened me.* "I interviewed her. I gave her my card. She wrote my home number on it, then the police found it on her and made a big deal of nothing. I just hoped she was coming to work here. We could have used the help."

"She didn't plan on working here long." Kathy gave a rueful smile.

"Why?" Patrick hadn't even known she was going to accept a job offer with them, but he'd been under the impression that she really wanted to make the move to Buffalo.

Kathy stood and returned to the break room counter. She refilled her cup and grabbed another sugar packet and a spoon. Back at her chair, she sweetened her coffee and took a sip, then nodded. "She told me she was about to come into some money. She planned to leave nursing when she did."

Patrick was surprised. "How—like an inheritance?"

"Maybe, but I don’t think so. Her parents were already deceased, and the rest of her family didn't have money. She promised to tell me more when she could. She was pretty excited about it."

"That's all she told you?"

Kathy squinted her eyes in thought, then smiled. "She said it would make her richer and more famous than Ichabod Johnson."

Patrick felt his forehead bunch in confusion. "Am I missing something? I've never heard of him."

Kathy laughed. "I haven't either. I said if that's how famous you're going to be, no one will know who you are either."

Patrick nodded, mulling over the perplexing information.

"Your lips are moving, but no sound is coming out. I think that's my signal this conversation is over. Are you coming to her service?"

"Sorry." He zoned back in for a second. "Yes. I'll be there."

Kathy stood. "I'd better get back to work. I hope the cops back off of Susanne and get smart soon."

Patrick didn't realize he hadn't thanked her or said goodbye until he realized he was alone in the break room. His mind was a million miles away, trying to figure out what had been going on in Whitney's life, where her windfall was coming from, and who the heck Ichabod Johnson was—if any of it even mattered.

---

WITH THE MYSTERIOUS Ichabod Johnson on his mind, Patrick extended his lunch to swing by the library. He parked in the closest spot and walked briskly to the door. His footsteps resounded as he went past the museum on the ground floor and down the stairs to the basement, where the library was housed. It was his daughter Trish's favorite place in the world when they had first moved to Wyoming. He used to drop her off and pick her up here frequently. He, too, loved the dank, musty smell and twilight atmosphere that lent an air of intrigue to selecting a book.

But that's not what he was here to do today, not really. He stopped at the front counter where longtime friend and librarian Cynthia Twain was working behind her desk. The library was fairly empty, other than a few employees re-shelving books.

"Dr. Flint, what a surprise." Cynthia had left her job as an elementary school teacher the previous year to run the library. Perry had been one of her students. Patrick had sat across from her at many parent-teacher conferences. "May I help you with something?"

He nodded. "I hope so. I need a quick shove in the right direction."

"I'm all ears." Which wasn't true, not literally. If she'd been a horse, he would've said her small ears were pinned back. The look was enhanced by her hairstyle —a tight, low braid hanging to the middle of her back. Her hair was completely white, although she still seemed youthful. Twinkling eyes. Bright skin. Athletic build.

"I heard a name today, and I was told this person is famous. But I've never heard of him. I'm wondering how to go about learning more about him."

"Well, the first thing to do is tell me his name." She poised a pencil over a small white scrap of paper.

"Ichabod Johnson. I don't know where he's from, whether he's alive or dead, or what he is supposedly famous for."

She put the pencil and paper down and flashed him a smile that revealed braces on her teeth. "You'll have to give me something harder next time. Ichabod Johnson is a famous Wyomingite. And he's dead. Or at least he's assumed to be dead. Although his wife still lives in the area. She and I went to high school together. Anyway, at the time he disappeared, it was on par with Amelia Earhart for us here in Wyoming. Some conspiracy theorists believe he's still alive, but he was a bit of a publicity hound so I doubt that he could live out of the public eye. He's still very popular."

*Well, alrighty then.* "I guess we moved here after all that happened and missed the excitement. Why was he famous?"

"He was a rich playboy who bought a big ranch here in Wyoming. As I recall, he traveled the world climbing mountains and acquiring rare and expensive things. He was an amateur archaeologist as well. Quite eccentric."

"A mountain climber, huh?" Small wonder that, as a Wyoming girl and a climber, Whitney had compared her potential upcoming wealth and fame to that of Ichabod Johnson.

"Yes. If I remember correctly, he was a solo climber. And it's believed he died nearby in the Bighorns. It was reported that had been his destination, anyway. There was quite a search for him, but no one found hide nor hair."

Patrick felt like he'd discovered buried treasure. "I can't believe I've never heard of him."

"He really captured the public imagination. Would you like me to pull some articles for you?"

Patrick almost told her not to bother, but then he realized that whether or not Ichabod Johnson had anything to do with Whitney's potential windfall or her death, he found the story of the eccentric mountain climber interesting on its own merits. "Thank you. I'll swing back by later this week if you don't mind."

The two of them parted ways. Patrick was so enthralled in thoughts of an eccentric solo Wyomingite mountain climber that he walked past his car and didn't realize it until he reached the intersection. Chagrined, he walked back to it, then managed to free just enough of his brain to make it safely back to work, where a harried Kathy met him at the door.

"Where have you been?" she asked.

"I just ran out for, um, an errand. What's the matter?" he asked, his mind racing toward mass casualties or the death of a prominent citizen.

"It's Susanne. She's been trying to reach you. And she sounded very, very upset."

# CHAPTER TWENTY-FOUR: BURN

SHERIDAN COLLEGE, SHERIDAN, WYOMING
*NOW:* MONDAY, JUNE 19, 1978

*Susanne*

SUSANNE ARRIVED fifteen minutes early to Professor Seth's office mid-day on Monday. She'd spent the morning stress-cleaning the house top-to-bottom while grinding all the enamel off her teeth and had ended it by checking in on Perry with Vangie Sibley.

"He just finished eating." Vangie's laugh lifted Susanne's spirits. "His head was bobbing. I swear he nearly fell asleep at the table. Blister is hazing him and Henry's wearing him out. He'll be dragging at football practice, I'm afraid."

"Thank you, Vangie. Give him a hug for me!" Susanne had said.

It was good news. Perry was safe, and Henry was a godsend. But her son wasn't her real worry. That honor was reserved for her fear that the police would arrest her. That she would go to jail. Be convicted and sent to prison. Innocent people were incarcerated all the time. She'd watched an investigative news program on it just a few weeks before.

She knocked on the frame of the open door, but Professor Seth wasn't in his office. She hadn't managed to work on the research she'd planned to the night before or that morning, but she was still eager to tell him about her progress. His feedback and direction were critical. Susanne walked back to the department secretary's desk. The gray head of the secretary was lowered, focusing on something she was reading in her lap.

Susanne put her fingertips on the woman's desk to get her attention. "Hi, Bertha. Is Professor Seth in?"

Bertha startled. Papers rustled in her lap. A newspaper, Susanne saw. The Sunday edition. "Oh! Susanne."

Bertha shoved the paper onto the floor under the desk. Literally, onto the floor, leaving no doubt in Susanne's mind about what she'd been reading. Her heart sunk. At least the humiliating argument she'd had with Whitney in the grocery parking lot wasn't in the Sunday stories. Next time the papers ran something on her, she was sure it would be included. Someone else's version. And it would make her look very bad.

Bertha looked across the hall. "He's, um—well, he's... he's in a meeting."

"Okay. I'll just get to work then."

"You might want to—"

The door to the department conference room opened. Professor Seth appeared, his eyes lighting on Susanne, his expression somber. Susanne peered into the room behind him. She spotted the familiar uniforms and faces of Buffalo's finest. The police were here interviewing Professor Seth. Tears stung the back of her eyes.

Professor Seth gave a barely perceptible head shake. Susanne understood. She should not speak. She shrunk back and waited for him to pass. He beckoned her, and she followed him down the hall. Behind them, she heard Appelt's arrogant voice calling for his next witness. She couldn't help herself and looked back. Bertha slipped into the conference room.

Professor Seth pointed Susanne into the office. She took the chair in front of his desk. He closed the door.

Then he sat, hands steepled. "Mrs. Flint. As you can see, we've had a visit from the Buffalo police today."

Susanne swallowed back the urge to cry. She would not cry. "I am so sorry. I promise, no matter what they are asking or saying, I didn't do anything to Whitney Saylor. My husband climbed mountains with her. It's horrible that she died. And all of this—I don't understand why it's happening."

"They are interviewing many people. Students, Bertha, me, other faculty. They want to know if you were here Friday afternoon. I hope you did not tell them you were."

She felt her forehead bunch. "Why would I tell them that? I didn't come to the college that day."

"Good. I felt it important to tell the truth but did not want to cause you trouble."

"How would that cause me trouble?"

"I was given the impression the police believe that is when Miss Saylor died."

Susanne pressed a hand to her mouth. Of all the times to take a day off. She'd driven to Billings, Montana to go shopping. Alone. "Did they say how she died?"

"They did not."

Susanne wondered if the cause of death had even been determined yet. She doubted it. If it was clear-cut foul play, she probably wouldn't be sitting here now, free. But surely they'd have that information soon.

"I hate to ask this of you, but would you consider taking your research home and working from there until this is, um, settled? It is quite a distraction, as you can imagine. For us and for you."

Susanne jumped to her feet. "Of course." She pointed at the stack of papers and documents in the corner on the floor. "I'll just grab these and be on my way." Now was not the time to seek input from Professor Seth. She would call him later in the week. She swooped down and lifted the stack. Papers shifted and tumbled to the floor. Her tears started to flow. She bent down, hiding her face. "I'm so sorry. I'm so, so sorry."

Professor Seth crouched beside her. He spoke in a low voice as he stacked and straightened the papers. "Shh. Mrs. Flint. You have nothing to be sorry about. It is I who am sorry. As a man from the Middle East, I come under more scrutiny than my colleagues. I must keep a low profile. Avoid even an appearance of impropriety. I wish you a speedy resolution and return, and my prayers will be with you." He handed her the papers.

"Thank you," she whispered. She took a deep breath and lifted her chin. She would exit with dignity. She dried her tears on the sleeve of her blouse, then stood and marched out of his office, down the long empty corridor, and out into the intrusive light of an unforgiving sun.

# CHAPTER TWENTY-FIVE: SLIDE

CLOUD PEAK WILDERNESS, BIGHORN MOUNTAINS, WYOMING
*THEN (NINE MONTHS EARLIER)*: MONDAY, SEPTEMBER 19, 1977

*Patrick*

AFTER AN UNCOMFORTABLE NIGHT in the cave, Patrick rose early. He crawled out and looked back over the rocky trail back to the summit. It wasn't officially sunrise yet, but there was enough light for him to see that the wind had worked in their favor. Most of the snow had blown to kingdom come, leaving bare rocks. He didn't have a thermometer, but his exposed nose and ice crystal breath recorded the temperature at well below freezing, which was good. It meant that no melt and refreeze had occurred. The path would be slick but not icy.

The sooner they left the better. Before it warmed up. While they were still well hydrated and not weak from fasting. Between the three of them they had harvested two full canteens of snow melt water through the night. He'd heard answering stomach growls from his cave companions that morning, though—they were out of food.

He imagined his wife and kids at home. Susanne would have reassured Trish and Perry, maybe pretending there'd been a change in plan she somehow forgot to tell them about. Perry probably would have believed her false promises. Trish would be too distracted by the teenage love bubble she was in with her boyfriend Ben for much to penetrate it. But Susanne would be eaten alive by worry. She wouldn't have slept a wink. He hated that for her.

When he made it off this mountain, he planned to hold her so tight she would laugh and tell him to stop. And he was re-evaluating mountain climbing. He didn't need summits. He needed his family.

"What do you see out there, man?" Loren came out of the cave and stood beside him. He was blowing on his cupped hands and stomping his feet.

Patrick pointed back the way they'd come. "A clear path to re-summit and catch the regular trail down."

"Sounds good to me. Man, I'm not even sure how we ended up here. Where we went wrong."

"I remember the way. And I can see it."

"You were delirious."

"Not the whole time. And I'm a homing pigeon." *Other than when you needed me to be, yesterday.*

Whitney exited the cave and stood on Patrick's other side, catching the end of the conversation. She pointed down the cliff at their feet. "What about those ropes? It looks like a descent route."

Patrick had noticed the ropes, too. They seemed to indicate a climber or climbers sometime in the past had traversed down the rocks from where they stood, skipping the summit. They looked old but not ancient. Weathered but not frayed beyond usability. "No way to know where they go. I like a sure thing."

A loud rumbling noise cut off their conversation. Patrick felt the ground beneath his feet shake. He grabbed Whitney by the arm on one side and Loren on the other.

"What's happening?" Whitney screamed.

"Rockslide maybe. Or an earthquake." Or both.

CRACK. The sound was like a gunshot, immediately followed by bouncing, tumbling, crashing rocks between them and the summit. All three climbers hit the ground on their narrow trail, hands over the back of their heads. The rock cliff only two feet away felt like it was pulling them closer. He turned away from it, leaning against the solid rock behind them. Whitney and Loren did the same.

As suddenly as the pandemonium had started, it stopped. A lone boulder crashed its way down the mountainside. It was probably the size of a Volkswagen Beetle although it seemed smaller against the expanse of rock. Then it grew deathly quiet. All Patrick could hear was their heavy breathing.

"Oh, my God." Whitney huddled against him. "Oh, my God."

Patrick stood, fearing the worst. He scanned below them but he didn't see any evidence of the phenomena they'd just experienced. Then he turned to look up the trail toward the summit. Dust was rising and, thanks to the omnipresent wind, dissipating. As it settled, Patrick saw nothing, but a different nothing. An *absence*. Where the trail had been, a whole section of rock floor had fallen away. On the far side of the abyss, boulders had stacked up, blocking the remaining.

Their return route was now impassable.

# CHAPTER TWENTY-SIX: MEET

BUFFALO, WYOMING
*NOW:* TUESDAY, JUNE 20, 1978

*Patrick*

"THERE'S A CALL FOR YOU, Dr. Flint." Kathy walked past him quickly, throwing the words over her shoulder. "I left the phone receiver on the counter." She pointed at the nurse's station.

"Thanks, Kathy." Patrick walked the opposite direction, toward the phone. His stomach tightened. He didn't get a lot of calls at the hospital. Susanne knew he didn't like his family bothering the staff to track him down unless it was an emergency. Had one of the kids been hurt—Perry stomped by a bull on his first day at the Sibley ranch? Trish in a car wreck? Or was it Susanne? *Susanne. Whitney. The Buffalo police.* "Who is it?"

"Some attorney." Kathy disappeared inside a patient's room.

Patrick steeled himself. Stu Ryan had been curt and final when he'd called Sunday night. Adamant that Susanne had been untruthful, despite her protestations. It was Tuesday morning, and they hadn't heard from him since. Why would he be calling now?

He put the receiver to his ear. He was getting tired of favoring his splinted right hand. The doctor part of his brain knew that after three days of healing it would barely have a fragile bone callus beginning to bridge the crack. He would be counseling his patients on how to deal with the severe pain that undoubtedly he was feeling. But the other parts of his brain told him to get tough. He could be extra careful. It would heal fine without it. "This is Dr. Patrick Flint."

"This is Gary Bolton." *Not Stu Ryan.* "I represent—or represented rather—Whitney Saylor. She left something for you."

Patrick didn't like the sound of that. The package in his underwear drawer suddenly seemed radioactive. He cleared his throat. "I'm not sure I understand." It seemed unusual for someone her age to have a will. He hated being mentioned in it. It looked bad. Very bad. And it couldn't be hidden beneath a stack of skivvies.

"If you come by my office in Sheridan, with identification, I can pass it along to you."

"Doesn't her will need to be probated first?"

"Oh, it's nothing like that."

"What is it then?"

"A ring of keys. She asked me to hold them for you before she died. She said you'd be coming to get them. Then, when she passed, I had to track you down so I could make sure you did."

Patrick wasn't a legal eagle, but if the attorney believed the keys were part of Whitney's estate, he wouldn't be giving them to Patrick. This still wasn't good, but it was less bad. Or he hoped it was. The only way to be sure was to collect them. "I'm on my way."

---

FORTY-FIVE MINUTES after the on-call doctor showed up to relieve him for his "emergency," Patrick sat across a cluttered desk from a bespectacled attorney. The man's sweater vest and bow tie marked him as someone who had migrated to Wyoming.

"Identification?" Bolton said.

Patrick handed Bolton his driver's license. Bolton scrutinized it with pursed lips, then nodded.

"Here are your keys." Bolton placed a fuzzy rabbit foot keychain holder with three keys into Patrick's palm.

Nothing about them looked familiar, but Patrick kept his face impassive. "Thank you."

"The buyer should be in touch soon. Was Whitney going to get a commission on your sale? Or was this a more ... informal arrangement?"

Buyer? Commission? *What's going on here?* It made no sense. Although a sale of ... something ... might be the source of the payout Whitney had told Kathy she was expecting. But sale of what? He wondered if Bolton really had no idea what the item was that the buyer was inquiring about.

For a moment, Patrick considered telling Bolton the truth. That he had no idea what the keys were to or what was being sold. That there was no way any of it belonged to him. It might extricate him from this mess. Plus, the right thing to do, legally, was to ensure Whitney's property went to her heirs. If it was Whitney's property. And if she had heirs.

But what if he was holding the literal key to Whitney's death? To removing Susanne from suspicion? He decided he should trust Whitney, like she said she had trusted him. Just long enough to try to figure this out himself. Why she mailed him the map. Why she left him the key. Why she'd told the attorney she was helping Patrick sell something.

He asked, "Did Whitney leave a will?"

"No. She lived paycheck to paycheck."

"Doesn't she have personal possessions, maybe something of sentimental value? How will those get to her heirs?"

"No family. The courts will figure it out, but it will probably be more trouble than it's worth."

All of this begged the question of why she had an attorney. But the rabbit foot keychain in his hand might hold the answer to that. It didn't hurt to ask. "What were you doing for Whitney? Besides hanging onto keys for me." Patrick offered up a smile. It felt hollow. This whole encounter with Bolton felt hollow.

"I've been representing her since the death of her parents. While she didn't have any inheritance left after their final debts were covered, it was still an ordeal with the courts and all. She turns to me from time to time with questions or issues." Bolton arched his brows. "Not that it's really my business, Dr. Flint, why Whitney was doing this for you. I assume you have your reasons for the subterfuge. I know who you are and that you are married. It's not my place to judge."

Patrick's cheeks burned. What was this man suggesting? He was too flabbergasted to protest. The only subterfuge had been Whitney's in suggesting that any of this had anything to do with Patrick. But there was no way Bolton was going to believe him. He'd stick to the essential issue. "I can assure you that you have no reason to judge. I'm a happily married man."

Bolton inspected a hangnail, then continued. "Whitney was of course working directly with your buyer. She gave him my contact information and asked that I act as a go-between. Here you go." Bolton pushed a yellow while-you-were-out note pad across the desk with two fingers. The blanks on the first page were filled with a name and phone number.

Patrick put his hand on the pad, then said, "May I?"

"All yours."

He tore the top page off the pad, cursing his purple and yellow bruised hand and the pain he couldn't ignore. It was a Wyoming area code number and a name. Carl Price. Patrick had never heard of him. Whitney was selling something to this guy that she'd led the attorney to believe belonged to Patrick. Something possibly secured by the keys in his hands. Where and what were the million-dollar questions. "Well, thank you. Is there any other information you have that might help me?"

"Information *from* me? No. But I'm still waiting on an answer from you to my earlier question."

"I'm sorry. Could you repeat it?"

"Was Whitney getting a commission? It might cover my final bill."

Patrick almost snorted. When Bolton had asked the question earlier, Patrick had assumed his intention was to identify any money or property that should pass to Whitney's *heirs*. He should have guessed, though. This was about passing money to Whitney's *attorney*. "We didn't have that type of agreement."

A cloud descended on Bolton's face. "Well, I hope you'll do the right thing anyway."

Patrick's eyebrows stretched up his forehead. He sat open-mouthed, unable to formulate a response.

"Well, I've taken up far too much of your time. Good luck to you, Dr. Flint." Bolton stood, all but shooing Patrick out with his hand.

Patrick didn't wait around. He exited quickly. He needed to think. And he needed to figure out what to do with the keys clutched tightly in his hand.

---

PATRICK SAT in his truck outside the attorney's office, rabbit's foot in his hand, rotating the keys, examining each one carefully. One looked like a standard front door key. Another smaller one could have opened a padlock. A third seemed likely to be a mailbox key. Not the big, heavy kind for post office boxes, but the flimsy little keys for private mailboxes in multiunit dwellings. His initial reaction was that he was holding a set of keys to Whitney's apartment. A spare set, he would think, since she'd given them to Bolton before her death.

This would be easy to verify. All he needed to do was visit her home. Only he didn't know where she lived.

He needed a phone book. He drove his truck north on Main Street until he reached a gas station. There, he went to the phone booth outside. As he had hoped, there was a covered phone book hanging in it. He looked Whitney up in the white pages, but he had nothing to write with, or on. Looking in both directions for watchful eyes, he found none. He told his inner Boy Scout to back off and ripped the page out. Then he got back in his truck and pulled a Sheridan map from his glove box. It took him nearly 10 minutes of slow perusing to find her street and to determine which block her address was in. Finally, he set off towards it.

He found a complex of two-story brick apartment buildings at the address on the filched page. The listing didn't have a unit number. But the little key that he believed was to a mailbox had a piece of paper taped to it and the number A212 written on it in tiny letters. Building A was easy to identify. He parked in front of it and found his way upstairs to a unit with 212 on the door.

The key fit easily into the lock. He felt a rush of elation at his successful sleuthing. But before he could turn the doorknob, he heard voices inside. One was strident and oh-so-familiar. He took hurried steps backward. Through a window in the stairwell, he could see into the back parking lot. And what he saw sent his heart to his throat. Police cars. Sheridan and Buffalo. Appelt was in Whitney's apartment. No way was he going in. No way was he letting them know about the keys.

He backtracked quickly without running. Sweat dripped down the back of his neck as he climbed into his truck. He put his truck in reverse. He had to get out of here before he was seen. *Please don't let them have seen me.*

As he navigated out of the neighborhood, his brain whirled with the new information. It made no sense that Whitney would leave him keys to her place unless there was something important inside, possibly related to the map she had sent him. To the sale she supposedly made on his behalf. But would it still be there after the cops finished searching?

He could only hope it would. There was nothing he could do until the cops were done. Not if he planned to keep all of this a secret.

*And there's no way I can tell them now after I didn't disclose the map Sunday night.*

But it wasn't only the police who were in the dark. He was headed back toward Buffalo, and the wife who would not be pleased at all about his newest entanglement with Whitney Saylor.

# CHAPTER TWENTY-SEVEN: LUMP

Sibley Ranch, Story, Wyoming
*Now*: Tuesday, June 20, 1978

*Perry*

By lunch on Tuesday, Perry was so whipped that he went to the bunkhouse for a nap instead of to eat. He couldn't understand it. He thought he was in shape for football. It was nothing compared to Henry Sibley, though. Even Blister was holding up better than Perry was. Henry had started working before Perry on Monday and was still working when Perry returned from football, but he'd been whistling and had a bounce to his step as he greeted Perry.

At dinner, Vangie had asked Henry if he'd like a beer.

Henry had laughed and said, "No way I can work at my best with that in my system. I'll save it for Sunday afternoon when I watch the Broncos. For now, food and sleep."

Perry suspected the interchange was staged for his benefit, but it hit home. If Perry wanted to be half the man Henry Sibley was, he'd do well to emulate him. But if he did, his older teammates would call him a wuss. Or worse.

He drifted out despite his turbulent thoughts, only waking when a knock sounded at the bunkhouse door.

Vangie's voice called out to him. "Perry, I have a phone call for you."

Perry sat up, stretching and scrunching his face to wake it up. "My dad?"

"No. He said he's your football coach."

A cold dread seeped down Perry from the crown of his head to the tips of his fingers. He jumped up and hurried after Vangie to the phone in the main house kitchen. Henry and Blister looked up from their food. Blister had a curious expression on his face.

Perry snatched up the phone and faced the wall. "This is Perry Flint," he said, using the script and tone his parents had drilled into him.

His coach's gruff voice blasted his ear. "Flint, this is Coach Cantrell. I've received some disturbing information about you. Is it true that you were inebriated Saturday night?"

Perry screwed his eyes shut. He paused. He had no option but the truth. "Yes, sir. I'm sorry, sir. It was a big mistake, and it won't happen again. I promise, my parents are plenty steamed at me."

"Is there anything you'd like to tell me about the incident? Like, who you were with, where you were, and how you got the alcohol?"

*Oh, no. He's looking for me to rat out Chuck and Billy.* They would never forgive him. Everyone would find out he'd snitched. He couldn't. He just couldn't. But he could take responsibility for himself. "Uh, no, sir. It was my mistake and mine alone."

"Here's the deal, Flint. I'm taking a chance bringing a runt like you up to varsity, no matter how talented and hard-working you are. But what the coach giveth, the coach can taketh away, and I'd be more than happy to bust your little hiney right back down to junior varsity and keep it on the bench this season."

"Yes, sir." Perry's voice was barely a whisper, but it was as loud as he could make it. How did the upper classmen get away with drinking when he got caught the first time he tried it?

"You're suspended for the week. I'll see you Monday for varsity practice. I'm counting on you to keep your word. If you learn your lesson, you could be a future leader of your team."

Perry felt like his guts had been ripped out by grizzly claws. He loved practice. He loved the games. He loved everything about football. Every second of it. "Thank you, Coach Cantrell." His voice sounded like a strangled cat.

He hung up the phone. His face was burning. He turned around to find Henry standing, arms crossed over his chest, waiting for him. "Well?"

He stood as tall as he could, which put him eye to eye with the rancher. The older man had been a heck of a bull rider in his younger days, Perry had heard, and the trophies and buckles lining the shelves in the living room attested to it. But the best bull riders were compact. Maybe if football didn't pan out, Perry would give it a shot. "Suspension. I guess I'm all yours for a couple of extra hours a day this week."

"Did he ask you to rat out your drinking buddies?"

"He did."

Henry nodded. "You owned up to it and took your punishment. I won't say that keeping quiet about your teammates was the right choice, but I respect you taking responsibility. Like a man." He turned and walked out.

Perry felt Blister's eyes on him, then he heard a second set of boot steps.

He was alone. He slumped against the wall for a moment, trying not to cry. If this was the first step in proving he was a man, why did it make him feel like a little boy again?

# CHAPTER TWENTY-EIGHT: SWALLOW

Buffalo, Wyoming
*Now:* Tuesday, June 20, 1978

*Susanne*

Back at home late Tuesday morning, Susanne sat at her sewing machine in the corner of her bedroom and stared at the pages in front of her, unseeing. She'd been folding it down and using it as a desk ever since she'd started back to school. When was the last time she'd even sewed with it? Definitely not in the last nine months. At least she was putting the table to good use.

The phone rang. She startled and squeaked. Afraid to answer it, she walked slowly into the kitchen. When she picked it up, she said, "Hello?" in a tentative voice, skipping her normal greeting.

Vangie whispered. "The coach called and suspended Perry for a week. Henry said Perry confessed and bore up well."

Susanne had told Vangie that it was Patrick who had called

Coach Cantrell and told him what Perry had done. Her shoulders sagged in relief. Not the police. Not a reporter. Not bad news. "That's great. Thank you."

"Hang in there. I'm praying for you."

"That means the world to me."

"Of course!"

The two friends hung up. Susanne considered leaving the phone off the hook, but she just couldn't. What if something happened to the kids or Patrick? She trudged back to her research, then had an idea. If she hid her car in the barn, she could refuse to answer the door if anyone came to it. She went back to the kitchen for her keys. Ferdinand trotted after her out to the car.

She let him sit in the back seat, a rare treat. "We're not going far, Ferdie."

His tail thumped frantically in reply.

Susanne drove through the open barn doors into the central area, where she and the happy dog parked it. She dragged the heavy sliding doors shut and snapped the padlock closed. Trish's truck was still here, but her daughter would stay holed up in her room all day. Answering the door when she wasn't expecting someone was not something the teenager deigned to do when she was reading. Susanne returned to her research, feeling a little more insulated.

After a few false starts, she dove into the reading materials. While not completely on target with Professor Seth's geopolitical relations angle, she indulged herself in an article about multiple grave robberies near the time of King Tut's original entombment. Susanne had believed that the tomb and its treasures had been intact, but that was far from the case. She scanned an inventory of all the items discovered by Howard Carter's team when they first opened the tomb in 1923. What was left behind after the robbers amounted to the richest burial ever unearthed in Egypt, despite Tut himself having been a fairly minor pharaoh. Punishment in antiquity for tomb robbing was severe. It was no small matter to rob a tomb at the time his was robbed. The evidence of the efforts to restore Tut's tomb made it appear to have been done in haste, like the robbers had been caught or feared they would be. In comparison, later robberies of other tombs cleaned out relatively all of the contents of the tombs opened, unlike Tut's.

Yet still, the team surmised the robbers had made off with many valuables. Carter found an inventory docket from the time of King Tut's funeral. Comparing it to the actual contents when he opened the tomb, he estimated that some sixty percent of the jewelry originally contained in the treasury caskets had been stolen, along with a whole series of precious metal vessels. Some of the items were rumored to have survived into modern day and passed through the hands of various wealthy collectors.

Susanne pressed record and described the robberies onto tape. Her stomach growled. She'd skipped breakfast, but she didn't even glance at the clock to see if it was lunch time yet. She was smiling, something she wouldn't have thought possible earlier in the day.

She kept reading, lost in a magical world she'd never imagined.

# CHAPTER TWENTY-NINE: BURN

Buffalo, Wyoming
*Now:* Tuesday, June 20, 1978

*Trish*

Trish slid to the grass and straightened her legs. She leaned forward to her toes, bouncing a little to deepen the stretch.

"Are they going to arrest her mother for killing her dad's girlfriend?" It was one of the other cheerleaders, apparently thinking Trish was deaf or asleep.

Trish closed her eyes and tried to pretend she didn't hear.

Jillian answered in a voice meant to carry. "I don't know. Trish doesn't believe her mom did it. Or that her dad was involved with Whitney. But where there's smoke, there's fire, you know?"

Trish jumped to her feet. "Enough! My dad was not cheating on my mother. My mother did not kill anybody. The cops don't even know whether Whitney was murdered. It may have been an accident or something. No one has been arrested. And keep your voices down if you want to talk about me behind my back."

She glared at four mouths and eight round eyes.

Jillian rallied first. "Whoa, Trish. We're sorry, you know? I'm sure you're right." She put her hands up. "Do you have a second?"

Trish wanted to say no. Jillian was the captain of the squad, though, and at practice, everyone deferred to her. She stepped toward Jillian and turned her back on the group. "What is it?"

Jillian lowered her voice, something she hadn't done when talking about Trish and her family. Trish didn't have to turn around to know everyone was watching and trying to listen in on their conversation. "Jimmy and Dabbo are still hiding out. I'm so scared they're going to get arrested. What are we going to do?"

Trish wanted to forget what they'd done Saturday night. She'd be happy never hearing Jimmy's name again in her life. "Stop. What if someone overhears us?"

Jillian wrung her hands and continued making a quiet scene. "Do you want to go see them with me tonight? I thought I'd take them some food."

"No!"

"Come on. It's not far, and I don't want to go alone. They're staying out at Jimmy's uncle's sheep wagon on the XYZ Ranch."

"I don't care where they're staying. I don't want anyone to know I ever went out with him. I don't ever want to see him again. It was not a date. It was a favor to you so you could see your boyfriend. So, please, don't bring him up to me again."

"We should help them, Trish. If they get caught, we get caught."

"I didn't do anything. You didn't do anything."

"Technically, that's not true. You orchestrated the whole getaway."

Pain shot through her chest. Trish clutched her shoulder. "Leave me out of anything to do with Jimmy Gross."

Jillian scowled at her. "What's wrong with you?"

Trish knew what was wrong with her. Jimmy, Dabbo, and Jillian were what was wrong with her. She'd had panic attacks a few years ago when she first moved to Buffalo. Her dad had taught her how to calm herself down through relaxation and deep breathing techniques. She hadn't had an attack in a very long time, not even after Ben left.

"I'm fine," she snapped. "Let's just get this practice over with."

# CHAPTER THIRTY: HEAR

CLOUD PEAK WILDERNESS, BIGHORN MOUNTAINS, WYOMING
*THEN (NINE MONTHS EARLIER)*: MONDAY, SEPTEMBER 19, 1977

*Patrick*

PATRICK KEPT his complete focus on Whitney as she backed down a boulder face-in, sliding her gloved hand along a section of rope. "Looking good," he said, his face unnaturally calm.

She looked fine, but Patrick was a bundle of nerves inside. The worst part of their semi-vertical descent was not knowing what lay ahead of them. Or below them, rather. Patrick had scoured the route with his binoculars for fifteen minutes before they'd started. It was easy to follow because of the rope stakes into the rock. But it disappeared around a pillar. He could only hope when they made it there, they wouldn't be at another dead end.

The second worst thing about the route was relying on old ropes installed by a stranger. Patrick didn't even trust work done by others when he witnessed it performed fresh in front of his own eyes. They had very little way to test the integrity of the ropes besides with their own body weight and lives.

Now he felt pretty helpless watching the young woman below him. Whitney had tried to insist on going first because she was the lightest, but Patrick had vetoed her. He wanted to claim the role because he was the oldest and most experienced. After all, he'd survived a rock slide and bouldering descent on Black Tooth Mountain a few years before, even if by the skin of his teeth. But the smart move was to send Loren first, as he was the lighter of the two men and Patrick the stronger. Loren had gone ahead, not without trepidation. Patrick went last, with a promise to haul all three of them back up to safety if necessary.

Whitney landed on a flat spot near Loren. She released the rope and exhaled sharply. "I think I'm getting the hang of it."

Patrick lowered himself after her, one careful step at a time.

The third worst thing about this descent was fear of one of them getting injured, and it would become the very worst thing if it actually happened. But if he thought about that too much, it would rob his attention from where it needed to be. On Whitney and Loren's safety.

The fourth worst thing would be more inclement weather. But so far, after starting a few minutes past the glorious sunrise to the east followed by a few hours of downward traversing, it had been the perfect mountain morning.

When he reached his companions, he said, "Please, God, let this be a shortcut." It wouldn't make this route preferable to the normal one, but considering a bright side would lessen their stress.

"No kidding." Loren started walking over mostly flat-topped rock in a nearly horizontal section. "This part's feet only." He threw a grin over his shoulder with his arms up. "Look, Pa. No hands."

"Eyes on the road!" Whitney shouted.

Loren just laughed in response.

"You're up," Patrick told her.

She nodded and walked after Loren, surefooted but slower and careful. Loren waited for her. The two moved along side by side, holding a whispered conversation.

Besides a few secretive asides, the two didn't act like a couple. There was no affection between them. While it might be early days, wouldn't they at least hold hands if not share a hug or a supportive glance in circumstances like these? If Susanne were here, he would have held her hand all night. He could understand Whitney and Loren's tension—heck, he felt it, too. This was a high stakes situation. They'd been weathered up on the tallest peak in the Bighorns, lost, and now they were taking an untested route that may or may not lead them back off the mountain, with the constant threat of more weather. He'd been medically compromised. All of them were hungry and out of food, and soon they'd be thirsty, too, if they didn't come to a water source before long. And if they did find water, he would be fearful of giardia, given his past bout of it. The damn bugs were probably lying dormant in his stomach waiting for a reunion with their friends. He'd been so sick on Dome Mountain he'd thought he was going to die.

*Get your mind on the positive, Flint.*

Taking advantage of the flatter section, he sped up, putting his feet down silently and controlling his breathing. He wanted to hear what they were saying, but he didn't want them to realize he was within earshot. Not that he was normally an eavesdropper. But because they were in this together, and he didn't want them discussing important issues or making decisions without his input.

"What were you doing in the cave so long?" Loren said.

"Securing stuff."

"We should have just brought it."

"Too heavy."

"But you've got..."

"Yes."

"Where?"

Whitney's head whipped around. "Oh, hey, Patrick. I thought you were further back. You're sure quiet."

Patrick smiled, even though he was irritated. "And a fast walker."

"Yeah, we saw that yesterday morning, ya old mountain goat." Loren hopped onto a taller boulder that required both hands.

Whitney and Patrick clambered over it, too. They rounded the pillar Patrick had seen from above. Just beyond it, Patrick got his first look of the next pitch, and it was a doozy. The route plunged downward, still marked by staked rope.

"Speaking of mountain goats, I sure hope we're not on one of their trails. Or a bighorn sheep trail, more likely in these mountains." Patrick rubbed his forehead. His mind returned to the conversation he'd overheard. What had they secured in the cave? Why hadn't they brought all their things? If they'd left something they needed, he hoped it didn't cost them their lives. And if it didn't, he reserved the right to be mad about it. Until then, he'd let the lovebirds have their secrets. What he wanted was down the mountain.

Loren put his hands on his hips and pushed out a breath, betraying his nerves. "Looks like it keeps curving around to our left." He pointed down the disappearing progression of rope. "Wish me luck." He grabbed hold of the rope with one hand and worked his way downward.

"It's so steep. Thank God for the ropes," Whitney said.

Patrick wondered who in the world would have staked them here when there was a perfectly good trail to the summit and down. Or there had been, until the rockslide that morning.

Whitney put her gloved hands on her hips. "Should I go now?"

"Let him get a little farther ahead."

"I'm starting to get overheated." Whitney unzipped her coat.

Patrick was, too. "Be careful. Loose clothing can cause accidents. I don't have anything to stitch you up."

"True." She raised the zipper. "I'll put a layer in my backpack when we get back on flat ground." She nodded at him. "Okay, see you at the bottom of whatever this section is."

*Calamity rock.* After all that had gone wrong, that should be the name for the route. "Be careful." Patrick watched her start her descent.

Just as he was about to begin his own, he heard her scream.

# CHAPTER THIRTY-ONE: FACE

BUFFALO, WYOMING
*NOW*: WEDNESDAY, JUNE 21, 1978

*Patrick*

PATRICK SQUEEZED Susanne's hand as the two of them stood several yards behind the last row of graveside mourners. Whitney's funeral had been a somber affair. At the cemetery, the atmosphere was marginally lighter, probably thanks to the chirping of meadowlarks, the call of a sandhill crane overhead, bright sunshine and clean, fresh air, and the abundance of flowers growing, wild at the edges of the facility and planted in front of tombstones. The newer ones, anyway. Some in this cemetery dated back to the 1860s. Life had been harder then, as witnessed by the stones of four young children who all died within a few days of each other in one family. He couldn't imagine how parents bore the weight of that crushing grief. Death was always sad business, but even more so for the young, and when death came unexpectedly and—in Whitney's case—potentially violently. Trish wasn't many years younger than Whitney. He needed to remind her and Perry how much he loved them more often. All the time.

A tear threatened. What held him back from saying it ten times a day? And whatever it was, would it make him feel any better if he never got the chance again? Of course not. He glanced at Susanne's beautiful profile. He would do better. With all three of these people that he loved more than life.

His eyes moved from his wife to the other mourners present. The only ones he recognized were Kathy and Wes. He'd known a few of the hospital personnel back at the church, but most of them hadn't driven out to the cemetery. His mind flashed back to Loren. *He would have wanted to be here.* But it quickly returned to how messed up all of this was. He'd barely known Whitney, really. Their entire friendship was based on the pursuit of a goal: climbing Mt. Rainier in two months. Whitney wouldn't be making that climb now. He wasn't sure if he would be either.

Then his gaze was drawn upward by something that seemed out of place. There, high in a cottonwood and mostly obscured by the proliferation of spring leaves, perched a white owl. The head was swiveling, but, as if sensing Patrick's interest, its eyes bored into his. Man and bird stood locked in a silent communication. *Why are you here so far from home?* Patrick thought, as if the nocturnal creature could hear him. *Why are you out here at all?* It seemed to say in return, and Patrick didn't have a great answer for that. Mourning for a friendship that wasn't what he'd thought it had been. Trying to gather information that would lead to his wife's exoneration, and his own. And because it would have looked really bad if he hadn't shown up. His eyes drifted back to Whitney's casket. He heard a thwump-thwump-thwump and looked back up into the tree. The owl was gone.

After the minister had finished his remarks and Kathy and another friend had spoken, the casket was lowered into the ground. The group began to disperse. Kathy and Wes joined the Flints.

"Nice service," Susanne said. "I'm sorry for the loss of your friend, Kathy."

Kathy thanked her.

Wes snapped his fingers. "Did you hear that little gas station in the center of town was robbed by two thugs with a baseball bat?"

Patrick shook his head. "It seems like there's a bad element moving in on our town. I think it's oil field workers."

Suddenly, a tall, muscular young man with a blotchy complexion was standing in front of Patrick, facing him. He opened his mouth to speak, his face angry.

Bolton was beside him and spoke first, interrupting him. "Were you able to retrieve your things and talk to the buyer, Dr. Flint?"

The other man frowned. "You two know each other?"

Bolton said, "Yes. I've been holding onto some keys for Patrick that Whitney gave me. And I was the go-between for her on a buyer for something of Patrick's."

"Whoa, whoa, whoa." The man's fists balled. "Keys to what? And what property?"

Patrick shifted to block Susanne's view of the conversation, hoping she couldn't hear it. He'd planned on telling her everything last night, but he'd ended up covering a later shift at the hospital in trade for the doc he'd called in during the day. She'd been asleep when he'd slipped into bed. Whitney's potential windfall. Ichabod Johnson. Bolton. The keys. He hadn't had the chance to fill her in on any of it. This morning, he'd balked. He wasn't sure what he was waiting for. Maybe until Whitney's death was ruled natural causes, an accident, or a homicide. Or he figured out what Whitney had been up to. He just didn't want to put Susanne in the middle, to cause her emotional distress, or to give her knowledge that the police could hold against her later. But holding off had clearly been a bad decision with Bolton about to spill the dirty laundry on the edge of Whitney's open grave.

This was not the way for her to find out about Bolton, the keys, and the supposed buyer for a mystery item Patrick still knew nothing about.

Bolton put a hand on the man's shoulder. "Anthony, I'll tell you all about it later."

Anthony, whoever he was, said, "Why would she give you keys? Why would she give you anything?"

"I'm sorry—but we haven't met." Patrick extended his hand, then wished he hadn't. He wasn't wearing the splint. An overly firm handshake could bring him to his knees. "I'm Patrick Flint."

But he needn't have worried. Anthony refused his hand. "I know who you are. You're the jerk my girlfriend dumped me for. The one whose wife killed her."

Bolton was shaking his head. "Patrick, this is Anthony Timms. He and Whitney dated."

"I'm sorry, Anthony, but you're mistaken. Whitney and I were nothing but training and climbing buddies, and my wife had nothing to do with her death."

Anthony lunged toward Patrick. "You were too old for her. She loved me." He put his hands on Patrick's chest and shoved him backwards.

Patrick stumbled and felt himself falling backwards. Falling into Whitney's grave. Falling toward a rough landing on an unsplinted broken hand.

A strong hand caught his elbow and jerked him upwards and to his feet before he hit the casket. Wes. Patrick was about to thank him when his eyes met Susanne's. Hers were flashing and furious.

Anthony was still shouting. "I want them out of here. They have no right to be here. And he shouldn't get Whitney's stuff."

Susanne turned on her heel and walked toward his truck.

Patrick ran after her. "Susanne, wait. Please. Let me explain."

She reached the truck door and pointed at him. "Your friendship with Whitney is like the gift that keeps on giving. Or the nightmare that will never end." Then got in and slammed the door so hard that Patrick was afraid the window would break.

---

THE RIDE HOME from Sheridan was tense.

"Start talking. That man. Bolton. How did you know him?" Susanne demanded.

Patrick told her about the call. About the meeting. He backed up and shared what Kathy had told him and what little he had learned at the library. He was glad for an excuse to keep his eyes on the road, so he didn't have to see the hurt and anger he was sure were in her eyes. He was about to tell her about his conclusions, such as they were, and finding Whitney's apartment, but she cut him off.

"It doesn't make sense, Patrick."

"None of it does. I need to talk to this supposed buyer. Figure out what it is Whitney told Bolton I sold to him."

"What is the key to?"

"Keys. There are three. One is to her apartment. I found her address and went and checked. One seems like a mailbox key. The third I have no clue."

"She gave you her spare keys."

"It appears that way."

"That's just awful."

"Maybe. Or maybe she had a reason. Maybe there's something there I'm supposed to find."

"This is getting so far-fetched." She smacked her palm on the dash. "Maybe this. Maybe that. Or maybe she just wanted you to show up in her bedroom and tell her you were leaving me."

His head drooped, eyes off the road for a second. He looked up and had drifted onto the shoulder. He swerved to correct. Susanne didn't react. "I know this is upsetting—"

"Upsetting? *Upsetting?* It's beyond upsetting. It's humiliating. It's hurtful. It's marriage threatening. It's threatening my freedom."

"And I'm sorry. I hate this. But I don't believe that's what she wanted. I know I could be wrong, but this whole deal with telling her attorney she was the go-between for me and a buyer on the sale of whatever this is—I have to believe it's related to that. Although why she involved me..." His voice trailed off.

The silence stretched to nearly a minute. When Susanne spoke, her voice was very soft. "You should never have let that...that...that *girl* get so close to you. Never."

"I agree with you, honey. Still, this is out of the blue."

"Not so out of the blue that Whitney's old boyfriend didn't tell the police about the two of you. Was that him at the grave yelling at you?"

Patrick nodded, feeling miserable.

"The one who told the police I fought with Whitney over her accosting me in the grocery parking lot."

"Yes. But it's just another example of how far out of proportion he portrays things."

"Or how out of proportion what she told him was."

"I can't disagree with that. It could be either. Listen, this is all bad, and I know I could have prevented it by partnering with someone else. But I'm asking you to trust me. I did not lead her on. I did not dishonor our marriage. I would have already told you about my meeting with Bolton if I hadn't had to work last night. I'm asking you to figure this out with me, not fight against me. For both our sakes."

"I don't think I have much choice. I'm the one under suspicion, after all. And all of this just makes me look even worse." She put her face in her hands. Then her head jerked up. "Do the police know?"

"I don't see how they would."

"What we haven't told them is beginning to pile up. I wish we had someone we could talk to. Stu fired us. Max is on the other side of this. We need to find another attorney before long."

"But we have each other." He held his hand out.

She didn't take it, just turned to stare out the window toward the Bighorn mountains flying by in a blur.

He put his hand back on the steering wheel.

They rode in silence for the next few minutes. Patrick exited the interstate into Buffalo. There, he noticed a black Cadillac behind them. He didn't think much of it until it turned on Fort Street and continued west. When it was still on their tail after they entered their own neighborhood, Patrick's hackles stood up.

"I think that Cadillac is following us," he said.

Susanne turned in her seat. "For how long?"

"I'm not sure. I just noticed it as we got off the interstate."

"Who is it?"

"I have no idea." He turned into their driveway, still hopeful the car would continue past their place, but it didn't. He braked hard. "Get in the house, quickly, and lock the door." He pulled his shotgun off the gun rack behind him.

"What about you?" Susanne said.

"I'll be fine. Make sure Trish knows to stay inside, too."

Susanne nodded, then she wrenched open her door and raced to the house.

Patrick got out slowly and held the shotgun across his midsection, barrel pointed toward the ground. He faced the Cadillac. It was a new model with tinted windows. He could see two people in the front seat, but not their faces.

The passenger's side door opened. A swarthy man a decade Patrick's senior climbed out. Not tall, but imposing, with big shoulders and a thick middle that wasn't fat. "Patrick Flint?"

"Who wants to know?" Patrick said.

The man snorted. "The one whose money you took. The one Bolton told you to call. The one who has not heard from you. The one who wants what he paid for."

Frantic barking and scratching drew Patrick's eyes to the house. Ferdinand was attacking through the sidelight windows by the door.

Patrick tried to recall the name from Bolton's while-you-were-out note. It was Carl. Carl something... Price. Carl Price. "You're Mr. Price?"

"That wasn't so hard for you after all."

"What are you doing at my home? I wasn't even aware you had my name."

"I didn't. You were talking to Bolton and that little whiner at the graveside service. I put two and two together. Then you led me here..."

He should have asked the more important question first. "What did you mean when you said I have your money?"

His voice rose. "We had a contract. I paid. You delivered a fake."

"I'm sorry, but I don't know what you're talking about."

The man dug around in his car and came out brandishing a sheaf of papers. "Does this look familiar?"

"Uh, no."

He stuck it in Patrick's face. "Are you saying this isn't your signature?"

The familiar handwriting was like a blow to Patrick's solar plexus. "It's my name. It's similar to my signature. But I didn't sign this document. Who did you give money to? Because it wasn't me."

"Your girl, Whitney. And I'm no idiot. I only paid after delivery. It looked like the photo, but my expert said it's a damn replica. I called her and she apologized and said it was an accident. That you got them confused in cold storage. Whatever that means."

Patrick floundered in the painful silence. There was nothing he could say. None of it made any sense. A replica of what? Confused in cold storage where? And why-oh-why had she involved him in this mess?

"Cat got your tongue, Flint?"

"Uh..."

"You get that she tried to pin this mess on you?"

"I'm not sure what you mean."

"I'm tired of you playing dumb. Let me make this crystal clear. You've got forty-eight hours to put the genuine article in my hands. After that, I not only want every cent of my money back, but I'll take something you treasure along with it." He grunted. "Like that nice wife of yours whose hand you were holding at the cemetery. Or maybe the pretty daughter watching us out the window. It'd be a shame for another woman to float up dead in the creek behind your house."

Patrick's eyes flicked to the second story window. Sure enough, Trish's face was at the glass. She stepped back when his eyes met hers. Susanne. Trish. This man was threatening them. Had he killed Whitney too when she didn't make good on the contract? When she'd swindled him? He felt cold and sick and powerless. "Can I, uh, have a copy of that contract, please?"

Price tossed it back in his car, laughing mirthlessly. He climbed in after it, then leaned out the window. "That's an original. You're not putting one finger on it. Forty-eight hours, and not a minute more." He made a twirling motion in the air and nodded at the driver.

The car reversed in a half circle and accelerated forward out of the driveway, throwing up rocks on Patrick's black funeral suit.

Patrick stood stock-still, feeling like he was sinking into quicksand. He rubbed his forehead, and he felt his lips moving as he tried to make sense of all the man had said. *Cold storage. A replica. Missing money. A plagiarized version of Patrick's signature.* Things just kept going from bad to worse to even worse. To catastrophic.

Patrick might not have had a motive to hurt Whitney before, but if he'd known about it when she was alive, he would have wanted to kill her. And if Susanne had known about it, she would have felt that same, only more so.

And that's when the police car pulled up, lights strobing.

# CHAPTER THIRTY-TWO: STAND

Sibley Ranch, Story, Wyoming
*Now*: Wednesday, June 21, 1978

*Perry*

After finishing up the afternoon's work, Perry decided to practice with the slingshot Henry had given him. He set up a row of soda cans twenty feet from the bunkhouse then moved back to the porch and took aim. The first shot he let fly completely missed the can he was aiming for. He was distracted. He'd missed the guys and practice the night before. Missed all of it with a dull ache. Once upon a time he would have called his best friend, John. They would have thrown the ball and goofed around. Forgotten about things. But John had been shot by gangsters and died up in the Bighorns the year before, right in front of Perry. It had been the worst thing that had ever happened to him. He hadn't found a friend like John since. He almost had in Kelsey Jones, but their friendship had turned into something more, only for her to break his heart and leave him alone again.

He set up another shot.

The bunkhouse door opened. Blister came out on the porch beside him. "Henry has you learning to shoot that thing?"

Perry focused on his aim. He tried to still his mind and relax the rest of his body into perfect stillness before he released the sling. This time he heard a satisfying PING as the can tumbled through the air a few feet and landed on its side in the drive. Only then did he answer Blister. "Sort of."

"I've never seen the point."

Perry shrugged and continued shooting. Each shot fired was hitting truer.

"So, Perry, what's the deal with your dad and the girl who died? Whitney."

Perry tensed up and his shot went wild. He turned to Blister. "They climbed together. That's it."

"Oh, man, the paper made it sound like they had some big thing between them."

"No. My mom and dad are pretty unhappy about all that."

"I'll bet your mom is pissed. I knew Whitney."

"You did?"

"Yeah. We used to be friends."

"Was she nice?"

"I thought so. But I'm not sure anymore."

"Why?"

"Things I'm hearing and reading. Seems like she wasn't the kind of friend I thought she was."

Perry grunted and returned to shooting. By the time he was out of the round balls, he was beginning to think he could be half decent with a slingshot. Blister helped him find most of the metal balls in the dirt of the drive.

Perry said, "I think I'd better grab a shower."

"You look like you might fall asleep in it."

Perry snorted. "I might."

"I'm going to the main house. Dinner will be soon."

"Yeah, I'll be over in a few." Perry saluted and went inside.

Five minutes later he was under the hot jets of the shower. Ranch work was dirty work, and the water circling the drain ran brown for close to a minute. His muscles ached. He leaned his forehead against the wall and let the water soothe his shoulders. Sleep sounded better than food at that point.

He got out, toweled off, and eyed the bed.

The front door opened. "Perry, you have a truckload of friends here." It was Blister.

Perry frowned. He'd told the guys at practice Monday night that he was staying at the Sibley Ranch to work for the week. But there was no one on the team he was close enough to that they'd visit him. "Okay. Tell them I'll be right out."

He threw on shorts and a t-shirt, then went outside. It was Chuck and Billy along with some of the other upperclassmen. His stomach got squirrely. He hoped they weren't here to hassle him. He looked at the main house. Blister was watching out the window. He grinned at Perry.

Chuck said, "Hey, Flint. Practice got canceled. We're headed over to Billy's place for a kegger. His parents are out of town. Hop in."

Perry winced. It was summer. All the windows were open. Anyone could hear Chuck from inside. He stepped closer and whispered, "Are you nuts? I'm grounded because of what happened Saturday night. And suspended. Coach Cantrell won't let me come back to practice until Monday."

"I don't see your parents out here. Or Coach."

Perry was glad for a built-in excuse. "The Sibleys might as well be my parents. They're best friends with them."

"You don't have to get sloshed. You can be our driver."

"I'm *grounded*."

"You're such a wuss, Flint. Maybe you're not the guy we thought you were." Chuck's look was taunting.

Perry's throat constricted. He needed the coach to trust him. He needed his parents to forgive him. But these were his teammates, and he needed them to like him. To include him. Then he remembered his parents would be out Friday night. Trish had told him about it Monday when she took him to practice. She was babysitting so his mom and Ronnie could do a girls' night. He wasn't sure what his dad was doing but gone was good enough. "Listen, no promises, but there's a chance my parents will be out Friday night. I'll be home. Maybe we could hang out at the creek where we found that dead woman last weekend."

"Whoa, like right where that girl died?"

"Where she was found dead. I don't know where she died."

"Way cool." Chuck shoved Perry. "I'll bring the beer."

That didn't mean Perry had to drink. "Okay. If they're going out, I'll call you Friday."

"Sweet." Chuck high-fived Billy. He turned back to Perry. "I guess you're not all bad, Flint. Thanks for not ratting us out to the coach."

"Yeah. Sure."

Perry watched them laughing and shoving each other as they walked back to the truck. Chuck cracked a beer and held it to his lips for a long chug as he backed around and drove out.

Perry shook his head, worried. Things in his life were getting more and more complicated.

# CHAPTER THIRTY-THREE: DEFY

BUFFALO, WYOMING
*NOW:* WEDNESDAY, JUNE 21, 1978

*Susanne*

SUSANNE WHISPERED TO HERSELF, feeling like her husband, who was notorious for the conversations he held with himself. "They are not here to take me in. They are not. They can't be. I didn't do anything." Despite all she had been doing in the last year to prevent them, she felt a migraine taking grip. Small wonder after the last few days. She kneaded Ferdinand's ears so hard the dog yelped and trotted away. She knew catching it early was important, so she went to the bathroom, filled a cup with water, and took one of her pills before going to the window to look out front.

Patrick was standing in the yard, hands on his hips. She couldn't believe he'd already taken his splint off, even though he had admitted that bones took six to eight weeks to heal, not six to eight *days*.

Appelt was sauntering toward him, his usual scornful look in place, while Welch lagged behind and looked like he wanted to be anywhere but there. Susanne had listened to Patrick through a window screen when he was talking to the man from the Cadillac earlier, but her grasp of the conversation had been spotty since she'd only picked up every third word. Part of her was terrified she'd be arrested if she went outside now. But that was outweighed by the part that had to hear every syllable and read every expression and bit of body language from the officers. This was her freedom, her life at stake.

"Stay, Ferdinand," she called to the dog, who had settled on the shag carpeting in front of the fireplace.

Her words had the opposite effect, but she was able to close the front door behind her before he reached it and set to whining and barking his concerns. She grasped the crook of Patrick's arm. He gave her hand a hug between his elbow and torso.

Appelt licked his lips and wiped his mouth. "Don't the two of you look fancy—been to Sheridan for a funeral?"

Susanne lifted her shoulders with a quick intake of breath. *Don't cower to him, but don't provoke him.* "Can we help you, officers?"

Welch smiled at her with a small nod.

Appelt spat brown liquid between his feet and theirs. "Medical examiner's report came back."

*Filthy, nasty habit.*

"And?" Patrick said.

"What do you think it told us?"

"How should I know? I didn't examine her."

"I thought your wife might have some insights she'd like to offer."

Susanne huffed. *Filthy, nasty man.* "Just get to the point."

"Cause of death was blunt force trauma to the back of the head."

"With what?"

"Dr. Evans is of the opinion it was a rock."

Patrick covered her hand with his. "Which is consistent with taking a tumble in a run-off swollen mountain creek."

"I think it's more likely a jealous wife hit her from behind with a rock myself. Does that sound about right to you, Susanne?"

She bristled at his use of her first name. What was his? She paused until it came to her tongue. "I can only tell you again I wasn't there and have no idea, *Cliff.*"

"Friday afternoon. You still sticking with that load of manure story that you drove to Billings by yourself to go shopping?"

"It's the truth."

"You sure you weren't up near the Grouse Mountain Trail meeting Whitney? Because, if you were, you should tell us now. You might be withholding information vital to this investigation. But if it leads to us finding a killer, we could probably forego obstruction of justice."

"Is that where she went in the water?"

"You tell us."

"I wasn't there. I've already told you where I was and that I don't know what happened to Whitney."

He shrugged. "We found her car up there."

"In the parking lot?" Patrick asked.

Appelt shifted his feet. "Near abouts. Believe me, we're combing for evidence. And we'll find it."

"I hope you find it. Because when you do, it won't have anything to do with our family," Susanne said.

Patrick's arm felt less tense. Like her, he had to have realized that the officers were still just fishing. Or, rather, that *Appelt* was. "So, what was the ruling? Accident?"

Appelt spat again. "Inconclusive. But that doesn't impact our investigation. I intend to prove she was murdered, and we all know who I'll be arresting when that happens."

Susanne knew who Appelt wanted it to be. This was a witch hunt. And she knew exactly what men like him did to witches—burned them publicly at the stake.

# CHAPTER THIRTY-FOUR: RESIST

BUFFALO, WYOMING
*NOW*: WEDNESDAY, JUNE 21, 1978

*Trish*

TRISH CLOSED the door to her room, a little tired after a late cheerleading practice. Tonight, their new sponsor had stopped by to ask if they'd like her to pay for them to travel to a cheerleading competition. Some rich lady whose husband was dead but looked too young to be a widow. Bella. She'd been a cheerleader for the Bison years ago. Trish didn't even know they had competitions for cheerleaders, but apparently they did. It made her a little nervous, truth be told, but at least she didn't have to ask her dad for the money to cover it. That would flip his lid. He was honestly the cheapest man alive.

She sat down at her desk in front of her window. The curtains were open to the night sky, and the breeze was blowing in. It smelled good. Like summer grass and the water of Clear Creek. She tilted her head back, letting the air cool her face, and wondered where her letter to Ben was. She pictured it on its long journey to Alaska. Truck to airplane to truck to ferry to truck to post office to him. She couldn't wait for it to get there. What she really wanted was to be able to talk to him on the phone. To hear his voice. She positioned a sheet of the monogrammed stationery in the center of the desk, pen poised over it. It felt so good to be able to write to him after all these months of not knowing how to reach him. She just wished she could tell him the whole truth about her week. She needed someone to talk to, but he was the last person she could tell about how scared she was and why.

There was a twanging sound at her window. Something had hit the screen. She flinched, then peered out. She was on the second floor, and there was no tree on the other side of the window. A bird, maybe? Sometimes they flew into the glass down by the kitchen. She'd never had one do it up here, but that didn't mean it wouldn't ever happen.

THWAP! The sound was even louder at this time. A bird wouldn't run into the window a second time. She felt uneasy. She was moving to the side—out of the path of flying objects—when she saw something hit the screen. TWANG!

A rock, not a bird. And that meant there was someone out there. Someone trying to get her attention. She had a bad feeling about it and hoped it was Marcy.

She stood and looked out. Standing below her partially illuminated by the light spilling down from her window was Jimmy Gross.

*What is he doing here?*

"Go away," she said, half whispering, half hissing.

"What's up, girl?" His voice was slurred. He sounded drunk. He took a staggering step toward the house.

"I don't want to talk to you."

"Don't be like that."

She grabbed the window. Night breeze or not, she now had something she wanted to shut out. The sound of Jimmy's voice.

"Stop! I have a question for you."

She paused, not responding. He could get her in a lot of trouble. It would be smart to hear what he had to say, as much as it pained her.

"I think we make a pretty good team. What do you think about that?"

"I think I don't ever want to see you again."

Jimmy bent over at the waist. At first, she thought he was barfing. Then she realized he was laughing. He straightened and wiped his hand across his forehead. "No, seriously."

She should have just shut the window. This was about nothing, certainly not about the situation he'd put her in the other night. Were her parents awake? Could they hear him? She wasn't sure which was worse—if they could hear him or if they didn't. If they heard him, maybe her dad would come out and chase him off with a shotgun. But there were no sounds from the room below her.

"I *am* serious. And you're right outside my parents' window. If you wake them up, they'll call the cops."

He put his hands in the air. "Excuse me, Sandra Dee." Then he laughed again and made a pistol out of his thumb and forefingers. He pulled the imaginary trigger. "But don't forget, I've seen the bad girl in you."

Trish felt sweat trickle down her chest. *I hate Jimmy Gross.* "Get lost, Jimmy. Go away and don't come back."

He laughed again. "It's a free country."

From outside the periphery of the light, she heard a second voice. Dabbo's. "Let's go, Jimmy. She'll regret this later."

Trish hugged herself. Maybe she should make an anonymous call to the police to turn him and Dabbo in. But they might tell the police about her. What she'd done. To reduce their own sentences, or just to be jerks. She wasn't willing to take that chance. Not yet.

She shut her window and locked it, glad she was high on the second floor.

# CHAPTER THIRTY-FIVE: ACCEPT

BUFFALO, WYOMING
*NOW:* WEDNESDAY, JUNE 21, 1978

*Jimmy*

JIMMY AND DABBO walked back to Dabbo's ride, which they'd parked along the road. The last thing Jimmy had wanted was Trish's stuffy dad to see headlights or hear the El Camino's engine. Stuffy. That was a good word for Trish, too, but she'd come around. She wouldn't have a choice. No girl was too good for him. Telling him to get lost? That wouldn't be happening. They were just getting started.

A car approached, bright lights pointed at them. Jimmy shielded his eyes with his hands, holding up a middle finger. The car slowed as it reached them.

"Jeez. No reason to blind us, asshole," he muttered.

"Some dumb-ass wanting directions, I'll bet," Dabbo said.

The passenger side was facing Jimmy as it pulled up alongside him. The window cranked down.

A voice said, "Did I just see you leaving the Flint home?"

"What's it to you?" Jimmy said, fists balling up. *Nosy bugger.*

"A lot actually. I'm looking for information."

Jimmy peered into the dark car interior. Was it a man or a woman? The silhouette was medium sized. The hair was short. The voice soft and midrange. It was impossible to tell. "That would cost you."

"As I would expect."

"What are you looking for?"

"I want to know where Patrick Flint goes and what he does."

Jimmy guffawed. "I'm not his keeper."

"Can you keep me informed or not?"

Dabbo elbowed Jimmy and whispered. "Jillian will help."

Jimmy nodded. "We can. How much?"

The voice named a number. It was more than worth it.

"I want twice that."

"Give me something valuable and I'll gladly pay it."

For a moment, Jimmy wondered what they were up to. Did they plan to hurt Patrick or any of the Flints? *Made sense.* Did it matter to him? *Nah.* He'd prefer they didn't hurt Trish before he claimed her, but cash was king. "How do I find you?"

The voice became a gloved hand out the window, extending a piece of paper. "Call. I'll come to you."

Jimmy took the paper. It was blank except for a phone number. He folded it and tucked it into his wallet. This sounded like easy money to him. The best kind. "Deal."

The window rolled up. The car drove away. Jimmy threw his head back and howled at the night sky.

# CHAPTER THIRTY-SIX: STALL

Bolton's Office, Sheridan, Wyoming

*Now:* Thursday, June 22, 1978

*Patrick*

Patrick and Susanne walked into Bolton's office side by side but miles apart. Patrick hated the disconnect between them. Maybe this trip would decrease the tension—they were on the same team, and with the police still pursuing Whitney's death as a murder, they were working toward the same goal. Clearing Susanne's name of suspicion. He needed her to believe it.

The first thing they'd done in Sheridan was cruise by Whitney's apartment. It was then that Patrick realized that a brown Ford LTD behind them looked familiar. Had he seen it in Buffalo? On the interstate? Or never and his mind was just playing tricks on him? It drove on past them as he'd braked to check the cars outside the complex.

The police had been parked on the street again, so he'd motored onward, stopping at a gas station to call Bolton for this meeting instead.

Now, Bolton's receptionist waved them past her with a nod, treating him like a regular, which wasn't great, given the circumstances. "Mr. Bolton is expecting you, Dr. Flint."

"Thank you," Patrick said.

The attorney's office door was open behind her. Patrick put a hand at the small of his wife's back.

Bolton looked up. A brief look of surprise crossed his face as Susanne entered. Patrick hadn't told him Susanne would be joining them. He recovered and stood. "Hello, Dr. Flint."

"I don't believe you've met my wife, Susanne Flint. Susanne, this is Gary Bolton."

Bolton held out a limp hand for hers. "Mrs. Flint."

"Mr. Bolton," she said, with the enthusiasm of someone picking out a casket. She pulled her hand away quickly.

He dragged a side chair in front of his desk so that there were two places for guests to sit. He gestured for Susanne to take one first. She did, eyes fixed on the side wall. Patrick took the other.

"Why the visit today?" Bolton said. Air escaped the seat of his chair in a hiss as he sat.

Patrick felt his forehead pucker. The reception was chilly. Far different from only days ago. "The keys you gave me. They're not mine. Did you realize that?"

Bolton lifted a shoulder and let if fall. "I made an assumption."

"Do you know what they're to?"

"I'd only be making assumptions again."

Patrick decided to meet cagey with cagey. No need to tell Bolton anything he didn't already admit to knowing, like where the keys fit. "I found a match for two of the three. I'm striking out on the last one."

"I'm sorry to hear that." Bolton didn't look sorry. In fact, he didn't look like he gave a flying fig.

*Time for a change of course.* Again, Patrick held back as much as he could. "I had a visit from Mr. Price. He said he'd given Whitney money pursuant to a contract. He felt ...swindled. He is demanding I deliver under the contract."

"Do you have a question?" Bolton was mincingly polite, in a deeply impolite way.

"Do you have a copy of it?"

"A copy of what?"

"The contract. Or the contracted item."

He shook his head, his eyes dropping to Patrick's sternum. "No. Sorry."

"Were you involved in this transaction?"

"You already know the full extent. I have nothing to add."

"What about the money? Do you know where it is?"

"Possibly in her bank account?"

Patrick didn't often feel violent, but he had a burning desire to break Bolton's nose. See if he still felt superior then. But it was beneath him. A fantasy, nothing more. He allowed steel into his voice, though. "Do you have the *balance* on her accounts?"

"Yes. So, I don't suppose it's there after all. They're next to zero. Unless she spent it already. Or it was a very small amount."

Patrick felt sure neither was the case. "Do you know what the contract was for?"

"I don't. But possibly you'll find everything you're looking for with those keys."

The conversation was doing nothing except frustrating Patrick more than he'd already been before. *A complete waste of time.* "We won't trouble you any longer." Patrick knocked the chair back as he shot to his feet, eager to get away from the smarmy attorney. Beside him, Susanne rose more slowly. He looked at his wife. She was staring at him like she was trying to read the hieroglyphics plastered all over the research she'd brought home from the college.

Bolton stayed seated. "I wish you the best of luck."

Patrick wanted to say, "Thanks for nothing," but he held it in and settled for a terse nod.

When he and Susanne were between Bolton's office and the reception area, she whispered, "I wish we could get in her apartment. But maybe the third key doesn't go to anything in there. Maybe Kathy would have some thoughts on what it might open?"

It was a good idea. And more words than she'd strung together in a row to him all that day. Was she thawing?

Patrick approached the receptionist. "May I borrow your phone for a call to Buffalo?"

"Of course. I was just on my way to the powder room." She pressed a button on her switchboard and handed the receiver to Patrick. "You don't need to dial anything to get out."

"Thanks." He waited for her to exit the area before calling the nurse's station at the Buffalo hospital.

Kathy answered, and Patrick dove right in. "This is Patrick."

"You're not working today. You should be enjoying your time off."

"I have a question for you. It's a weird one."

"Try me."

"Where do you think Whitney would have kept something important? Or valuable?"

"Hmm." After a few seconds of silence, Kathy said, "Maybe a safe deposit box?"

He bounced the keys and rabbit foot in his hand. It was definitely not a safe deposit box key. "Did she have one?"

"I don't know, actually."

"Anyplace else?"

"Under her bed?" Kathy laughed. "Seriously, let me think. She wasn't dating anyone—she dumped her last boyfriend. But she was a little paranoid."

"In what way?"

"She thought someone had been stalking her. Notes. Hang up calls. Noises outside. I know she was super cautious as a result. And I told you she thought she was about to be rich and famous."

"You did." Patrick turned to look at Susanne. She must have seen the puzzled look on his face because she mouthed *what?* He'd have to explain later. But this was the first time he'd heard anything about a stalker. Why weren't the police all over that? He would call Appelt and make sure they had the information.

Kathy was continuing. "So, I guess she had a reason to hide things. But she never said so. This is all speculation."

"Did you tell the police about the potential stalker?"

"I did, actually. They didn't seem very interested."

"Keep going."

"Really, the only things she cared about besides her job and her friends was climbing and her gym membership.

Patrick paused, thinking. Climbing. That was him, mostly. At least since last fall. But gyms had nothing to do with him. He didn't have a membership. Then a thought sparked for him. Gyms had lockers. Lockers had locks. Locks used keys like the one on this ring. "Thanks, Kathy. You've given me lots to think about."

"What's this about?"

"An unusual bequest she made to me. It's more like a puzzle. I'm sorry, but I have to go. Hopefully I can tell you more soon."

"All right. Now you've got me curious." She laughed again and hung up.

Susanne said, "Well?"

"Whitney may have had a stalker."

"That's good for us."

*If the police pursue it.* "Yes."

"Do we have a plan?"

He smiled at her. "It may not be a good one, but we do. And this one will all depend on you."

# CHAPTER THIRTY-SEVEN: FALL

CLOUD PEAK WILDERNESS, BIGHORN MOUNTAINS, WYOMING
*THEN (NINE MONTHS EARLIER)*: MONDAY, SEPTEMBER 19, 1977

*Patrick*

WHITNEY'S SCREAM raised the hairs on Patrick's neck. He craned to see her, but she was behind a bulge in the rock.

"Are you okay?" he shouted.

"Yes, I think so." Her voice quavered. She didn't sound okay.

"What happened?"

"Slippery spot. My feet went out from under me. Thank God for these ropes. And that one of my gloves didn't come off."

Patrick's breath hitched. "How many points of contact do you have?"

"Two now. I found a foothold. But I lost a glove."

The ropes would be tough in this cold weather. "Do you have anything you can wrap around your hand?"

She was silent for a moment. He pictured her, only five or six years older than Trish. One bare hand in space. One gloved hand clutching an ancient rope and footing she probably didn't trust anymore for one of her boots while the other foot kicked at rock looking for a place to hold her weight. It was a terrifying image.

Finally, she said, "I have a bandana. But I need to get to flat ground first. I—I'm climbing again. I'll be more careful."

Patrick started after her, trying to regulate his breathing. Everything had spiked when Whitney screamed. His respiration, his heart rate, his adrenaline. "Are you hurt?"

"Maybe bruised a little. And I wrenched my shoulder. It still holds weight, though. No cuts, no breaks, no bumps on the head. I'll be fine."

He wanted to keep her talking. He also wanted to catch up with her, although that wasn't rational. He needed to give her space. Not rush her. There was nothing he could do to help her except encourage her, coach her. "Take it easy. We've got all day, you know."

She laughed. "I want dinner in town tonight."

"Boy, does that sound good."

The two of them climbed in silence for a few minutes. An eagle screamed below them, and the wind whistled through the rocks. Patrick shimmied over the boulders that had blocked his view of Whitney and Loren. When he was safely around them, he caught sight of her head below him in its bright red cap.

"Looking good," he said.

"I hope it's not much further."

"Me, too."

Their route continued past another rounded corner. He was only a few yards above and to the side of her now. He was careful never to let himself climb directly over her, but he hoped his presence was a comfort. As they finished the turn, he gazed out and down. The reflective surface of Mistymoon Lake was like a mirage. It was also close to a miracle and not that far away. He could see a path over to it below where he and Whitney perched against the mountain.

*We're going to make it. This crazy route is actually going to connect us back to the trail. Thank you, God, and whoever installed these ropes. Thank you, thank you, thank you!*

But then he looked at the base of their pitch. Something was down there. On the flat ground. A non-boulder pile of color. He scanned the mountainside below them, searching for Loren, fearing the worst, and then confirming it.

His breath was sharp, involuntary. Audible.

"What is it?" Whitney asked.

He couldn't tell her. He needed her safely down before she saw it. "Scraped my hand. It's nothing."

But it wasn't nothing. It was Loren's body crumpled at the foot of the rocks below them.

# CHAPTER THIRTY-EIGHT: UNEARTH

YMCA, Sheridan, Wyoming
*Now:* Thursday, June 22, 1978

Susanne

Susanne sashayed into the women's locker room at the YMCA with her big purse over her shoulder, like she knew where she was going and what she was doing, neither of which was true. All she did know was that she felt conspicuous. Had it been her imagination, or had the gray-bearded man at the front desk looked like he recognized her? He might, because the Sheridan paper had run the article insinuating she'd murdered Whitney.

Patrick explained to the old guy that they were new in town and wanting a tour. Not technically a lie since they lived in Buffalo and definitely wanted someone to show them around. Halfway through the tour, Susanne had excused herself to the bathrooms, pleading female problems, to the horror of their guide. He'd scurried off with Patrick to the men's locker rooms.

The plan had worked perfectly so far.

Unfortunately, Susanne didn't know which locker was Whitney's —if any—which meant she had to start testing locks. She started on the top row and worked from left to right, moving fast. One after another, the key did not fit.

"Come on, come on," she muttered.

The work was mindless, and hers wandered. She realized her emotions had steadied. In the last half hour, her anger with Patrick had ebbed. He'd opened up to her. She wasn't *in* control, but she was *taking* back some of it. With her husband. If she found something horrible today, it wasn't his secret. It was their problem. *And he wouldn't have me looking if he believed there would be something in here that would hurt me.* She believed that down to her toes.

She finished the top lockers on all the walls of the locker area and moved down a row. There were four rows. This was taking too long. Patrick's guide would send a woman in after her, and she wouldn't be able to explain what she was doing. She'd look like a thief, in addition to being a publicly accused murderer. But she couldn't move any faster.

Second row done, she moved on to the third. She'd had a few false alarms, where the key fit perfectly but didn't turn. Now she was leaning over, which slowed her down. Midway through the row, the key slid in easily again. *Don't get your hopes up.* She sucked in a breath, then turned the key, and the lock released.

Susanne gasped softly. She couldn't believe it had worked. She squatted down and peered in. There were two black duffel bags inside. She pulled the front one out. It was heavy and filled with something much harder than gym clothes and a towel. She retrieved bag number two. It was even heavier. Then she patted inside the locker all the way to the back and in the corners, careful not to miss anything—not after all of this. But there was nothing else in there.

She was dying to know what was in the bags, whether it might exonerate her, but there was no time. She had to get moving. The bags were too big to carry out over her shoulders. Someone might notice she'd come in with one homemade denim hobo bag and was leaving with two gym bags in addition. But her purse was extra, *extra* large. She'd sewed it herself, to carry her books at school. She set it on the ground and stuffed the gym bags into it. While heavy, the bags weren't overly full. One poked out the top of the purse, but they pretty much fit.

She lifted the purse and put the strap over her shoulder. It bit into her flesh. She knew the strap was strong, but possibly not strong enough. She wound her arm around the body of the purse and supported it in her hand, hugging it to her side. Her shoulder hurt less, at least.

It would have to do.

She hurried into the hall on a rush of adrenaline and emotion.

Patrick and the guide were waiting for her. The guide averted his eyes.

Susanne batted her eyes. "So, sorry. You know how it goes. I mean, I guess you don't. But, ah, anyway, I'm sorry to make you wait."

Patrick was eying her bag. He tapped a forefinger on the face of his watch. "I hate to rush you honey, but we're late."

"I understand. A shame to cut the tour short, but we can come back another time." She turned to the man. His neck was splotchy with embarrassment. He must not have grown up with sisters. Or have a wife and daughters. *Good for me today.* "Thank you for showing us around."

Patrick repeated her thanks and the two walked out briskly together.

When they had exited, Patrick said, "Well?"

She couldn't help the excitement that crept into her voice. "Found it."

"What is it?"

"Her locker. The bags in it. I haven't opened them yet."

They reached his truck. Inside, Susanne put the top bag on the seat between them. She unzipped it. She gasped. Even her wildest imagination couldn't have conjured up the sight before them.

"Is that what I think it is?" Patrick asked, eyes bulging.

Susanne pulled out a bundle of hundred-dollar bills. Then another, and another. She brought out the second bag.

It was more of the same.

She did quick math in her head. "If you think it's a million dollars, I'd say you're right. But what was a nurse in her early twenties doing with this much cash stuffed in a gym locker?"

"Whatever it was, I'm guessing it's a pretty good motivation for murder."

And now it was in their truck. Susanne packed it back in the bags and tucked them under her legs, feeling suddenly like a buck dead in the sights of a hunter's rifle.

---

PATRICK TURNED the wrong way out of the YMCA parking lot.

"Where are you going?" Susanne asked. "Home is in the other direction."

"I keep thinking about what Price said to me last night. About Whitney telling him that whatever it was she was selling him was in cold storage. What does that suggest to you?"

"Something that goes in the freezer."

He nodded. "What do you put in a freezer, usually? I mean, food, obviously, but what food?"

"Things you aren't going to use any time soon. Sometimes because they'll ruin if they aren't used immediately. Other times because you need to store them for a long time and they're in the way in your refrigerator." She lifted a finger. "So, cold storage can mean things that aren't going to be used for a long time. Or it can mean things you have to keep frozen."

"Or things you want to hide, because who looks in a freezer, right?"

"Maybe."

"I just can't see how something Whitney would have in her possession that's worth a million dollars would need to be in a freezer. But I'd like to see inside hers."

A Buffalo police car passed them going the opposite direction. Susanne averted her face.

"It wasn't Appelt or his partner Welch. I didn't recognize them."

Susanne looked ahead again. Whitney's apartment complex came into view. Earlier, there had been law enforcement vehicles parked outside her building. This time, there were more empty spaces, and no obvious police cars.

"Coast looks clear."

"They could be driving unmarked cars. Or personal vehicles," she said.

"True. Want to stay in the truck while I check in case we run into cops inside?"

"And have them run into me outside? They could haul me off and you'd never know what had happened to me."

Patrick parked the truck on the curb. "I'd have a good guess."

"I'm going in with you." A Bisons ball cap was hanging from the gun rack behind their heads. She put it on, tucking all her hair into it. She pointed at his sunglasses in the ashtray. "You wear those."

He slid them on. "How do I look?"

She grinned. "Like Harrison Ford."

"Who?"

"Never mind. Now, let's do this." Susanne's heart was pounding. She imagined police around every corner. The words, "You're under arrest for the murder of Whitney Saylor." Handcuffs. Fear. Shame.

Patrick put his hand under her elbow. "As much as I love your hair, you'd look cute with short hair, too."

His touch was soothing. His teasing tone a balm. "Flatterer."

He led her up a set of outside stairs and onto the second floor.

"You've been here before?" She couldn't keep the edge out of her voice. Actually, the complex looked familiar to her, too. But most of them in Sheridan were cookie cutter replicas of each other. She'd visited a few with study partners in the last year.

"Only Tuesday. And I got out of here pronto when I realized the police were inside her place."

"They took long enough. They've had it since Saturday."

He stopped at number two-one-two and put the key in the lock. "No crime scene tape on the door. They must be done."

"Let's hope so."

"Do you want the honors?" Patrick asked.

Susanne liked this new paradigm. A deferential Patrick. Herself cast into an action hero role, rescuing bags of cash out of gym lockers, and breaching the ramparts of the apartment they'd come to search. With a little smile, she made her way in and over to the kitchen. The apartment was small, and it looked like a tornado had torn through it. Lamps were overturned. Trash emptied onto a tabletop. Items stacked outside of cabinets on counters. It was hard to visualize a young woman living here. To see past the mess to the personal touches she'd added. A photograph of her, Patrick, and the other guy —the one who'd fallen—atop Cloud Peak hung askew on the wall. Her blood heated, but she told herself to relax. It was a proud memory, and Patrick wasn't the only man in it with her.

She kept her tone light. "Are the police usually this messy?"

Patrick circled the living room. He used the toe of his cowboy boot to lift the corner of a tweed couch cushion off the floor. "Well, we know they've been in here for the last few days. What we don't know is whether anyone else has, before or after them."

Susanne opened the freezer compartment to the refrigerator. It was filled with packets wrapped in aluminum foil. She picked one up. It mushed in her hand. "This isn't frozen." She pushed on another with her fingertips. "This one either. Someone turned it off or unplugged it."

""It should be easier to open everything up then. To look for whatever it is we're supposed to find."

He had a point. "I need to turn it back on, though. It will rot and leave an ungodly mess and stench for whoever has to clean in here." She opened the refrigerator. The cold was turned on. She followed the cord. "Unplugged." She rectified the power situation, then returned to the freezer compartment. The contents looked like they'd been through a tumble dryer. Not the way Susanne kept her own. She assumed Whitney wouldn't leave hers in shambles either. "Someone's already been through it." She hoped it was the cops.

"Our turn now."

Susanne peeled back the aluminum wrapper around the first package. "Meatloaf." She wrapped back up. Then she wondered why she'd bothered with the re-wrap. No one was coming back to this apartment. No one would ever eat this meatloaf. What she should be doing was throwing the contents into the trash. Or taking it home in a cooler. She did hate waste, after all. But none of it belonged to her. And clean-up wasn't her role. But she could use some help. "Why don't you re-wrap them?"

Patrick sidled up to the counter. She handed him the items as she finished with each. Meat, leftovers, homemade bread, a whole cheesecake. Nothing that would be subject to a contract, much less a contract for $1 million.

"No hidden jewels or contraband, I'm afraid."

Patrick clucked. "A bust."

Susanne shook her head as she stuffed packets back into the freezer. "We don't know what isn't here now that was before. Maybe the police or the bad guys already found something Whitney intended for you."

"Or maybe it was never here at all, and I had the wrong idea for cold storage."

His body was so close she could feel his warmth. When was the last time they'd hugged? The friction between them had been so high the last few days. "At least we've closed this off as a line of inquiry." She turned to him, leaning in.

He put his arms around her and rocked her, dropping light kisses on the top of her hair. She closed her eyes and soaked it in.

After a minute, Patrick said, "Might as well look around while we're here."

"Hopefully the police aren't on their way back from a lunch break."

"Nah. They took down the crime scene tape."

"It seems like we've amassed another long list of things we aren't going to tell them."

"I hate it, but you know they'll claim it's just further evidence against you. We can't take it to them until it's exonerating."

Susanne couldn't have agreed more.

Together they rummaged each room, but quickly. Susanne looked through pictures of Whitney receiving her diploma, attending a dance wearing a giant corsage on her wrist. There were nurse's uniforms and cowboy boots. Expected things.

"I'm not finding anything suspicious."

Patrick shook his head. "Me neither. How about we get out of here?"

Susanne stepped out into the hall while Patrick locked up. A voice jerked her attention away from her husband.

"I told the police you'd been here before. And here you are again."

Susanne whirled. A bespectacled woman with corkscrew curls was holding a robe tightly around her tiny frame. "Excuse me?"

"You. You're the one the police say killed Whitney. I saw you here." She shrank back through her doorway. "I was just telling the truth." And then she slammed the door before Susanne could ask her what the heck she was talking about.

But then it pummeled her. A memory. These apartments. Why they looked familiar.

"Susanne? What is going on here?" Patrick said.

His worried voice barely registered with her. Susanne walked to the door on the far side of Whitney's unit. She'd been here before, yes. But not to see Whitney. She knocked on two-thirty-one.

"Coming," an accented voice called.

"Do you know the people who live there?" Patrick asked.

Susanne held up her hand.

The door opened. A lovely Arabic woman smiled out at her. Susanne took in the long white tunic over slacks. Casual. A nod to the traditional in the western world.

"Yes?" the woman said.

"My name is Susanne Flint. I work for Professor Seth at the college. I'm sorry to bother you. I dropped some papers off once for him, and I wanted to confirm this was where I did it."

The woman nodded. "You have the right address. But why are you checking?"

Susanne waved a hand to minimize the issue. "My husband—that's him behind me, Dr. Patrick Flint—and I were in the building, and I just knocked on impulse. I'm really sorry to disturb you. Are you Mrs. Seth?"

"I am."

"Welcome to Sheridan. Your husband is a wonderful professor and boss."

"Thank you kindly."

Susanne backed away, trying to ease the awkward moment. "So nice to meet you, and sorry to bother."

"Likewise." The woman's face was creased in a confused but not angry frown.

The door shut.

Susanne turned to Patrick. "I've never been to Whitney's place. But her neighbor is only partly wrong. I've definitely been here before."

"That's good, I think."

He was right. And he was wrong. Because she'd still never be able to disprove that she didn't go to Whitney's when she came to Professor Seth's place. If the police didn't believe her before, they certainly wouldn't now either.

# CHAPTER THIRTY-NINE: HOPE

KETCHIKAN, ALASKA
*NOW:* THURSDAY, JUNE 22, 1978

*Ben*

"SEE YOU LATER, CAP." Ben Jones had stayed to clean up the boat and was the last person off *Fishy Business* besides the captain.

Ben's boss grinned under his walrus mustache "Have a good one. But not too good. I want to get an early start tomorrow, when the monster fish are just struggling home after a wild night."

"Yes, sir."

Ben's footsteps echoed on the dock. There was a softness to the air. The days were getting longer. June in Ketchikan was turning out to be as good as it could be without Trish here with him. The three-story blue boarding house across the street seemed to be leaning toward him, welcoming him home. He hurried over to it and up the front steps, hoping there'd be a letter from Trish waiting for him.

There had been nothing from her yesterday or the day before. He wasn't sure how long his letter should have taken to get to Buffalo. How long a reply from her would take to reach him.

"Anything for me?" Ben sauntered in, hoping to give the impression of nonchalance, even though he was as nervous as a seal pup being circled by a killer whale.

Cleve, the housemaster, pulled at his gray-bearded chin. "Are you expecting something? I can watch for you, but I don't think there's anything here for you today, boy-o."

Ben slumped. The words like a bucket of cold water. "No, that's OK."

"I think Mary Gail served salmon croquettes for dinner. You know you're her favorite when she saves you a covered plate. Be sure to swing by the kitchen or it will break the woman's poor heart." He smiled wide, revealing his broken front tooth.

Ben nodded and shuffled toward the dining area. He could smell the salmon. In Ketchikan, he could always smell the ocean and the salmon.

Cleve's voice rang out in a teasing lilt. "Wait a second. I almost missed this. A letter. Addressed to Ben Jones. All the way from Wyoming, don't you know. Would you be looking for something from a Trish Flint?"

Ben spun around, feeling a rush of warmth in his face. Trish. Trish had written back to him. "Not funny. Give it to me."

The housemaster laughed and held the letter above his head. "Say 'please,' then, why don't you."

"Please, before I have to whup your butt."

Cleve lowered the letter and wiggled the fingers of his other hand. "Oh, scary—you and what army?" Then he winked and held the letter out.

Ben snatched it and raced up the stairs and toward his room, feet pounding on the wooden treads. Dinner could wait. He threw his door open and slammed it behind him so hard the cheap pictures on the wall rattled. He tossed his work bag in the corner. Flopped stomach first onto the bed. Only when he was there, alone, did he dare verify that what Cleve had said was true. The return address read "Trish Flint. Buffalo, Wyoming".

His heart was pounding crazy fast. His breaths were coming in short pants, and he felt lightheaded. He sniffed the letter, hoping for a whiff of the girl in his dreams. It was sweet. Like her perfume. Like her. He held it to his chest and closed his eyes. Slowed his breathing. This was it. This was the moment he would find out whether Trish could forgive him. Whether she had moved on from him or not. Whether she still loved him.

Part of him was scared to read her words. Maybe he should just hold the paper she had touched and addressed to him? Never read it. He could feel connected to her. If it was bad news, he wouldn't have to feel how much it would hurt.

But a bigger part of him was dying to tear it open and dive in.

He settled between the two extremes inside him, peeling back the sealed flap with care. He didn't want to risk damaging a single word, but his finger was too big to slide inside and pry it apart. It seemed to take forever to open the dumb envelope. Finally, the flap was fully released. He pressed it flat then extracted the single sheet of stationary. He'd seen it before. Monogrammed stationary that her parents had given her for her birthday. Her name at the top of the page. She'd written him a love note on the paper once. He'd kept it, but it was back at the Sibley's ranch in Wyoming.

He took a deep breath then began reading, whispering the words aloud.

Dear Ben:

First, I am so glad you are all right! And that you wrote to me! I have missed you more than anything, and I love you so much. You completely got the wrong idea about Wyatt. He is not my boyfriend. I never went out with him. He is dating Perry's old girlfriend Kelsey, and they were stuck at our house because of a blizzard. There is no one for me but you, Benjamin Jones. Please call me. Please give me a phone number to call you. Please come see me. Please write to me.

Please just, well, please just don't forget about me. I don't care if you go to college. I don't care if you live in Alaska. I just want it to be you and me again, forever.

I am wearing your ring. You are my one. The only one for me. I can't wait to hear from you and to see you again.

All my love,

Trish

The words were like water. Like air. He hadn't known he wasn't breathing but he could breathe again. He jumped to his feet. He needed to call her. He didn't have a phone in his room, but there was one in the lobby. Cleve would let him use it. He'd give him the money to pay for it right now. He pulled a roll of cash out from between his mattress and box springs. A twenty should cover it. He shoved the money back in, then sprinted down the stairs.

Cleve raised an eyebrow. "I didn't know if it was you or a herd of your Wyoming buffalo on those stairs."

Ben thrust the twenty at him. "Can I make a long-distance call?"

The housemaster pulled a wry face. "Would this be a call to a certain girl back home?"

"Yes. Can I do it?"

Cleve picked up the phone from the desk and brought it over to the counter. He took the twenty. "I'm guessing you'll want to run a tab then."

Ben was already dialing. His hands were clammy. His finger slipped from the dial and he had to start over. He tried again, finally getting through.

"Hello?" a female voice answered.

"Trish?" But he knew it wasn't her as soon as he said it. It was Mrs. Flint.

"No, this is Susanne Flint. May I take a message for her?"

"Um, yes, ma'am. Could you tell her Ben called?"

"Ben? Our Ben?" Mrs. Flint's voice got louder and higher pitched.

Did Trish's parents hate him for how he'd left things? He might in their place. He would win them back. He would prove to Trish and her parents that he had his head on straight now. "Yes, ma'am. Ben Jones."

She laughed, and she sounded happy. *Oh, man. That's a relief.* "Of course I will. She's at cheerleading practice. Can I have her call you back?"

Ben read her the number of the lodging house phone.

"That's not in Wyoming."

"It's the number for the boarding house where I live. In Alaska. Ketchikan. I have to work early in the morning. Could you tell her I'm available tomorrow night?"

"Of course. She's babysitting Will Harcourt at our house at six o'clock. He goes to bed by eight."

Ben did the time conversion in his head. That would be seven o'clock. He'd have more than enough time to finish work and eat dinner before the call. "I'll just call her then. If that's okay with you, Mrs. Flint."

"Of course. It's great to hear your voice, Ben."

"Thanks, Mrs. Flint. Yours, too."

Ben hung up, grinning from ear to ear.

# CHAPTER FORTY: EXULT

BUFFALO, WYOMING
*NOW*: THURSDAY, JUNE 22, 1978

*Trish*

"DID everyone bring me back the parental permission slips, signed?" Bella Crooke asked the cheerleaders. She was a little older than Trish's mom but seemed cooler somehow. Long blonde hair tied back in a low ponytail. Oversized glasses. Freckles. Lots of freckles. Stylish in a boho shirt with a denim skirt and boots with big chunky heels.

The girls all passed in their forms.

Trish waited until they'd finished then walked up to Mrs. Crooke. "I, uh, I'll get mine to you next week."

"Is it going to be a problem getting permission from your parents, Trish?"

"No. I just—well, they were really distracted this week. I didn't want to bother them. I'll get them to sign over the weekend."

Mrs. Crooke lowered her voice. Her eyes looked sympathetic. "Problems at home?"

"Sort of."

"Anything you need to talk to someone about? I'm a good listener. I want to be here for you girls."

Trish looked into the woman's bright green eyes. It would help so much to talk about what had happened at the gas station, and after. A grown-up who would know what to do. But she couldn't. It might put Mrs. Crooke in a bad position between her and Jillian. Or she might feel an obligation to inform the school. Worse, the police. "Uh..."

Mrs. Crooke put her hand under Trish's elbow. "I heard about the woman in your creek. Your dad finding her. I read the article about the police suspecting your mother. All of that must be very hard."

Trish drew back. She hadn't been thinking about that, but she knew how her parents felt. Her mom had been painted in a false light. Her reputation damaged. Talking about it with anyone was like betraying her own family. "We're fine. She didn't do it."

"But the pain she must feel. With what your father was doing."

Now Trish jerked away. "He didn't do anything. I'll get the forms to you Monday."

"If you say so, honey." Mrs. Crooke turned to the others. "I'll see you girls next week. I can't wait for you to show the rest of the country what you've got at this competition."

After she'd left, Jillian starting yattering on about team spirit and getting fired up. She did this at the end of every practice. Trish had decided Jillian just liked hearing the sound of her own voice. She stared out at the mountains, barely registering Jillian's voice. Her mind drifted to Alaska. To Ben.

Jillian bounced up and down on her toes. "We only have Friday morning practice before we're off for the weekend, girls. I expect you all to be practicing and ready to show me perfection on Monday." She made a disgusted sound. "Trish, are you listening to me? Because I'm talking to you."

Trish jerked to attention. "Practice all weekend. Yes, I heard you." She couldn't quite keep the annoyance out of her voice. After the horrible night with Jimmy, Dabbo, and Jillian, it was hard to take Jillian seriously as a leader. She just wanted to get home and check the mail for a letter from Ben. It was too soon. She knew it was too soon. But she couldn't help hoping for a miracle.

"Who peed in your Post Toasties? This squad is all about being perky. I need your perky back."

Trish was not about to tell Jillian a single detail about how she felt or her personal life. Honestly, she worried Jillian was behind the visit last night from Jimmy. She might have been there with Dabbo, waiting in the car. And Trish definitely wanted to keep things about her and Ben quiet—only let her true friends know. Friends like Marcy. She hadn't even told her parents about his letter or her answer. She would have to soon, but right now, the whole thing felt fragile. She'd been through all the heartbreak and humiliation one girl could take. She'd tell them when everything seemed more solid.

She laughed. It sounded fake, but it was all she had in her. "I was just thinking about babysitting tomorrow night. It's not going to be much of a weekend off for me."

"Tell me where you're going to be babysitting, and I can bring something and someone to cheer you up." Jillian shimmied her shoulders. "A little MD 20/20."

The other girls laughed. They always laughed on cue for Jillian. *A bunch of suck-ups.* This all would have been so much better if Marcy had made the squad, too.

*Not on my life.* "I'm keeping a deputy's son at my own house. Please don't. You'd not only get caught, but she might throw you in jail, too, for minor in possession." Amongst other things. Like conspiracy after the fact. And she might take Trish with her.

"Well, you're no fun, loser." Jillian pouted. "Who's up for a little weekend warm-up fun with me tonight?"

Several girls slapped high fives and followed Jillian off the football field.

Jillian turned when she reached the track ringing the field. "Trish?"

Trish had hung back on purpose. She shook her head. "Not me. I've got to drive out to Story to pick up my brother."

"Another loser. Fine. But you're missing out."

---

BACK AT HOME after picking up Perry, Trish walked in and found her mother sitting in the dark living room, her dad at the kitchen table with his head buried in something he was working on. Perry tromped up the stairs. He made huffing sounds as he climbed. She ignored him. So did her mother. She heard him mutter, "Fine," as he closed the door to his room.

"I've been waiting for you," her mom said.

Trish felt a flicker of panic. *Oh, my gosh.* Had the police come to arrest Trish for what she'd done the other night?

She tried to appear calm even though inside she felt like a fire alarm was going off in her head. "Hey, mom."

"We got a phone call here tonight."

In the low light, Trish couldn't see her mother's expression. *How to play this?* "Oh?"

"From a young man."

Not Jimmy. Please not Jimmy. "For me?"

"Yes, for you."

"Who was it?" Trish's voice squeaked. A tell. A giveaway. She swallowed back bile.

"Is there something you'd like to tell me first?"

"Umm, I'm not sure what you mean?" *Not in a million years.*

"I mean like how long have you been talking to Ben?" Now Trish could hear the smile in her mother's voice.

Ben! Ben had called. That meant her letter got to him. And he'd called! That was a good sign, wasn't it? Involuntarily, Trish clapped her hands together and clasped them in front of her chest. "Oh, my gosh! When did he call? What did he say? Did he leave his number?"

Susanne laughed. "He said, 'would you tell Trish I called,' when I told him you weren't here. He left his number, but he has to work early in the morning. He's calling you tomorrow night after you put Will down to sleep."

Trish fought back a wave of disappointment. She wished she could call him back right that second.

"So, are the two of you back together?"

"I'm... I'm not sure." Were they? Trish hoped so. But she'd have to wait twenty-four hours to find out. Right now, that seemed like an eternity.

# CHAPTER FORTY-ONE: DIG

Buffalo, Wyoming
*Now:* Thursday, June 22, 1978

*Perry*

Perry had nearly cried with relief when Trish pulled into the driveway at their house that night. He was home. His stint of work at the Sibley ranch was over. It felt like a month since he'd been here instead of only four days. If he never threw another bag of feed or bale of hay, it would be too soon.

He lugged his bag upstairs, happy that it included the slingshot Henry had given him. It had an old school coolness to it. Perry was pretty good at it. He planned to keep practicing. Just before he reached his room, Trish squealed over something his mom told her. He heard the word *Ben*. More of that drama? *Whatever*. He wanted a shower and bed. But he was too hungry. He had to get food first. He threw his bag on his bed and reversed course.

When he was back downstairs, he shouted, "I'm home!"

His mom had moved to the kitchen table beside his dad, who glanced up. Trish was rolling around on the living room floor playing with the dog. The dog who didn't look up as he walked past them.

"Oh, hey. Welcome back, Perry," his dad said.

Perry hadn't expected a brass band, but he had thought his return merited a little more than that. "Is that any way to greet your prodigal son?"

His mom still didn't respond, but his dad said, "You weren't exactly working like a slave and living with pigs."

Perry frowned. Is that how the prodigal son story went? "What do you call unpaid labor? And do cows count?"

Neither of his parents answered, although his mom half-smiled. Her face looked droopy. Tired. Then Perry remembered that only a few days before the police had hauled her off to jail, and that, according to Vangie, the police were still considering her suspect. There had been a big article in the newspaper that all but said so. It had seemed so far removed from him out at the ranch, away from town and his family. He felt bad for her. Bad that he'd forgotten about it.

Trish walked past him into the kitchen, straight to the refrigerator, Ferdinand right behind her. She was smiling, which was weird. "What's for dinner?"

His mom's head snapped up. "Oh! I hadn't even thought about it. Why don't you run get us some hamburgers?"

Now Perry knew something was really wrong. His parents never chose to eat out unless it was a special occasion. A normal Thursday night definitely didn't qualify. Then he took a closer look at the table. Between his parents were two black gym bags that Perry didn't recognize. One of them was unzipped partway. Inside the bag was rolls and rolls of cash.

He moved closer to the table, grabbed one and held it up. "Whoa! What are you, like Richie Rich?"

Trish spun away from the refrigerator. "What?"

His dad snatched the money away from him and stuck it back in the bag. He zipped the bag the rest of the way shut.

Perry gestured at the bag. "How much money is in there?"

His mom pulled it to her chest and wrapped her arms around it.

He felt his own eyes widen and eyebrows rise, like he was a cartoon version of himself. "You guys are acting weird. What did you do, rob a bank?"

"Of course not!" His mom's voice was snappy.

"You're going to have to tell us something," Trish said. "We both saw that roll of money."

*A darn sight more than one roll.*

His mom and dad shared a long look. Then his dad said, "You have to keep this a secret."

Trish shivered. "You're scaring me. I hope you robbed a bank. I hope you didn't murder somebody to get that."

His mom gasped. "Absolutely not." Then she sighed. "But you know that Whitney's death has caused us some trouble."

"*You* some trouble," Trish said. "I don't think the cops are after Dad."

His dad shook his head. "You're right. They're not. But when your mom is in trouble, it's my trouble, too. And there have been some developments."

Perry didn't like the sound of his dad's voice. He sounded scared. His dad was never scared.

"Whitney left me some keys. When we opened up one of the locks, we found the money."

His mom rolled her top lip between her teeth. Everyone was quiet. Perry didn't know what to say. Trish was staring at the bags.

His mom finally said, "Money like this can mean problems. Big problems."

"It can be dangerous. Like it was for Whitney. That's why we need you guys to never, never mention this. Not to anyone," his dad said.

"I won't," Trish said.

"Me either." Perry grabbed for the bag again and this time his mother let him take it. He unzipped it. The top gaped open. What he saw made him back up, like it was a snake about to bite him. "Holy moly! I've never seen this much money. Is it real? How much is in there?"

Trish looked in. She drew in a quick breath. "People would kill for that much money."

"Maybe they did. And that's why we all need to keep this a secret." His dad had a stern look on his face. "At least until we figure out what to do with it."

"We should keep it," Trish said. "You could buy me a plane ticket to go visit Ben."

Perry's stomach growled. "Can we use some of the money to buy the burgers? And can I drive?"

His dad's eye roll was a big fat no. It had been worth a try.

"Does Ronnie know about it?" Perry asked.

"Not yet. No one does outside this room."

"What's in the other bag?" Trish said.

"More of the same."

"So, we're rich?"

His dad gave her a squinty-eyed look.

"Kidding. Are we going to be safe with it here?"

"We are, because you and Perry and your mom and I agreed that no one but us will know."

Perry opened the second bag and dug around in it. Ferdinand dropped his chin on the table to watch. It was crazy to think he was up to nearly his elbow in rolls of money. The outside bills were hundreds. Rolls of hundred-dollar bills. No one would believe him even if he was allowed to tell. Then his hand brushed against something hard. Not like a roll of bills hard. Hard like a rock, but smoother. He pulled it out of the bag and held it up under the light fixture. It was a ring. An oval thing with a gold band. It had odd symbols and stones in it.

"This is weird." He turned it in the light.

"Where did you get that?" his dad said.

"It was just in that second bag. Under the money."

His mother took it from him. She frowned. "Those look like hieroglyphs."

Perry knew what hieroglyphs were from his social studies class. Everything about Egypt was a big deal this year. "Maybe Whitney went to one of the King Tut exhibits. It kind of looks like the stuff Steve Martin wears when he does that song."

His dad stood up and started pacing. His lips were moving.

His mom was still staring at the ring and turning it in her hand. She rubbed her fingertips across the surface. "It looks very old." She closed her fist around the ring. "And very expensive."

None of this was making any sense to Perry. But then again, his parents were pretty weird a lot of the time. He knew though that this money and this ring were a really, really big deal. Scary big.

# CHAPTER FORTY-TWO: CONNECT

BUFFALO, WYOMING
*NOW:* THURSDAY, JUNE 22, 1978

*Patrick*

AFTER TRISH AND Perry left to pick up the burgers, Patrick walked onto the back deck. Susanne followed him. He rubbed his forehead. His mind was racing. The creek that had carried Whitney's body burbled. A breeze rustled the leaves. In the distance, he heard the hoot of an owl. Summertime sounds. Peaceful sounds. But they did nothing to still the turmoil inside him.

"Patrick, what was that girl into?" Susanne whispered.

He sighed. "Seems like nothing good."

"Do you think she was supposed to sell them that ring? Is that what she held back?"

"Is it worth a million dollars?"

Susanne put her hands on the railing and leaned out into the evening air. "If it's authentic, it could be valuable. But I'm no expert."

He marched along the deck behind her, doing a crisp about-face at each end. "It seems impossible that a Wyoming nurse in her twenties would have authentic Egyptian antiquities in her possession."

"Maybe she inherited it from someone? Or it was a gift?"

Patrick threw his hands up. "It's anybody's guess. I know so little about her."

Susanne nodded. "Let's start with what we do know."

Patrick ticked on his fingers, still pacing. "She's a mountain climber."

"Yes. And she's friends with Kathy."

"Right. Kathy introduced her to me. Which is how we came to climb Cloud Peak together." Patrick smacked a palm to his forehead. "I'm an idiot."

"Why?"

"I have to get up Cloud Peak." It was still early in the season for an ascent. He couldn't go alone. It was never wise, but especially not with his hurt hand and the probability of snow, cold, and maybe even ice. Patrick's mind always went to the same person first when he was up against the worst Wyoming could throw at him. "With Wes."

But even with Wes—whose knowledge, mental toughness and creativity, and innate wilderness skills were unsurpassed by anyone Patrick knew—it would be iffy.

They could always turn back. *We can, but we won't.*

"Whoa. That's extreme. And sudden. Why?"

"Because of cold storage. Thinking about what was important to Whitney, which is climbing, cold could refer to mountains."

"Okay... I still don't get it."

"I'm not sure I do either, but let's step back and look at everything together. She sent me a map of our climb. She left me the keys to this money from Price and the ring. She led Price to believe I could get his merchandise out of cold storage for him. Putting all that together, she's telling me to return to the cave."

"But why? What's in there?"

"I'm not sure. I didn't see anything when we were there. But I was sick. I was out of it. I do recall she and Loren were acting strange. I chalked it up to their relationship. Since then, the mountain has been covered in ice and snow. Maybe she found something up there. Maybe she left it there in cold storage." He made air quotes with his hands.

"Which means she wouldn't have been able to get to it until the snow melted."

"Right."

"Isn't there anyone else who'd know? What if you get up there and you're wrong?"

"I wish there was. I think I have to take the chance."

"But it's too early to make that climb. At least wait until July."

Patrick remembered Price's threats. There was a very real possibility he had murdered Whitney, and his money was sitting on their dining room table. "I don't think it can wait."

"I don't like it. You can't go. You just can't."

"Susanne, he threatened to make sure you and Trish ended up like Whitney if I didn't have it for him this weekend."

Her mouth made an O. Then she nodded. "We can't let him hurt Trish."

Patrick put his arms around her. "Or you." He kissed the top of her head, then hurried back inside, grabbed the telephone, and called his friend.

# CHAPTER FORTY-THREE: MISS

CLOUD PEAK WILDERNESS, BIGHORN MOUNTAINS, WYOMING
*THEN (NINE MONTHS EARLIER)*: MONDAY, SEPTEMBER 19, 1977

*Patrick*

PATRICK LOWERED himself another handhold down the rock face of the peak, the image of Loren's crumpled body at the base of the pitch planted firmly in his mind. There was no sound coming from below. He didn't dare call out to him. Whitney's climb was already difficult because of her cold hand, which was also taking abuse from the rough, old ropes. He needed her down before she figured out that Loren had taken a fall. A bad fall.

Whitney screamed. *She's seen him.* "Loren! Loren!"

Loren didn't answer.

"Patrick! Loren's on the ground. He's not moving! He's not answering me!"

Patrick used his calmest voice. "We'll take care of him."

"Oh, my God. Oh, my God. Oh, my God." If she didn't pull it together, she'd hyperventilate.

"Whitney, I need you to get your breathing right." *I don't need another fall and a second patient.* "Loren needs us."

"You're right. You're right. Okay. You're right." She still sounded panicked, but he could tell she was trying. "I'm ready. I'm starting back up. He needs us." She inched down the boulders.

"That's good. You're doing much better."

"Yes, better. I'm better."

"Do you feel steady?"

"I, I'm okay."

"Make this the slowest and most careful part of your descent, okay?"

"Okay. Yes. Slow and careful." Her teeth were chattering. Her movements were jerky. But she didn't rush, and her breathing slowed.

"Looking great. Maintain three points of contact. Only a few more feet now."

If her face and trembling body pressed against the rock counted, she had closer to five points of contact at all times. She covered the last few feet at a glacial pace. Then she jumped off the rock wide of Loren and fell to her hands and knees. "Ow!"

"What's the matter?"

"My ankle. It smarts, but I'll be fine."

Patrick landed on his feet. He knelt by the younger man, who was face up in front of an odd bell-shaped rock. With his hand on Loren's shoulder, Patrick watched the rise and fall of his chest. Then he started scanning him for injured places, starting with his head, which was resting in a pool of blood. Patrick winced. A large pool of blood.

"He hit his head," Whitney hobbled over to them.

"He did." He probed Loren's skull gently with his fingers, his mind racing. He couldn't find a fracture, but he did find a bump at the site of the external wound. Closed head wounds could be deadly, but the swelling wasn't too bad. At least not yet. He continued searching for issues, working his way down Loren's neck and back. Without x-ray equipment, he could only identify the most obvious breaks or misalignments. What he wouldn't give for a stretcher, a couple of EMTs, and an ambulance full of life-saving equipment and supplies. That, and a different location. Preferably one across the street from the doors to the emergency room. While he was making a wish list, how about a nurse and climbing partner who hadn't just injured her ankle?

*How in deepest Hades will I get these two down the mountain?* And to think only twelve hours before they'd faced the same problem with him and the effects of his dehydration.

Loren groaned.

"He's waking up!" Whitney put her weight on one leg and lowered herself to her knees beside Loren. She gripped one of his hands in hers.

After a few seconds, Loren fluttered his eyes. They rolled back in his head a few times before they opened to slits and fixed on Patrick's face.

Patrick knew better than to get his hopes up, but this was a positive development at least.

"Shee-yut." Loren's voice was weak and thready.

Patrick smiled at him. "Welcome back."

"What happened to me? Where am I?"

"You took a shortcut. Airborne to the base."

Loren's eyes clouded. He frowned, looking confused.

"Are you okay?" Whitney asked.

"My head. It hurts. Real bad."

"I imagine you've got a whopper of a concussion," Patrick said. *And maybe more.* "Can you wiggle your fingers and toes?"

Loren did as Patrick requested. *Good.* At least in his current position, there didn't seem to be a serious spinal or neck injury affecting his extremities. That could change when they had to move him, possibly knocking something broken disastrously out of alignment. Patrick didn't even want to think about it.

Patrick held up two fingers. "How many fingers am I holding up?"

Loren's eyes crossed then straightened. He rotated his head slightly. Then his eyes rolled back in their sockets again and his body jerked a few times.

"Loren! Loren!" Whitney shouted, leaning over his face.

Patrick was less surprised that Loren had lost consciousness again than he'd been that Loren had woken at all. "We learned that Loren's chief complaint is his head and that he has movement in his extremities. That was useful."

"But he's unconscious again."

"That might be for the best, at least right now. The way down is going to be difficult and painful."

She nodded. Tears rolled down her cheeks, drying quickly into salty tracks in the cold mountain air.

Patrick swallowed. He had to make some decisions. He could hurry down and send a helicopter back for Loren—Whitney would have to stay with him. Left alone, Loren could die of hypothermia or fall prey to an animal attracted by the scent of his blood. They could carry him out on a stretcher, possibly? But he doubted Whitney could carry her end stably with her ankle injury. Maybe Patrick could drag him on a travois? That option seemed the highest risk of causing further damage. Maybe he could decrease the risk by immobilizing his neck and spine? Of all the ideas he'd come up with, he leaned toward carrying him out with Whitney. He could tear up his shirt and wrap her ankle. Give her some painkillers.

But they were still above the tree line. Even finding wood to immobilize Loren and build a makeshift stretcher was going to mean Patrick had to hike partway down and back up. That being the case, he needed to get moving immediately. Their rescue operation would take the rest of the day.

"Patrick?" Whitney was staring at him. "You're talking to yourself."

"Sorry. I was making a plan to get us back to West Tensleep Lake.

Let's staunch Loren's bleeding and finish checking him for injuries we can address up here." He took off his backpack and dug through it for his first aid kit. He tossed a bottle of Extra Strength Tylenol and an ace bandage with clips to Whitney. "Let me know if you need help with your ankle. We need you in the best shape possible. I'll work on Loren."

She nodded, and Patrick turned to Loren with a small pack of gauze.

But then he heard a distinctive sound. The clang of metal on stone.

*Horseshoes! Someone was near the peak on horseback!*

"Do you hear that?" Whitney said.

"I do." Patrick craned his neck, searching for the source. It didn't take long to find it. It was a line of horses coming around Mistymoon Lake. His heart leapt. The horses might be lifesavers for Loren.

"Look," he said, pointing."

"Thank God," Whitney breathed.

Patrick stood and cupped his hands around his mouth. "Over here," he shouted.

Whitney whistled and waved her arms.

But the riders didn't react. The line of horses continued walking toward the established summit trail.

"Do you have a flare gun?" Patrick asked.

"No!" Whitney said.

Patrick didn't either. He shouted again. And again. And again.

"They don't see us!" Whitney said.

Patrick said, "Can you go after them while I take care of Loren?"

Her face was stricken. "My ankle. But I can take care of him."

Patrick nodded. "I'll be back." He raced down the slope toward the lake.

# CHAPTER FORTY-FOUR: LUMBER

Cloud Peak Wilderness, Bighorn Mountains, Wyoming
*Now*: Friday, June 23, 1978

*Patrick*

Patrick was thankful he and Wes had started at sunrise—they needed all the daylight available for the climb. Sunrise was four thirty in the morning this time of year, although on the western side of the Bighorns, sunrise was more an attitude than a phenomenon of light. They were still stumbling along in near dark. But it wasn't all bad. The temperature was above freezing. The first few miles of the trail from West Tensleep Lake weren't challenging. They had encountered some icy mud puddles the size of lakes, but no tough footing or taxing sections yet. Patrick's mountain climbing training was more than a match for these lower elevations. And if Wes was gassed, he didn't show any signs of it.

They'd hashed out a pretty good plan on the drive across the

Bighorns. The West Tensleep route was an out-and-back trail to the summit. Experienced climbers in good physical condition could do it in one day, conditions permitting, if they kicked off early.

Patrick and Wes wanted to give themselves the best possible chance to achieve that.

But while they anticipated decent weather, they felt certain they'd encounter mud, snow, and ice. Hence backpacks twice as heavy as Patrick would normally carry. They were toting tents, sleeping bags, clothing layers, and crampons for traction. Double food and water rations plus rock climbing gear. Shovels and ice picks were strapped to their packs. Not to mention they'd be making an unorthodox ascent off-trail to the cave because of the rockslide last year that had blocked the path between the cave to the summit.

If they could even *find* the route to the cave. Whitney's hand-drawn map was helpful, but it wasn't detailed. Patrick hadn't been at his best that day. His memory was spotty.

He would do his best now, though. But even with their best and everything going right, the expected trail conditions plus the extra weight made it unlikely they'd summit *and* make it back down in one day. And that was assuming his hand didn't slow them down. Although he normally hated taking medications unless absolutely necessary, Patrick had taken heavy-duty painkillers as they left the parking lot. He'd brought a baggie of those as well as an extra Ace bandage to match the one he'd carefully wrapped his hand in, over a skintight glove. He had to balance his need for mobility and mental clarity with the opposing need to protect and stabilize the hand and keep pain at a minimum. Now, he hiked with his hand held above his shoulder. He felt like a slightly loopy goofball, but normal arm motion slung blood into the hand. His unorthodox posture wouldn't counteract that completely, but it would help minimize the swelling this little adventure was going to inevitably cause.

They'd been on the trail for two hours or more when Wes's teasing voice rang out only a few feet behind Patrick. "Need me to carry anything for you, Sawbones?" Wes alternated between Doc and

Sawbones as nicknames for Patrick, based on his mood. Sawbones indicated a level of jolliness that portended doom for Patrick's ego.

"Nah. I'm good," Patrick said.

"Seen any human footprints?"

"Not since those down by one of the creek crossings."

"Shoot, you mean you missed those by Lost Twin Lakes? Maybe I'd better lead so you don't run us up on a Yeti."

Patrick had been too caught up in the moose munching water plants at the edge of the water, backlit by the sun which had finally made it over the mountains. "I'm not worried about Bigfoot. I'm worried about people from behind us."

"Nobody but us is crazy enough to try to summit this early in the season."

"The people I'm worried about don't have to summit. They just have to wait for us to do it."

Wes laughed. "That's kinda like that old joke about outrunning a grizzly bear."

"You don't have to outrun the bear, you just have to outrun your buddy. I'll have you know I feel good about my chances in that case. I was a sprinter in high school."

"I'm no slouch myself, Sawbones. These long legs eat up the ground."

"It would be optimal not to cross paths with any grizzlies or their human equivalents."

Wes snorted. "Whitney sure got you in some trouble, didn't she?"

"You don't know the half of it."

"Don't you think I should, seeing as you're putting my life at risk today?"

Patrick had explained some of it in the car, after Wes had napped half the drive and before they'd made their climbing plan. "Old guys like me need all their breath for the climb." But he laid out the rest of the story anyway.

When he was done, Wes let out a long, low whistle. "So, you think Price is coming after us?"

"I hope not. I didn't tell anyone I was coming up here except you."

"I just can't believe if this whatever-it-is is so valuable that she'd have left it behind."

"Me neither. Not unless it was too big to carry. But if it was too big then, it's too big now."

"Speak for yourself." Wes jogged backwards past him, flexing his long arms.

"Popeye would tell you to eat more spinach." Patrick slowed to let Wes in front. "Your turn to lead. Just pick up the pace. The sooner we get up and down this hunk of rock, the better."

# CHAPTER FORTY-FIVE: SPILL

Buffalo, Wyoming
*Now*: Friday, June 23, 1978

*Trish*

Trish didn't think twenty-four hours could pass any slower. She wanted the night to come so Ben would call. But here she was stuck in stupid *morning* practice with Jillian's chirpy voice barking orders. Was there any worse way to start a day than listening to her? Straighten your legs on that split. Raise your arms on your V. Jump higher. Smile bigger. Yell louder.

She couldn't concentrate on this when she was floating on a cloud of giddy anticipation.

"What's up with you, Trish?" Jillian was right in her face.

Trish shot her arms into a crisp T. "Sorry. Did I mess up?"

"No. I just want to know who put that dreamy look in your eyes."

The other girls let out long ooooooo's in unison, like backup singers.

Trish smiled. She couldn't help it. She was just too . . . happy. The thought was crazy. She hadn't been happy since—well, since Ben had left Laramie and her for Alaska. She blurted it out before she could stop herself. "Ben and I are getting back together."

"What?" Jillian screeched. "The hot older guy who did a stint in juvie? Wait, wasn't he in there for kidnapping you with his crazy dad and uncle?" She socked Trish in the arm. "And here you were acting like you were too good for Jimmy."

"He's not like that." Jillian had the facts about Ben's past correct, but the gist of it was completely not her Ben. He was a good person. He knew right from wrong. He had principles. And he loved her.

"Okay. Sure. Well, do you want to go out with us girls tonight?" She waved her arm at the other cheerleaders. "I mean you did say you're getting back together, not that you already are. One last fling."

"I can't. He's calling me tonight." And she was babysitting. Which she'd told them yesterday, but Jillian didn't pay attention to anything that didn't involve her or make for good gossip, so naturally she'd forgotten.

Jillian turned to her fan club and put the back of her hand to her forehead. "Trish has to sit at home with her parents and pine away by the phone tonight waiting for her bad boy ex to call her."

"For your information, my dad is climbing Cloud Peak, and my mom has a girls' night out." Jillian was starting to make Trish mad. She looked at her watch. It was time for practice to be over. "Is it time to go?"

Jillian did a round-off into a back handspring and then a back flip. She loved to rub her tumbling skills in Trish's face. When she finished, she was facing Trish and the rest of the squad. "We're done. Trish, tell Ben I *can't wait* to meet him."

This time, Trish was the first to leave practice, jogging under the goalpost and into the parking lot with a sour taste in her mouth. She didn't want Jillian to have anything to do with Ben. She liked most of cheerleading so far. But the one thing she didn't like, she was learning to hate.

Jillian.

# CHAPTER FORTY-SIX: OBFUSCATE

BUFFALO, WYOMING
*NOW:* FRIDAY, JUNE 23, 1978

*Susanne*

SUSANNE HEARD a car pull up out front through the open windows. She loved this time of year, when she could let the cool temperatures sweep through the house. Everything smelled clean and new. A yawn escaped her. Half the night she'd dreamed about that ring in the gym bag. She'd woken up convinced that she'd seen the design on it somewhere in the stack of research she'd brought home from the college. Probably not, though. She wasn't an expert in hieroglyphs. It was likely they were just similar to something she'd seen in the King Tut papers.

She peeked outside, thinking the vehicle might be Trish home from cheerleading.

But it wasn't. It was the same car that had followed Patrick and her home from Whitney's funeral. The one Patrick called Price. The one Patrick said had threatened her. And, worse—Trish. The thought of anyone using their kids to put pressure on them, of anyone hurting their kids, made her feel sick. At least Perry was asleep upstairs. He wouldn't get out of bed until she went to his room and beat a wooden spoon in a pot to wake him. Trish was gone, although she might arrive back home any minute.

The sick feeling got worse. She had to handle this alone, and she had to handle it quickly. But Patrick hadn't expected Price until the weekend. They'd thought she had no reason to worry, because by then Patrick would be back, hopefully with the item Price believed he'd paid for.

Well, she sure didn't want that man in her house. Ferdinand ran to the door, whining. She didn't have to be completely alone. Grabbing the leash from its hook by the back door, she went back to her giant dog and clipped on his lead. He jumped and twirled with excitement, slinging slobber as he spun. She threw her shoulders back, lifted her chin, and marched out to the front steps with her dog beside her, trying to rise above the fear lapping at her.

A lone man exited the passenger side of the car, leaving the driver behind. He strode toward her, dark-skinned. Thick. Hair thinning. Eyes mean.

"May I help you?" she said.

"Nice dog." The man smiled, but his voice was hard. Ferdinand stiffened beside her, then strained forward against the leash. "I'm here for the man of the house."

"He's not here."

"That's a shame. Because he's supposed to have something for me."

"And what is that?"

His face turned red, and he stalked back to his car, returning with a piece of paper which he shook in her face. "This. He damn well has this for me."

Ferdinand began to growl, low in his throat, long whiskers quivering.

Susanne ducked away from his fist, pulling Ferdinand with her. "Did you want me to see that? If so, you'll need to either let me take it or hold it further back from my face."

With a snarl, he shoved it in front of her. "Don't touch it."

She only got a glance before he snatched it back away. It was just long enough for her to see a detailed rendering of stick figure wearing an oval breastplate with hieroglyphs and what she assumed were precious stones. There were handwritten notes in the margins, but she didn't have time to read them. *Jesus, Joseph, and Mary. It matches the ring.*

"Ring any bells with you?"

"I've never seen that before." Which was true. She'd seen the matching ring, but not that breastplate.

His tone grew even more menacing. "Your husband has my money, so I think my associate and I will come in and look around. Just to be sure you're telling the truth."

Her heart was beating so hard in her chest that it hurt, but she stood taller. She couldn't let them in. They'd rip the house apart. They might hurt her or Perry. Trish might come home while they were there. And there was the matter of the big bags of cash and the ring that matched the breastplate in the drawing. They'd find it if they looked hard enough. She and Patrick had hidden it in a cooler in the garage, but they hadn't had time to figure out a secure place for it offsite. To keep him out, she had to give him something.

"Yes, I do mind. I told you I've never seen it. But I do know that Patrick has gone to get it."

The man's eyes narrowed. "Gone where?"

"He wouldn't tell me. All I know is Whitney left him some cryptic instructions, but he thinks he figured them out."

"When will he be back?"

"When he finds it."

He stuck his finger in her face. This time, she didn't draw back, and she expected the tip to poke her in the cheek at any moment. Ferdinand couldn't stand it anymore. He lunged forward and snapped at the man.

"Control this cur."

"He doesn't like people threatening me."

"I don't make threats, lady. If you don't tell me where he is, I'll go find him myself. And if he doesn't have what I paid for—well, don't keep his dinner warm. Because he just might not be coming back. And then, I'm coming back here with my colleague. We'll find something we like, even if it's not the goods I purchased." He leered at her, and she prayed for Trish to stay late at the school after practice. "That's a promise."

She held perfectly still as he turned on his heel and stalked back to his car, fists clenched, and shoulders hunched.

As the car drove away, her whole body started to shake. She had to call for help. But the Buffalo police weren't her allies. Ronnie would understand and believe her, but she'd taken the day off to go shopping in Casper with her mother. She wouldn't be back until time for their girls' night out date that night.

Susanne flexed her hands until the shaking stopped. She was on her own. But that didn't leave her helpless. In fact, suddenly, she had an idea of exactly what to do next.

# CHAPTER FORTY-SEVEN: PIECE

BUFFALO, WYOMING
*NOW*: FRIDAY, JUNE 23, 1978

*Susanne*

BACK IN THE HOUSE, Susanne went to work. Because didn't she have a treasure trove of information about Egyptian antiquities sitting in a tall stack beside her sewing machine table? She'd never been more excited to pull up a seat at it than today.

She hefted the top section of the papers onto the tabletop and set the ring beside it. If she could put stock in her own dreams, she'd seen something like the design on it—and possibly on the breastplate in Price's drawing—buried in these pages. She picked up the ring and studied it carefully. There were images inside the oval and outside it in a raised, rope-like border. The hieroglyphs stamped in the border were too small to identify. Not without a magnifying glass, and she wasn't sure she even had one.

But she could work with the larger images. Going clockwise around the oval she saw something that reminded her of the bottom few rows of a chess or checkerboard. In the first quadrant on the right was a bird with a tall feather on its head, with a small mound in front of and behind it. In the bottom right, what she would describe as a shepherd's hook. It was colored in alternating sections of copper and off-white. The bottom image was a pole rising out of a tri-colored base. Bottom left, she had a harder time with but decided it reminded her of a fancy shower head. Far left, she was certain was the symbol of life in ancient Egypt, known as the ankh. It was a cross with a loop above the center post. And in the top left quadrant, a horizontal line like the teeth of a serrated blade. Or, keeping it closer to home, like the peaks of a mountain range.

This is what she was looking for. Something that matched these images or came close to them. She didn't know what they meant. She wasn't a scholar of ancient Egypt. She took a steadying breath and scanned the first page. Then the next. She saw ovals that reminded her of the ring, but nothing that matched it. The ovals were identified as *shenus*.

"What is a shenu?" She'd never heard of one and didn't remember the word from her earlier reading.

Much of the terminology in the articles and inventory was new to her. She kept going, enthralled by the ancient subject matter and its relation to the object beside her, in present day Wyoming. She was on the hunt for an answer, and, when she stumbled across it, she gripped the ring in her hand, caressing the shenu with her thumb. Napoleon's soldiers, on expedition to Egypt, discovered circular symbols that reminded them of the cartridges, or "cartouches," used in their guns. But the Egyptian name for what became known to them (and later to the world) as a cartouche is *shenu*, a word derived from the verb sheni which meant "to encircle," like the shen rings. And this shenu was the place holder for the name of the pharoah. Whether circular or an elongated oval as it became over time, it held within it the hieroglyphs in the pharaoh's two most important names, his birth name and his throne name, which represented the king's realm—everything encircled by the sun.

The shenu was used in decorative ways and also a protective symbol for the king. In the Eighteenth Dynasty, royal sarcophagi were constructed in the shape of the shenu. Howard Carter had found a box in King Tut's tomb with symbols on the lid that were Tut's name, as well as finger rings made in the shape of the cartouche. *Like the one in my hand?* She needed to compare her ring to pictures.

She set it down and began flipping through the pages faster, scanning photographs and descriptions, looking for anything that sounded like the images depicted in the shenu on the ring beside her. It was hard for her to resist slowing down and digging into the fascinating material. Over and over, she forced herself to continue, glancing up at the clock on Patrick's bedside table. Time was passing far too quickly.

The front door opened and shut. She hadn't heard a vehicle pull up. She started to rise, heart rate accelerating. Was Price already back? And then another thought, possibly worse. Is it the police?

"Mom?" Trish called.

She sat back down. It was only Trish. She sighed, relieved. "Working. Do you need something?"

"No. I'm gonna take a shower and go to Marcy's, okay?"

"Do your chores first."

"Okay."

She returned to the pages, using her finger to keep her eyes moving but focused. Her finger stopped before she realized what she was looking at. Then she gasped and stabbed at the page. It was a picture of a knob from a box found in King Tut's tomb. And it looked so very much like the ring. She put the ring shenu-up beside the picture and studied the two side-by-side. The images inside the rope border were to her untrained eye a perfect match. She compared them again, unable to find any differences.

She ran her finger over the ring. "This makes no sense." King Tut's shenu on an authentic looking ring hidden in a bag of money in Whitney's YMCA gym locker in Sheridan, Wyoming? How?

Assuming for a moment it was authentic, where would it have come from? Maybe someone stole it from the exhibit. But she hadn't read anything or heard anything about a theft. Professor Seth would have mentioned it. It would have created an international incident. INTERPOL would be involved in hunting for it. David Brinkley would be talking about it on the *Nightly News*.

No, a recent theft didn't seem possible.

"Bye, Mom," Trish shouted. The front door clicked shut.

Too late, she mumbled, "Bye."

She set the document aside. She shouldn't jump to conclusions. If the shenu on the ring matched King Tut's shenu, that was one thing. It could be a knockoff. Same with the breastplate in Price's drawing. Cheap imitations to cash in on the King Tut frenzy around the world. What she needed was evidence that a ring and a breastplate with the shenu were amongst the original items in Tut's tomb and had gone missing at some point in history.

But by the end of her first pass through the materials she hadn't found any.

Perry knocked on her door frame. "You look a little crazed, Mom." He motioned to the top of his head.

She patted her head. Her hair was poofing out of her head band. She didn't bother to smooth it down. The clock read one p.m. She raised her eyebrows. "Are you just getting up?"

He grinned. "Nah. I've already put in a hard day's work outside."

Her brows shot up, and she half-smiled. "Liar."

"Okay. I just got up. I'm still recovering from working with Henry."

"There's a list of chores on the table for you."

"Mo-om..."

"What? You think we did them for you while you were gone this week?"

"I was gonna go throw the ball with some of the guys."

"After you're done."

He dropped his head back. Eyes closed, mouth open. "Fine." He wheeled and disappeared.

She started her second pass through the papers, going slower this time, looking for the original inventory made by Carter and anything that would prove the ring and breastplate existed. Maybe she'd missed something. Her stomach growled an hour later. She was thirsty. She needed to go to the bathroom. But she just couldn't stop.

Another hour passed before she found the two words she was looking for in an article about tomb robbing: ring and breastplate. She bit her lip and whispered, "Now we're talking."

She started from the beginning. It was a piece she had skimmed earlier in the week that covered grave robbing in ancient Egypt, and how the relative lack of successful forays into Tut's tomb left what would otherwise have been a fairly minor tomb a treasure-trove by comparison. But his grave had been plundered several times in the years immediately following his entombment. From what Carter and his team could tell when they opened it, robbers had accessed the entire tomb, removing lids on boxes without resealing them. While they couldn't be certain, Egyptologists were of the opinion that Tut's sun god statue was missing a breastplate and at least one ring, both theorized to bear his shenu. This was due to other pieces of jewelry, amulets, and weaponry found on or near the statue. A ring and breastplate should have been with them and were obvious in their absence.

The real question wasn't whether they existed—all the researchers agreed they should have, citing the inventory—but whether they *continued* to exist. Often the ancient grave robbers broke down their stolen goods. The items were less likely to get the thieves tortured and executed if they were unidentifiable, and they had substantial value in their component parts. Gold, colored glass, and precious gems.

If the ring and breastplate remained intact, they had been kept a secret and passed down through generations of collectors. The article cited numerous rumors about collectors paying outrageous prices and stashing them in top secret private collections but offered no proof or conclusions. Their whereabouts—their very existence—remained a mystery.

Susanne sat back in her chair. A ring like this had existed and might still. A breastplate like the one in Price's drawing had been real once upon a time and might be now. She literally felt as if her brain had turned to sludge and wouldn't move another inch forward.

This was bigger than she'd ever imagined in her wildest dreams.

Or, in this case, nightmares. Because if they were authentic, they were more valuable to obsessed collectors than mere money... or human life. And her husband was at that very moment climbing up a mountain to potentially bring down an item that could get him killed.

# CHAPTER FORTY-EIGHT: GOSSIP

BUFFALO, WYOMING
*NOW*: FRIDAY, JUNE 23, 1978

*Trish*

TRISH STOOD in line at the ice cream stand on Main with Marcy. It wasn't a stand really. It was inside a little building, but it was only open in the summer. A temporary store. The line extended all the way out to the street and down the sidewalk. To Wyomingites, cold ice cream in the summer was a big deal after a long, cold winter.

"This is taking forever," Marcy said. "I have to get home sometime this year. I'm expecting a call." She waggled her eyebrows.

"From your *boyfriend*?" Trish bumped her friend with her hip.

"Don't call him that. You're going to jinx it."

"Are you going to see him tonight?"

"That's why I have to get home and talk to him. I'm hoping I will. You're babysitting, right?"

"Yes. Little Will and I will have the house to ourselves."

"Wait. I thought your mom was having a girls' night out with Ronnie? Where's your dad?"

"Climbing Cloud Peak with his buddy Wes."

"Your dad is weird."

"No argument from me on that. But he actually has a reason this time."

"There is no reason for it. Especially not when there's still snow up there." Marcy jerked her head back toward the mountains.

From this angle, they couldn't see the peaks because of the looming bulk of the front range, but Trish knew what she meant. "Okay, this is a huge secret. Can I trust you?"

Marcy rolled her eyes. "Duh."

"You know that woman who died, the one everyone says was after my dad?"

"Whitney Saylor is the only thing anyone is talking about in this town. That and your mom. That, she, uh, you know. Killed her. Which I know she didn't, but anyway, go on."

Trish could forgive her for repeating the gossip, because how could Marcy have kept from hearing about it? And because it was just to her. "This is super confusing, but Whitney sold something or maybe she was supposed to—I'm not sure—but it was super valuable, and someone paid her a lot of money for it. And she told them my dad had it. Only he doesn't. But he thinks he knows where it is."

"May I have your order please?" the boy behind the counter was a year behind them at school. His face turned bright red when he recognized them. It made his freckles less noticeable.

"Double scoop of strawberry, in a cup, please," Trish said, putting her money in front of the barely open window.

"Double chocolate in a cone." Marcy laid her money beside Trish's.

"Okay, I'll have it out to you in a jiffy."

After he left Marcy frowned. "Who says jiffy, you know?" Then she shook her head. "So, where is this mystery item your dad is looking for?"

"Somewhere up on Cloud Peak." Trish shrugged. "In a cave or something where he spent the night last year."

"In a cave with Whitney?"

"I guess. Her and the other climber. You know. The one who bashed his head in."

"What is he looking for?"

"I have no idea." That hadn't struck Trish as odd before, but it did now that she thought about it.

"Then how will he know if he finds it?"

"You're the one who said my dad is weird."

"Yeah. Like really weird."

"Your ice cream," the boy said, handing Marcy's cone first.

She took it. "Come to mama."

He handed Trish a bowl and plastic spoon. "And here's yours." His voice broke and squeaked.

She felt sorry for him and gave him a big smile. He turned away quickly. Trish felt the weight of eyes on her. She glanced around. That mean cop Appelt was in line behind them. He was staring a hole into the back of Trish's head, but he looked away when Trish made eye contact with him. She turned back to Marcy, trying to shake off the icky feeling he gave her.

"You and baby Will have the place to yourself. Cool. Want me to call you? I mean if I'm not on a date."

Trish smiled. "I don't think so."

"That's so rude!"

Trish laughed and told Marcy about her plans to talk on the phone with Ben after Will went to sleep.

Marcy squealed and socked her.

Then the girls walked along Main Street, arms linked at the elbow, eating their ice cream, chatting, and with the memory of Appelt fading from Trish's mind. After a few minutes, Trish realized the feeling of sunshine inside her was the closeness she was regaining with Marcy. She wanted to open up to her. She needed to tell someone about the guillotine she felt hanging over her head. About the visit the night before from Jimmy and Dabbo. And the horrible night with them and Jillian at the gas station.

She stopped to throw away her empty ice cream cup and spoon then turned and took a surprised Marcy by both hands.

"Are you about to ask me to marry you?" Marcy said. "Because I think I'm already taken."

Trish's eyes welled. Now she was the one surprised at herself. "I need to talk to you."

"You're scaring me now."

Trish wiped her eyes with one hand but held on to Marcy's with the other. And she told her friend what had happened and the guilt she was carrying, about Ben and about her involvement.

When she was done, Marcy hugged her tight. "It's going to be all right. It will be."

Trish put her head on her friend's shoulder and sobbed. She had so much on the line, but she really, really wanted to believe that.

# CHAPTER FORTY-NINE: DIG

Buffalo, Wyoming
*Now:* Friday, June 23, 1978

*Susanne*

Still breathless from her discovery about the missing ring and breastplate bearing King Tut's shenu, Susanne called Professor Seth's office. It was Friday afternoon. Sometimes he left early on Fridays. It rang seven times before he picked up.

"Hello, Seth here," he said.

"Professor, it's Susanne Flint."

"Susanne. I hear you met my wife."

"Yes, uh, she was very gracious about my interruption. I have a question for you."

"I hope I can be of assistance to you. But first I must ask how you are?"

"Surviving. It's a long story. Maybe my question will answer yours, in part."

"Go ahead, then."

She described the ring and the breastplate, the pictures of the King Tut buttons with his shenu, and the article about the items scholars believed existed and were stolen from his tomb. "I know it seems illogical that what I have could be real, but how would one be able to tell if an artifact is authentic?"

He hadn't interrupted her once during her disjointed, excited tale. "Where did you say you got these items?"

"I only have the ring. The woman the police accused me of killing—she left it for my husband in a bag of money. A whole, whole lot of money. And a man came to our house twice this week threatening us if Patrick doesn't hand over what he paid her for. Patrick thinks he might know where to find the breastplate—which he doesn't know is a breastplate, I only just figured that out—and has gone there. It seems impossible, doesn't it? I mean, I just don't see a way this could be real."

"I've never seen evidence that anything is truly impossible. Only that it exceeds our imaginations. Yet I must tell you how extremely unlikely it is to be from Tut's tomb, for so many reasons."

"Yes. I understand."

"As to your question, authentication might start with specialized testing of the metal and other elements to determine their age and composition. It's not something you or I could do with our naked eyes."

"Okay." She'd expected an answer like that.

"Another important piece of this sort of puzzle is tracing its ownership. Who held it before this woman did and so on, working backward in time."

"That makes sense."

"Do you think you can put that together?"

Before he'd asked the question, her answer would have been no. But her tired brain suddenly took her back to Patrick telling her about his conversation with the librarian, Cynthia Twain, about a wealthy climber who'd disappeared in the Bighorns years before. A rich climber who was also an amateur archaeologist and collector. And that Whitney had mentioned him to Kathy. "I don't know. But I think I know where to start." What time did the library close on Fridays? It was already nearly four o'clock.

"And where is that?"

"I'll let you know. Now, I'm sorry, but I have to go. Thank you so much!" She depressed the phone hooks to end the call and released them immediately to get another dial tone. She didn't have time to find the phone book and look up the number. She dialed information and asked for the library.

The phone rang. After three more rings, she hoped she hadn't used up all her luck catching Professor Seth in his office. "Come on, come on. Pick up. Please pick up."

A woman answered. "Johnson County Library, Buffalo branch."

"Hello. I'm wondering what time you close?" Susanne said.

"In five minutes."

"Oh, shoot!"

"Is there something I can help you with?"

"My name is Susanne Flint. I'm—"

"Hello, Susanne. This is Cynthia Twain. I believe your husband was in earlier this week. And your daughter Trish has been our most loyal patron for years."

"Actually, I'm calling about the same topic my husband talked to you about."

"Ichabod Johnson. Yes. I have some articles at the circulation desk that are ready for him. That was an interesting conversation."

"I'm on a wild goose chase. And I'm pressed for time. I was hoping to make it in before you closed. I'd love to see those articles. And maybe ask you for help."

"I hope it's not insensitive to ask whether this has anything to do with what I've read in the paper this week?"

Susanne winced. "It is related, yes."

"If you'll tell me what you're looking for, maybe I can pull it for you. I don't have to be anywhere for another hour."

"Oh, my. Yes, thank you. Thank you so much. I'm looking for information on any Egyptian artifacts he owned. Or, I don't know, anything special to him that he might have taken on a climb."

"Taken on a *climb*?"

"Yes. I know it sounds odd, but..."

"The weirder the question, the more fun the research."

"Am I correct his body was never found?"

"That's correct. I re-read the articles when I copied them for Dr. Flint. It was big news at the time. The theory was he was buried in a rockslide."

"And this was when?"

"Mid-1960s."

"All right. How about I drive to you now?"

"That's perfect. I have Dr. Flint's articles, and I might even have something related to your question by the time you get here. Or not. That's the way research goes."

*How well I know that.*

---

FIFTEEN MINUTES LATER, Susanne rapped on the locked library door. Cynthia Twain appeared a minute later, smiling, and ushered her in.

Cynthia's cheeks each had a bright mark. Slap red, Susanne's father would have called it. But in her case, it looked like excitement. She walked as she talked, and Susanne followed. "I don't know if I found what you're looking for, but I did find *something*, and I'm having fun. I'd already cross-referenced everything we had on Ichabod Johnson in our card catalog. The bulk of the information is held at the University of Wyoming's library, unfortunately, but we carry a fair amount of it on microfiche. That's where I got the articles for Dr. Flint." She smiled and adjusted her blouse, looking like a proud mother hen. "But I have something else I want to show you." She gestured at a chair in front of a microfiche projector. "Have you used microfiche before?"

"Many times. I do research at Sheridan College for my job." She took the offered seat.

Cynthia's mouth dropped a little before she corrected herself. "I had no idea." Her expression took on a look of something new. Respect, maybe? Kinship?

Susanne nodded. "I work for a geopolitics professor. And I get course credit as well as a small stipend."

"That's wonderful." Cynthia turned her attention to the microfiche reader. "Well, I already loaded what I found and have it pulled up for you to read. You asked about Egyptian artifacts and climbing with them. I tried to call his wife and ask her, but she didn't pick up. But I ran across this one little thing from his journals. I don't know how it even got catalogued, really. We got lucky."

Susanne squinted to decipher the handwritten words on the screen. She read aloud. "I don't feel like I climb alone. I always wear my treasures, one over my heart and the other on my pinky finger. They connect me to all those before me. When I look out from a peak, they make me feel like I am sovereign over everything my eyes can see. A pharaoh whose kingdom is the entirety of the world touched by the sun." *A ring and a breastplate that made him feel like a pharaoh. Reference to a shenu.* His words weren't definitive, but they couldn't have been clearer to her.

"That's all I could find. Is that helpful?"

Susanne wiped tears from her eyes. "It is a link in a chain. A very important one."

"I'm just tickled to hear that. And it really is related to Whitney Saylor's death? She came in here, you know. Researching Ichabod Johnson's climbs."

"When?"

"Oh, it was a few weeks ago."

*Wow*. Susanne pointed at the screen. "Can I make a copy of this?"

Cynthia brandished a stack of papers. "I made you and Dr. Flint a packet already. It has all the identifying information about the journal and where to find it, too."

Susanne surprised them both by throwing her arms around the older librarian and giving her a brief, heartfelt hug. "Thank you. More than you'll ever know."

"Of course. Good luck to you."

Susanne left the library and ran to her car. Was it better or worse to know the stakes behind Patrick's climb? She was so glad she hadn't told Price where Patrick had gone. *Dear God, don't let him find out from someone else.*

---

SUSANNE APPLIED a final swipe of soft rose lipstick, hands trembling. The doorbell rang. She smoothed her top and grabbed her cardigan from the bed before heading for the door. She slipped the sweater on as she threw open the door.

Ronnie was standing hand in hand with her toddler, Will. The little blond boy launched himself at Susanne's knees.

"Oomph! Wow, what a bruiser you've got here, Ronnie." She crouched to look Will in the eye. "Did you and Mommy have a fun day?"

He grinned, nodding, then barreled past her to greet Ferdinand, who solemnly slathered Will's face in kisses. Will giggled then wrapped his arms around the dog's neck.

Ronnie moved inside. "Mommy spent too much money. Will screamed his way through JCPenney, but I prevailed all the way to the cash register."

Trish came running down the stairs. "Will! Hi!"

The little steam engine released the dog and barreled at her. He met her at the bottom step, where she sat, and he crawled into her lap. "Story. Story."

Trish laughed. "I haven't babysat you in weeks and that's the first thing you have to say to me, huh?"

"You get your story reading skills from your dramatic father," Susanne said. She felt a jolt in her midsection at the thought of him. She hated the thought of him camping out on that mountain overnight. She needed to know he was safe, but there was no way to contact him. *Maybe they'll make it in one day. He could surprise me later tonight.* She could hope, but she doubted it.

Trish looked up. "Oh, Mom—Perry said to tell you he may bring a few friends home with him from football."

Susanne nodded, her mind still on her husband.

"Are you okay?" Ronnie said.

Susanne tried to erase the worry she was broadcasting. "Lots to talk about at dinner."

"More of the same with the Buffalo police?"

"Not really. But... in that vein."

Ronnie nodded. She handed Trish a diaper bag. "This has everything you need, even books, bath toys, and dinner. Bath at seven. Bedtime at seven-thirty. No more than two books."

Trish picked up Will and swung him in a circle. Ferdinand barked and did a yoga pose, front legs extended and chin to the ground, tail wagging. "He'd have me read all night if I'd let him." She set the boy on the ground.

"Mo'! Mo'!" he screamed.

"You've gotten too heavy, munchkin."

Ronnie ruffled Will's hair. "Well, you can read to him before bath, too, if you'd like."

"Yay for us, Will!" Trish held up a hand for him to high five.

He smacked it with enthusiastic force.

"He's getting strong."

"Yes, he is." Ronnie cocked her head. "You're in a good mood, Trish Flint."

Trish blushed. "I am."

"Any special reason?"

"Ben called. We're, um, we're maybe getting back together."

"That's great. I'm happy to hear it."

"Okay, Trish," Susanne said, mindful of the time. "We'll be at the Occidental. I don't think we'll be there too long—"

"Speak for yourself," Ronnie said. "I'm having wine with dinner. And dessert."

*Maybe a glass of wine would do me good, too.*

"See you guys later." Trish stood, with Will holding her hand and pulling her toward the back door. "I think we'll go outside for a bit."

"Bye," Susanne said. She grabbed her purse and headed for the door.

Just before she shut it, Trish said, "One more thing. I almost forgot. Some guy called for dad earlier. I made a note with his number. I told him dad was climbing Cloud Peak and couldn't call him back until at least tomorrow. He said dad would know what it was about."

Susanne's blood turned to an icy sludge in her veins. "What was his name?"

Trish shrugged and slipped out the back door. "I can't remember. It's all on the kitchen table."

Ronnie touched Susanne's elbow. "We're going to be late for our reservation."

Susanne stared back at the table, at the note of the phone call. There was nothing she could do about it now that couldn't wait until later.

Maybe nothing at all.

She blinked several times. "Right." Then she headed out the door into the dusky evening.

# CHAPTER FIFTY: CATCH

Cloud Peak Wilderness, Bighorn Mountains, Wyoming
*Then (nine months earlier)*: Monday, September 19, 1977

*Patrick*

Patrick ran after the mounted search team at the base of Cloud Peak, struggling to lift his knees in his heavy boots. If he had a prayer of intercepting the riders, he had to cut between the trails. He veered across a rocky open area. The footing immediately became more treacherous. Rocks seemed like boulders to his fatigued thighs. The boots he'd bought for their light weight felt like lead strapped to his feet. He shouted at the group. The combination of wind and elevation made the effort futile, sucking his voice into the ether.

He had to run faster. It was going to require Herculean effort. His dehydrated muscles were rebelling. They were bone-weary and sore from the climb the previous day. He was exhausted after a fitful sleep on the rock floor, fighting stress dreams and frigid temperatures.

But desperation fueled him. He and Whitney needed help to get Loren down to a hospital, and they needed it sooner rather than later. There was very little Patrick could do for him on the mountain. The young man could die up here.

*He might die no matter what.*

Just then, one of the riders turned in the saddle to look in Patrick's direction. Even from the distance of hundreds of yards, Patrick recognized Wes Braten's face and lanky, gangly body. Patrick waved his arms over his head. Wes waved, pointing at him and saying something to the others in his group. The other horses drew to a halt.

Patrick felt like weeping with relief.

He shielded his eyes with one hand. Besides Wes, he recognized a few members of the local search and rescue squad by their jackets. Normally, he only encountered them when they were helping EMTs bring in someone injured from the mountains. At the back of the pack was a smaller figure with a tow head. Perry, he realized, and a good pain gripped his heart. The boy was grinning and waving.

Patrick shook his head. A rush of pride made his eyes water. His son, his little boy, was not so little anymore. He averted his face so that Perry wouldn't see his tears.

He strode toward the group as they rode toward him.

Thirty seconds later, he could hear Perry shouting, "Are you okay, Dad?"

Patrick didn't know how to answer that question. He was fine, but with Loren's head injury, how Patrick was faring was irrelevant. But he made an OK sign with his thumb and forefinger.

Wes was close enough now to speak without yelling. "Hey, Doc. You ready to head back so Susanne can tell Perry and me what heroes we are for bringing you home alive?" His eyes were twinkling.

The thought of his beautiful wife and falling asleep in the warmth of her arms was dizzying. Patrick had always known mountain climbing was inherently dangerous, but he'd never experienced anything like this. His group could have perished over and over in the last twenty-four hours. Loren was lying unconscious at twelve-thousand-feet elevation in rough terrain. Whitney was sheltering him, but she was hurt, too. Patrick's mortality hung on him like a shroud. He'd have to think seriously about whether to continue with the sport. There'd be plenty of time to make up his mind about that later, though. Now, he had to try to get Loren off this mountain alive.

He swallowed back his fears and focused on the calm, measured confidence Loren and Whitney needed from him. "Thank God you're here. One of our group took a fall. A bad one. We need to get him down to the hospital."

"A fall from where? You're way off trail." This from the leader of the search and rescue group, Dale Douglas. The man had to be pushing seventy, but he was fit, tough, and had legendary experience in the Bighorns.

"It's a long story. Follow me." Patrick was already striding back toward where he'd left his companions.

# CHAPTER FIFTY-ONE: HIJACK

BUFFALO, WYOMING
*NOW:* FRIDAY, JUNE 23, 1978

*Trish*

TRISH LOWERED Will onto the pallet she'd made for him in her parents' room. The toddler was exhausting but fun. She'd chased him up and down their long first floor hallway about one hundred times. After dinner and a long, warm bath with lots of bubbles and the bath toys Ronnie had brought for him, Trish had read him two stories. He'd fallen asleep before the end of the second one. It was all she could do not to lay down beside him and sleep, too.

But she didn't. Because she had a date.

She left the door open a crack so she could hear Will if he cried, then went into the kitchen and sat by the phone. She had unplugged the phone in her parents' room so it wouldn't wake up Will when it rang. She stared at it for a few minutes. *Come on, Ben. Please call.*

Ferdinand whined at the back door. She got up and let him out.

She made herself a glass of cherry Kool-aid, which she still loved even if it was for kids. She paced. She stared out the window into the twilight. She cradled her head in her arms at the table, facing the phone.

And then it rang.

She jolted upright and grabbed the receiver. "Hello?" she said, forgetting to use the phone manners her parents insisted on.

"Trish?" That deep voice.

Tears welled in her eyes. "Ben. Yes, it's me."

His voice sounded thick. "Hey. It's, uh. It's been too long."

"It's just so good to hear your voice." She pressed her forehead against the cool glass of the window.

"I loved your letter."

"And I loved yours!"

He cleared his throat. His voice was soft. "I'm sorry, Trish. I really am."

She swallowed a lump in her throat. "I know. And I am, too. But none of that matters to me anymore now that you've called."

"Me, either."

"I've missed so much of your life. I want to hear all about it. Tell me about Alaska."

"Okay. It's pretty cool." Ben told her about his job on *Fishy Business*, the captain and crew, what it was like to live by the sea, and the funny people in his boardinghouse. "I eat a lot of salmon. I like it here. But I miss you."

"It sounds great. But I miss you, too."

"I want to hear all about you, too."

The thought of telling him about cheerleading meant Jillian. That made her think of Jimmy, Dabbo, and the gas station. She wanted to put that off. "Long distance is so expensive. Maybe I should write you a letter?"

"I'd like that. So, you're babysitting Will?"

"Yes. Mom and Ronnie are having a girls' night out at the Occidental for dinner. My dad is climbing a mountain. And Ronnie's husband Jeff is on a trip for his job."

Ben laughed. "Your mom? On a girls' night out?"

"I know! So funny!" It was good to laugh with him. New yet familiar. Comfortable but different.

"I want to figure out when we can see each other. But you're right. These calls are really expensive."

"I can call you back. So we split the cost."

He gave her his phone number, which she wrote down like the most precious note she'd ever taken, even though she already had it from her mom. Writing it in her own hand felt like a promise. "Okay, I'll just—"

The front door opened hard, banging against the inside wall. She turned, expecting to see Perry, or maybe Perry and his friends. To hear their laughter. To smell their sweaty post-practice bodies.

But it wasn't Perry. It was Jimmy, with Dabbo right behind him.

She lowered the phone and put it on the counter behind her, some instinct telling her to hide it. "You can't just barge in here."

"Looks like we did, though." Jimmy swaggered into the kitchen. "Jillian told us you'd be home. Does your pops keep any beer in the frigde?"

She shrunk back from him. "I told you never to come back here. You need to get out, now!"

Dabbo laughed. "Whoa, darling. You're hurting our feelings."

Ferdinand launched himself at the back door, barking and snarling. How she wished she hadn't put him out.

Jimmy pulled two glass bottles of beer out of the refrigerator and riffled through drawers until he found a bottle opener. He popped the caps off and handed one to Dabbo. "I assume you don't want one, Sandra Dee? Or maybe you do. Jillian told us you're not the goody two-shoes you pretend to be. Something about a bad boy. And here I thought you were into me."

"I'll never be into you. Leave or I'll call the cops. I swear I will."

"What, and admit you drove a gas station robbery getaway car? I don't think you will. But that's beside the point. We are leaving."

"Good."

"And you're coming with us."

Her whole body froze, cold and unmoving. "What? No, I'm not."

"We're not asking. We're telling. Because you're going to give us a hand tonight."

"A hand at what?"

"Ducane's Liquor Store is going to donate money to our escape fund. You're going to help."

"No. No I'm not. I won't!"

"Oh, yes you are."

She backed away, toward the door to the deck. If she could get outside she could make a run for it. They didn't know the area like her. Ferdinand would protect her. But Will... She hesitated, and it was enough for Dabbo to intercept her.

Dabbo laughed, blocking her exit. "You can make this easy or hard. Hard is more fun for us."

Jimmy grinned. "Good girl likes it rough, you think, Dabbo?"

Trish weighed her options. They seemed wilder than usual. Drunk or high or something. They were criminals that she had to keep away from Will. She couldn't call the police, but maybe Ben was still on the line and could hear her. Hear them. *And all the horrible things they'd said. What would he think?* If he could hear them, then he had the information to help her.

It was her only hope.

She raised her voice. "If I go with you to Ducane's now, will you bring me home when we're done?"

Dabbo leered at her. "When we're done with something."

She shuddered. What did Jillian see in him? He was disgusting.

Jimmy was suddenly on her. He grabbed her around the waist. She kicked and screamed and beat at him with her fists, but he carried her under his arm like she was weightless. "This isn't a negotiation. Dabbo, get the door."

Trish bit his shoulder, digging her teeth in through his t-shirt.

"Ow!" He threw her to the floor then straddled her, fist raised. "Enough. If you want to make this hard, we can. But we'll make it hard for everyone. That brat you put to bed in your parents' room when we were watching through the window. Your little brother. That ugly dog."

Trish screamed and flailed. "You can't do this." But her heart wasn't in it anymore. Jimmy and Dabbo were awful. She couldn't let them hurt the people she loved.

Jimmy's voice was smug. "Really? Cuz it looks to me like we just did."

# CHAPTER FIFTY-TWO: SUMMON

KETCHIKAN, ALASKA
*NOW*: FRIDAY, JUNE 23, 1978

*Ben*

"TRISH? TRISH!" Ben screamed into the phone but there was only silence on the other end of the phone. When those guys—Jimmy and Dabbo—had first burst in and she'd dropped the phone, he'd called her name, then he'd realized that what he needed to do was listen and not make noise that would cause her any trouble.

But now they'd taken her. The terror he felt was indescribable. Terror and hopelessness. What could he do?

"Ben?" Cleve was shaking him. "What's wrong, boy-o? You look like you've seen a ghost."

"My girlfriend. Trish. She was just kidnapped, while we were on the phone."

"What? Are you pulling my leg now?"

"No." He lifted his eyes to meet Cleve's intense gaze. "I wish I was, but I'm not."

"You'd better call the cops, then." He shook him again. "Call information and get them to connect you. Hurry, boy."

Ben knew another number by heart, though. Marcy. Trish's best friend. He'd called Trish there so many times that it was burned into his brain. He thought about his juvenile delinquent reputation back in Buffalo because of his family and his time in juvie. Better for Marcy to call the cops than him. "I've got a better idea."

"Whatever it is, do it fast."

He nodded then hung up the phone and dialed Marcy's number as Cleve watched him.

"Hello-oo. This is Marcy. Who's this?" Marcy's voice was high-spirited.

"Marcy, this is Ben, calling with an emergency."

"Who?"

"Ben Jones. I need to talk fast."

"Oh, my God! Ben! What's wrong?"

"I was on the phone with Trish and these two guys burst in and—and they kidnapped her. Their names were Jimmy and Dabbo."

"What?! They took Trish? She knew they were bad news."

Ben's mind tried to go back to the strange conversation he'd overheard and all the questions it had left in his mind, but he couldn't let it. He had to stay on track. "They're taking her to rob Ducane's Liquor Store. But listen—Trish said her mom is with Deputy Ronnie at the Occidental. Could you call the police and then go find her and Mrs. Flint?"

"I was just about to leave to go out with my boyfriend. But I'll go. I'll go now."

"Call the police first, Marcy."

But Marcy had already hung up the phone.

# CHAPTER FIFTY-THREE: MAN-UP

BUFFALO, WYOMING
*NOW:* FRIDAY, JUNE 23, 1978

*Perry*

PERRY HERDED his football buddies around the Flint house and through their backyard. "This is an outdoor-only event, you guys."

"What if I have to take a leak?" Chuck said.

That drew laughs from the other guys.

"Plenty of trees out here and bushes along the creek."

Chuck burped long and loud enough to wake the dead, much less Will who Perry knew was asleep inside. "Cool. And you promise this is where that chick died?"

"It's where my dad found her anyway."

"That's crazy, man."

What was crazy was bringing these guys to his house. Perry had wanted to do something to show he could still be cool and hang out with them, even if he wasn't drinking. So, he'd promised them a tour of the infamous site where his dad had found Whitney. The guys swore they'd leave in an hour, before his mom was due to be home. They said they understood this was just show-and-tell with bring-your-own-brewskies. But if they got too drunk, would he really be able to get them to leave? He was their babysitter. He wasn't imposing enough to be their bouncer. And even if Perry was sober his mom wouldn't like it that everybody else was drinking. One of the juniors crushed a beer can and tossed it into the yard. *I need time to clean up after them, too.*

Maybe this had been a bad idea.

"So, is it true your mom killed her because she was..." Chuck made a lewd thrusting motion with his hips, ". . . with your dad?"

Perry's fists balled. "None of that is true."

"But she was murdered. That's what it said in the paper. And she was fine. I saw the pictures."

Perry didn't bother answering. He took a few deep breaths, trying to manage his temper. Forget what his mother thought. He was probably going to have to bust someone in the chops soon if they kept talking about his parents like that. If she didn't ground him, he'd end up in jail.

Yes, this had really been a bad idea.

# CHAPTER FIFTY-FOUR: HUNKER

Cloud Peak Wilderness, Bighorn Mountains, Wyoming
*Now:* Friday, June 23, 1978

*Patrick*

It was mid-afternoon before Patrick and Wes reached Mistymoon Lake and set their packs on the rocky ground. The summit loomed over them.

"Think we should push on?" Wes said.

Patrick calculated the hours left in the climb. He flexed his hand. The swelling wasn't too bad. He had decent movement, and he could tolerate the pain.

"You're talking to yourself, Doc."

"Yeah, I needed to consult with the smartest man on the mountain."

Wes snorted. "And what did he tell you?"

"It'll take us several hours to get to the cave. It won't be easy." Patrick pointed at patches of snow up the rocky mountainside.

"Now that we're here, do you think you can find your way up?"

Patrick slow nodded. He actually felt more confident about the route. He drew it with his finger in the air. "Yeah. I think so."

"We've got the advantage of facing the sunset. It's going to be light up here for another five or six hours. I think we've got time. Camping in a cave would be far out, too."

Patrick raised his eyebrows. Hearing his Wyoming friend say far out was comical. "Or we could get stuck halfway up there just as we're losing light."

"Nah. We'd have time to turn around if things looked bad."

Patrick had reached the opposite conclusion in his own mind. He'd told Susanne that he and Wes would overnight at Mistymoon Lake if they were running low on light. Camping at a lower elevation was the conservative thing to do. Still, Wes wasn't wrong.

"C'mon, Sawbones. Worst case scenario, we come back here to sleep. Best case, we make it much quicker tomorrow."

Patrick couldn't argue with the logic. "Fine. But if we're doing it, we need to quit jawing and burning daylight."

Wes pulled two sandwiches from his pack and tossed one to Patrick. "Can you walk and chew sandwich at the same time?" He shrugged his pack back on like it was empty and strode out.

Patrick struggled into his and jogged a few steps to catch up, nearly choking on PB&J in the process. He sent up a silent prayer. *Okay, Big Guy. I'm on the side of the angels here. Show us the way.*

# CHAPTER FIFTY-FIVE: STAKE

Buffalo, Wyoming
*Now:* Friday, June 23, 1978

*Trish*

Trish tried to shrink into herself to avoid contact with Dabbo and Jimmy, but she was sandwiched in between them in the front seat, and she couldn't get any smaller. Their bodies were hot and humid. The El Camino smelled like sweat, beer, and pot. If there was a Hell, she was in it.

In some ways, it reminded her of the night a few years before when Ben's uncle and father had taken her from a campsite and dragged her up Dome Mountain. It had been awful. But Ben had been there. She'd ridden on horseback with him to the remote campsite. Even though he hadn't let her go, he'd been nothing like Dabbo and Jimmy. He'd wanted to help her. He'd felt terrible about what his family was doing and tried to protect her. In the end, he'd told the truth to the cops about what they'd done, too, and paid a big price for not much more than being born into the wrong family.

Ben was a good person. Jimmy and Dabbo were losers. Dangerous losers. They'd even threatened to kill Ferdinand unless she put him in the garage where he couldn't attack them as they left with her. He'd howled like a demon as Dabbo had driven away with her in the car.

Now, Dabbo swerved to park across the street from Ducane's Liquor Store.

"You don't have to do this," Trish said.

Jimmy jabbed her in the ribs with his elbow. She held in a yelp. No way was she showing any more weakness in front of them. "Nice try."

Dabbo switched off the engine. "We just need to wait for the right moment. When there ain't no potential heroes shopping in the store."

Trish was relieved they didn't plan to put customers at risk. It wasn't much, but it was something. But after fifteen long minutes with a steady stream of customers, the atmosphere in the car grew tense. More tense.

Jimmy said, "This is bull crap. Maybe we just need to call it a night."

"And what—wait for the police to find us while we cram the three of us into that shitty sheep trailer on your uncle's ranch? It's bad enough with just you," Dabbo said.

"You can sleep outside. Trish and I need some alone time." He drew out the word alone and made it sound disgusting.

*We most definitely do not.* If it came to that, she'd fight like a demon.

"Are you turning pansy on me, Jimmy?"

"Someone's going to notice us out here. I don't want to get caught."

Trish watched as a pair of customers exited the store. The two guys were laughing, and one socked the other in the shoulder.

Seconds later, they were in their truck, backed out, and drove off, leaving the parking lot empty. She kept silent. Maybe Dabbo and Jimmy were arguing too much to notice.

"What do you think, Sandra?" Jimmy said. "Want to get out of here?"

She did because she didn't want to be the getaway driver for a liquor store robbery. She didn't because she dreaded what they'd try to do to her next. If they went ahead with the robbery, she could drive off and leave them. Or run to the nearest store and hide in the bathroom.

"Well, well," Dabbo said. "Looks like it's batter up time. The store's empty. You guys ready?"

Jimmy thumped his chest. "Born that way. Sandra?"

"Me?" Trish squeaked.

"You didn't think we'd leave you out here alone?" He snorted. "You'd be off like a shot."

She licked her lips, terrified now that her escape plan was off the books. Well, she'd just have to come up with a new one.

# CHAPTER FIFTY-SIX: ALARM

Buffalo, Wyoming
*Now:* Friday, June 24, 1978

*Susanne*

After a no-thank-you bite of the fried Rocky Mountain oysters Ronnie ordered at the Occidental Restaurant, Susanne finished telling the deputy her story. The whole story, leaving nothing out, and building up to the isolation of Patrick and Wes up on Cloud Peak. How there were some very motivated people—guilty of conspiring to traffic in stolen antiquities, if not murder—potentially aware of where they were and what they were doing.

"I can't involve the Buffalo police, for obvious reasons," Susanne said, subtly pushing the plate of bull testicles closer to her friend. She looked away. Anywhere but at the unappetizing appetizer that she could swear smelled like the animals they'd come from. The restaurant had preserved an old west feel with the décor. And what passed for a fancy restaurant back then meant aged wooden tables with cloths draping over them. Flickering candles. Paintings of genteel scenes rather than cattle drives. Lace doilies. Chairs with spindly legs.

Ronnie wiped her mouth. "It's outside their area anyway. County is the way to go. Us or Big Horn, since they're on the Big Horn County side of the mountains. No one will be able to get up there tonight. I'll mobilize someone to go with me first thing tomorrow morning, right after we finish dinner, all right?"

Susanne felt a fluttering sensation. A lessening of the weight on her spirit. She would have preferred earlier, but she knew that it wouldn't help Patrick and Wes to send officers into an unnecessarily dangerous situation. "Thank you."

"And after that—well, it may be time to call the feds. Trafficking stolen antiquities that may belong to a foreign government falls far outside Wyoming's jurisdiction."

Susanne wondered if she could trust federal law enforcement any more than local. Present company the exception, of course.

The door to the restaurant banged open. An agitated young female voice was demanding the hostess let her in to see Ronnie and Susanne. Susanne frowned. The voice was familiar.

"I'm not joining them. I have a message for them."

Susanne craned her neck to get a look. It wasn't just the voice she recognized but also the face.

"I'll pass it along for you," the hostess said. She sounded pleasant but firm.

Susanne stood so quickly she spilled the Chablis glasses. "Marcy—what is it?"

The hostess turned to Susanne. "I'm so sorry for the interruption, Mrs. Flint."

Susanne motioned Marcy over, ignoring the hostess.

"Mrs. Flint. Deputy Harcourt." Marcy gulped in a shuddering breath. "Ben just called me. He was on the phone with Trish when two guys came in the house and took her."

Susanne gasped. "The ones who got Whitney."

Marcy shook her head. "I don't know about that. It was Jimmy Gross and Dabbo Kern. They're friends of Jillian's."

"But why..."

Ronnie drew two twenties out of her wallet and dropped them on the table. "Does he know where they were taking her?"

Marcy nodded vigorously. "Ducane's Liquor Store. They were going to rob it. They were forcing her to help them."

"This doesn't make sense," Susanne said. Why would someone kidnap Trish to drag her into a crime?

"Tell us more on the way."

"Are you taking us to Ducane's?" Marcy's eyes were wide.

"No. The Flints first to drop you guys off. Someone has to take care of my child."

Susanne gasped. "Will!"

"Ben didn't say anything about him. That's good, right?" Marcy's eyes were huge.

Ronnie flashed her badge at the hostess. "Emergency. Our apologies. I left payment on the table." As she led Susanne and Marcy out, she broke into a run and called over her shoulder, "I don't know anything except that we need to get there as fast as we can."

Susanne grabbed Marcy's hand. *Trish. My baby girl has been taken.* She pulled the girl into a run and chased after Ronnie.

---

SUSANNE WAS REELING from the bombshells Marcy was dropping on the drive home.

"Jillian pulls the wool over most people's eyes." Marcy was leaning over the seat back between Ronnie and Susanne. "But she's not a nice person. She tricked Trish into going on a blind date with Jimmy last weekend. And then Jimmy and Dabbo robbed that gas station and forced her and Jillian into helping them get away."

Susanne gasped. Ronnie reached across the front seat and took Susanne's hand in hers.

"Trish has been, like, sooo scared about it ever since. She's scared of Jimmy and Dabbo, but she's also scared she'll get in trouble too which would ruin her chances for scholarships and stuff."

Susanne put her fist to her mouth, holding in sobs. Her daughter had been scared and hadn't confided in her. She was keeping secrets. Big ones. And pretty poor company. It was beyond disturbing. It was heartbreaking. And now those horrible men had her, which was *terrifying*.

Ronnie turned into the Flint's driveway. Several trucks—only Trish's belonging to a Flint—were parked in the driveway.

"Who are all these people at our house?" Susanne said.

"With my little boy." Ronnie threw open her door and was out almost before she'd put the vehicle in park. She left the motor running.

Susanne and Marcy once again ran after Ronnie. Susanne could hear laughter and shouting coming from the backyard. She was torn whether to follow her ears or to get inside. But Will was more important than whatever was going on out there. As was the possibility that Trish was inside or had left a note or clue. And then she heard another sound. Howling. Deep, wolf-like, hair-raising. It was coming from the garage. *Ferdinand!* She'd go see about him as soon as they checked on Will and looked for Trish.

"Trish made a pallet for Will in my bedroom," Susanne said as they entered.

Ronnie sprinted down the hallway.

Susanne was right behind, shouting. "Trish? Are you here? Trish?" She didn't expect an answer, but it was still crushing not to get one.

Ronnie threw open the bedroom door and was kneeling on the carpet crooning when Susanne reached the room. "Shh, my sweet boy. There you are. Go back to sleep. I love you."

Susanne stopped in the doorway, emotions warring inside her. Relief that Will was okay and panic about Trish.

Ronnie stood, a finger to her lips. Will rolled over, made a sleepy sound, then sighed. Ronnie pulled the door shut. "I need you to keep Will for me."

"Maybe Marcy could? I want to go with you to get Trish."

"You can't. And I need an adult here. Not a teenage girl. Not with everything going on."

Susanne's insides churned. She hated it. And Ronnie was right. "Okay. I've got him."

"I need to call this in. Then check the area by the phone."

They moved quickly to the kitchen. Ronnie made her call. Perry was coming in the door from the deck with Marcy.

"Mom, I can explain." Perry frowned "Is that Ferdie howling? Where is he?"

"Garage, I think. Just tell me what's going on," Susanne said. "Did you see Trish?"

"I never saw her. I saw her truck and thought she was inside with Will. And my friends are loud. I guess that's why I didn't hear Ferdie. I'm really sorry, Mom."

Susanne advanced on her son. "Are you drunk?"

"No. I'm not drinking."

"Good. Check on Ferdie and let him out. Then get your friends to leave. Take my car and give Marcy a ride back to her car, then come straight back."

"I don't have a license." He jerked his head at Ronnie.

Ronnie didn't look up from her search of the kitchen and dining area. "I won't tell if you won't."

Perry looked like he would give his mom another argument. His jaw worked a few times. His Adam's apple bobbed. Then he said, "Yes, ma'am," and headed for the garage.

Marcy bit her lip. "Thank you. Keep me posted, okay?"

"I will."

"And someone should call Ben. He was panicked."

Susanne nodded. “I will.”

Ferdinand came scrambling into the kitchen. His eyes were wide and wild. He was slobbering in long strands of drool. He didn’t stop to greet Susanne, just ran frantically around the house.

*He’s searching for Trish.* It was the last straw for Susanne’s battered emotions. She sank into a chair at the kitchen table, her legs no longer strong enough to hold her up.

Marcy and Perry called their goodbyes and left through the back door.

Ronnie finished up her search, shaking her head. “Nothing here, unfortunately. I’ve got to go.”

“Find my baby, please.” Susanne’s voice broke.

“I will. And keep mine safe.”

Susanne nodded, holding back tears as Ronnie left. *Dear God, help her bring my daughter back to me.*

The house had never felt so empty.

# CHAPTER FIFTY-SEVEN: FLIGHT

Buffalo, Wyoming
*Now:* Friday, June 23, 1978

*Trish*

Dabbo was swinging his bat in a circle by his side, narrowly missing liquor bottles on either side of him. Jimmy stood beside Dabbo pointing a gun at the wide-eyed cashier who was standing behind the checkout counter.

"Put every cent you've got in the girl's bag. Her name is Trish Flint. Her daddy is a bigwig in town, but she's in love with my friend here and has taken to a life of crime," Dabbo said, then snickered.

Jimmy gave Trish a shove with his free hand. She stumbled behind the front counter, near the scared, skinny man. She held out a bag, hands shaking. She wanted to argue with Dabbo. She wanted to explain that Dabbo was a big liar to the cashier. Most of all, she wanted to apologize that this was happening to him. She couldn't do any of it, though, and tears began rolling down her cheeks.

The cashier turned to her, holding the cash register drawer. His splotchy face was ashen. He dumped the money into the bag. Coins rattled. Some of them fell to the floor. Trish looked down as a quarter rolled under a cigarette display case.

His eyes met hers. "Are you okay?" he mouthed. His face was turned away from Jimmy and Dabbo.

He was being held up, and he was worrying about her. She prayed they didn't hurt him. He was such a nice guy.

She acted like she was glancing at the back of the store. "No," she breathed.

"Hurry up," Jimmy shouted. "Is there any more cash?"

"N-n-n-no, sir."

"Get down on the floor then. Hands over the back of your head. Don't move for five minutes. If you stand up, I'm coming back and blowing your damn head off. Maybe not tonight. Maybe not here. Our surprise reunion will just be something for you to look forward to." He waved the gun at the cashier and Trish.

The cashier was frozen in place, still holding the drawer. His eyes darted around like he was trying to think of a way to fight back.

Jimmy screamed, "Now, dumb-ass! Get on the floor! And Trish, move that pretty little tush. You're driving."

The cashier lowered himself to the ground. He turned to Trish at the last second. He mouthed, "I'll call the police."

She didn't dare acknowledge him save for one dip of her head. She backed away, every step closer to Jimmy and Dabbo making her skin crawl more.

"You first," Jimmy said.

She ducked her head and exited the store, very aware of the bat and gun in the hands of Dabbo and Jimmy behind her.

As soon as they were outside, Dabbo whooped and whipped his bat in a circle over his head. It made dangerous rushing sounds as it cut through the air. "Like taking candy from a baby." He started to run toward the El Camino. Jimmy ran up behind Trish and poked her between the shoulder blades. She broke into a jog with the jangling bag bouncing off her legs. It was heavy. *It's going to leave bruises.*

"Trish, we're just like Bonnie and Clyde and... their ugly sidekick," Jimmy said.

Dabbo snorted. "Funny, man."

At the car, Dabbo hopped in the backseat this time. He positioned his bat over the front seat. Trish gripped the steering wheel, the bat uncomfortably close to her ear. Jimmy turned to her from the passenger side, gun pointing lazily at her feet.

She closed her eyes. *If only this was just a bad dream.* "Why am I the one driving?"

"So we can duck out of sight. You taught us this last time. They're looking for two dudes and a girl. Not one girl."

"Plus we can say you were holding us hostage," Jimmy said, laughing.

"And we can ditch you if we're caught. All good stuff."

Trish was sorry she'd asked. "Where do you want me to go?"

"We've got money for a nice mo-tel now. Let's drive on up to Billings for a fun night and see which way feels right tomorrow." Jimmy leered at her, waggling his eyebrows and doing something weird and disgusting with his tongue.

She couldn't bring herself to look at him. "Can you... can you drop me off at the edge of town? I helped you."

"Drive, Trish." Dabbo thumped the bat on the seat. "No more talking."

She swallowed back a huge lump in her throat. Her eyes were burning, but she didn't dare cry. She had to be able to see where she was going. Turning on the blinker, she accelerated onto the road.

"Look at how good you're doing, sweet thing. Following all the traffic laws so you don't draw attention to us." Jimmy reached over and squeezed the bare skin of her knee.

She flinched, wishing she had on jeans instead of shorts.

"A little jumpy though. You need to get that under control. Or maybe not. It might be fun later."

Headlights appeared in her rearview mirror.

"Let's take the back way out of town," Dabbo said. "I want to stop at your uncle's place and grab a few things, Jimmy."

"Fine by me. Turn left here, Trish."

As Trish turned, she watched her mirror. It was a deputy's truck. A Johnson County deputy. Somehow, she had to get the deputy's attention.

But how?

# CHAPTER FIFTY-EIGHT: TUMBLE

CLOUD PEAK WILDERNESS, BIGHORN MOUNTAINS, WYOMING
*NOW*: FRIDAY, JUNE 23, 1978

*Patrick*

"TELL me we're going the right way, Sawbones," Wes panted.

Patrick hammered a piton into the rock. "Trust me. I'm a veritable homing pigeon." He had been putting in the pegs as they ascended to create a climbing anchor to clip their lines on and arrest any falls. He didn't want either of them to put it to the test.

Some climbers wouldn't have bothered with the climbing anchors as the rock Patrick remembered descending nine months before wasn't completely vertical. He wasn't taking any chances, though.

Wes had more rock-climbing experience than Patrick, but neither of them was an expert—something they'd proved to themselves last summer on a guys' weekend to the Tetons where they'd chickened out of an attempt on the Grand Teton after a scary fall on an easier route up Disappointment Peak. Their dual dive had been farther than they'd anticipated, because two of their pins had come out of the rocks. Luckily, neither of them had been hurt seriously. Some scrapes and bruises for them both in a fall that could have killed them. At the time, Wes said it had proven to him that man was not made to fly. Both of them felt the need to change their underpants afterwards. But Patrick felt like that fall had made them smarter. And today, they were determined not to repeat history.

Besides, if Patrick took them off course, who knew what they'd encounter. They could end up needing the climbing anchors. *Safety first, always.*

"Prove it. Tell me where we're going."

"Up." Truthfully, Patrick wasn't one hundred percent sure the path he'd mapped by eyeballing the edifice above them would land them on the ledge to the cave. But it felt familiar. And he was certain they'd started at the right spot. The bell-shaped rock had imprinted on his brain when he'd tended to Loren after the younger man's tragic fall.

But he couldn't let his mind stray back to that. To what unforgiving rock did to the relatively fragile human cranium.

Wes grunted. Patrick took off and climbed like a geriatric version of Spider Man, keeping three points of body contact on rock at all times, one of those points painful enough to keep him alert. He'd kept his hiking boots on since this was as much steep bouldering as rock climbing, but he'd opted to shed his gloves for better feel and grip on the rocks, going so far as to unwrap his bum hand to remove the glove under the bandage. He'd tested the fingers and hand. They weren't too awful, so he'd rewrapped the bandage.

Of course, now his hands were like clubs of ice with the broken one pounding.

He stopped to hammer in a piton, rubbing his hands together and blowing on his fingers first.

Then he raised his body slowly up the boulders for a few yards and stopped to hammer in another peg for the climbing anchor.

Coached himself to ignore the pain. Repeated the process. Repeated it again. Over and over until his shoulders and thighs were quivering and his mental instructions weren't doing anything to quiet the internal scream from every new grip of his injured hand. The western sun at his back was like a laser. Sweat trickled down his neck.

He used his sleeve to wipe perspiration off his forehead before it ran into his eyes. "If we don't reach the trail in fifteen minutes, we're going to have to go down."

"Agreed." Wes sounded out of breath, which was a first. It worried Patrick. To him, Wes was more machine than man when it came to handling altitude and exertion.

He set another peg then reached for a new handhold. He hauled himself up a few inches and looked to his right. He caught a glimpse of the trail along the ledge. *Hallelujah.* Further in the distance, he saw the cave. *Double hallelujah.* He hadn't led them wrong, and rest time was coming soon.

And then the rock beneath his hands shifted.

# CHAPTER FIFTY-NINE: SUSPEND

BUFFALO, WYOMING

*NOW:* FRIDAY, JUNE 23, 1978

*Susanne*

FIVE MINUTES after a herd of inebriated teenage boys had left, Susanne watched Perry drive away with Marcy from the window in the living room. She stood with one hand on Ferdinand's head. The dog was still clearly agitated. *You and me both, Ferdie.*

The phone rang. She ran to answer it. Ferdinand panicked and dove in front of her. She fell forward, knocking over one of the chairs and catching herself on the kitchen table. "Ferdie, back." Her command did no good. He pressed his giant body against her leg.

"Hello?" Her voice was a shout into the receiver.

"Susanne, are you okay? It's Kathy." Kathy. Patrick's co-worker. Wes's girlfriend. Susanne's friend, more and more lately, although

Susanne felt odd about it now, given that Kathy and Whitney had been best friends.

"Oh, Kathy. No. I'm really not."

Kathy's voice registered surprise. Then concern. "What's the matter? Is it the guys?"

"Not really." She debated telling her about the predicament she suspected they could be in. She decided to stick with the more clear-cut topic first. "It's Trish. She was babysitting at our house. Two... thugs... showed up and took her."

"What? Your daughter was kidnapped?"

Susanne filled in the rest of the story quickly.

"Oh, my gosh! I can't believe this. But you know Ronnie will find her and bring her home."

*From her mouth to God's ear.* "Yes. Yes. I have to believe that."

"Would you like me to come over?" The sincere offer brought fresh tears to Susanne's eyes.

"You're so sweet. But I'll be okay. I'm just sitting by the phone and watching the door. And praying."

"Well, I can pray, too."

"Yes, please do."

"Have you heard from Patrick?"

"No. Patrick told me to expect this to be a two-day adventure."

"Yes. Wes told me that, too. Still, you know. I just thought I'd call and check in case they were home and still at your place."

Susanne sighed. She owed Kathy the truth, if for no other reason than she could use her prayers on that topic as well. She took a deep breath and then spilled the whole story. When she stopped, Kathy was speechless for a moment.

"Kathy? Are you there?"

"I am. I'm thinking. I—I'm going back through memories to see if Whitney gave me any clue these things were going on. And Susanne—she didn't. I had no idea."

"I'll admit I was hoping that if I told you, you'd realize you knew something that would help."

"She'd been excited about coming into money lately but secretive. I'd seen her less. I'd chalked that up to my relationship with Wes, though. And Egyptian artifacts from King Tut's tomb?" She laughed mirthlessly. "That's about the last thing I would have guessed was going on with her."

"I'm worried about Patrick and Wes. People know they're up there. If the guys after this breastplate try hard enough, they'll figure it out. I told Ronnie about it, before all this happened with Trish. She said she'll go up there in the morning with another deputy."

"Do you think this is related – Trish and Whitney's... treasures?"

It had never crossed Susanne's mind. She put her forehead in her palm. "I honestly don't see how it could be. Other than through this cruel twist of fate. Too many bad things happening at once."

"Ronnie going won't be a priority compared to Trish's situation."

Air seeped out of Susanne's lungs. She hadn't thought of that. So many cues her exhausted, stressed brain wasn't processing well. "Oh, my gosh. You're right. Normally, I'd call Wes in this situation. Honestly, the fact that it's Wes with Patrick is what I've been hanging onto for comfort. Patrick is always telling me there's no one he'd rather bring to a rockslide or a knife fight."

"He is pretty amazing. They'll be fine. And Ronnie will make sure someone checks on them."

"You know what? I'll see if Henry Sibley will go after them. Just to be on the safe side."

"Great idea!" For all her earlier confidence, Kathy sounded relieved.

Perry was suddenly standing directly in front of Susanne. She jumped back, startled. He'd walked right in without her even hearing him. If he had been anyone else—well, she didn't even want to think about it. *I'm not at my best. I am so far from my best.*

"Send Henry after who? When and where?" His serious face and the lower pitch of his voice surprised her. He sounded like a young man. Not her little boy.

"Your dad and Wes. Up to Cloud Peak tomorrow morning."

"Because of that money you found?"

"Yes. Because of all of the stuff related to that."

Perry nodded, his mouth in a firm line. "Okay. I'll go with Henry."

"That's not a good idea."

"Yes, Mom. I know the way to where they're going. I went with the group last September, when Dad and Whitney got stuck up there with the other guy that fell. Henry wasn't there. He doesn't know the way."

Perry's logic was actually sound. And Henry wouldn't let anything happen to him. "Maybe."

"I'll call Henry when you're off the phone. And then I'll get geared up. I'll have to get Dad's guns ready."

In her ear, she heard Kathy say, "Oh, my. He's all grown up."

She ignored Kathy. "You're going a little overboard with the guns."

He shook his head. "You and dad made sure I know how to handle guns and shoot good. Plus, you taught us to always be prepared. Henry and I have to be prepared. Otherwise, why are you bothering sending us up there?"

Again, his logic held up. But that didn't change the fact that he was fourteen and it made her nervous. "I'll call Henry. He can make the call."

"Okay. But tell him I want the horse I rode this week. Duke is great but he's not as tough. This is a hard ride."

She rolled her lips together to keep from blubbering like a baby. Literally, it felt like she was watching Perry transform into a grown man before her eyes. It was wonderful. And, she wasn't ready for it. Not at all. "Kathy, I'll call you when I know more."

"Please, do. And I'll keep praying."

Susanne depressed the phone hook for a few moments then let it go. When she had a dial tone, she called Henry.

# CHAPTER SIXTY: AWE

CLOUD PEAK WILDERNESS, BIGHORN MOUNTAINS, WYOMING
*NOW*: FRIDAY, JUNE 23, 1978

*Patrick*

PATRICK SAW SKY, then heard clattering rocks and his own breath expelled with force as his body slammed into rock and shirred off it. Then he was spinning and careening into Wes. By the time he had a chance to be scared, the two of them were balanced against the steep rock, both holding the line with two hands. Neither of them spoke. Everything grew quiet except their heavy breathing. He just thought his muscles had been quivering before. Now his whole body was shaking so violently it was making him nervous about losing his grip.

After a few seconds, Patrick thought about the weight of their bodies on the climbing anchor and pins. After their experience on Disappointment Peak, he didn't want to trust them a second longer than he had to.

He found a handhold, then a foothold. Then he dug his fingertips into a crevice and shoved his toe into another. *Better.* Then he remembered he had a broken hand, because it reminded him. Funny, terror had been the best painkiller yet, even if the effect hadn't lasted all that long.

"What were you doing, trying to go back down? That fifteen more minutes wasn't up, Sawbones." Wes's face telegraphed exhaustion, but his grin was in place as he re-established his own contact with terra firma. "But I do admire a quick descent."

Patrick was sure his own face looked worse. In fact, it stung and ached from where he'd broken his fall with his cheek. "It will take fifteen minutes just to wrap my head around nearly dying."

"You stare death in the face every day."

"Other people's deaths. By the way, I wasn't trying to cause yours." Patrick put his doctor's hat on and gave Wes a once-over. He didn't look like the falling rock had done him any damage.

"Could have fooled me."

"I have some good news. I was in eyesight of the cave before my position gave way."

"Whoa, boy. Am I ever happy to hear that! Time to climb and get this over with!"

Patrick eyed the pitch above them. He needed to end up near to but not exactly in the same place. He decided he didn't need to reset the pins to achieve his goal, just hammer in one more near the top. He blew all the air out of his lungs several times, then sucked in good clean oxygen and lifted his foot. *Here goes nothing.*

Five minutes later, he and Wes were standing side-by-side, looking back out over Mistymoon Lake.

Patrick leaned on his knees with one hand. He put the other atop his head, letting blood drain back out of it. "That was anticlimactic, and I'm damn happy about it."

"You and me both. Helluva view from this angle." Wes shook his head in amazement.

The lake's surface reflected a perfect replica of the brilliant sunset in orange, reds, golds, and purple far below. Treetops, pristine patches of snow, and the amazing perspective of land falling away in a steep jumble of rock. Patrick felt almost like he could fly. "We've definitely got the penthouse apartment for the night." He unclipped from the climbing anchor rope and slipped out of his gear.

Wes did the same, then Patrick led him to the cave.

"It's low-ceilinged in front, as I recall, but it opens up inside. Follow me." Patrick retrieved a flashlight from his pack, then turned it on and pushed the pack inside ahead of him. He crawled after it, grabbed it, and rose to his knees in the chamber. He shone the light around the walls. It was his first really good look at it. He'd been too knackered on his last visit. He didn't even remember using a flashlight. Just drinking and sleeping. He did have memories of flashes of light from Whitney and Loren. *Flashlight.* Then another thought struck him. *Or camera.* Whitney had brought a camera and taken pictures at the summit. Maybe in here, too.

There was the noise of grunting and the rustling of blue jeans against a dirty rock floor. Then Wes was beside him, still on his hands and knees.

"Tight squeeze for a skyscraper like me," he said.

"As I recall, Whitney and Loren went even further in, through there." Patrick gestured to the darkest spot in the wall, which, as his eyes adjusted, morphed from dark spot to passageway leading away, deeper into the mountain. "I just collapsed out here and slept."

"Why don't you check it out, and I'll guard the door."

"I'm sensing claustrophobia."

"Is that a big fancy word that means enclosed places scare the pants off me? If so, yes."

Patrick chuckled. "I have an idea. Why don't I check it out and you set up dinner?"

"That works."

Patrick ducked through the passage, which was lower than the antechamber, but not as low as the crawlspace into the cave from the outside ledge. He passed through it bent over. He played the light around ahead of him. It was only a few yards before the ceiling rose and the walls opened onto a chamber, larger both in height and width than the one before it.

Then he sucked in a quick, amazed breath.

It wasn't the size of the room that astounded him. It was the sight before him. A sight he'd half hoped, and half dreaded seeing.

A human skeleton—still partly dressed in tattered clothes—listed in a seated position facing the passageway. Patrick stepped closer. A backpack bearing the teeth marks of small rodents lay a few feet away from the skeleton. A crack in the skull and several large, loose stones nearby, one with a dark and ominous stain. From the relaxed posture of the skeleton, it was most likely a natural cause of death from a fallen rock. A stunning golden oval was strapped across the remains of a flannel shirt. It was studded with gemstones that glittered in his flashlight beam. He shook his head, only half believing what he was seeing. And it was ringed with Egyptian characters that looked strikingly familiar to the ring Perry had found in the bag of money the night before.

He sank to his haunches, elbows on thighs, and cradled his face, staring in wonder at this stunning object lost in time and space.

# CHAPTER SIXTY-ONE: LIBERATE

BUFFALO, WYOMING
*NOW*: FRIDAY, JUNE 23, 1978

*Trish*

TRISH WATCHED the deputy vehicle behind them out of the corner of her eyes. She'd had a few seconds to think about how to get the attention of the deputy without getting herself killed in the process. She turned off her headlights.

"Hey! What are you doing?" Dabbo said.

"Sorry!" She jerked the steering wheel like she was disoriented, then turned the headlights back on. "I'm nervous with a bat against my head and a gun pointed at me."

"A slight exaggeration, but I get your point." Dabbo moved the bat closer to center of the seat. "Jimmy." He mashed his hand downward.

Jimmy sighed and made a show of putting the gun in his lap, although it was still pointed in Trish's general direction.

Trish stepped on the brakes. "Sorry! Sorry! I was trying to slow down. I don't want to get pulled over for speeding."

"Shit. If you can't get it together, you're going to need to pull over and let one of us drive," Jimmy said.

"I've got it. I'm okay." She accelerated a little too quickly to regain a normal driving speed but then let off the gas and stayed five miles below the fifty-five-miles per hour limit. She snuck a look in the rearview. The distance between them and the deputy vehicle had grown, but it was making the left turn after them. She felt along the steering column for the hazard button that was supposed to be there if this car was anything like the one Marcy's mom drove. *Yes. Found it.* Then she scanned the controls until she found the air conditioner.

She drove normally for a moment. "I need air conditioner."

"It's not hot in here," Jimmy said. "Except for me, and that's not something an air conditioner can fix."

"It's probably just my nerves, but it's making me dizzy." She set the air conditioner to full blast then turned on the hazard lights as she brought her hand back to the steering wheel. "Do you want radio?"

"Don't touch my dials, sweetness." Jimmy flipped on the radio to a station that was blasting a hard rock band singing about climbing a stairway to heaven.

Between the noise of the radio and the air conditioner, Trish felt sure the guys wouldn't hear the click-click-click of the flashers. Which had been her goal. But there was definitely a pulsing light emitting from Dabbo's car. She peeked in the mirror at the deputy. It had closed the following gap.

*Please turn on your light thingy and pull me over. Please please please.*

Like the deputy was on the same secret wavelength as her, the wig wags came on, strobing blue. Not only was it a signal to pull over, it covered the light of her own hazard flashers. Not that she needed them anymore. They'd done their job.

Dabbo shielded his eyes from the reflection of the blue light in the rearview. "Shit. We've got a cop on our tail." He turned back to look at it. "Looks like it's time to floor it."

Trish didn't have to fake the fear in her voice. "What? No. I'm not a good enough driver for a high-speed chase."

"He said floor it. Now, do it!" Jimmy yelled.

"Well, I'm putting my seat belt on first then." She did as she warned, then mashed down the accelerator. There was no way she was running from the deputy. What she needed was the perfect place to take the El Camino off the road. Something flat without a deep Wyoming ravine or boulder the size of the Rocky Mountains in their path. And she had better find it before she had to navigate any of the crazy curves she knew this road was famous for. A stretch ahead looked promising except for a barbed wire fence strung between metal t-posts. Well, a fence was better than a giant rock or a cliff. *I can do this. I can do this. I don't have a choice, so I can do this.*

She gripped the steering wheel as hard as she could with both hands then steered off the road.

"What the hell?" Jimmy screamed.

The terrain had looked flat, but nothing in Wyoming was truly flat or debris-free. The car went airborne. Jimmy's body flew upwards. Trish heard a loud sound as his head crunched into the ceiling. Then the El Camino landed like a dying elephant, crunching down on its shocks with a screech and a groan. Dabbo flew halfway across the front seat. Just as the car started to bounce up, the hood crumpled, and the car came to such a grinding halt that Trish knew they hadn't hit a t-post. Her head smashed into the steering wheel. *Boulder?* Glass shattered. Her head whipped backwards. The seat caught her by the neck, but it seemed like her head just kept going.

And then there was nothing but pings, pops, stillness, hisses, and a few moments where she lost her sense of reality.

She sat up, dazed. For a moment, she didn't know where she was or what had happened. Then it came rushing back. Jimmy and

Dabbo. The liquor store. The El Camino. Crashing into something completely unyielding.

She looked around her. She was alone. She looked down. Broken glass coated the front of her body. Red broken glass. She was bleeding. Out the front window, she caught a glimpse of Dabbo helping Jimmy off the hood of the car, slinging his friend's arm over his shoulder and half dragging him away. They disappeared into the darkness.

The driver's side door opened beside her. She gasped. Had they come back for her?

"Trish? Are you okay?"

Trish doubled over with relief, glass crunching. It was Ronnie. "I thought you were with Mom." Her voice came out in a thready whisper.

"Until Ben called Marcy. She came to find us."

The impact with the steering wheel had scrambled her brains. "Ben. Marcy. That's good. What happened?"

"You hit a very large boulder."

"I never saw it."

"The grass is already really tall. Can you get yourself out of the car?"

Trish nodded, wincing.

"Good you had on the seatbelt."

"I put it on so I could wreck on purpose." Trish's head was clearing and starting to hurt. She touched her forehead. *Ouch*

"That's my smart girl." Ronnie unbuckled her seat belt and gave Trish her hand. "Ready?"

A sudden panic gripped her. "Wait! Will!"

"He's fine. Your mom is with him."

"Thank goodness." Trish struggled out, with Ronnie's help. Broken glass rained from her clothing onto the floorboard and ground. When she was vertical, the world tilted and spun. Flashing lights in all directions. Her entire head throbbed. "I feel sick."

"I've got you."

Trish vomited. Strong hands held her by the waist. *Misery. Pure misery.* But she was safe. When the heaves ended, she stood again, becoming aware of the pasture stretching out before her toward the dark shadow of mountains in the distance. *Dad.* He was up there somewhere.

"If you're okay to walk, let's get you in my vehicle. I'll call for an ambulance. Then I have to go after them."

Trish started shuffling toward Ronnie's truck. "Jimmy and Dabbo."

"Yep."

"They robbed Ducane's. They made me help."

"Yep." Ronnie guided Trish into the passenger seat. Then she went around to the other side and radioed for help, first confirming their location. "Two white males have run from the scene of the accident on foot. The kidnap victim is in my vehicle. Send an ambulance. I'm going after the suspects." Ronnie holstered the mic. She looked at Trish. "Lock the doors."

"Jimmy and Dabbo. They were headed to XYZ Ranch. It belongs to Jimmy's uncle. They said they've been staying in a sheep wagon out there."

Ronnie nodded. "When I get back, we'll talk more."

Then she trotted off into the darkness. Trish leaned her head back against the headrest and closed her eyes.

---

IT HAD BEEN VERY LATE when Ronnie picked Trish up from the ER—where Trish had been cleaned up and her forehead stitched. Kathy was on shift and tended to her personally, carefully picking each sliver of glass out of Trish's skin and making sure she took the painkillers and antibiotic the on-call doctor prescribed. The doctor didn't think she had sustained a concussion, but he cautioned her mom on the phone of the symptoms to look for. The painkillers were helping, but her neck and back were as sore as her head now, and she felt each glass cut like stings from a hive of bees.

It was even later when Ronnie and Trish pulled up in front of the Johnson County Sheriff's Department. After midnight-type late. Trish's dad had always told her nothing good happened after midnight, at least based on his experience working big city emergency rooms when they'd lived in Irving, Texas. She had always thought he was just trying to scare her and Perry into good behavior. But in the last week, she'd had progressively worse experiences the later it had gotten. And when she looked back on her last year, there was a strong correlation to bad things and late hours. She wasn't going to admit it to her dad, but he might be on to something.

Trish was nervous as she took a seat. The two Buffalo cops who'd been after her mother sat across from her. The ones who had hassled her when she and Goldie were in the neighbor's backyard. Ronnie hadn't told Trish they'd be here. The two of them hadn't even had a chance to talk the incident through completely.

Ronnie moved to stand behind them and mouthed, "It will be okay."

Trish heard the door shut. She turned and saw her mother walk in. Tears sprang to her eyes. Relief was quickly followed by fear, though. Her mom was here because Trish needed her, but she was putting herself at risk with these cops. More risk than Trish faced.

Her mom sank into the chair beside her. She reached for Trish's hand under the table and gripped it hard.

Trish squeezed back. "Who's with Will?"

"Perry," her mom whispered.

"Thank you for coming."

Her mom smiled at her. "I'm so glad you're okay."

"Thanks to Ronnie."

Susanne nodded, and they both looked at the deputy.

Ronnie said, "Trish, this is Officer Appelt and Officer Welch."

"I've met them before," Trish said.

Ronnie walked to the head of the table where she leaned with hands splayed, palms down. "This evening, Trish Flint was kidnapped from her home by Jimmy Gross and Dabbo Kern. They coerced her into accompanying them into Ducane's Liquor Store, which they robbed, and into driving Dabbo's car away from the scene of the crime. I became involved because Trish was on the phone with Ben Jones at the time of the abduction, and he overhead the whole thing. He called her friend Marcy and asked for her help. Marcy tracked Mrs. Flint and me down. She told us that not only had Trish been taken, but that earlier in the week, she'd been on a blind date that had ended with the same young men robbing a gas station, which had scared Trish so badly that they were able to coerce her silence. Marcy told us the two men would be robbing Ducane's. Trish was injured in the incident and has spent the evening at the ER." She nodded at Trish. "Do I have that right?"

"Yes."

"Anything you would add?"

"I'm sorry I didn't turn them in after the gas station robbery. I was scared."

"Did you have anything to do with robbing the station?"

"No. Jillian and I were shocked when it happened. We thought they'd just stopped to put gas in Jimmy's car. But I did help them not get caught, because I didn't want to get in trouble with them. I know that's wrong. I understand I may be in a lot of trouble because of it. My parents raised me to tell the truth, even when it's hard."

"They raised you to the tell the truth even when it's hard?" Appelt said. "Hmm. Maybe that means your mother will tell us what she did to Whitney Saylor?"

Trish hung her head. She'd been afraid of this.

Ronnie pointed at him. "Out of line and off topic."

He raised his hands and looked away.

Ronnie nodded at her. "Thank you for your honesty, Trish. What happened next?"

Trish said, "Well, before tonight, Jimmy showed up at my house and was hassling me a few nights ago. Throwing stuff at my window and refusing to leave me alone. I told him I didn't ever want to see him again. Dabbo was with him. I told Jillian the same thing. Not about her. That I never wanted to see Jimmy again. Or Dabbo."

"Did you know they'd be coming to your house tonight?"

"No! And they literally carried me out of the house and threw me in the car. I fought, but they threatened Will. Your—Deputy Ronnie's—son. He was in my parents' bedroom because I was babysitting him."

"And then what happened?"

Trish stared Ronnie in the eyes, embarrassed to look at the male cops with what she had to say next. "They parked outside Ducane's. They talked about making me go to Billings with them after... afterwards. They said a lot of disgusting things they were going to do to me."

"I'm sorry."

"Then when the store was empty they made me go inside with them and hold a bag. Jimmy had a gun. Dabbo had a baseball bat. The same bat he used in the gas station robbery, I think. He had one then, too, anyway. The cashier was really scared but he was nice. He asked me if I was okay." She stopped and her lips trembled.

Ronnie turned to Appelt, then to the other cop. "For the record, I talked to the cashier, who called 911 after the robbery. He confirmed Trish was an unwilling participant."

Trish nodded. "Back at the car, they made me drive. As we were leaving, I saw a deputy's truck, so I started trying to attract attention. Going fast then slow. Stomping the brakes, turning off and on the lights. Then I turned on the air conditioner and radio so I could activate the hazards without them hearing it."

Ronnie smiled at her. "Which I saw, since it was me in the truck behind the El Camino she was driving." She looked from one Buffalo cop to the other. "I initiated pursuit, cautiously, since I suspected a kidnap victim was in the car with the suspects. After I put my lights on, the El Camino sped up. Then it ran off the road."

"I crashed on purpose. I hit my head pretty hard. Jimmy and Dabbo ran off. Then Ronnie came."

"I got Trish out of the car and determined she was stable. I put her in my vehicle, called for an ambulance, and went after the suspects."

Appelt held his hand up. "Thank you, Harcourt. Sounds like Trish is dead to rights for robbery of the gas station and obstruction of justice."

Susanne's palm smacked the table. "She's a seventeen-year-old girl who was involved against her will."

Appelt sneered at her. "What's your excuse?"

Ronnie stood. "Enough. Trish, did you give me information that might lead to the capture of Jimmy and Dabbo?"

"I think so. I told you that they said they'd been hiding out on Jimmy's uncle's ranch in a sheep wagon."

"The XYZ Ranch?"

"Yes. They told me they wanted to stop there to get their stuff before they split town. It's where we were headed before I wrecked Jimmy's car."

Ronnie nodded. "I've talked to the sheriff. Ducane's is outside the town limits of Buffalo, which normally falls into our jurisdiction. We won't be asking the county attorney to press charges against Trish, but we will be including kidnapping with armed robbery for Jimmy and Dabbo who are in county lock-up as we speak."

Trish sat forward. "You caught them?"

"Yes." Ronnie smiled at her. "And we got the money back for Ducane's."

Appelt sneered. "Good for the county. I'll be asking for charges against Miss Flint for the gas station robbery. A little time in juvie might overcome her bad parental influence. Or, who knows—as mature as she is, maybe she'll be tried as an adult."

Trish's heart sank. She had been a candidate for an academic scholarship. Would she even get to go to college? She clenched her teeth to keep from crying. She didn't want to give him the satisfaction.

Susanne jumped to her feet. "You're unbelievable."

Ronnie grabbed her elbow. "Susanne... "

Eli Welch shook his head. "I'll be opposing you, Appelt."

Appelt laughed. "The man of few words speaks."

"I'll have plenty to say to the chief. Just none of it will be about charging Ms. Flint."

Appelt glared at him.

Ronnie put a hand on Trish's shoulder. "Unless you're making an arrest, Appelt, we're out of here."

Deputy and Buffalo cop locked eyes for long seconds. They ticked off inside Trish's head, loud and sharp. Her headache was returning with a vengeance.

Finally, Appelt waved his hand in disgust. He stormed out of the room. Trish turned and threw her arms around her mother.

# CHAPTER SIXTY-TWO: PLEAD

BUFFALO, WYOMING
*NOW:* SATURDAY, JUNE 24, 1978

*Trish*

UNABLE TO SLEEP in the next morning between her headache and nerves, Trish stared at the phone like it was a rattlesnake. She put her hand out then pulled it back. She paced the kitchen, then returned to the phone. Went and got herself a glass of orange juice, drank it, then sat at the table, paralyzed. Finally, she whispered, "Just do it, dummy." She stood and snatched the receiver out of the cradle. She dialed the number she'd written down the night before.

A strange male voice answered. "Hello and isn't it a fine morning to be alive. What can I do for you?"

Startled by the cheerful greeting, Trish licked her lips, then said, "Um, I'm calling for Ben Jones?"

There was a pause. Then the friendly voice turned teasing. "Ben? That tall, dark, and handsome young man from Wyoming?"

"Yes."

"And you would be...?"

"Trish Flint."

"Trish Flint. I do believe I've heard him speak of you before. I'm at the front desk, but I thought I saw him headed down to breakfast. Let me see if I can find him." There was a clack like he'd dropped the phone on a hard surface. Then silence. For a long time. A bell dinged loudly, close to the receiver.

"Excuse me? Some help please?" someone said.

More time passed. There was an exasperated sigh. Then she heard male voices in the background.

"Yes, sir, what can I do for you?" It was the man who had answered the phone.

A second male voice said, "Finally. I've been waiting."

Scraping noises. Breath in the mouthpiece. "Hello?" Ben's voice.

Trish felt sick with apprehension. "Ben. It's me. Trish."

"I've been so worried! Are you okay?"

"I called you as soon as I could. A lot has happened."

"All I care about is that you're not hurt."

She took a deep breath. "I hope that's how you'll feel after I tell you the whole story."

"What do you mean?"

"Those guys. Dabbo and Jimmy. Last night. And before. It's a lot. It's not all good."

"Just tell me, Trish. Tell me everything."

But if she did, would it be the end of them? She closed her eyes and started at the beginning.

# CHAPTER SIXTY-THREE: DOUBLECROSS

Cloud Peak Wilderness, Bighorn Mountains, Wyoming
*Now:* Saturday, June 24, 1978

*Patrick*

Every muscle in Patrick's body ached and a good number of them were cramping, too. Those pains paled in comparison to his throbbing hand, though. Climbing in mud and snow was hard work, and he'd always hated down as much as he loved up. He and Wes had been pushing so hard since daybreak, they didn't even banter—not enough breath. They hadn't taken a single break in the two hours of their descent so far either. It was steep, technical, icy, and dangerous from the cave down to the lake—even with the climbing anchors they'd put up the day before—and required one hundred percent concentration.

Especially because Patrick didn't dare fall. He was carrying something arguably more valuable than his own skin and bones in his backpack, wrapped carefully in his sleeping bag and excess clothing items. Tucked inside with the bejeweled chest piece was a small weatherproof pouch from the back pocket of the skeleton's threadbare blue pants, too. It held a driver's license and some cash. The ID bore the name Ichabod Johnson. Closing out several elements of the mystery that had been dominating his and Susanne's life was satisfying, although it made Patrick hyperconscious of the immensity of the unresolved issues that kept him up half the night. Literally, life and death issues.

But now that they were back on the trail, his bladder was close to bursting. He didn't want to wimp out before Wes, but he needed to take a leak. *Soon.*

They reached the tree line—a wonderful confirmation of their progress—at around ten thousand feet. He was about to call for a break, when a man stepped from behind a rock formation on the uphill side of the trail. A man with a gun pointed at Patrick's center mass and a balaclava over his face. The man clearly wasn't wearing it for the weather, which had warmed as Patrick and Wes came off the peak and was up to a balmy forty-five or so.

"Stop," the man shouted. "Not another step."

Patrick complied. Quickly.

Wes stepped on Patrick's heel. "What in holy Hades is going on?"

The man's voice shook. "Both of you. Stop. Put your hands up."

"Seriously?" Wes muttered.

Patrick put his hands up. The voice. The wiry frame. It seemed impossible. "Loren? Is that you?"

No answer.

The last Patrick had heard after Loren was care-flighted to Denver was that he was tackling long-term recovery back in his hometown. He'd beat the odds by surviving clot removal surgery for a subdural hematoma. If you'd have asked Patrick whether the young man could climb a mountain to hold up Patrick and Wes nine months later, he would have said it was possible, but not probable.

Wes stepped forward. "Loren? That friend of Whitney's that

fell? I brought you down the mountain last September, man. What are you doing pointing a gun at us?"

The gun wavered, then corrected. Loren—if it was him, and Patrick felt very sure it was—pulled back the hammer.

"Whoa, whoa," Patrick said. "No need to escalate things. Can you just tell us what's going on here?" Although Patrick could guess.

Loren's voice was a screech. "Just give it to me. I won't hurt you. I'll just tie you up. Someone will come looking for you before long."

"Give what to you?"

Loren ripped up the balaclava with his free hand. For a moment, his eyes were covered. Patrick considered rushing him, but the distance between the two of them was too great. The moment passed. Loren stalked toward them, four giant steps closing the gap. The clean-shaven face Patrick had known before was covered by a thin beard below dark-circled eyes. "You know damn well what I'm talking about. How'd you find out about it? Did she tell you? She swore she wouldn't. It was ours. Mine and hers. We were going to split everything."

Wes snorted. "Patrick and I wanted to be the first to summit this season. We ain't got nothing but toilet paper and peanut butter and jelly sandwiches."

"That's BS!" Loren screamed. "Whitney figured out it was worth a lot of money. I just needed to get back up here after the snow melted and I'd recovered enough and bring it down. Then sell it."

Patrick lowered his hands to chest level. "You know she already sold it, don't you?"

He glared at Patrick.

"She passed a fake on to the buyer, and he's angry. Really angry. He wants what he paid for."

His face reddened. He cursed under his breath. "Well, maybe that's why she was killed. Because people found out she was a liar and a cheat."

"What do you know about that?"

Loren's voice grew reptilian. For the first time since recognizing him, Patrick was afraid that the younger man really had it in him to shoot the gun. "How do you even know about that supposed sale, huh? You weren't part of our deal. You were never part of it."

Patrick threw his hands up in the air. "Whitney dragged me in right before she died." He didn't want to divulge too much, but he needed to try to persuade Loren to back off. "The buyer thinks I have what he paid for. He's going to hurt my family if I don't take it to him."

"Where's the money, if he paid?"

Patrick stared him in the eye. He needed a supremely convincing lie just in case he didn't walk out of this confrontation alive. Because if he told the truth, Loren would be on the Flints' doorstep next, putting Susanne and the kids in a danger they'd never see coming. "Her lawyer had it."

Loren shook his fist. His gun hand wobbled. "Now that she's dead it's mine. The money. All of it."

*Now that she's dead it's mine.* Loren could have double crossed Whitney with a blow to the back of the head knocking her straight into Clear Creek, just as she'd done him by selling a fake antiquity and not telling him about the transaction. Maybe he'd realized Whitney was cutting him out. Patrick kept his voice calm. Sympathetic. "It doesn't sound like she treated you right. I'm sorry."

Loren paced back and forth, muttering unintelligibly under his breath. Every few steps Loren would jerk the gun up and re-aim it at Patrick.

Patrick needed to break Loren's downward spiral. "I wouldn't blame you if you killed her. After what she did to you."

Loren stopped. "Give me what's mine and I'll let you go."

*He's losing it.*

Wes sighed. "Just give it to him, Patrick. Let the goons come after him instead of you."

A lone hiker came up the trail behind Loren. A woman with long blonde hair and a face full of freckles. She didn't appear to notice the stand-off and was walking right into danger.

"Ma'am," he shouted. "Stop. We've got a situation."

She smiled. "Good morning, gentlemen. Wonderful day for a climb." She kept walking, closing in on Loren.

Patrick launched his body. He had to get between her and Loren's gun. But he was too late.

As she drew near Loren, the woman drew a gun from a belly holster, raised it, rotated it, and cracked Loren over the head with it. "Timber," she said.

Patrick drew up short of her. Loren toppled to the ground.

"Thank you, kindly," Wes said. "He was a bee in our bonnet for sure."

Patrick stepped toward her, hand outstretched to shake hers. "You're a godsend. I'm—"

"Shut up." Rather than holstering her gun, she'd rotated it again. The business end was pointing at Patrick. Her hard, calm voice was chilling, though, especially in comparison to Loren's anxious, strident whine. "Throw your backpacks down. Lay on your bellies and leave a good five feet between you. Now."

Patrick quickly pondered the odds of being held up twice on the Cloud Peak trail in one day, much less at the same time and in the same spot. They were as close to zero as you could get unless you factored in the cargo in his pack. *This is getting really old.* He needed to stall. And he needed Loren's gun, which had fallen near Loren's body.

He said, "Excuse me? You must have us confused with someone else. We're just trying to go home."

"Dr. Flint? Quit talking. My husband died on this mountain, on one of his stupid vision quests. Ike did love to get loaded on peyote and play dress up in his ridiculous Egyptian baubles. So, it isn't like I was completely surprised when I heard what that little nurse was up to."

Patrick's brain was doing an Olympic-worthy gymnastic floor routine to catch up with her. "Ike? You mean Ichabod Johnson?"

"No one who knew him called him that. Stupid family name."

*Aha.* "You're Mrs. Johnson then."

"Almost. I wasn't about to take that generic last name when I married him. I'm Bella Crooke. Otherwise known as the legitimate owner of the hunk of metal and gems you're carrying."

She fired at the ground by Patrick's feet. The noise was deafening. Rock chips ricocheted, digging into his calf. Patrick jumped sideways liked a scared jackrabbit only half as fast. Then he froze. A thwump-thwump-thwump of feathers against air startled him. For the briefest of moments, his eyes tracked a snowy owl. A sense of peace washed over him. As if coming from the owl, thoughts entered his awareness. *Patience. Win with your brain by mastering your emotions.*

"Down, now," Bella said.

He heard a thud, then saw Wes laying prone. "No problem, Miss Crooke."

Patrick threw his backpack down and himself on the ground near it, as close as he could get to Loren without being obvious. He looked up at Bella. Was he looking up into the face of Whitney's killer? It didn't matter. What mattered was slowing down and using his brain to find the opportunity that would get them out of this mess.

*Thank you, owl friend.* And then he started to pray.

# CHAPTER SIXTY-FOUR: CHASE

West Tensleep Lake, Bighorn Mountains, Wyoming
*Now:* Saturday, June 24, 1978

*Perry*

Perry didn't like the number of cars in the trailhead parking lot. He saw his dad's truck, an LTD, a Cadillac, and a few others, including a familiar looking yellow Ford Pinto that had seen a lot of rough miles. The sunrise hadn't crept over the mountains yet. In the near-dark, he mounted the horse Henry had brought for him—Blue, a roan gelding that Perry had ridden at the ranch. "That Pinto. Have you seen it before?"

Henry latched the trailer. "You double-check your gear?"

Perry nodded. He had a rifle in his scabbard with extra ammo. A knife in the saddle bag that carried his rain and cold weather layers as well as water and snacks. He'd even brought the slingshot Henry had given him, which he'd tucked in his pocket, mostly to make Henry laugh. It had worked. "All good."

Henry swung a leg over his horse and motioned for Perry to lead the way. Just when Perry figured Henry hadn't heard his question, the rancher said, "Looks like the one Blister drives."

"Isn't he back at the ranch?"

"I think so. Let's put some miles in while the trail's easy. Put ole Blue in drive."

Henry had explained to Perry that week that horses had a gear they could travel in all day, easier than walking and much faster. The easy trot. Perry clucked to the animal and squeezed with his lower legs. Blue responded immediately.

Soon, all Perry could hear was the puffing breaths of the horses and the clank of their shoes against rock. The lower part of the trail from West Tensleep Lake was heavily wooded with twists, turns, steep downhill, and even steeper uphill. Blue picked his way through the rocks in the low light without a stumble, slowing to a walk where it made good sense without having to be asked, and sucking down water at some of the stream crossings.

When Perry had ridden this trail with Henry and the Search & Rescue team last September, they'd walked the horses. Even walking, the group had cut the ascent time nearly in half with their mounts. This time, Perry could barely believe how fast the first few miles flew by. He kept thinking Henry would call a break, but he didn't, and the horses didn't seem to need one.

"How do they handle this altitude so well?" he hollered back to Henry.

"God made them for it better than us, that's for sure. They feel it, but they're in good shape from working. The ranch is at a mile high. But they still don't acclimate as fast as a dog."

Perry thought about hiking up in Cloud Peak Wilderness with Ferdinand. Henry was right. Ferdinand sprinted around like a crazy fool, like he didn't feel the elevation at all. "Are we going to give them a breather?"

"They're getting a little rest on their walk when they drink. I'm keeping an eye on Blue. He's not even showing a lather yet. I'll let you know when it's time."

Perry rode on. They hadn't passed anyone, and he began to wonder if the other cars were for campers instead of hikers. He hoped so. Best case scenario, they just rode up here and escorted his dad and Wes down. Took in the scenery his dad loved so much. Got a little suntan on their faces. He pushed his cowboy hat further down on his head at the thought. What he didn't need was a goofy sunburned nose when he returned to practice Monday. Three black shapes shuffled out of the woods and across the trail a few hundred feet in front of them. One large and two much smaller. It took him a few seconds to register it was a mama bear and two cubs.

"Black bear and cubs ahead." He pointed to the left where they'd disappeared into the woods.

"Hold steady and be alert," Henry shouted.

Blue didn't falter as they approached the spot where the bears had crossed the trail. Perry was just about to reach down to pat his neck and praise him, when the adult black bear charged out of the trees at the horses. She stood on her hind legs and growled a warning.

Perry felt the telltale bunching of the muscles in Blue's body a split second before Blue rocketed forward like he had afterburners. He'd just had time to grab the saddle horn before the horse took off. Perry's head snapped back but he didn't let go. He worked his center of gravity back over Blue's and lowered his upper body. He didn't dare fall. Not on this rocky trail with a mad mama bear behind them. Not when it might be the last he saw of Blue for many hours.

Behind him, Henry's horse was drumming the trail at a full gallop as well. He heard Henry calling, "Whoa there, easy now."

The hoofbeats receded. Perry couldn't look behind him, but if Henry was slowing, it was time to ask the same of Blue. Honestly, Perry hadn't minded putting some distance between them and the mad mama. "Whoa, Blue. Whoa." Most of his horsemanship had flown out the window when Blue bolted, but it came back to him now. He sat up in the saddle, letting his weight slump into his rear. He released his leg pressure, lifted the reins, and eased them and his weight slightly back at the same time. If he pulled too hard he knew he risked Blue rebelling. A determined horse could just clamp the bit in their teeth, stretch their neck against the reins, and keep going. Blue would stop because he was convinced it was safe to trust his rider, not out of blind obedience.

At first the horse ignored Perry. Perry used a soothing tone. "Hey, there, boy. It's okay now. Whoa. Whoa."

Finally, Blue eased up. His gallop slowed to a lope, then a trot, then a walk.

"Good boy." Perry patted his neck. "Good Blue."

Henry rode up beside him. "Did that get your blood pumping?"

"Man, oh man, did it."

"It got the horses pretty lathered, too. How about we walk them until the next water, then we'll all take a break."

"Hopefully in a bear-free area."

Henry chuckled. "She didn't want to hurt us. She just wanted us to leave her babies alone. Mamas in the wild are as tough as they come."

Perry wasn't so sure about the not wanting to hurt them part, but he did know how tough mamas could be. In the wild and in his own house. He saw the morning sun glint off a wet surface ahead. "There's a creek crossing."

They dismounted on the far side of the creek. The two horses immediately drank then set to munching grass. Perry's butt was numb and his legs wobbly from the miles in the saddle. *I think I'm in worse shape than Blue.*

Henry tossed Perry a canteen. They took turns drinking, then ate muffins Vangie had made for them. Perry was going to miss her baking skills. His mom was great, but she wasn't much of a cook, and she never baked, except occasionally chocolate chip cookies. Usually, she just left the raw dough in the refrigerator with a family spoon stuck in it.

"Have you been up Cloud Peak before?" Perry asked.

"Nope. Never been a climber. And I work too much."

"I think we're pretty close to this big lake at the bottom of the peak."

Henry capped the canteen. "Looks like it. The vegetation is changing. We're coming up on the tree line. You ready?"

"Yes, sir."

The two of them walked toward the horses, who had wandered off a few yards to nibble grass, each of them with a lead rope dragging the ground to make catching them easier.

Just then, a loud CRACK shattered the silence, echoing off the rock faces in the peaks above them. The horses reared, spun, and sprinted back down the mountain trail.

Perry's heart galloped with them, and it felt like it was lodged in his throat. "Was that a gunshot?"

Henry frowned. "Could be a rock breaking off. But I don't think so. I think gun."

"Dad. Wes."

Henry nodded.

"Was it far away?"

"Hard to say the way sound travels up here. My best guess is a quarter mile away."

"The horses..."

Henry worked his jaw side to side as he shook his head. "The shot was too close on the heels of the bear. They got nervy. We won't catch them."

"We're going to be slow."

"Worse. We're going into a gunfight unarmed. The firearms are on the horses."

The blood drained from Perry's face. How were they going to protect his dad and Wes?

Henry put his hand on Perry's shoulder. "We're going to need to get up there without being seen or heard. Stay behind me, be quiet, and keep covered."

"Yes, sir."

Henry headed up-trail at a brisk walk. Perry took one last look after the horses, then hurried after him.

# CHAPTER SIXTY-FIVE: STANDOFF

CLOUD PEAK WILDERNESS, BIGHORN MOUNTAINS, WYOMING
*NOW:* SATURDAY, JUNE 24, 1978

Patrick

PATRICK WATCHED Bella Crooke walk to the edge of the trail and peer into the void. The drop-off on that side was a sheer cliff. The trail itself in this section was fairly wide, but the uphill side was boulder strewn with only sparse, scrubby trees at this elevation. He would have loved to rush her and push her over, but she'd hog-tied Wes and him before her reconnoitering, each with their wrists belted behind their backs. *Amazing what a grown man will let you do when you have a muzzle to the back of his best friend's skull.* It was a good bit less than comfortable. Painful, in fact, for his broken hand to be pulled against the other. He was engaging all the muscles in his lower back to relieve some of the pressure. But what he wasn't able to do was reach Loren's gun. Even if he'd wriggled over on his stomach without Bella noticing, he wouldn't be able to grab it and would only be drawing Bella's attention to it when she returned.

*Think positive. As soon as I get my hands free.* Both he and Wes had knives and weapons in their backpacks, too, if they ever got the chance to dig for them.

Wes whispered under the cover of the ever-present wind. "You weren't wrong about us meeting up with opposition, Sawbones, but I don't recall Loren or Johnson's widow either one making it onto your short list of possibilities."

Patrick harrumphed, spitting dirt. Wes wasn't wrong. How had he not seen this coming? He wondered if either Loren or Bella had been the stalker that Whitney had told Kathy about. Or drove the Ford LTD he'd seen following him a few days before. But there were more pressing questions at the moment. "I don't like the way she's scouting that cliff. What do you think she's up to?"

"I can promise we aren't going to like it."

Bella marched back over to Loren. She nudged him with her toe. He groaned. She knelt and used his belt to hog tie him. *One woman half Wes's size has taken down three armed men.* He thought about the owl and the message earlier. Brain and patience over brawn and hurry. If Bella was any indication, it was a successful strategy.

Bella grabbed Loren by his belted extremities and began trying to drag him uphill and across the trail. It was immediately clear that she wasn't going to progress quickly. But then Loren woke up.

"What the hell? What are you doing?" His strident whine was back, but he began to fight for his life.

Bella drew her gun on him again. "Stop. Don't make me shoot you."

"What are my options? Where were you dragging me and what were you planning to do to me, huh?"

She stared at him with dispassion. Then she lowered her gun. "You can't be so dumb as to think I'll let any of you live? Or leave your bodies to be found on this trail?"

Patrick was definitely not that dumb. But he wasn't feeling very smart either because he couldn't figure a way out of this. Bella had been eying that cliff and trying to drag Loren to it. Seemed like she wanted to send them to their Maker where it would be months before they were found, if ever. *Stall her. I need more time to think.*

"What are you going to do, just return to your normal life? After you kill three men and take back your husband's stolen antiquities?"

"Three men and one woman. It was never supposed to be like this. I just wanted my property back. No one needed to die. But I have resources and a place to go. It's time that I need. Time to cross the northern border."

*She did kill Whitney. I knew it.* Knowing it was satisfying but it didn't help them now. What were they going to do? Speed roll on top of Bella? He could stand and charge her, but she'd shoot him. Even if he and Wes did it at the same time, it wouldn't be much of a challenge for her to pick off one and then the other of them.

*God, if I don't make it out of this, please watch over my family. I hope I showed I loved them enough that they'll always remember it. But I would highly prefer a miracle and stand ready to be eternally grateful if you'll send one.*

She waved the gun at Patrick. "You. I'm going to cut you loose, and you're going to carry Loren for me. Or drag him. I don't care. And if you make one false move, I'll shoot you."

Part of Patrick wanted to protest not to make him part of her scheme. But the other part just wanted her to cut him loose. "Fine."

"Be still." She removed the belt from his wrists.

His arms dropped to the ground, needles of pain stabbing them.

"Stand up."

It wasn't easy or immediate, but he complied, with her gun pointed at his midsection.

"Arms in front, wrists together."

Again, he complied. She eyed his wrists, and he could see she hadn't thought it through. She had to approach his hands in order to secure him. She and the gun would be vulnerable. Hogtieing him had been less difficult, as she was able to kneel in his back with the gun digging into his neck to tie his hands. He'd even been cooperative.

*I will not cooperate again.* Better to force her to shoot him than to give in now.

They faced each other, neither speaking, neither yielding.

And then there was a PING sound. Something hit her in the head. She pitched forward onto her knees, then over face first into the trail bed.

Patrick didn't wait to find out what was going on. Moving as fast as he could, he grabbed her gun, shoved it in the front of his waistband, and did the same with Loren's in the back. Then he took his belt from the ground beside her and tied her like she'd done to Loren.

He spun, drawing his gun and holding it in the down ready position. He crouched, making quarter turns as he searched for the next attacker. Who would it be? Price? One of his "colleagues?" Or was there yet someone else with a stake in this game?

"Don't shoot!" a man yelled.

Patrick knew the voice, but right now, after two attacks on this trail, he trusted no one. He turned to face the direction the sound was coming from. "Show yourself. Slowly, hands empty and up."

"Patrick, it's me."

Patrick didn't lower his gun.

"Dad!" a younger voice yelled. "Dad, it's Henry and Perry. We're coming out."

*Henry and Perry?*

Then it clicked. The voices matched. "What the heck? How the heck?"

The rancher and Patrick's son emerged from behind a stand of rock, hands up. Patrick lowered his gun.

"Susanne sent us. She was worried some guy was going to come up here after you."

"He hasn't yet, but everyone else has."

"Did you see me, Dad?" Perry said. "I got her."

"That was you?"

Perry held up a slingshot.

"Holy cow! And thank you!" He met the two men and put one arm around his son, still unwilling to relinquish the gun.

"Thank Henry. He's the one who convinced me they were useful to keep around."

"Weren't you armed?"

Henry laughed. "We were until our horses ran off with our weapons."

Patrick pulled the second gun from his waist and handed it over to Henry.

"Yeah, this would have come in handy."

"Who is she, Dad?"

"Whitney's killer. She was married to the guy who owned the ring and some other stuff Whitney was trying to sell."

"Where is he?"

"Dead. Up there." Patrick pointed. "In a cave."

Wes snorted. "When this love fest is over, can someone cut me loose?"

"Don't be a baby, Braten." Patrick walked over and unfastened the belt around Wes's wrists.

Loren was being awfully quiet. Patrick used his foot to roll him onto his back.

"Ow." Loren turned his face away.

"Aren't you going to cut him loose?" Perry said.

"Nope. He was the first bad guy to come after us. Perry, Henry, meet Loren. He was the other climber with Whitney and me last year."

Perry came over to take a look but stopped and put his hands on his hips. "Henry, come see."

Henry joined them. Loren turned an angry face in their direction.

"Well, I'll be goldarned." Henry sounded disgusted. "If it isn't Blister."

# CHAPTER SIXTY-SIX: RECONCILE

BUFFALO, WYOMING
*NOW*: SUNDAY, JUNE 25, 1978

*Patrick*

A MERE TWENTY-FOUR hours after Wes, Henry, Patrick, and Perry had brought their two prisoners down the mountain to Deputy Ronnie and one of her colleagues—with no further incident and without the aid of Henry's horses, who were waiting for them back at the trailers—Patrick was tying his black Percheron gelding Reno to the hitching post by their barn. Perry dismounted from his smaller paint, Duke. Of the two Flint offspring, Trish was more of the rider. But Perry had surprised Patrick that morning when he'd asked his dad to ride with him. Maybe a few days working with Henry Sibley had rubbed off on him.

The two of them had talked about their little adventure some, but mostly they'd been quiet together. It had been peaceful ever since

Ronnie had called to tell them the Buffalo police had taken Price in for questioning that morning. Patrick had things he needed to talk to Perry about, but he'd swallowed the parental urge, not wanting to spoil a single second. An unexpected gift of outdoor time one-on-one with this young man who had been his little boy just a blink ago.

That is, Patrick had swallowed it until they'd arrived home.

He loosened the cinch on Reno's saddle. "I hear from your mother that you had a little get-together Friday night. Without permission."

Perry glanced at him, as if evaluating how much trouble he was in. "You weren't here to ask." Then he mirrored Patrick's motions, unsaddling Duke.

"Just a spur of the moment thing, huh?"

"Mostly."

"You could have asked your mother."

"She was with Ronnie."

Patrick thought the story smelled a little fishy, but it was impossible to disprove. He zeroed in on the last important element. "She said there was beer here when she got home."

Perry pulled Duke's saddle and blanket off and carried them in to the tack room saddle trees. Patrick followed with Reno's tack.

On their way back, Patrick said, "Perry?"

"I told the guys I wouldn't drink. Some of them brought beer. It was never in the house. They took it down to the creek."

"Was everyone drinking of age?"

"Most of them were seniors."

"That sounds like a no."

"I can't stop them. And Dad—" Perry slipped Duke's bridle off and turned to Patrick— "I have to decide who I'm going to be to my teammates. Which is one of them. But I can be the one who hangs out with them and is fun even if I don't drink. I can make sure guys stay safe and get home. I thought this would be a good way to show it, since the entire team knows about me getting suspended and sent to work with Henry all week."

Patrick nodded. It wasn't perfect, but it was a decent compromise. "They've given you a hard time?"

"Yeah. Some. But I didn't rat any of them out, so they laid off."

"You know, sometimes you have to tell the hard truth about other people. If their actions get them in trouble, that's on them."

"I know, Dad. But they didn't hurt anyone."

"Except you."

"Don't you tell me all the time not to blame other people for my mistakes?"

Patrick rolled his lips to keep from smiling. *Touché.*

"Besides, I couldn't be the tattletale. Dad, I need it to be okay this time."

Patrick mulled it over. It was a tough call. The parent in him wanted his kid to tell the whole truth. The former high school football player in him would have done the same thing as Perry. Would still do the same thing if he had it to do over again, even with hindsight and years as an adult and parent. Hadn't he just withheld truths from the police because he thought it was the right thing to do for his most important teammate, Susanne? Withheld them until he figured out the right way to solve the problem within his team. *Talk about the whole truth...* The hard truth.

And then he smiled. Perry was finding his way. He would trust in the solid core of what he and Susanne were teaching their son. The truth is the world is made up of shades of gray. Rarely is an answer black or white—if only it was ever that easy.

He slung Reno's bridle on his shoulder and led Perry back into the barn. "All right, this time. But we're not talking absolutes here. Sometimes you gotta let the truth out."

They hung the bridles on their hooks.

Perry sighed. "I know, Dad. It's part of figuring out how to be a man."

Patrick walked a few steps behind him toward the house, his eyes suddenly wet. Perry had matured a few years this week.

Susanne opened the door as they approached. "We just had a visit from the Buffalo Police."

Patrick frowned. "Appelt?"

"No. The nice one. Welch."

"What did he want?"

"The ring and breastplate. Again."

"Did you give it to them?"

She shook her head and backed up so the two male Flints could enter the house. "I reiterated that we are in legal possession of them, that they are not part of the commission of a crime within their jurisdiction, and that we will gladly return them to their rightful owners, if it can be determined who that is."

Patrick laughed. "How did he take that?"

"Well, his mouth hung open, and then he left with a hangdog look. Then I called my brother." Susanne's brother Frank was an attorney in Texas.

"Good thinking."

"He said we don't have a legal obligation to give them to the local police. But I have an idea about what we should do with them before this becomes a bigger problem."

"And that is?"

"Breakfast is ready. While you guys eat, I'll tell you."

Perry was already in the kitchen scooping eggs and sausage onto a plate. He grabbed a piece of grilled, buttered toast and carried it to the table between his teeth.

Patrick loaded up his plate and took a seat. "Where's Trish?"

"Marcy's." She refilled her coffee and poured Patrick a cup. "My boss called."

Patrick sucked in a breath. Susanne's banishment from the college had been humiliating. "And?"

"He wants me back immediately. Tomorrow."

"That's great, honey!"

"Even better, he'd like me to document the artifacts and how I came to realize what they were. He'd like us to co-write a journal article."

"Congratulations!"

She beamed. "I'm going to take them to the college tomorrow. We'll get some good photographs and he'll do some preliminary work to establish their authenticity."

"Which you can't do if the cops have them."

She put her finger on her nose and winked. "And which brings us to what I think we should do with them, especially since this article is going to gain global attention."

"The whole situation is already breaking news across the country. Maybe even the world. So, what's your idea?"

She leaned in and said, "Remember that friend you made last winter snowmobiling with the guys up at Clear Creek Lodge?"

Patrick grinned. He liked where she was going with this.

# CHAPTER SIXTY-SEVEN: ACT

Buffalo, Wyoming
*Now*: Tuesday, June 27, 1978

*Susanne*

The plane gliding over the runway at the Johnson County Airport was sleek but nondescript. Having been in planes with Patrick when he'd taken off and landed there many times, Susanne knew the runway was plenty long to accommodate the government plane. It landed and taxied to the hangar. She and Patrick stood arm-in-arm on the tarmac breathing in jet fumes as the Secretary of State descended the plane's steps.

Cyrus. A friend of Patrick's ever since they both attended a guys' winter sports weekend in the Bighorns that had gone awry. Perry, too actually. Cyrus had helped the Flints' dear friend escape the Iranian Secret Police and assume a new identity as Abraham Farhad, providing medical care on Wyoming's Wind River Reservation. Now they counted Cyrus amongst their friends as well. They'd received a card from him at Christmas, and he'd written to Patrick recently about attending the annual men's trail ride over the Bighorn Mountains.

Hugs were exchanged, then Patrick handed Cyrus a package. "I'm glad to get these off our hands."

"And I'm looking forward to seeing what good we can do with Egypt by negotiating their return," Cyrus said with a grin. "I'm glad Susanne thought to call me about them."

"Are you staying in Wyoming long?" Susanne asked.

"Just long enough to extend the thanks of a grateful nation. Patrick, I'm looking forward to that trail ride. See you there?"

Patrick glanced at Susanne. She nodded. She wasn't thrilled with yet another activity that took him away for days on end, but the ride drew movers and shakers from across the country, and he'd been coveting a spot in the group for a few years—as long as it didn't interfere with any mountain climbing plans. "I'll see you then."

More handshakes and hugs, then Cyrus boarded the plane with the invaluable package tucked casually under one arm. He stopped and saluted them before the jet door closed. As it slipped away—a ghost, in and out so fast it had almost been invisible—grit pelted Susanne's cheeks. She put a hand up to shield her face. Patrick grasped the other one and gave it a tug, chinning toward the parking lot.

They walked out with their hands swinging between them like teenagers.

Susanne jostled him with her hip mid-stride. "I almost forgot to tell you—big news in Trish's world. Jillian was kicked off the cheerleading squad because she was helping Jimmy and Dabbo collect information on us that they were selling to Carl Price."

Patrick tilted his head back and whooped. "I can't tell you how happy that makes me. That girl and everyone in her orbit is bad news."

"Agreed. But this is the biggest part of that news. They moved up the first alternate into the vacated spot on the squad. Guess who it is?"

"No idea."

"Marcy!"

Patrick dropped her hand and they both got in the car, which was unlocked. Because they lived in Wyoming. "That's got to make both of them really happy."

"Definitely. Now, if she and Ben can just get through this rough patch over the Jimmy Gross thing, all will be well. God willing." Susanne closed the passenger side door. "Next stop, my favorite place. The Buffalo Police Department."

"You're sure you want to go?" Patrick steered them out of their parking space and toward the exit.

"I wouldn't miss this for the world." She and Patrick had done the real work that Appelt had shirked in favor of harassing and badmouthing her. She couldn't wait to make him retract his accusations.

"Good. Max will be meeting us there with an update."

She fanned herself and laughed. "Aren't we important to rate that."

"I think he feels pretty bad about how the whole thing went down."

"More like he thinks I might talk him down to your sister. Are the two of them ever going to tie the knot?"

"She doesn't want to move to Wyoming. He doesn't want to live in Texas."

"Wow, sounds familiar."

Patrick reached for her hand with the fingers of his newly casted hand. It had killed him to admit weakness, but he'd wrecked it climbing Cloud Peak. The bones had been re-set before Dr. John had plastered it. *Talk about no pain, no gain!* "Have I told you lately how much I appreciate your change of heart about that?"

"Not nearly often enough."

Max stood waiting for them in front of the police station.

Susanne decided to play it aloof. He hadn't supported them much. He could have. He might have made the right career choice, but not the right family choice. Let him sweat.

But Patrick didn't hold out. "Max, glad to have a minute alone with you. We have a legal question."

"No, you can't sue the department. Susanne was never arrested or charged." Max winked at Susanne.

Patrick laughed, but she didn't. "It's a little matter of money. Cash. A lot of it."

Max swept them inside, nodding at a dapper man staffing the front desk. He opened the door to a bare bones conference room ringed with pictures of police chiefs-past. "Ah, the money. So, here's the thing. Mr. Price swears he never gave any money to Whitney or anybody else for antiquities or anything illegal, immoral, or ill-advised. Ever. In his whole life. And there's no record of where Whitney got the money. Who from or for what."

"But surely you agree it was for the ring and breastplate?" Susanne moved to the far side of a conference table and stood with her hands on the back of a chair.

"I only agree with what I can prove. And if I could prove it was ill-gotten, we'd return it to the rightful owner. If there was one."

"Does it go to the government, then?"

"Oh, how I wish. But we can't find cause for that. And we've tried. Very hard."

"I guess it goes with her estate then. The heirs will be happy."

He shook his head. "Her attorney has signed an affidavit that Whitney gave him keys and instructed him to give them to Patrick for Patrick to obtain some locked-up property. She didn't give him the keys for safekeeping. But to give it to Patrick. Before her death."

Patrick's jaw hung open like a fly trap. "What does that mean?"

"It means it falls outside her estate."

"Are you sure?"

"Her attorney is. That doesn't mean her heirs won't try to sue for it. But I'm pretty sure they won't win."

"What do we do with it then?"

Max drummed his thumbs on the table. "I'd say hold onto it until the statute of limitations runs out on any suits the heirs might file. After that, my best advice is to invest in gold. Like the bars. Store them in the basement. Hedge against inflation."

Patrick frowned. "No, seriously. What should we do with it?"

"I am serious. No one else has a claim to it. It's yours."

"But we don't want it!" Susanne said. All that dirty money. Money that nearly got her charged with murder. That led to Whitney's murder. And tied them forever in some indebted, crazy way to her memory. Susanne didn't want that at all.

Patrick's brows shot up. "We don't? I don't think we even talked about it."

She narrowed her eyes at him. "We don't."

"All right then. We don't."

Max shrugged. "Then donate it to a worthy cause. Just get some tax advice first. And a suggestion—I'd put it in a safety deposit box until then, or someone might come looking for the money he says isn't his, if you get my drift. And make a very public-if-premature announcement about a large donation to a worthy charity."

Susanne smiled, close-mouthed. "Part one is done. Part two is a good idea."

The door opened. The chief of police joined them. Susanne had never met the man before. He was as thick through the middle as he was tall with a serious face and nearly black eyes.

"Dr. Flint. Mrs. Flint. I'm Leonard Peabody." He shook their hands and sat down. "The department is so grateful to the two of you. Mind you, I'm not pleased you put yourselves into danger. We would have gotten to the right conclusion on our own, but—"

Susanne glowered at him. "If by "we" you mean officers like Appelt, then I highly doubt it."

"I don't actually. We have other fine officers. And Appelt is no longer employed by the city."

Susanne was speechless for a moment. The good kind of speechless. "May I ask why?"

He had the good grace to blush. "It appears he had a personal interest in Ms. Saylor. An interest that was unreciprocated."

Susanne looked at her husband. His eyes were as wide as hers felt.

She said, "Don't tell me. He was the one leaving her notes and spying on her?"

"Sadly, yes. And got caught destroying the evidence. I know he was overzealous. Introduced facts into the case that came from himself alone. I am afraid this may have been why."

"Like what?"

"It seems that he was the original source of the rumor that your husband had a romantic relationship with Whitney."

Susanne was glad to hear he'd been fired, but she'd still relish the opportunity to take her own pound of flesh from his hide. Painfully. Slowly. Publicly. And she knew as the daughter of her very southern mother that she never would. "Does that mean I'm officially off the hook with respect to Whitney?"

His eyebrows arched. "Of course. I thought that was a given."

"And I thought that would come with some sort of apology."

Max jumped into the awkward silence between Susanne and the police chief. "Loren Freemason will be prosecuted for assault with a deadly weapon. We're not going to pursue robbery since the breastplate didn't belong to you or Wes, Patrick."

"That seems like a really bogus distinction."

"We only pursue what we believe we can make stick."

Susanne said, "I don't love that, but I have a little sympathy for him. It turns out Whitney was an even greedier pig than he was. Taking advantage of him when he was injured and selling their find out from under him. It's really a miracle he wasn't the one who killed her."

Patrick nodded. "Or that it wasn't Carl either after she tried to swindle him. Amazing what money can do to some people's ethics. She wasn't the same person Kathy introduced me to anymore."

"Just one of the reasons I don't want that dirty money from Carl. What's going to happen to him?"

Max looked relieved to get the floor back. "He'll be charged with threatening your family with serious bodily harm, if you'll both testify."

"We will," Patrick and Susanne said at once.

"And Bella Crooke will be charged with the first-degree murder of Whitney Saylor."

"Did she confess?" Patrick asked.

"No. It's not a slam dunk, but we're building a strong case against her. For starters, we found a useful connection. Cynthia Twain, the local librarian, went to high school with Bella. They maintained a friendship through the years. Cynthia came forward yesterday. She said she called Bella after Whitney visited the library to research Ichabod's climbing, because she got the impression Whitney had a lead on where Ichabod died. She thought Bella would want to know. Bella's phone records include that call from Cynthia to Bella shortly before Bella placed a call to Whitney."

Susanne gasped. "Cynthia was the link between Whitney and Bella?"

"We don't believe it was intentional."

"I'll bet hearing from Bella was what spooked Whitney into sending me the map and having Bolton give me the keys," Patrick said.

Susanne rolled her eyes. "Amongst other reasons. Like, she wanted Carl on your back instead of hers. And maybe wanted to draw you into her scheme for personal reasons."

Patrick rubbed his forehead. "Bella was following me last week."

"What?"

"I just realized. When we left West Tensleep, there was a brown Ford LTD there. That's what was following me around town."

Max flipped through a few pages in his folder. When he looked up, he was nodding. "She definitely had one. Chances are, it was her."

"What else do you have on her?" Susanne asked.

"We found her fingerprints in the passenger seat of Whitney's car. We have phone records between the two of them, initiated by Ms. Crooke. And the good widow received a speeding ticket on Highway 16 on the day the coroner targeted as the day of Whitney's death, only a mile from where Whitney's car was found. Means, motive, and opportunity. We'll get there."

Susanne wished the case was stronger. She and Patrick had zero doubt the woman was guilty. She didn't want the killer back on the streets, especially since Patrick and Perry were instrumental in her capture and arrest. An epiphany struck her like a lightning bolt. "What Whitney wrote on Patrick's business card—'His wife knows. She threatened me.' That was about Bella."

Patrick grinned at her like he was amazed at her genius. "I'll bet you're right!"

"But it still doesn't make sense to me, why she went after Patrick and Wes. She didn't need that breastplate. If she'd just laid low, she never would have been caught. Or she could have made the move to Canada if she thought the police were on to her."

Max grinned. "You would think. But it turns out she was broke. She and her husband had run through all their money with their extravagant lifestyle. She'd been selling off all their assets to pay creditors and to live on. Even their ranch was mortgaged to the hilt."

"She was going to try to sell the antiquities herself!"

"It appears so."

"What is going to happen to Ike Johnson's body?"

"The ME declared his death accidental and will return the body to the family. Bella said climbers would want to do a memorial service, but she's not going to be out on bail to participate if I have my way."

"I'm not so sure, given that he was wearing stolen artifacts, that people will be enthusiastic about celebrating his life."

"We shall see."

Patrick stood. "Do you need anything else from us?"

Everyone else followed suit.

The chief shook his head. "Not a thing. Thanks for coming in."

Susanne nodded. "You'll excuse me if I don't say it's my pleasure. This whole situation has been anything but. I do appreciate the information, however."

Max smiled. "You'd never believe how many people feel exactly that same way."

"Oh, you'd be wrong there."

"Well," Chief Peabody rose, although he didn't seem much taller than when he was sitting, "Take care, Dr. and Mrs. Flint."

Again, handshakes were exchanged. Patrick and Susanne were on the road home a few minutes later.

"What are you thinking?" he asked her. "Your forehead is all scrunched up."

"I was serious when I said I don't want that money."

"I don't either. Not the bulk of it. And I think we could have a great time as a family coming up with a list of charities to donate it to. But I would like to keep a modest finder's fee—something we could use on the family, given the toll this took on all of us."

She tilted her head. "What did you have in mind?"

# EPILOGUE: MARVEL

Treasures of Tutankhamun Exhibit, Seattle Center's Flag Pavilion, Seattle, Washington
*Two months later*: Saturday, August 26, 1978

*Patrick*

Every muscle in Patrick's legs ached as he finally, finally climbed the steps into the Seattle Center's Flag Pavilion. Recovery from his successful ascent of Mount Rainier was going to take a few days. But he'd pushed through it to stand in line since six a.m. with Susanne, Trish, and Perry for tickets to the Treasures of Tutankhamen exhibit.

Funny that before the ordeal on Cloud Peak, Perry would have had little interest in coming. Trish, either. But since then, their whole family had been swept away with the nation's King Tut fever.

Their excitement had reached a whole new level when they'd learned the authenticity of the ring and breastplate had been confirmed. Perry thought they should have asked for a reward. Patrick was just glad they'd made it through the ordeal with their lives. At first neither of the kids had been in favor of giving Whitney's money to charities, but after a few days they'd made a game out of the selection process. Competition and campaigning was fierce amongst the family for each person's favorites. But no one had objected to Patrick's suggestion that they use a small part of it to come see the Treasures exhibit.

The four of them made their way through the pavilion, in collective awe with the other visitors. But it wasn't long before Perry's interest flagged. He was singing "King Tut" and doing the dance, like he was made of rubber.

"Can it, shrimp. This is a serious art exhibit," Trish hissed at him.

Perry kept dancing and singing. When he'd finished the performance—which other people had joined in with—he bowed... to applause. Then, grinning at his irritated sister, he said, "Why are you such a grump? Wait, because you're you. Never mind."

"Mo-om. Dad. Make him stop."

"Perry," Susanne said, a warning in her tone.

Patrick smiled. Was there anything better than this? Trish was acting a little irritable, but he chalked it up to her being a teenage girl. She had given him and Susanne a graduate course in how to deal with her species in the last few years.

All too soon, their tour of the exhibit was drawing to a close.

"What was your favorite part?" Susanne asked them as they walked away from the exit doors.

Before any of them could answer, a tall young man stepped in front of them. His hair was longer. His skin darker. His eyes wiser. But the expression on Ben's face when he looked at their daughter was just the same. Wonder. Longing. Love.

"Ben." Trish shot a look at her parents, as if checking to see if they were mad.

Had Susanne known Trish had arranged for Ben to meet her? Because there was no way this was happenstance. Patrick raised his eyebrows at his wife in question. She shrugged, appearing surprised but smiling. The ache is his cheeks told him he was, too.

"Trish." Ben's eyes flicked to the others. "Dr. and Mrs. Flint. Perry." Then back to Trish. "I'm sorry I'm late. I drove as fast as I could after I got your message. It took me four days."

She tossed her hair, and Patrick saw the glow in the blue eyes that were a copy of his own. "No more excuses."

Ben must have seen the look in those eyes, too, because his lips curled upward, and he closed the last few feet between him and Trish. "None. Ever." He stopped. "May I hug your daughter, Dr. and Mrs. Flint?"

Susanne laughed and wiped tears from her eyes.

Patrick crossed his arms, fighting leaky eyes of his own. "You'd better, if you know what's good for you."

Perry whooped and said, "But no PDA. This is a *serious art exhibit.*"

Ben and Trish met halfway, crashing into each other so hard that it was almost like watching Perry with the tackling sleds at practice. But neither of them faltered. Arms circled backs, heads bowed to meet. Faces disappeared into shoulders.

Patrick cleared his throat. "Ice cream for five on me."

He threw one arm around Perry's shoulders and gave him a noogie with the other hand, smiled at his wife, and in the shadow of the Space Needle led his happy family toward Pike Place Market.

***

For more Patrick Flint and family while you wait on #9 in this series, you can find them in cameos in:
BIG HORN (A Jenn Herrington Wyoming mystery) and several books in the Detective Delaney Pace series.

---

BIG HORN: Nora Roberts meets Yellowstone. https://pamelafaganhutchins.com/products/big-horn-jenn-herrington-wyoming-mystery-1-ebook

HER SILENT BONES: If Jack Reacher and CJ Box's Cassie Dewell had a love child, it would be Detective Delaney Pace. https://pamelafaganhutchins.com/pages/detective-delaney-pace-series

*For Eric, every damn time, and I will never be sorry I'm not more original. Without him, there are no books. It is as simple as that. The keys to Pamelot are his love and his partnership. IYKYK.*

# ACKNOWLEDGMENTS

When I got the call from my father that he had metastatic prostate cancer spread into his bones in nine locations, I was with a houseful of retreat guests in Wyoming while my parents (who normally summer in Wyoming) were in Texas. The guests were so kind and comforting to me, as was Eric, but there was only one place I wanted to be, and that was home. Not home where I grew up, because I lived in twelve places by the time I was twelve, and many thereafter. No, home is truly where the heart is. And that meant home for Eric and me would be with my parents.

I was in the middle of writing two novels at the time: *Blue Streak*, the first Laura mystery in the What Doesn't Kill You series, and *Polarity*, a series spin-off contemporary romance based on my love story with Eric. I put them both down. I needed to write, but not those books. They could wait. I needed to write through my emotions —because that's what writers do—with books spelling out the ending we were seeking for my dad's story. Allegorically and biographically, while fictionally.

So that is what I did, and Dr. Patrick Flint (aka Dr. Peter Fagan— my pops—in real life) and family were hatched, using actual stories from our lives in late 1970s Buffalo, Wyoming as the depth and backdrop to a new series of mysteries, starting with *Switchback* and moving on to *Snake Oil*, *Sawbones*, *Scapegoat*, *Snaggle Tooth*, *Stag Party*, *Sitting Duck*, and *Skin and Bones*. With *Skin and Bones*, I started with my father's real life klutziness (the marmot story and broken hand are basically real but involved an armadillo) and the clarity about his priority—my mother—that near death on a mountain climb brought him. Throw in a few murders, red herrings, threats to life and limb, and over-the-top adventures, and these books nearly write themselves!

I hope the real life versions of Patrick, Susanne, and Perry will forgive me for taking liberties in creating their fictional alter egos. I took care to make Trish the most annoying character since she's based on me, to soften the blow for the others. I am so hopeful that my loyal readers will enjoy them, too, even though in some ways the novels are a departure from my usual stories. But in many ways they are the same. Character-driven, edge-of-your-seat mysteries steeped in setting/culture, with a strong nod to the everyday magic around us, and filled with complex, authentic characters (including some AWESOME females).

I had a wonderful time writing these books, and it kept me going when it was tempting to fold in on myself and let stress eat me alive. For more stories behind the actual stories, visit the blog on my website: http://pamelafaganhutchins.com. And let me know if you liked the novels!

Thanks to my dad for advice on all things medical, wilderness, hunting, 1970s, and animal. I hope you had fun using your medical knowledge for murder!

Thanks to my mom for printing the early manuscripts (over and over, in their entirety) as she and dad followed along daily on the progress of the first few books.

Thanks to my brother Paul for the vivid memories that have made Perry such an amazing fictional kid.

Thanks to my husband, Eric, for brainstorming with and encouraging me and beta reading the *Patrick Flint* stories despite his busy work, travel, and workout schedule. And for moving in to my parents's barn apartment with me so I could be closer to them when they needed us.

Thanks to our five offspring. I love you guys more than anything, and each time I write a parent/child (birth, adopted, foster, or step), I channel you. I am so touched by how supportive you have been with Poppy, Gigi, Eric, and me.

To each and every blessed reader, I appreciate you more than I can say. It is the readers who move mountains for me, and for other authors, and I humbly ask for the honor of your honest reviews and recommendations.

Thanks mucho to Bobbye for the fantastic *Patrick Flint* covers.

*Skin and Bones* editing credits go to Karen Goodwin. You rock. A big thank you as well to my proofreading and advance review team.

SkipJack Publishing now includes fantastic books by a cherry-picked bushel basket of mystery/thriller/suspense writers. If you write in this genre, visit http://SkipJackPublishing.com for submission guidelines. To check out our other authors and snag a bargain at the same time, download *Murder, They Wrote: Four SkipJack Mysteries*.

## BOOKS BY THE AUTHOR

Fiction from SkipJack Publishing

**THE *PATRICK FLINT* SERIES OF WYOMING MYSTERIES:**

*Switchback (Patrick Flint #1)*

*Snake Oil (Patrick Flint #2)*

*Sawbones (Patrick Flint #3)*

*Scapegoat (Patrick Flint #4)*

*Snaggle Tooth (Patrick Flint #5)*

*Stag Party (Patrick Flint #6)*

*Sitting Duck (Patrick Flint #7)*

*Skin and Bones (Patrick Flint #8)*

*Spark (Patrick Flint 1.5): Exclusive to subscribers*

**THE *JENN HERRINGTON* WYOMING MYSTERIES:**

*BIG HORN (Jenn Herrington #1)*

*WALKER PRAIRIE (Jenn Herrington #2)*

**THE *WHAT DOESN'T KILL YOU* SUPER SERIES:**

*Wasted in Waco (WDKY Ensemble Prequel Novella): Exclusive to Subscribers*

*The Essential Guide to the What Doesn't Kill You Series*

**Katie Connell Caribbean Mysteries:**

*Saving Grace (Katie Connell #1)*

*Leaving Annalise (Katie Connell #2)*

*Finding Harmony* (*Katie Connell #3*)

*Seeking Felicity* (*Katie Connell #4*)

**Emily Bernal Texas-to-New Mexico Mysteries:**

*Heaven to Betsy* (*Emily Bernal #1*)

*Earth to Emily* (*Emily Bernal #2*)

*Hell to Pay* (*Emily Bernal #3*)

**Michele Lopez Hanson Texas Mysteries:**

*Going for Kona* (*Michele Lopez Hanson #1*)

*Fighting for Anna* (*Michele Lopez Hanson #2*)

*Searching for Dime Box* (*Michele Lopez Hanson #3*)

**Maggie Killian Texas-to-Wyoming Mysteries:**

*Buckle Bunny* (*Maggie Killian Prequel Novella*)

*Shock Jock* (*Maggie Killian Prequel Short Story*)

*Live Wire* (*Maggie Killian #1*)

*Sick Puppy* (*Maggie Killian #2*)

*Dead Pile* (*Maggie Killian #3*)

***The Ava Butler Caribbean Mysteries Trilogy*: A Sexy Spin-off From *What Doesn't Kill You***

*Bombshell* (*Ava Butler #1*)

*Stunner* (*Ava Butler #2*)

*Knockout* (*Ava Butler #3*)

Fiction from Bookouture

***Detective Delaney Pace Series:***

*HER Silent BONES (Detective Delaney Pace Series Book 1)*

*HER Hidden GRAVE (Detective Delaney Pace Series Book 2)*

*HER Last CRY (Detective Delaney Pace Series Book 3)*

Juvenile from SkipJack Publishing

*Poppy Needs a Puppy (Poppy & Petey #1)*

Nonfiction from SkipJack Publishing

*The Clark Kent Chronicles*

*Hot Flashes and Half Ironmans*

*How to Screw Up Your Kids*

*How to Screw Up Your Marriage*

*Puppalicious and Beyond*

*What Kind of Loser Indie Publishes,*

*and How Can I Be One, Too?*

**Audio, e-book, large print, hardcover, and paperback versions of most titles available.**

# ABOUT THE AUTHOR

Pamela Fagan Hutchins is a *USA Today* best selling author. She writes award-winning mystery/thriller/suspense from way up in the frozen north of Snowheresville, Wyoming, where she lives with her husband in an off-the-grid cabin on the face of the Bighorn Mountains, and Mooselookville, Maine, in a rustic lake cabin. She is passionate about their large brood of kids, step kids, inherited kids, and grandkids, riding their gigantic horses, and about hiking/snow shoeing/cross country skiing/ski-joring/bike-joring/dog sledding with their Alaskan Malamutes.

If you'd like Pamela to speak to your book club, women's club, class, or writers group by streaming video or in person, shoot her an email. She's very likely to say yes.

You can connect with Pamela via her website
(http://pamelafaganhutchins.com)
or email (pamela@pamelafaganhutchins.com).

## PRAISE FOR PAMELA FAGAN HUTCHINS

**2018 USA Today Best Seller**
2017 Silver Falchion Award, Best Mystery
2016 USA Best Book Award, Cross-Genre Fiction
2015 USA Best Book Award, Cross-Genre Fiction
2014 Amazon Breakthrough Novel Award Quarter-finalist, Romance

***The Patrick Flint Mysteries***

"Best book I've read in a long time!" — Kiersten Marquet, author of *Reluctant Promises*

"*Switchback* transports the reader deep into the mountains of Wyoming for a thriller that has it all--wild animals, criminals, and one family willing to do whatever is necessary to protect its own. Pamela Fagan Hutchins writes with the authority of a woman who knows this world. She weaves the story with both nail-biting suspense and a healthy dose of humor. You won't want to miss *Switchback*." -- Danielle Girard, *Wall Street Journal*-bestselling author of White Out.

"*Switchback* by Pamela Fagan Hutchins has as many twists and turns as a high-country trail. Every parent's nightmare is the loss or injury of a child, and this powerful novel taps into that primal fear." -- Reavis Z. Wortham, two time winner of The Spur and author of *Hawke's Prey*

"*Switchback* starts at a gallop and had me holding on with both hands until the riveting finish. This book is highly atmospheric and nearly crackling with suspense. Highly recommend!" -- Libby Kirsch, Emmy awardwinning reporter and author of the *Janet Black Mystery Series*

"A Bob Ross painting with Alfred Hitchcock hidden among the trees."

"Edge-of-your seat nail biter."

"Unexpected twists!"

"Wow! Wow! Highly entertaining!"

"A very exciting book (um... actually a nail-biter), soooo beautifully descriptive, with an underlying story of human connection and family. It's full of action. I was so scared and so mad and so relieved... sometimes all at once!"

"Well drawn characters, great scenery, and a kept-me-on-the-edge-of-my-seat story!"

"Absolutely unputdownable wonder of a story."

"Must read!"

"Gripping story. Looking for book two!"

"Intense!"

"Amazing and well-written read."

"Read it in one fell swoop. I could not put it down."

## ***What Doesn't Kill You: Katie Connell Romantic Mysteries***

"An exciting tale . . . twisting investigative and legal subplots . . . a character seeking redemption . . . an exhilarating mystery with a touch of voodoo." — *Midwest Book Review Bookwatch*

"A lively romantic mystery." — *Kirkus Reviews*

"A riveting drama . . . exciting read, highly recommended." — *Small Press Bookwatch*

"Katie is the first character I have absolutely fallen in love with since Stephanie Plum!" — *Stephanie Swindell, Bookstore Owner*

"Engaging storyline . . . taut suspense." — *MBR Bookwatch*

## ***What Doesn't Kill You: Emily Bernal Romantic Mysteries***

"Fair warning: clear your calendar before you pick it up because you won't be able to put it down." — *Ken Oder, author of* Old Wounds to the Heart

"Full of heart, humor, vivid characters, and suspense. Hutchins has done it again!" — *Gay Yellen, author of* The Body Business

"Hutchins is a master of tension." — *R.L. Nolen, author of* Deadly Thyme

"Intriguing mystery . . . captivating romance." — *Patricia Flaherty Pagan, author of* Trail Ways Pilgrims

"Everything about it shines: the plot, the characters and the writing. Readers are in for a real treat with this story." — *Marcy McKay, author of* Pennies from Burger Heaven

## ***What Doesn't Kill You: Michele Lopez Hanson Romantic Mysteries***

"Immediately hooked." — *Terry Sykes-Bradshaw, author of* Sibling Revelry

"Spellbinding." — *Jo Bryan, Dry Creek Book Club*

"Fast-paced mystery." — *Deb Krenzer, Book Reviewer*

"Can't put it down." — *Cathy Bader, Reader*

## ***What Doesn't Kill You: Ava Butler Romantic Mysteries***

"Just when I think I couldn't love another Pamela Fagan Hutchins novel more, along comes Ava." — *Marcy McKay, author of* Stars Among the Dead

"Ava personifies bombshell in every sense of word. — *Tara Scheyer, Grammy-nominated musician, Long-Distance Sisters Book Club*

"Entertaining, complex, and thought-provoking." — *Ginger Copeland, power reader*

## ***What Doesn't Kill You: Maggie Killian Romantic Mysteries***

"Maggie's gonna break your heart–one way or another." *Tara Scheyer, Grammy-nominated musician, Long-Distance Sisters Book Club*

"Pamela Fagan Hutchins nails that Wyoming scenery and captures the atmosphere of the people there." — *Ken Oder, author* of Old Wounds to the Heart

"I thought I had it all figured out a time or two, but she kept me wondering right to the end." — *Ginger Copeland, power reader*

# BOOKS FROM SKIPJACK PUBLISHING

**FICTION:**

**Marcy McKay**

*Pennies from Burger Heaven*, by Marcy McKay

*Stars Among the Dead*, by Marcy McKay

*The Moon Rises at Dawn*, by Marcy McKay

*Bones and Lies Between Us*, by Marcy McKay

*When Life Feels Like a House Fire*, by Marcy McKay

**R.L. Nolen**

*Deadly Thyme*, by R. L. Nolen

*The Dry*, by Rebecca Nolen

**Ken Oder**

*The Closing*, by Ken Oder

*Old Wounds to the Heart*, by Ken Oder

*The Judas Murders*, by Ken Oder

*The Princess of Sugar Valley*, by Ken Oder

**Gay Yellen**

*The Body Business*, by Gay Yellen

*The Body Next Door*, by Gay Yellen

**Pamela Fagan Hutchins**

### *THE PATRICK FLINT SERIES OF WYOMING MYSTERIES:*

*Switchback (Patrick Flint #1)*, by Pamela Fagan Hutchins

*Snake Oil (Patrick Flint #2)*, by Pamela Fagan Hutchins

*Sawbones (Patrick Flint #3)*, by Pamela Fagan Hutchins

*Scapegoat (Patrick Flint #4)*, by Pamela Fagan Hutchins

*Snaggle Tooth (Patrick Flint #5)*, by Pamela Fagan Hutchins

*Stag Party (Patrick Flint #6)*, by Pamela Fagan Hutchins

*Spark (Patrick Flint 1.5): Exclusive to subscribers*, by Pamela Fagan Hutchins

### THE *WHAT DOESN'T KILL YOU* SUPER SERIES:

*Wasted in Waco (WDKY Ensemble Prequel Novella): Exclusive to Subscribers*, by Pamela Fagan Hutchins

*The Essential Guide to the What Doesn't Kill You Series*, by Pamela Fagan Hutchins

### Katie Connell Caribbean Mysteries:

*Saving Grace (Katie #1)*, by Pamela Fagan Hutchins

*Leaving Annalise (Katie #2)*, by Pamela Fagan Hutchins

*Finding Harmony (Katie #3)*, by Pamela Fagan Hutchins

*Seeking Felicity (Katie #4)*, by Pamela Fagan Hutchins

### Emily Bernal Texas-to-New Mexico Mysteries:

*Heaven to Betsy (Emily #1)*, by Pamela Fagan Hutchins

*Earth to Emily (Emily #2)*, by Pamela Fagan Hutchins

*Hell to Pay (Emily #3)*, by Pamela Fagan Hutchins

### Michele Lopez Hanson Texas Mysteries:

*Going for Kona (Michele #1)*, by Pamela Fagan Hutchins

*Fighting for Anna (Michele #2)*, by Pamela Fagan Hutchins

*Searching for Dime Box (Michele #3)*, by Pamela Fagan Hutchins

**Maggie Killian Texas-to-Wyoming Mysteries:**

*Buckle Bunny (Maggie Prequel Novella)*, by Pamela Fagan Hutchins

*Shock Jock (Maggie Prequel Short Story)*, by Pamela Fagan Hutchins

*Live Wire (Maggie #1)*, by Pamela Fagan Hutchins

*Sick Puppy (Maggie #2)*, by Pamela Fagan Hutchins

*Dead Pile (Maggie #3)*, by Pamela Fagan Hutchins

***The Ava Butler Caribbean Mysteries Trilogy*: A Sexy Spin-off From *What Doesn't Kill You***

*Bombshell (Ava #1)*, by Pamela Fagan Hutchins

*Stunner (Ava #2)*, by Pamela Fagan Hutchins

*Knockout (Ava #3)*, by Pamela Fagan Hutchins

*Poppy Needs a Puppy (Poppy & Petey #1)*, by Pamela Fagan Hutchins, illustrated by Laylie Frazier

**MULTI-AUTHOR:**

*Murder, They Wrote: Four SkipJack Mysteries*,

by Ken Oder, R.L. Nolen, Marcy McKay, and Gay Yellen

*Tides of Possibility*, edited by K.J. Russell

*Tides of Impossibility*, edited by K.J. Russell and C. Stuart Hardwick

**NONFICTION:**

**Helen Colin**

*My Dream of Freedom: From Holocaust to My Beloved America*,

by Helen Colin

**Pamela Fagan Hutchins**

*The Clark Kent Chronicles*, by Pamela Fagan Hutchins

*Hot Flashes and Half Ironmans*, by Pamela Fagan Hutchins

*How to Screw Up Your Kids*, by Pamela Fagan Hutchins

*How to Screw Up Your Marriage*, by Pamela Fagan Hutchins

*Puppalicious and Beyond*, by Pamela Fagan Hutchins

*What Kind of Loser Indie Publishes,*

*and How Can I Be One, Too?*, by Pamela Fagan Hutchins

**Ken Oder**

*Keeping the Promise*, by Ken Oder

Made in the USA
Coppell, TX
24 April 2024